PRAISE FOR *NETTLEBLACK*

CW00665694

"A joy to be invited into the rau~~d~~
Nettleblack. Nat Reeve's novel pres~~e~~
where subterfuge, scurrilousness, s
the pages. All told with wit, flair and ~~heart~~ ~~a true~~ ~~-----~~
**– ELEY WILLIAMS, AUTHOR OF *THE LIAR'S DICTIONARY* AND
*ATTRIB. & OTHER STORIES***

"Fresh, witty, and wildly original, *Nettleblack* is an unforgettable
debut that brings a world of subversive characters to brilliant life, and
announces the arrival of a unique new voice."
**– PRETI TANEJA, AUTHOR OF *AFTERMATH* AND *WE THAT ARE
YOUNG***

"*Nettleblack* arrives breathlessly, wholly itself, yet also winding down the
strange and brilliant bent lanes previously ridden by Sylvia Townsend
Warner and Robert Aickman. It's a gorgeous bicycle basket of a novel
wherein there are many things that delight my big gay heart, including
bicycles and the divided skirts in which to ride them; ferrets and novelty
rat pyjamas; surprising cravats and haircuts; full tilt journalling for
justice (and love); scandalous novels; self-naming; swooning; sisters,
and running away from – and towards – them; and a cornucopia of true
love, of every kind and queerness. A heart tonic in a dark time, *Nettleblack*
will sweep you up unawares and carry you along in its headlong plots
and desires, just as the Dallyangle Division does to Henry – and like
Henry, you may find that it changes, and even saves, you, or at the very
least, makes you ecstatic."
– SO MAYER, AUTHOR OF *A NAZI WORD FOR A NAZI THING*

"*Nettleblack* plunges the reader head-first into an immersive and
absorbing world of Victorian demi-monde derring-do, told by an unforgettable narrator. Henry Nettleblack avoids a (married) fate worse than
death by hiding amongst a band of intrepid thief-catchers, experiencing
a thrilling (and queer) coming-of-age outside the boundaries of conven-
tional society. Nat Reeve's debut sizzles and crackles with confidence,
offering a timeless tale of LGBTQ people finding family wherever they
can. A delight!"
– ALLY WILKES, AUTHOR OF *ALL THE WHITE SPACES*

Published in 2022 by Cipher Press

Ink Court
419 Wick Lane
London, E3 2PX

Paperback ISBN: 978-1-8383900-6-8
eBook ISBN: 978-1-8383900-7-5

Printed and bound in the UK by TJ Books Ltd
Distributed by Turnaround Publisher Services

Cover Design by Wolf Murphy-Merrydew
Edited by Ellis K.
Typeset by Laura Jones
Map by Alexis Somerville

www.cipherpress.co.uk

Supported using public funding by
ARTS COUNCIL ENGLAND

NETTLEBLACK

NAT REEVE

**OR; THE PIONEERING MISADVENTURES OF
THE DALLYANGLE DIVISION, AS COMPILED
IN A MOTLEY SERIES OF RATHER
FRANTIC DOCUMENTS**

Cipher press

Dramatis personae (figs, can I quite say that?), as given by Henry Nettleblack

HENRY NETTLEBLACK, *interchangeably known as Harriet or Henrietta, occasionally known as Henry Hyssop, perennially known as my own incompetent and feeble self*

My family
EDWINA NETTLEBLACK, *my eldest and most fearsome sister*
ROSAMOND NETTLEBLACK, *my middle sister, of questionable morals*

The Dallyangle Division
KETURAH ST. CLARE BALLESTAS, *the Director, wielder of indefatigable composure*
SEPTIMUS, *where do I even begin?*
CASSANDRA BALLESTAS, *the Director's daughter, keeper of the records*
GERTIE SKULL, *the locus of misbehaviour*
MILLICENT MUSGROVE and **OLIVER SKULL,** *feral co-workers*
MATTHEW ADELSTEIN, *a prodigal's worst nightmare*

Other assorted humans
PIP PROPERTY, *cravat designer, astonishing dandy, eschewer of genders*
LORRIE TICKERING, *Septimus's brother, a tailor by day and tenor by eventide*
NICK FITZDEGU, *a rat breeder*
LADY ELVIRA MILTONWATERS, *a noble neighbour*
ADELAIDE DANADLENDDU, *a governess in the employment of the Ballestas family*
MAGGIE and **NORMAN SWEETING,** *recreational burglars of the most frightening nature*
MORDRED, *a ferret*

Many more figures will doubtless appear in this parade of chaos, and I can only prostrate myself at their feet for failing to record

Contents

PAGE

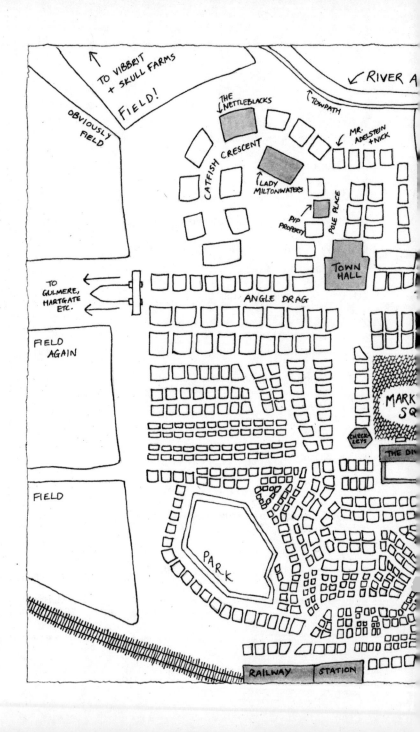

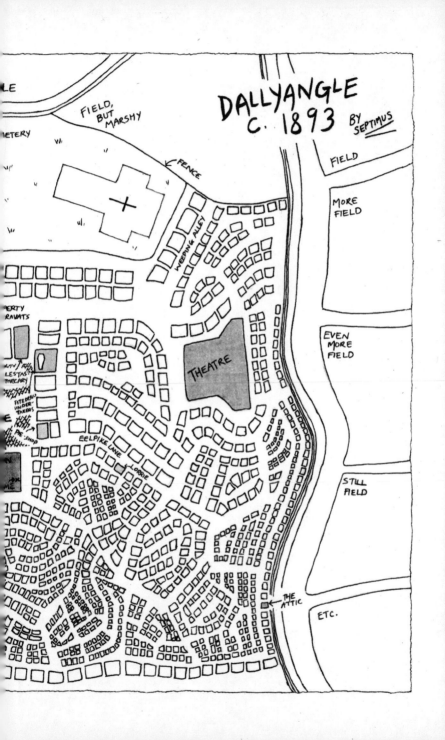

1.

IN WHICH SOME STRANGE DECISIONS ARE MADE ON MY BEHALF

NETTLEBLACK'S TINCTURE

A BLESSING TO THE MILDLY UNWELL!

SOLD AND POSTED EVERYWHERE IN 3 / 4 ½ INCH DECORATIVE BOTTLES!

PREPARED TO A SECRET FAMILY RECIPE, WHICH HAS BEEN PROVIDING RELIEF TO CUSTOMERS IN THEIR DROVES SINCE 1740.

There is no better remedy in the whole world for persons suffering from:

Melancholia	Constipation	Slight Injury
Headaches	Internal Weakness	Sore Throats
Monthly Complaints	Quack Remedies	Twisted Ankles

AND ALL

Painful, Nervous and Drugbaffling Cases.

(For more Dangerous Cases, Nettleblack's Tincture may be taken as supplementary pain relief, as all medical professionals will doubtless recommend.)

Read the following unimpeachable and unsolicited Testimonials, and then silence the voice of Incredulity, discard Prejudice, and seek a means of relief.

Mr. Vernon Vibbrit, Professional Photographer and Guinea Pig Breeder, writes: —"There is no room for doubt that I have derived benefit from the ready availability and prompt consumption of your Reliable and Effective Tincture. I need no longer complain of head-aches in the dark room. Your Tincture is truly a boon!"

Dr Florence Breall, of Girton College, Cambridge, claims: —"I cannot but speak in the highest praise of Nettleblack's Tincture. A versatile and invigorating medicinal supplement which every family in the land should own – though I imagine they do already!"

AND MOST IMPORTANTLY

Miss Edwina Nettleblack, eldest daughter of the late Mr. Morgan Nettleblack, declares: —"Though the Nettleblack family are no longer overseeing this Useful and Trusted business, I may assure you personally that our successors hold to the Impeccable Standards my ancestors have maintained over the centuries!"

WITH PRICES STARTING AT THE ASTOUNDINGLY AFFORDABLE
2/9, NETTLEBLACK'S TINCTURE IS TRULY WITHIN
REACH OF ALL!

Find this Benevolent Essential at your nearest Chemist, Apothecary or News Agent. A Free Descriptive Pamphlet will also accompany your first purchase!

Excerpt from the Last Will and Testament of Morgan Nettleblack

Draft, dated 16th April 1880
Nettleblack House
Southgate (<u>not</u> Penclawdd anymore, please note!)
Gower Peninsula
Wales

Nettleblack House, along with my English dwelling (5 Catfish Crescent, Dallyangle, Surrey), shall first pass into the care of my wife, *Eira Imogen Nettleblack, née Jenkins*, and from thence to our eldest daughter, *Edwina Rhiannon Cornelia*. Likewise, the Nettleblack fortune, remaining shares in <u>Nettleblack's Tincture</u>, and all my other worldly goods shall be inherited first by *Eira*, then *Edwina*. No living male relatives shall dispute this inheritance (even if they try it – which they will – but they're not getting it this time either!).

[N.B. – amend this phrasing in subsequent drafts, Morgan. A Will is not the appropriate receptacle for sardonical gloating. And surely only 'living relatives' can dispute an inheritance? – Eira.]

The aforementioned *Edwina*, having obtained the fortune,

[N.B. – where have I gone, Morgan? Am I suddenly dead? – Eira.]

will hold two thirds of it in readiness for when her younger siblings come of age. On their twenty-first birthdays, our daughters *Rosamond Pleasant Myfanwy Earlyfate* and *Harriet Morfydd Hyssop* will each take their third of the estate in their own right.

[N.B. – Morgan, are you sure this works? Does this include the houses? Are you cutting them in three as well? Recall, if you will, that you have a beautiful and pertinent copy of King Lear on your bookshelf – as I should know, given I bought it for you myself. – Eira.]

I trust that *Edwina*, our beloved daughter and our bright young schemer, will use her newfound wealth and independence to the fulfilment of all our family's highest hopes.

[N.B. – you can't put 'bright young schemer' in a Will! Nor is our desire to enter the ranks of the nobility – or, indeed, your failure to do so – a matter to bring up in the midst of a binding legal distribution! And you, Mr. Pencut, Solicitor – you let him write this? Have you lost your professional spectacles? Are you simply stood beside my dear idiot husband, twitching your thumbs, whilst he scribbles and scrawls and flicks ink over his nose? – Eira.]

Under no circumstances is any of the aforementioned – houses, money, shares, everything Eira and I have, all of it! – to pass to any other relations, especially not on my brother Rhys's side, unless all three Nettleblack daughters and their descendants be deceased or unable to hold the responsibility. ~~Which they are not No They are All three are possessed with precisely the correct amount of~~

The girls can handle it. And they will. They're having the lot, and I know that Edwina will be more than capable of making something better of it.

[N.B. – Morgan. Sweet Morgan. We must make sure to have a very serious conversation about these ideas of yours before you make your final draft – for the girls' sakes. – Eira.]

SIGNED (just in case, Eira!) –

MORGAN NETTLEBLACK

MICHAEL PENCUT

GARETH WYN EVANS

* * *

Addendum (25th June 1880).

In the absence of any other surviving drafts, the sentiments expressed by the late Morgan Nettleblack in this document, in the presence of witnesses, are to be taken as reflective of his last wishes. One can only assume that the 'very serious conversation' suggested by the late Mrs. Nettleblack did not have time to take place.

M. Pencut, Solicitor

Correspondence (of doom)

Miss Edwina Nettleblack
5 Catfish Crescent
Dallyangle, Surrey
October 23rd 1893

My dear little Dwina,

          You have often spoken to me of your concerns regarding your youngest sibling (that hussy Rosamond, alas, an absolute lost cause!) – and I wonder if I don't have something of a solution for you. As your incompetent staff failed to hear my knock – really, dear girl, if you are to smooth this transition into our set, you must find yourself some decent servants! – I send this note in the hope of a prompt and delightful reply.

You met my uncle – the Marquess – back in '87, before the ruckus around young Rosamond caused so much upset (fortunately for you, *he* has never met *her*). Well – he has invited a party of us to Alberstowe Hall next week. I could, with a bit of wrangling, get your youngest sister (the less disgraceful one – I forget her name) invited as my guest, and chaperone her for a sojourn of – shall we say a month's duration, commencing on the thirtieth? I'm sure I can contrive to keep the girl there for longer, if necessary.

I believe, under such circumstances, even your poor little sister – do remind me, it begins with a H? – could hardly fail to secure herself a respectable match. I plan to inveigle her into my uncle's pheasant-shoot – you tell me marksmanship is an area in which she excels – she simply can't fail to impress!

Doubtless this little intervention will provide you with some much-needed respite –

Believe me your devoted friend, and neighbour –

Lady Elvira Miltonwaters

6

Myself – or, at least, my journal, which amounts to a far more coherent and articulate version of myself than I fear I'll ever quite manage in person

Sunday, October 29th, 1893

To be blunt: I must escape. It's either that or keel over smiling at Lady Miltonwaters's feet, and destroy both mine and my family's prospects. Neither of which – figs! – are remotely safe in my hands.

A *country visit!* In some terrifying marquess's estate! For a month! With pheasant-shoots! And Lady Miltonwaters my chaperone! Granted, I have no quarrel with Lady Miltonwaters – I have only the vaguest idea who Lady Miltonwaters is. I know nothing of Edwina's friend other than her rank, and her elegant housefront, and her supposed profusion of single male relatives, and their universal fondness for courtships enacted *en plein air* – with firearms in hand, and dead pheasants toppling from the sky!

How in figs' name could Edwina sentence me to this?

I would have said as much, and quite entirely refused to participate in the aforementioned insanity, had Edwina not been – well, her own undiluted petrifying self – and my disposition not been far too nervous to convincingly articulate open rebellion. I haven't, to put the finest point on it, actually made my distaste for the scheme known to the eldest sister in question. Not in so many words. As if I could summon anything half so giddying as *words*, in the face of Edwina!

This journal, I ought to specify, is in no way representative of my capacity to engage in any manner of verbal sparring – or verbal pleading – or indeed verbal conversation in all of its variants. The world has never received even a sentence of the gumption I write with. I'm far too indelibly sealed in everyone's minds as a spineless child with incongruously excellent cravats. Not that I intend to let my ineloquence win again in this instance.

Not that I have much of a plan to conquer it besides – well, running away.

It must be noted that I did attempt to reason with *someone* in my impossible family, before any thoughts of absconding from it seized my mind. Not Edwina, of course. She had been the one to hurl the ghastly news at me, over boiled eggs and white rolls and Mother's porcelain cups with their tiny swirls of painted nettles, as we sat to a cold tremulous breakfast with an empty chair between us. She'd even shown me the fateful letter – a letter dated from the previous *Monday* – which was only calculated to horrify me further. I had spent the week oblivious and giddy-headed in the company of an overexciting new novel, idiotically delighted that the book had made it into the house past Edwina's approval. Sweet plums, of course she must have meant *Life and Limbs: a Comic Romance of the Medical School!* to be a distraction. If I'd known I was being marked for doom with every page I read – if I'd been aware of the scheme before it had blossomed –

But it surely can't be too late to stop it, even now!

Edwina was far too fearsome to openly question – but, at least for the moment, she was out of the way, pacing fit to gouge holes in her study floorboards. It gave me just enough clatter to conceal my own steps as I darted past her door, crept the staircase double-pace in search of Rosamond.

Figs, but calling on the aid of my middle sister was, in hindsight, wildly overambitious of me. I quite should have known this. I *did* know this, though I was far too pheasant-haunted not to try. Adolescent Rosamond conquered two languages and a fresh-built country house to bring me up in comfort, but adult Rosamond has snatched far too much of her own comfort to worry anything more about mine. She's not wanted to linger in a room with me since – certainly since I returned from Girton – and as for holding a conversation –

Plums! There wasn't another choice!

As I'd suspected, Rosamond was eyebrow-deep in self-indulgence when I found her. The downstairs drawing-room is her usual haunt for her long lazy mornings; it faces the wrong way to catch the sun, and the velvet window-drapes snake from floor to ceiling to block any rogue light from sneaking round. It would still be a dark place even if the light had been able to weasel in. Every piece of furniture, every strip of flocked wallpaper, every polished mantelpiece and skinny-legged tea-table – everything droops with the gloomy green and black hues to which Edwina cleaves with such heraldic passion. The hush of the room only makes it more funereal: a silver clock occasionally trills out pieces of time, but not a scrap of street-noise can breach the legion of full-drawn curtains.

Of course, hushed and dark is nothing if not Rosamond's favourite English habitat. She'd commandeered the largest chaise and huddled down on it, a pallid-skinned parcel of bones underneath the family portrait that glowered down from the wall behind her (not that she much resembles the portrait anymore). Even in the gloom, she was easy to pick out against the dour green brocade of her improvised bed. She'd wrapped herself in an uncut bolt of Morris fabric – where she got it, I quite haven't the faintest – and lit an extravagant fire in the nearest hearth, badly, the smoke licking the edges of the crest on the mantelpiece. One sallow bare foot stuck out from the chaotic twirl of pattern, far smoother at the heel than it used to be.

I swallowed, regretted it on the instant. The stale air was thick as the curtains, veined with coal-smoke and something alarmingly reminiscent of the liquor cabinet. If the situation hadn't been half so dire, I would have bolted there and then.

"Rosamond – I – it's – me – I'm – erm – entirely at stake!"

One strangled sentence was enough to set her groaning, eyelashes twitching against the brocade. "Paid siarad, Henry, rwy'n moyn cysgu heddi."

I twisted my cravat, by way of her neck. She knows my fluency is slipping, and she knows Edwina won't have Welsh in Surrey, and – oh, persimmons, as if she cares! She's forgotten she was ever fond of me. It would hardly be unprecedented for yet more of her former self to leech out of her head.

"Please – I – this is important!"

Another groan. "Pam? Ydyn ni'n mynd adre?"

"What?"

"Home," she spat, half-word half-cough. "Are we going home? Is Eddie declaring us free of this Surrey backwater?"

I'd not nerve enough for an especially verbose answer, but I could just about manage a gesture. I dashed to the back of the room to scrabble amidst the velvet drapes, on a desperate hunt for the curtain-pull. Edwina surely wouldn't object to my opening *these* curtains, as long as I kept the street-facing ones shut. "No – it's – I've – look – please get up – "

She hissed as the light hit her, bruising all the colours on her Morris fabric to a distinctly unrespectable brightness. Perhaps it was a surprise that I'd not simply sprinted away the moment she hurled Welsh at me.

"Wyt ti – *fine* – whatever is it now?"

I ought to have begun soberly, to have embroidered her eloquent descriptions of pheasants, and zealous noblewomen with rifles slung over their arms, and faceless noblemen looming behind them, and fearsome aristocratic houses with pitying scrutiny dripping from every wall. Rosamond dealt with all the problems in my tiny world, back in Wales – she dealt with them in Welsh, mostly, whilst I cowered behind her in a lambswool blanket and stammered feeble diolchs! But we weren't in the least in Wales now, and the almost-interest crackling in her drawl had sparked my hysteria tenfold.

A fig for sober beginnings. I confess I rather shrieked at her.

"It's – just – Edwina!"

Rosamond shunted vaguely upright, bare feet swinging over the polished wooden floor, yanking the fabric about in crumpled imitation of a dressing-gown. Her jet-black curls were flat on one side, pressed too long against the chaise, and the swirling acanthus of the brocade had patterned itself to red spots on her pale face. She looked – if not quite concerned, at least partially intrigued, and her bloodshot green eyes were raking over my features, pupils flickering in the spasmodic firelight. This was quite possibly the most encouragement I'd had from her in years.

"Eddie. Of course it is. Alright, then, chwaerlet – beth sy'n bod?"

I gaped at her. This phrase I remembered. She'd murmured it to me a thousand times, from when I was a child sobbing in my mourning skirts, right up to my seventeen-year-old terror as our carriage first drew up outside the Surrey house. And I'd tell her what was wrong, whatever it was, however long it took and however brokenly it came out, and she'd listen.

"Edwina – erm – she's summoned a rather horrendous plan – or – her friend has – Lady Miltonwaters – you know – our neighbour – "

She snorted. "Ah, yes. The kindly mistress to Eddie's obliging maid."

"Well – the two of them want to – erm – send me to her brother's – cousin's – uncle's – oh, plums, I don't know! – some relation – with a title – their country estate – for a month – and – erm – they're quite not intent on letting me leave until – figs! – until I've – I – "

"Until you've married us into the nobility," she muttered darkly. I was feebly grateful she'd spared me the trouble of wrestling out the sentiment myself.

"Quite – yes – and they've been arranging it all week – but she – erm – she only told me this morning – "

"*There's* our sneaky sister!" Her grimace, of all things, had a kind of sour admiration tinging its edges. "Not a word to the youths until it's too late."

"But – but surely it isn't too late? I – I can't do it – I don't want it – it'll be Girton all over again – worse than Girton – and – look – please – harness your innate defiance – and – erm – help me do something about it!"

Four years ago, she would have sprung off the brocade, flung on her clothes and sorted the madness. The ghost of her, on the wrong side of my eyes, promptly did as much. It was wishful thinking, and idiotic of me to let it sting, but I quite thought I heard the slap of her feet on the wood, the drag of the fabric at her heels, the parti-lingual yells of challenge to our indomitable sister.

Then I blinked. She'd already flopped back over the chaise.

"Rosamond?"

I'd lost her face. Her free hand dragged itself through a bramble-bush of black hair, snagging every tangle. "Henry, reasoning with Eddie is *so* much effort."

Nectarines, I could cheerfully have upended the very furniture she sprawled on! – had I the strength, and the courage, and all the attendant capabilities. "But – but – I – I'm – I can't – !"

Her hand flapped like a carp-tail, a limp-fingered banishment.

"Please! I haven't words to talk Edwina out of it – and our neighbour's relations are all going to despise me – and I quite don't want to woo a living soul! – especially not through the medium of – erm – tweed and firearms and aristocracy and pheasants – "

"Paid poeni," she mumbled, still insouciantly prostrate. "I taught you to shoot. You aim like a demon. The pheasant bit will hardly be difficult."

"That's quite not the point!" I wailed at her – my voice too shrill not to spiral through the house, my mind too desperate to notice my mistake. "The last time I staggered out to meet the world, I – well – I – you know – you saw – I – I couldn't – and I quite can't do it now! And why must it be me? Why – I mean – why aren't you coming – how do you get out of it? Why does it not apply to you?"

"An excellent point, Henrietta Morfydd Hyssop!"

Figs.

Penance for my shriek, and prompt as ever. Edwina had appeared with horrendous punctuality, sturdy and stern in the doorway, a pillar of spinach-coloured tweed up to her gold chignon, her high collar neatly lined with grey wool. She began, as she usually did, by stringing out my middle names; it's a favourite affectation of our sister-despot. I haven't heart nor nerve to remind her that my unabridged first name is supposedly Harriet. I grant that, four years into our cohabitation, I really ought to have broached the subject – but the longer I leave it, the more terrifying it gets, and disagreeing with her is frightening enough as it is.

"Oh – erm – yes – quite!"

This spluttering insanity was, of course, myself. Faced with the petrifying thing that is unexpected human interaction, I lose all capacity to speak in anything more than tangential monosyllables.

Edwina bustled undaunted past my flailing response, as was her wont, splicing the room in three strides to take up station between myself and Rosamond. Her eyes lashed from my sister to me in two sharp breaths, then settled on Rosamond – and would have skewered her to the brocade with a glare of reprimand, had my sprawled sister been sufficiently upright to notice her doing so. Presumably Edwina had spotted the incongruous heap of coals in the fireplace – the pale juts of bare shoulders – the tumble of uncut fabric – the alarming lack of chemise, or corset, or indeed of any decorous clothing whatsoever.

"Rosamond Pleasant Myfanwy Earlyfate!"

A snigger for every name, muffled through whorls of hair. "Bore da, Eddie!"

"You know I do not care for your absurd nicknames," Edwina snapped. "What are you doing? Are you not ashamed, three-and-twenty as you are, to find yourself still undressed at this hour?"

With perfect, vicious insouciance, the mantelpiece clock trilled half past eleven. Rosamond giggled in tandem, launched herself up the chaise-back like a rag-doll, until she could meet Edwina's incredulous stare with a lazy grin.

"Dearest sister, you can't have it every which way. You said *no tight-lacing* – edrych! No laces!"

Edwina glowered at her for a moment, then gritted her teeth. Her voice was tight and pinched, threading a warning through each word. "It does not matter. It does not. Well – I trust you have been made aware of Henrietta's good news?"

"I might have heard," Rosamond muttered. "You're still Miltonwaters's lapdog, then?"

Edwina blinked, frowned, pressed on. "Lady Miltonwaters has made a most generous offer, and I intend to see it through as swiftly as possible. Everything can move far more quickly now that we have confirmation from the Marquess."

"Confirmation from the Marquess," Rosamond echoed dryly. "What a phrase."

"The insanity of Henrietta's upbringing will finally bear respectable fruit," Edwina continued, lifting her voice over the interruption like a skirt from the mud. "And our family's legacy will be secured!"

Rosamond smirked. "What – you mean that our separate legacy of curing all painful, nervous and drugbaffling cases via herbs in a bestselling bottle *isn't* enough to ensure our infamy?"

"No," Edwina retorted crisply. "That is the very legacy we must distance ourselves from. We are no longer *trade* people."

She dipped stiffly to one knee, her neat tweed skirts folding about her, lifted a pallid hand to pluck the dark curls out of Rosamond's face. "Father sold the business so that we might have this chance

– and we will take it! We will transcend our origins! We will enter the ranks of the nobility!"

Rosamond swung out of her reach with an extravagant groan, all her hair flung straight back to its former chaos. "We will quote our mother verbatim!"

Edwina sighed, stepped sharply away from her efforts at the chaise. Figs, but I could well have told her it was an impossible task to neaten Rosamond's edges, however stressful they were to observe – if I had the nerve to tell her anything.

"As Lady Miltonwaters's companion, Henrietta will be introduced to a host of eligible suitors – an introduction which shall happily coincide with a practical demonstration of her most successful accomplishment. You brought her up shooting targets – wooden targets, yes, and unmoving, but pheasants can hardly be so very different. For all we know, it might even be easier than the task of Girton."

She glanced at me then, a stark sparse look that had me cringing back a step. "Now, Henrietta – as your sister's sole waking purpose is to pour scorn upon the endeavour, I suggest we – "

"Wait a bit!"

Rosamond swallowed, grabbed the chaise-back in both hands and heaved herself to her feet, her fabric swinging about her ankles. We could only stare at her – plums, and she quite intended us to – as she closed her eyes, sucked a breath between her colourless lips until her eyelashes fluttered, steeling herself. For what? For – figs, and I hardly dared think it, but – were all these interjectory theatrics the preamble to saving me? Had she seen me, really seen me, when she gazed at my face earlier – at my cadaverous complexion, at the terror that must have been unmistakeable in my eyes? She might have tried to dismiss me when it was us alone, but Edwina was here now, and the battle was already underway –

"Has it not occurred to you that Henry doesn't want to do this?"

Edwina blinked at her. Rosamond quite didn't let her snatch a retort.

"Any more – " – and her eyes opened, glinted, narrowed – " – any more than I did?"

That momentary surprise vanished. Edwina's irritation had been struck from the moment she saw Rosamond resplendent in her decadence, and now it went scrambling up her stiff tweed gown, over the bulge of her leg-o'-mutton sleeves, across the crested brooch at her pale palpitating throat.

"Why do you think that Henrietta would wish to cast off the chance she has so graciously been granted, and emulate your selfish descent into spinsterish morbidity? What have you been saying to her?"

Rosamond was feverishly radiant with all the unabashed defiance I wish I had, sauntering up close and smirking into the whiplash of elder-sisterly menace. I haven't the faintest why, but Edwina's imperious coldness has never in my recollection intimidated her.

"Well. I don't imagine you asked Henry's opinion before you planned this marry-off-the-youngling reprise, and it doesn't look like you've asked her since. You didn't even tell her it was happening until twenty seconds ago – "

"I did not tell her until it was fully arranged." Edwina pursed her lips for the heady scent in Rosamond's words, but – peaches, no! – stood her ground. "I did not want to raise her hopes only to dash them. There was no guarantee anything would come of it. It is a miracle that Lady Miltonwaters was able to persuade her uncle to disbelieve the rumours, and distinguish Henrietta's good character from the unsavoury tales concerning your own."

"You say that, Eddie, but I *know* you. And I know Henry. Considerably better than you do, if you set seventeen years against four – "

"That does not give you the right to poison her against this!" Edwina spat. "Our parents did not entrust you with the responsibility of arranging these matters for her. They gave that to me. *You*, if you wish to make any useful contribution, should be commending her for attempting to ameliorate her last social failure – certainly not discouraging her from the idea! Or do you want some part in this too? Are you simply disappointed that I could not volunteer you for the visit as well?"

Rosamond shattered into shrill peals of laughter. "You think I'm *jealous?* Dim diolch o gwbl! Mistress Miltonwaters would never have me, and I'm glad of it!"

Edwina broke their stare at last, striding away to the mantelpiece, her hands knotted to smarting at her waist. "I do not have time for you to ruin anything else. I cannot provide you with such opportunities – with any opportunities – whilst you parade your appalling practices of reckless profligacy and speaking Welsh – "

"We *are* Welsh!"

" – and consummately dishonouring your family's brightest hopes!"

I'd snuck halfway to the door before either of them remembered the proximate existence of a younger sibling. Their bristling squabbles can last for hours, and are never the least bit encouraging to witness. Not that this feeble retreat of mine was even slightly successful. Edwina was far too swift, whirling into the doorway, her skirts thwacking dust-motes out of the drab October light. Her glare crashed over me, the kind of glower that conjures up her voice to snarl at the back of my mind – and I could well imagine what she must have been thinking of my pitiful state. *You've no constitution, no spine, no conversation, no charm, not even a scrap of Girtonian intelligence – is it too much to ask of you to manage* something, *without falling under the sway of your irredeemable slatternly sister?*

"Why are you running away, Henrietta Morfydd Hyssop?"

Words instantaneously deserted me, my name included.

"Oh – I – erm – "

"She's escaping you," Rosamond suggested cheerily.

"Enough of this!" Edwina snarled. "Evidently, our sister had the good sense to eschew your venomous company in favour of attending to preparations in the solitude of her bedroom! Am I correct, Henrietta?"

I'd hoped my subsequent spasms would be interpreted as a decorous nod. Figs, but I ought to have known it wouldn't be enough. Edwina simply stared at me, entirely bewildered – and evidently all the more exasperated for it.

"Well? Speak up!"

"Yes, Henry," Rosamond echoed wryly, somewhere hazy and sickly-scented behind Edwina's glare. "Do speak up. Last chance!"

But Edwina got there first. "Be quiet, you! Henrietta, I understand that it might seem a daunting prospect, but there is truly very little demanded of you. Everything has been arranged. Lady Miltonwaters is taking charge of it all. She will be more than able to settle things for you. You have no need to worry. Yes?"

My throat quite closed.

Where would one begin? What reasons would I even have to give, that could stand up against the sternness of her neat crisp sentences? There weren't reasons – there was just Edwina's scowl, and she didn't care in the least about reasons, certainly not any reasons I might try to summon – and all the cautions that had sounded perfectly sensible no longer seemed to exist – there was quite no space in which to fit them –

There wasn't anything. It was as much as I could do just to drop my gaze.

"Well, I tried," Rosamond drawled into the smothering silence. "Pob lwc i ti, Henry. If you're never going to do anything more than Eddie's every whim, let's hope you can at least succeed at *that!*"

Edwina's hands were on my shoulders in the next breath, cold fingers pinching in my collarbone, pulling me close as she snapped over my head. "I won't have you talking to Henrietta like this, is that understood?"

Figs – but –

"Come away, Henrietta. Let us leave her to her sulking."

And the chance was lost. Edwina marched us out in tandem, her hand still clenched on my shoulder, too swiftly to allow for any further disobedience. I had one last snatched glimpse of Rosamond before she crumpled back over the chaise – and she gave me little more than an unrepentant shrug. At the rate Edwina was hustling me along, I was half-afraid she meant to drag me all the way up to my room and lock me in; it was a feeble relief when she released me at the foot of the stairs, and set herself to folding a bundle of unmended skirts on the hallway table. She snagged me in one more glare, shrinking the bundle fold by sharp fold –

"I must deliver these to our tailor. In the meantime – stay away from your sister. You *will* have your chance, and no one will spoil it for you."

And she slammed herself out of the house before I could manage a word.

So – figs – in the wake of that – well. It only makes sense – doesn't it – that I'll have to spoil it for myself?

2.

IN WHICH I RESPOND BY MAKING SOME INFINITELY STRANGER DECISIONS OF MY OWN

More of my journalising

Later, quite possibly the next morning (certainly the earliest hours of it)

Plums. Well. I did it. I – oh, sweet nectarines, I don't entirely know what it is I've done – but I have most thoroughly and irrevocably done it nonetheless.

Edwina had stalked away to the family tailor, Rosamond had disappeared into her attic, and I had the afternoon to myself. I suppose it can hardly be claimed I didn't adhere to Edwina's demands. I certainly spent the time *attending to preparations* in my bedroom, albeit preparations of a rather less acquiescent and respectable sort.

The first thing was to note everything down – for my defence, if nothing else, though I quite hadn't an idea of who would ever read it. I wrote my journal by gloomy gaslight, which caught every shard of the string foliage engraved in the glass of my desk-lamp, whilst the rest of the house darkened around me; even the brief paltry light of the late-autumn day was barely enough to illuminate the page. The fields and coppices beyond my window congealed into the twilight outside, until the panes were slick and sodden with night, the sort of dismal tempestuous rain that flings itself sulkily in every direction at once. I could glimpse nothing beyond, no details but the host of insects that gathered about the sash: spindly harvestmen on the inside, their jagged legs like tiny cracks in the pane, and a moth the size of my thumb, rattling along the casement. Mordred hadn't been in today, clearly.

By the time I dimmed my desk-lamp, the rest of the preparations were done. I'd retrieved the portmanteau from beneath my bed and anonymised it as best I could. Given that Edwina had compelled its maker to pierce the leather with a metal crest, the disguising process had principally involved melting an entire stub of sealing-wax over the telltale nettle-leaves. This improvised vessel I had filled with the plainest clothes I could prise from my wardrobe – the second plainest, I should say, after I had selected the most supremely quiet garments for myself, right down to a penny-collar and wholly patternless cravat. I dredged my Wales greatcoat from its hermitude at the wardrobe's end, and stuffed its capacious pockets with necessary sundries: a pen and ink-bottle, this journal, and the unsmudged perfection of a new fifty-pound note. The latter – with a smart of guilt, I must specify – I'd filched from Edwina's study drawer; she controls the family money, and she won't let Rosamond or I anywhere near it after the ferret incident.

It wasn't just the money that plucked at my conscience. There was a squirming part of me that baulked, even now, at slicing Edwina's plans to such tatters. But what was the alternative? To confess it – here, if nowhere else – my preparations for escaping were not simply the work of one afternoon. I'd kept the suitcase close since at least Girton, in the dreadful anticipation of such an eventuality. Though I'd hoped Edwina would have been sufficiently disappointed by Girton to leave me alone.

But now – this new scheme with Lady Miltonwaters – strangers, scorn, impatience – an unknown noblewoman proffering me out like the spindliest of choice delicacies – hordes of sneering dandies watching me do my best to avoid a live target with whatever ghastly firearms they possessed – if ever a situation were nightmarish enough to spark me to desperate measures –

In short: I left. I had to. I abandoned my sisters' house in Catfish Crescent, sprinted headlong across neighbouring Pole Place, and essentially vanished as best I could into the damp cobblestoned streets of Dallyangle, Surrey.

That, at least, is a very smooth overview of quite how all of this came to happen. It's a skeleton structure for a spread of madness, if you will. To be entirely precise, the madness began before I even made it out of the door.

Persimmons, but it was dark. Gloom is quite the house's natural state – there's very little in the black-and-green for light to catch on – but it had thickened tenfold this evening. Squinting down the staircase was like peering into an inkwell. A few strange shards of – not light, so much as greyer darkness – lay scattered on the steps, marking the panes of the nettle-patterned window that lines the stairwell. There couldn't even have been a light on down there. The only light in the house had been the pallid desk-lamp in my bedroom, and that I had extinguished. I quite didn't dare take a taper down the stairs with me, even so.

There is entirely nothing easeful, no matter how nightmarish the alternative, about inching down two flights of stairs in peat darkness, in your own house, when any sound – beyond the shallow flick of your breath, and the rain, and the distant scrape of the moth at the windowpane behind you – is very likely to send you toppling down the steps in guilty palpitations. The brittle trill of the drawing-room clock, scratching out eleven-thirty, nearly wrung a cry from me. It was late enough, or so I hoped, for both of my sisters to be either resoundingly abed (Edwina) or resoundingly gallivanting somewhere else (Rosamond). The chill of the air was reassuring: if the fires had been put out, there surely couldn't be anyone lingering awake?

I was almost down the staircase when it happened. The shadowy angles of the entrance-hall were nearly upon me, and my greatcoat was all but done with murmuring treason against the banister –

But there was something ahead of me. Stark pale in the darkness. Looming – watching – on the polished floor beneath the last step.

It was quite all I could do to keep hold of the portmanteau. Everything was still quiet, damp rain-splattered quiet, beyond my choking breaths. There was a strange sharp musk to the air now, thick as oversteeped tea.

Plums. Of course. It had to be Mordred.

I should mention that Mordred is a ferret. Edwina prefers to call him an *ermine* – it's more aristocratic, I suppose – and he's been something of the family pet for the last two years. He was Rosamond's final unsupervised purchase, apparently from one of Dallyangle's innumerable farmers; quite as she'd intended, Edwina was furious, but far too proud to dismiss the animal and let the joke win out. Mordred decided, perversely, to despise Edwina on sight – though it does tend to be she who makes a point of attending to his needs – and yet is more than happy to curl up on the chaise with Rosamond and sleep for hours at a stretch. He's a charming tyrant to me, mostly because I allow him to sit on my shoulder, nibble my cravats and steal my handkerchiefs without objection (yes, quite, I can't even menace a ferret).

I've an odd, ill-advised affection for him, even so. The creature is all too aware of my many insufficiencies, and determined to compensate for them: he'll kill any clothes-moth that breaches my wardrobe, and absolutely will not permit a rodent to sneak into my bedroom unchallenged. It is, I must confess, the most effective camaraderie I've had in years. The very mustelid puts Rosamond to shame!

I sighed, crept down to him.

"Mordred – erm – I'm escaping – the sisters have – gone madder – am I making sense?"

Mordred smirked. Sleek as an eel, he slid up the step and shinnied into my greatcoat pocket. My shaky attempt to lift him out again only resulted in a crisp nip to the finger. Figs, but I had no other suitable rain-based attire!

So there I was: a Nettleblack heiress, full twenty-one years of age, whisper-pleading with a ferret on my own family staircase.

"Mordred! I – you can't just – I can't steal you! Please – I – I don't know where I'll go when I leave – pomegranates, I might even end up back in Wales – but my options will be – erm – entirely more limited – if anyone finds out about you!"

He swept his warm little head along the back of my hand, a swathe of reassurance. Also a slight threat.

"You'll – erm – scream the house awake – if I leave you behind – won't you?"

Another smirk (I promise ferrets can smirk). I swallowed.

"Quite. Well – if you insist – "

He fell asleep halfway across Pole Place, a pale swirl in the last of my pockets.

I was considerably further away from my house than Pole Place when the next of that night's calamities struck. I'd decided, by way of an opening gambit, to try and walk to the railway station, and use however much of my fifty pounds was necessary for a ticket to London (how much do these things cost?). From there, in theory, it would be a frantic hunt for another train that could take me – well – there had to be somewhere, somewhere that wasn't here – anywhere that quite didn't require me to be married – or even myself!

This all seemed, in my hazy hysterical state, far too marvellous a plan to defy. Now, I can only look back and wince.

Walk across Dallyangle! On my own! In the middle of the night! When I'd not the faintest idea which direction I ought to walk in – when the grim-weathered gloom smudged the town into utter inscrutability – when Edwina barely ever let me out of the house to learn any of the routes! I'd lived on Gower until I was seventeen, in Girton until I was twenty-one. I knew nothing of Dallyangle beyond the fields and forest-patches that hemmed the town at my bedroom window, and the carriage-ride to church in Edwina's boxy brougham! Edwina was well-acquainted with the place – she'd lived here with Mother long before we joined her – and Rosamond snuck out in the night sometimes, even if she swore she did nothing of the sort, but I – plums, I only knew there *was* a railway station in Dallyangle because Edwina didn't need the brougham for her trips to London! My journeys to Girton had been all pomp and carriage – I'd never even seen a Surrey train!

The more I walked, the more my feeble optimism shrivelled in my ribs. The streets weren't lit beyond the odd dim lantern-hook, the heavy dark of the fields seeped through every crack in the housefronts – and, purely to spite me, it was still snarling with rain. Five minutes of dizzy staggering saw me drenched, sodden fringe dripping into my eyes, ungloved hands frozen to claws (ferret, incidentally, still defiantly asleep). Even so, I don't recall that I ever considered retracing my steps. I didn't think, certainly not in comprehensible sentences, just shivered and stumbled and trusted a semi-fictional railway station to manifest around every new corner – not that it ever did.

I tumbled into a peat-black lane with the appalling name of Weeping Alley – a backstreet, with no doors or entrances to speak of. The backs of rickety tenements lined the path on one side, damp cottages trimmed the other, and the lane itself seemed to lead quite to nowhere, with nothing but marshy fields ahead behind a flimsy token of a fence. It looked, at first blurry glance, quite as sensibly empty as every other street I'd encountered. Not that it was easy to make anything out in more attentive detail; there were no lantern-hooks further into the lane.

And yet – there was certainly something, some flicker of move-ment inside – the first movement I'd seen in the streets beyond my own staggering feet. I peered in, stumbling forward for a better vantage-point. Perhaps it was some kind of important path, even despite its gloomy state? Perhaps that brittle fence was a gate – a gate out of the town –

Then my limbs weren't entirely mine anymore. Something lunged out of the darkness, a shadow springing forward to horribly solid form – and wrenched me into it, yanking me down the alleyway, my boots dragged almost clear of the cobblestones. The shock of it thrust at me like smelling-salts, shattered all the world out of words. There was just a scent, violent and earthy, like the fields outside my window when the ploughs have turned them over – but pressed hideously close, and possessed of far too many limbs. Arms, amphibious and rain-spotted in heavy waxed sleeves, scrabbling for purchase at my elbows – calloused ruddy hands pinning my wrists like a bouquet –

Then a shove that knocked me breathless, until the sharp brick wall of the tenement stung through the back of my greatcoat.

"Don't just stand there – get the case!"

Not a poltergeist, but a person – two persons – their shapes splitting as my eyes steadied to the thickened gloom. I squinted for their faces quite as much as they scowled at mine: a woman and a man, weatherbeaten at the skin and rustic at the voices, the same lilting Dallyanglian accent of Edwina's servants. They'd dressed for the weather far better than I had, solid from the floor up in their waterproof coats, bulky wool scarves in murky grey knotted tight about their necks. More to the point, they both towered over me, brawnier-armed than I'd ever thought plausible to imagine.

I twisted my head about, towards where the alleyway's entrance had been – though the spread of these assailants' shoulders was far too sturdy for me to writhe past – and there was quite nothing. No lights had flickered on in any of the shadowy buildings. No footsteps came running at the sudden flush of voices. No carriage-wheels clattered on the cobblestones. Not even the sharp stab of a police-whistle cut through the silence, which still hung clotted and close about us, beyond the rasps and splutters of our breaths.

Was it possible that *no one* would hear it, see it, if this goblinous pair devoured me now? Had Edwina and Rosamond simply made Dallyangle up? Was the town nothing more than a mass of oblivious empty shells, with not a single animating spirit behind the shut windows and tight-drawn curtains?

Still nothing came. It truly was just me.

Figs.

"Please – do – take the case!" I stammered. "It's – erm – it's not even mine – well – quite – I – I mean – I didn't pack anything ostentatious – "

The woman cut me off, for which I could hardly blame her. *Didn't pack anything ostentatious!* The longest words you've managed in years, and this was what your mind supplied?

"She looks rich. It'll be brimful. Get on with it!"

The man bit his lip. Not that this apparent glimmer of doubt hindered him from snatching at my suitcase handle, more than vigorously enough to prise it from my fingers. "You sure, Maggie?"

The woman (Maggie, presumably?) snorted. "Call it a special treat. Our fitting reward for a job well done."

"Even if the case's got a crest?"

Peaches. A full stick of sealing-wax had been spent covering up that wretched adornment, and all to not the slightest scrap of avail.

"A *crest!*"

Maggie dragged me up to her eyes, frowned for a better look. Another few inches and my feet would leave the stones. "What'd you say your name was?"

My voice was, quite understandably, a squeak. "I – I didn't?"

She wrenched at her pocket, wrestled something free in a shiver of metal. It was a pair of scissors – but far larger and thicker at the blades than any I'd ever seen, with a terrifyingly sharpened edge for such a clumsy-looking tool. Not that she was clumsy with them in the least: in one practised tweak of her fingers, she'd spread the blades wide, tipped them with horrendous insouciance towards where I shrank back against the wall. "Well?"

Well! And all I could imagine, deranged though it may have been, was the two pastoral criminals hearing *Nettleblack* and marching me back to Catfish Crescent, quite possibly in the company of a ransom demand, in what Edwina would surely regard as my most spectacular social failure yet –

"I – erm – it's Morfydd!"

Maggie blinked. "Say again?"

"I – it's – erm – it's Welsh – "

The man (Not-Maggie? Until he gives me his name, it'll have to do) scowled. Cracked open at his feet, my unfortunate suitcase was fast becoming a water feature. "You ladies done with your introductions? Maggie, unless you fancy another Div brawl – "

"Just shut the case and keep watch," Maggie snapped. Her hand lashed up the back of my neck, twisted me about to face the wall, wrenched on my hairpins until my scalp and I were smarting in unison. "Nice fat plait. Perfect!"

I gasped, swallowed a breathful of sopping brick-dust. The wall scraped across my cheek, sodden and freezing – and the scissors, the ghastly scissors, what had she done with them?

"No – wait – please – "

"There we go!"

Then her fingers vanished, left me slumped and bewildered, the rough skin of the bricks still pressed to my face. I set my hands to the wall – it was the only thing of any solidity that quite still seemed to exist – and pushed myself about, until I had Maggie back in my sight again, slipping the scissors into her pocket. I suppose I really ought to have tried to sprint then, life and all, ducked through the jostle of their burly elbows and fled – but her grin held me transfixed. She flung me a cheery wave, something damp and dark and snaky dribbling from her fingers.

The chill dashed up my neck. The chill – and the revelation.

"Give it back! I – you can't – that's my *hair* – you can't just *cut it off* – I'm – *pineapples!*"

Maggie sniggered, twirled my plait around her wrist like a mitten. Now that she had her prize, she seemed almost inclined to be convivial.

"'Fraid that's not how hair works, dear. You could always buy it back – I bet your glossy brown ringlets'd fetch top price on the market!"

The *market?*

Could I shriek for the constable? Did this town even have constables? Did this town have anything by way of benevolent human presence?

"Now, Morfydd, what're you hiding in those pockets?"

This fresh humiliation – and Maggie's fist at my arm, squeezing the rain from my coat sleeve as she tugged me close – snatched me out of my petrified daze. *Those pockets* – those pockets with everything of importance and value stuffed into them – those pockets, which I clearly did not think through back in the safety of the house! Am I so resoundingly incapable of managing a shred of practical-mindedness – of world-wisdom – of self-preservation – of anything, in short, beyond indignant fruit and wanton fear?

"Bloody hell – look at this!"

Maggie wrenched my fifty pounds free with a guillotine grin, lashed the money to her palm with my hair (merciful kumquats, but that wasn't a phrase I ever thought I'd pen in my conscious existence). Barely a moment's pause, and she was scrabbling at my other pocket, her breath thick as wool on my bare neck.

My other pocket – containing journal, pen, ink-bottle, and ferret. Ferret.

"Wait!" I spluttered. "Don't – I – he'll – "

It was the only warning I had time to offer. Maggie ignored me, jostled Mordred out of his slumber, and was promptly reproved with all the needlepoint agony of a ferret's teeth.

To confess it plainly, wretchedly: he nearly bit off her index finger. By the time she yanked her hand back, the digit was mauled beyond repairing, splattered in blood and wrenched half-apart from the knuckle. When I mused on the ferret's penchant for chivalry, this was entirely beyond what I'd wished to anticipate.

Maggie screamed. Not-Maggie screamed. I screamed. Mordred screamed, a feral white snarl over the edge of my pocket, curled atop my journal like a wyvern.

Somewhere terrifyingly close at hand, a fifth shout shrilled through the rain.

Oh, better and better! *Now* the town finds its limbs!

"I am so sorry," I blurted wildly. "You must forgive the ferret – erm – he – he was raised in a very tolerant house – "

Not-Maggie hurled me the full width of the alleyway. "You're not helping! Maggie – what the – how – you're bleeding – "

"For the Dallyangle Division!" someone yelled, mere cobblestones away.

Maggie lunged for my lapels with her unscathed hand, both sleeves bloodied to the elbow. "I'll have them throttle the beast!"

I scrambled back. "He – he quite won't let you!"

"Just run, Maggie!" Not-Maggie roared at his maimed colleague, concluding the insane quartet with admirable ferocity. "Case – tin – hair – scarper!"

And they were off like two slightly incapacitated shots, leaping the fence to tumble into the shadows of the field beyond. There was no hope of following their path any further, not once the darkness had gulped them down.

New footsteps hammered into the alley. Blood splattered my sodden greatcoat. My hair – I felt it, my shaking fingers tracing the back of my neck – had been cropped for the scaffold, and barely straggled to my jawline.

The money was gone. My clothes were gone. There wasn't a route out of Dallyangle in sight or probability. Not a route – except – bergamots – except the very route I was currently in the process of escaping from – a route that started with Lady Miltonwaters's carriage and ended in certain matrimonial doom –

I slumped against the wall, gasping for breath. Someone seized my shoulders. I could only presume it was a policeman, ready to escort me shorn and contrite to my sisters' hearth, the ignominious conclusion to a harrowing evening –

Then I looked up, and felt my jaw slap my collar.

I'd assumed policeman, or parish constable, or whatever Dallyangle had by way of law enforcement. I'd barely seen anything of Dallyangle – how was I to know? And yet – the apparition before me was too slim and angular to be any kind of policeman. She was a young Black woman, wide-eyed above the relentless freckles across her nose, staring at me with – figs, with *impatience* twitching at her features. Her strange attire didn't even slightly resemble a policeman's garb, but it was unmistakeably some kind of uniform. Spirals of peat-coloured hair skittered out from under her broad-brimmed hat, her stiff brown jacket had been vigorously waterproofed from its copper buttons to its high burgundy collar, and there was a lantern hooked to a loop in her belt, streaking her cropped walking-skirt with yellow folds of light.

But – what – who – what – ?

"Where did they go?"

I blinked at her. She shook me.

"Those two – did you see which way they went?"

My fingers twitched, the feeblest indicatory gesture. She didn't appear to notice. Her next gambit was a little gentler, words spat out slowly to make sure I caught them.

"Can you at least tell me what happened?"

Yes. No.

Robbery – haircut – sisters – pheasants –

I answered with the first words that made it to my teeth:

"I wish to join – whatever you are!"

Then I deciphered my own sentence, and promptly fainted.

I woke up with only half an idea who I was, and not even half an idea where I'd been spirited off to. There were chimes and groans from a clock nearby, far tinnier than the delicate trill of our mantelpiece clock, nudging us past midnight. Something simmered under my eyelashes with an appalling brightness, especially considering the lateness of the hour. Woodsmoke clustered thick against my skin, woodsmoke and warmth – all the vague comfort of a nearby fire.

The rest was less comforting. Closer than the rain, which clattered against – windowpanes, it must have been – there was another steady drip, regular and sharp. There was sharpness at my elbows too, the scratch and splinter of fresh-cut wood, jostling through my shirtwaist.

Shirtwaist. My – if I – where had my greatcoat gone?

The brightness cracked my eyelids, blared a room into focus. It was a little smaller than our drawing-room, with a far lower ceiling, its stark whitewashed walls catching the glare from half-a-dozen gaslights nailed in at eye-level. There was a huge desk, tall enough for a dresser and almost as wide as the room itself, the shining wood meticulously polished – and topped with a thick leather ledger, splayed open, an ink-pen balanced precariously on the pages. My greatcoat swung from a coat-stand beside two broad double doors, attended by a smudge of rainwater on the floorboards below – the source of the brittle drips. I was rain-smudged myself, drying off by slow stiff degrees – sprawled on a rickety wooden bench that lined one of the horrendously bright walls –

But I wasn't alone. In point of alarming fact, I appeared to be using the bench's – no, the room's – only other occupant as some sort of pillow. I blinked, sharpened the face above mine: dark navy eyes and a crease of a frown, pinching me in taut scowling scrutiny.

"Figs!"

I sprang up, regretted it, crumpled back onto the bench – upright, this time. She – it was a she – was still frowning at me, more nonplussed than intent now.

"I – I'm so sorry – consummately not intentional – I – erm – apologies – all of them – many – "

My erstwhile pillow managed a wary smile. She was quite startlingly handsome, even in the ghastly glare of the late-night lamps: brawny at the shoulders, rosy-skinned and sun-brazened with health I'd not seen at close quarters for an alarmingly long time, and – and *phenomenally* chignoned! Her reams of thick chestnut hair had been painstakingly whorled up with a myriad of pins; they were by no means expensive pins, but they glinted all the same in the untimely gaslight.

"Not a problem, miss. 'Long as you're alright."

Then she glanced away, her smile tweaking to a glower, muttered a coda to herself. "There! I can do your public-facing charm *just* as much as the rest of 'em!"

Of course I stared. Her hair was the very antithesis of the sodden foundling-crop mine had just become, she had a face more exquisite than any I'd ever seen, and now she appeared to be soliloquising some deep relentless strife that made not the slightest edge of sense. At least, I assumed it to be a soliloquy – there was no one else in the room for her to strike up a conversation with. If anything, she appeared to be discoursing to her notebook, a weatherbeaten paper-backed thing with cheap black covers, its splayed pages scrawled with capitals and underlinings in smudgy pencil.

For all its battered state, the notebook seemed to have entirely absorbed her, and it felt quite impolite to gawp as she communed with her own furious annotations. I hauled my gaze away, cast about the room for something else to look at – and got, to my alarm, rather a lot to scrutinise. From where I was sat, I could make out both front and back of the enormous desk, everything from the crisp-paged calendar announcing the date to the plate of – peaches, of a half-eaten wheel of cheese? – hidden beneath the counter. There was a wood-burner tucked behind the desk, gnawing through a heap of logs, the floor about its raised legs scattered with splinters and moss.

Stacked up on the stools beside it were more books, some of them ledgers to match the open volume, the top one unmistakeably a copy of *Life and Limbs: a Comic Romance of the Medical School!* And beyond the stools – opposite the bench – there was a gaping threshold without a door to it, twisting round into the darkness of a skinny corridor, from which were issuing all manner of strange rustlings and scrapings.

What in figs' name *was* the place?

Sheer desperation set words in my throat, though I was more than a little afraid of interrupting my only companion's peculiar self-reflection. "I – erm – well – sorry again – could I just enquire – I haven't the faintest where I – erm – am – at present – "

Her gaze snapped back to mine, far too eager-eyed for the late hour, her fingers pinching the notebook shut. The words, when they came, roiled off her tongue like an aria, strict to rhythm and slick with rehearsal.

"Well! Welcome, miss, to the Dallyangle Division! Hurl upon us all sinister activity and midnight menaces, and you'll see 'em resolved in a trice!"

Quite why she needed to advertise me such services didn't seem clear – though they were, admittedly, precisely what I needed. Persimmons, having one's hair and suitcase-based life stolen by two terrifying thieves with nineteen functioning fingers between them certainly qualified as a *midnight menace!*

"Oh! I – erm – right! Thank you! That – actually – yes – "

She narrowed her eyes at me, a stare quite as scalding as it was suspicious. The practised polish of her previous utterance dropped, returning her voice to its original sharpness – certainly sharper than the Sweetings' broad accents, with chisel-cut edges that sounded almost cockney. "That's why you're here, ain't it? You ain't a public menace – 'least, I don't think so."

I didn't know whether to be flattered or incredulous. I suppose, given my current appearance, I had little right to either extreme. "I – what?"

"Is it the Sweetings you've met with?" Lemons, she was scowling again, up and across the ragged edges of my shorn hair. "Brother and sister. One of 'em's called Maggie."

I gaped at her. "I – how can you know that?"

She grew a full two inches, still sat on the bench, her face struck somewhere between pride and exasperation. "'Cause I'm a Division Sergeant, and chasing 'em down's part of my job!"

Her words and her clothes thwacked me in the same instant. She was all in brown, short jacket buttoned to her chin, her collar and cuffs a deep burgundy – the strange effect finished off with some peculiar variation on rational dress, in the form of tall boots and tailored trousers, cut from the same sturdy fabric and darned at the knees. It was hardly the neatest of outfits – certainly nowhere near as elegant as her hair – the colours were faded, the collar-edges wearing away, the fabric speckled over with scrapes and stains – but it suited her to an astonishing extent. *Disconcerting* was the word: disconcertingly bizarre, disconcertingly compelling – and, most disconcerting of all, disconcertingly *familiar* –

"Javert! Stop terrorising the new recruit!"

A new voice sprang at us from across the room, complete with a new human emerging from the gloom of the corridor. It was another woman, dressed to match my latest perturbing acquaintance – although she wore the jacket with a walking-skirt – sepia-faced and freckly under unpinned black curls, dangling a flimsy sheet of paper from finger and thumb. There was an answering snarl from my interrogator, but in that moment I'd not the nerve left to glance back at her. I'd been wrong in my first assumption – this weary-looking woman with the paper wasn't new – I recognised her face, her wry voice – I'd seen her before –

I'd yelled that nonsensical request for immediate employment at her, seconds prior to my spectacular swoon in Weeping Alley.

Abruptly, horrendously, I remembered everything.

"Recruit?"

The – what had she said, the Division Sergeant? – with the beautiful chignon – whose name, surely, could not be cribbed straight from *Les Misérables* – plums, but she sounded quite as horrified as I felt. "She ain't even minimum height!"

"Forgive me if I don't exactly trust your assessment." The other woman skirted the desk, hauled me off the bench with her free hand, dug her nails into my arm to keep me upright as I staggered. The skin of her hands was quite pockmarked with freckles – no, with ink, a pattern of dashes and commas pinwheeling from her wrists to her fingernails. "Come on, Divisioner-to-be, I haven't got all night."

"But – wait – I – erm – "

The woman on the bench sprang to her feet, eyes stark wide with incredulity. "Does the Director know about this, Cassandra?"

"She will." Cassandra flung her a withering smirk. "But that'll be for me to tell her, and you to seethe about."

Nectarines, her colleague was seething already. "I thought she wanted you to try lookout tonight. I thought *you* wanted to try lookout!"

Cassandra rolled her eyes. "If I ever thought lookout and I would be bosom companions, I can't see it now. I looked out, and I saw the Sweetings – but they bolted, and there's no way of following them, and the rain's only getting worse. Home comforts may be worlds beyond your daily routine, but I'm not drenching myself to a fever for a hopeless chase."

"I knew it'd be the Sweetings!" the other burst out. "Why didn't you go after 'em?"

"Had to rescue the bright-eyed new apprentice, didn't I? Come back and snarl at me the day you work out how to deal with those two single-handed. Or – maybe even – the day you actually spot them in time to try it."

The other woman's navy eyes glinted, and the chignon twitched – but she was evidently too furious to speak. I glanced between the sparrers, swallowed yet more panic. They clearly despised each other, they were both taller than me, and if brawls ensued I'd not survive to hear the next clock-chime. Not that Cassandra appeared inclined to push the battle from words to blows. Next to her rival's wiry strength and weathered uniform, she looked soft as a quill, with only one night's speckling of raindrops to mar the smooth edges of her clothes.

"Oh, and Javert?"

"Septimus," her nemesis snapped. "For the last time, I ain't your damned fictional policeman – "

"The Director's waiting for you," Cassandra interrupted, all insouciance. "Do try not to get yourself suspended again, *Septimus*."

Septimus (was that her name? I suppose, if she said it) gritted her teeth. "I think you'll find it was unpaid leave – "

"I think you'll find I'm the one who proofreads the Director's Record," Cassandra tossed back, sneering, "So I know exactly what it was."

Septimus flushed. "You don't know a thing – "

"I know the foundling prodigy's lost her touch, and I know *I've* got someone to interview. Run along to the Director, now!"

Cassandra marched off before I could snatch another glimpse of the combusting chignon, sweeping me along like a parasol, spitting practicalities through her teeth. "Ignore her, she's our resident downward spiral. Thinks a mad name's a substitute for an appealing personality. My name's Cassandra – Division Sergeant Ballestas, really – but you might as well call me Cassandra, everyone does insist on it – and if you manage to meet my standards, I'll be one of your superiors in the Dallyangle Division."

She flung us forward into the murky corridor, wheeled me about until the last of the reception-room vanished from view. There was a row of doors lined up on our left side, the first with a sliver of light spilling from beneath it, the others half-discernible further down – there were no gaslamps here to light our path. Even for all its brightness, the first room had been ominous, and the sudden profusion of shadows only made it worse, until I could hardly snatch the breaths to keep up with her hasty stride. Was this the moment to confess the lot? Was this – figs – was this the moment to twist from her grip and run?

"Take a seat!"

We'd reached the second door in the passageway, and she bustled me into it, kicking the door wide with one sturdy boot. Whatever this room's previous use had been – judging by the remnants of hooks on the walls, I guessed either tack room or torture chamber – vague efforts had been made to transform it into an office, with brittle shelves full of ledgers and loose papers, and a stack of stained teacups lining the skinny legs of a desk. Plums, it was still every penny dreadful Rosamond had ever lent me. The metal poking from the walls was peeling with rust, and the sallow desktop had its own scratching of stains, which I fervently hoped were merely the work of an inkwell. Another brace of gaslights had been haphazardly nailed in at head-height, but they hadn't been lit; there was a piece of torn paper stuffed into one of the glass casings, hollering *don't turn on, they will explode!* in jaunty inked capitals. The only light in the room came from the tapers dotted about the shelves and desk, their flames swooning fit to rival even my earlier performance.

Cassandra threw me into a spindly wooden chair, bristled herself down opposite me with her sheet of paper, hooked a loose curl behind her ear, and grabbed for the nearest of many battered ink-pens. The tapers trembled for her every movement, raking clawed shadows from the hooks on the walls.

"Alright. Want to join us, you say?"

And in that instant – sodden and half-mad – still reeling from the loss of my very existence – scorched at the eyebrows by that encounter with Septimus and her formidable hair – and frantically dodging thoughts of all that my sisters would do if they discovered it – I was either too polite, or too terrified, to want anything else.

"Well – quite!"

Cassandra, gangly and elegant in her strange uniform, allowed herself full thirty seconds to study me properly. Her freckled face slowly crumpled into a turbulent combination of scepticism and irritation, a good quarter of it directed solely at my cravat. I knew the look all too well. There was nothing to do but stare at the nearest inkstain, my toes curling in my boots, the jagged edge of my truncated hair dripping icy gnat-bites down the back of my neck.

"Right. Well. Whatever you are, you're on my head, so we'd better make the best of you. And you're *new* – unsolicited – which is something, at least. Name?"

Yes! She hadn't instantly thrown me out!

Cassandra cleared her throat, nudged me back into panic. *Name?* I was far too twitchy to try anything ostentatiously Welsh again. Edwina had always bungled my first name, so that was a possibility – but it wasn't as if I *liked* the name Harriet – and if I spluttered out *Nettleblack* everyone in Dallyangle would know it –

"Henry!"

Her eyebrows melted into her hairline. Figs, I could hardly blame her.

"Really. Just like Javert named herself Septimus, I suppose."

Neck-deep in my own mire, there was nothing to do but force a petrified smile. "Well – in a manner of – anyway – it's Henry – erm – Hyssop?"

My other middle name. Herbal as it was, it was at least not famously associated with a certain household tincture.

"Henry Hyssop."

"Yes! I – well – my – my parents just – erm – were – eccentric – "

She flicked a hand at me. "Alright, alright. At least you've got a surname. What are your parents?"

"Dead," I stammered, like a consummate fool. "I – I mean – well – yes – "

"My condolences." Her sympathy was dry as paper, and quite as ironical as the flourish with which she scrawled down my impromptu alias. "Anyway. Age?"

"Oh – I – erm – twenty-one – "

"Mm. Older than you look. Height?"

Plums, how was I to know? "I'm sorry, I – I haven't the faintest – "

She rolled her eyes. "Didn't come prepared, clearly. Fortunately for you, I'm not Javert. Get up – I'll measure you."

I skittered off the chair, tipped onto my toes, prayed my skirt and the shadows and the looming desk would mask my doing so. *Minimum height,* Septimus had said, and I was the shortest of my sisters by half a head. I must have been near the end of the test – and I was hardly having this oddly-named version of myself getting thrown out of the Dallyangle Division before she'd fully signed up!

The Dallyangle Division. At what point was I going to venture that feeble, small-voiced, petrified enquiry: *what actually are you?*

Cassandra, for her part, appeared to be grappling with a conundrum of her own. I had been expecting her to produce a tape measure, or perhaps gesture me towards one of the metal-studded walls to mark out my height – but she clearly had no such intention. She fumbled in her desk-drawer, extricated a ruler – a skinny wooden thing that couldn't have been longer than twelve inches – glanced from it to me in several increasingly panicky stares – held it up, as if she meant to toast me with it – then dropped it straight back into the drawer. I blinked at her, and got a valiant shrug by way of answer, a quick jerk of the head for me to sit down again, a wry grimace as she did the same.

"It's probably fine," she muttered, after several seconds of dazed silence on both our parts. "We're desperate, and I've had it just about up to *here* – " (*here* being a violent hand-gesture towards the ceiling, quite possibly level with the minimum height) " – with Javert quoting my mother at me."

I blinked. "I'm sorry?"

"Apology appreciated," she smirked irritably, apparently disinclined to elaborate. "Look – Hyssop – Henry – whatever – is there anything you *can* do? Please?"

Well. I'd been asking myself the same question for twenty-one years.

"Oh – erm – I – I can read – write – draw – paint in watercolours – badly – embroider a handkerchief – more or less – play the pianoforte – not well – "

And this genteel spiel was, of course, more than enough to bring the whole *Rights of Woman* crashing down on my sheltered head. Cassandra looked ready to upend me through the door. Was there nothing else I knew – anything less accomplished?

"I'm also – erm – very proficient with firearms?"

Sweet nectarines, the irony!

Cassandra flung a groan up past her quivering tapers, lolling back in her chair in an attitude of exhausted despair. "And what good will that be, when the Div don't carry weapons? How's your constitution? Physical strength? Capacity to shrug off bad weather?"

I paled. Mercifully, she didn't demand further answer than that.

"Look, just sign here," she declared through a sigh, skidding a form across the desk. She'd put my name in quotation marks. "You've got to be useful somehow. And there's a free bed in the dorm."

I gaped at her. "I – what – am I expected to reside here?"

"Oh, no. We sleep in the fields, mostly." She sniggered for her own sarcasm, pen-nib dripping ink on the dotted line. "The Dallyangle Division's no longer an out-of-the-living-room affair – we have *lodgings* now. Apprentices sleep here. Anything higher sleeps in its own home, if it's sensible, or under the desk in its office, if it's Javert. Did you not know this? Do you know anything about being part of the Division?"

"I – erm – well – "

Plums, how to put this delicately?

"I've only very recently been – erm – made aware that I – erm – had such an option – I've – ah – not encountered a – a police with ladies – "

"We're not the police!"

She straightened up in her chair, cleared her throat, reeled off the rest as if it were a poem for a drawing-room – much like the way Septimus had introduced the Division to me, not that I imagined Cassandra would appreciate such a comparison. "Dallyangle doesn't need them, not while it has us. Hurl upon us all sinister activity and midnight menaces, and so forth. And there'll be no metropolitan interference here, now that we're providing public protection for our town's particular needs – or something like that – and it's all thanks to our brilliant Director. Haven't you heard of her? Or... any of this? Are you not from around here? Have to say, I can't place your accent."

In the face of all these brilliant women, I could hardly admit that I'd simply never been permitted to walk the Dallyanglian streets alone – or, for that matter, to attend to anything in Dallyangle beyond its nobility. As for my voice – well, figs – when one thwacks a South Welsh lilt against the affected elocution of the English upper classes, the result is certainly rather difficult to place.

"I – erm – well – I've just come back from studying at Cambridge – "

Her tired eyes quite popped. "Real Cambridge? Girton College?"

"I – quite – "

To my astonishment, she struck up a triumphant laugh. "Well, what do you think of *that*, Javert? I've only gone and hired a Girton girl! That is – " – and her grin wavered – " – if you're sure you want to sign?"

Pheasants and proposals or spontaneous Divisionry.

Have stranger choices been made?

But – I'd come this far, hadn't I? And it was hardly hurting anyone! And – surely slipping myself into some sort of structure – something pioneering and useful, if what they all said was to be believed – surely that was a start? The panicky stab of thought – *you can still sneak back to the house* – struck me between the eyebrows, but I frowned it off before it could settle. Coward that I was (well, am), I couldn't entirely bear the thought of braving the stormy witch-hour streets again.

Was this what decided me? I could claim it was that noble desire to serve a useful purpose, but in wretched honesty it was a bit of both. I signed, blotted the pen to turn *N* into *H*, and Cassandra shook my hand.

"Welcome to the Dallyangle Division, Henry Hyssop," she drawled. "I can assure you, you're in for the rollick of your life."

3.

IN WHICH A PLACE THAT QUITE CAN'T EXIST DEFIANTLY CONTINUES TO DO SO

To further pursue my insanity

I had barely a breath, in that stunned shadowy moment, to think on what I'd done, before all thoughts were abruptly curtailed by the sound of a door opening – well, to be precise, smashing open with clang fit to set the walls shaking. Cassandra dragged herself to her feet, shot me an eye-roll, stalked out into the corridor to meet the carnage with astonishing sangfroid. Given that I'd toppled half off my chair already, it seemed only prudent to follow her lead.

"It *does* make sense! You've got to trust me!"

The yawning door – the one at the top of the corridor – flung out a splash of gaslight, illuminating the passageway like a magic lantern, catching all the colours of the two figures beyond Cassandra's sprightly curls. It was Septimus again, whirling about to plead with another woman – taller and older than the others, her skin deepest brown and her hair tight-bunched in a bun, her pristine uniform starred with a gleaming silver badge. She seemed quite profoundly disinclined to indulge whatever strange request had been proffered to her, pinning on a calming smile with alarmingly quick precision, her hands neatly clasped at her waist.

"Septimus. I appreciate your zeal, but we cannot employ this – this tactic of yours again. Pip Property is not personally involved in every crime ever to have struck Dallyangle."

"But they'll know something! And if you'd just let me question 'em again – you're the Director, you can authorise it – *and* you're the one who said we shouldn't be afraid to use our abilities, 'long as the town required 'em – "

"But this isn't about the town, is it?" the Director interjected. "This is about you, continuing to neglect the good sense that made your name. We will discover the author of these letters, and we will unmask whoever sees fit to harass us – but we are not dragging that cravat designer back into our affairs."

Brilliant was what Cassandra had called the Director, this fearfully controlled leader with her polished badge and elegant gold-rimmed spectacles. Looking at her, I could well believe it. Edwina, perpetually stressed and dragging the Nettleblack fortune from her shoulders – she was another *brilliant* woman, as our parents and our servants had all agreed, and the fact that she looked completely tormented by her own brilliance only enhanced its credibility. The Director was the same, though her calm façade was far more convincing than Edwina's. She kept her brilliance perfectly poised, balancing on that careful self-control – and if you'd not lived with a sister similarly hounded by just how highly everyone thought of her, you'd never have noticed the edge to that armoured smile.

"So – in a shocking turn of events – we're not chasing after Property tonight," Cassandra smirked, grasping behind her to shunt me forward. Unsurprisingly, considering the blazing row unfolding a metre down the corridor, I wasn't inclined to let her. "But *one* of your Division Sergeants has done something right this evening! I've only gone and – "

"Property could give us a lead!" Septimus insisted, still doggedly intent on the Director. "That's if they ain't the one writing the letters! It makes a mort of sense for 'em to want us disbanded – "

The Director set her teeth. "Because you provide ample reason. Which you would do well to stop doing."

"It's the moral of Javert's existence," Cassandra remarked loudly, her sardonicism slightly more panicked, her fingers still flitting blindly in search of my arm. "Anyone in a fancy cravat must be harbouring terrible secrets!"

Oranges. I was sporting a fancy cravat at that precise and incriminating instant, and my mad past self had apparently seen fit to trap it under a penny-collar.

"Septimus," the Director sighed, patting her on the shoulder with one measured flick-of-the-wrist – or quite possibly preventing her from springing at Cassandra – "Enough of this. The Division has its duties, and you need to start prioritising them again."

Cassandra snickered. "Do you hear that, Javert? No more burglaries on your lookouts, eh?"

The Director glanced around, lifting her voice high over Septimus's retort, with such shrivelling disapproval in her tone that both Cassandra and I wilted. "Cassandra, is there some reason you are stood here offering unhelpful witticisms, when you should be – and who is your companion?"

Every gaze in the corridor slid in my direction. The Director, in a rather objectionable flash of brilliance, edged a step to the side to unblock the stream of gaslight from her room, until it lit me up like a bedraggled votive. Given that I'd spent the last ten seconds feverishly wrestling the cravat from my neck, it was all I could do to manage a countenance of approximate composure.

"She's our latest recruit to the Division," Cassandra declared, triumphant at last. "I found her in Weeping Alley, and – hear me out – I've just signed off her paperwork."

"*What?*" Septimus spluttered.

I curtsied, face flaming, utterly devoid of words. Three shadowy silhouettes gaped back at me. The Director swallowed, arched her eyebrows, radiating forced calm frantically enough to steady every quivering flame in the building.

"Your reasoning, Cassandra?"

I could only be grateful she hadn't asked me.

"Well – I know it looks mad, but we can train her up – and she wanted to join! And she's not a Skull – she's not just clung on from one of the old cases – she's a proper Spontaneous Dallyanglian Citizen, choosing to make a career of the Division! The very thing you've been hoping we might start to get!"

Septimus looked more inclined to protest than words can do justice to – but the Director held up a curt hand to silence her, glanced me over with wary curiosity. "Is this true, miss?"

"I – erm – I – quite – "

"It is!" Cassandra blurted, not without a scowl for my paltry efforts. "And I chose well! She went to Cambridge!"

The Director's voice was a perfect tritone of shock. "The University of Cambridge? And you have a – that is to say, you completed your studies there?"

She had plainly been on the brink of asking what my qualification was, as if I'd sat the London exams instead of a Tripos. Edwina's choice of institution for me had been based rather more on proximity of nobility than ability to receive a degree – although, with my grades, I probably never would have obtained one regardless. Figs – not that admitting as much would have been at all wise –

"I – yes!" I stammered hastily. "I – at Girton College – I – quite – do you – erm – do you know it?"

The Director's golden eyes twitched behind her glasses, and I felt my stupidity on the instant. "Yes. I know it. And I know that the university makes a point of refusing to offer its female students any qualification for their efforts. I am intrigued that you chose to study there regardless – was there some resource that only the College could provide?"

Nectarines, tread carefully. Do not mention tinctures, or inheritances, or sizeable donations. "Oh – erm – no – I – I just – my family – "

"Ah." Her smile sprang back, sharp at the edges, the determined politeness stopping just short of her spectacle-frames. "Family connections. I see."

She frowned a moment, the distracted brow-furrow of someone making a note. I expected the inevitable *what family?* – and was already scrabbling to find some credible profession for the fictitious Hyssops –

"Anyway," she declared briskly. "You have a name, I presume?"

I could only blink at her.

"Answer the Director," Cassandra hissed, with a stare that plainly threatened to make me eat my enlisting form in the event of non-compliance.

Words. Coherency. Please?

"Oh – well – I – it's actually – just – Henry – erm – Hyssop – yes – quite – so do call me that – "

"Henry Hyssop," the Director finished dryly, fastening off my insanity like a French knot. "Well, Miss Hyssop, we have all manner of idiosyncratic names here, so I suppose in that respect you are a perfect fit. And, as Cassandra says, you are precisely what the Division has been hoping for – a new recruit from beyond our usual circle, evidence of broader neighbourly engagement with our cause."

I nodded as wildly as my penny-collar would permit me. "Quite – exactly – erm – yes – "

"Excellent. I am Keturah St. Clare Ballestas, Director and founder of the Dallyangle Division – although I imagine you know that."

Ballestas?

She caught my bewilderment, the startled stares I was now skeining between her and Cassandra, and sighed. "Cassandra is my daughter, Miss Hyssop. She is also one of my two Division Sergeants – that's what we call our senior authorities now, you see. Cassandra keeps track of the paperwork and runs the desk, and Septimus takes the lead in our practical work."

Septimus jerked an irritable nod at me. "Miss Hyssop."

"Practical work," Cassandra muttered wryly. "Does it still count as practical if she's *at* the crime, but looking the other way?"

Of course it struck her colleague like a match. "One more snipe, Cassandra – "

"Enough!"

The pair snapped to silence – Cassandra wide-eyed, Septimus with a mutinous glare. The Director looked halfway to another steely reprimand, until some unexpected thought yanked it back, left a sudden shrewd smile in its place.

"Septimus. Cassandra is right. You require a new focus."

Cassandra grinned, a little bemusedly. "I – yes, that's what I said – "

"Miss Hyssop might have a privileged education, if not the degree to show for it – but she won't know where to start with working for the Division. You, Septimus, will be training her. She can assist you – the present task is certainly difficult enough to merit it."

Figs. Septimus looked ready to smite. For my own part, I fear my expression was quite as horrified as hers.

"But – I ain't – you can't – !"

"Think you'll find she can," Cassandra cut in. Her spare hand scuttled up my back, locked on my collar, waved me about like a handkerchief. "Surely you've always wanted an assistant? Someone to follow you round and point out any obvious crimes you might not otherwise notice?"

And weigh you down, she may as well have said. "I don't need an assistant! She'll only get – "

"I think you do," the Director interrupted sharply. "You'll take her out with you tomorrow. Tonight, you'll sort her uniform and her space in the dormitory."

"Why so furious, Javert? She's got practical hair, she'll make you look tall – "

"I *am* tall!"

"Do your best, Septimus." The Director held her gaze, let the smile drop centimetre by centimetre, until everything of her face was a keen warning stare. "Don't let me down this time."

Septimus blanched. "But – "

The hand at my neck shoved, and I went skidding headlong into the thunderstruck Division Sergeant, squeaking apologies into her jacket. Cassandra's voice sauntered after me, sharp with triumph: "Best of luck, you two!"

Before anyone could stammer forth a shred of audible reason, Cassandra had waltzed off in the direction of the reception-room, and the Director was marching back to her office with all the studied care of a grenadier guardsman. She left her door open, doubtless to ensure that her eavesdropping would be noted, and that her subordinate would be rendered unable to dismiss me. The narrow strip of gaslight penned Septimus in with me like – oh, figs, is a caged lion too wantonly hyperbolic?

I swallowed, clung to my elbows. It was the closest I could manage by way of a heat source. The wood-burner's tendrils hadn't curled out this far, and the corridor was draughtier than Cassandra's ramshackle office, enough to press the clammy shoulders of my shirtwaist tight to my skin. I wanted quite nothing more than to dash into the reception-room and snatch up my greatcoat, though I doubted the poor sodden garment would be of any use whilst the drips from its hem were still audible. More to the point, I'd no idea whether I was allowed to get the coat – or wander off – or do anything, in short, until Septimus had summoned some words for me. She'd turned away, her fingers drumming on the pocket where she kept her notebook, staring out the damp-printed floorboards with enough fervour to poke a hole in them. I'd quite no idea how to draw her back out – and, by the look of it, she hadn't the faintest how to even look at me. For a long moment, nothing spoke but the Director's pen, scratching over paper in her office.

Even so. For all the quiet, my head was a veritable cacophony. Full-fledged panic was back in earnest and hollering at my temples. If I left it much longer – if I committed to this ruse – my absence would be noted. Edwina would be sure to wake me early tomorrow – today? – before Lady Miltonwaters's arrival, anxious to choose some gleaming green-and-black outfit for me. She would have my bedroom door open the instant I didn't answer – to all the stark hollowness of the empty bed, the undrawn curtains – and the moment she struck a match to investigate further – the moment she realised there wasn't a shred of *Henrietta* left to meet Lady Miltonwaters on the front steps – she'd surely do as anyone would in a town with no police – and enlist the Dallyangle Division to hunt me down –

"Right!"

It was all I could do not to topple out of my skin.

"Oh – yes – Sept– erm – I mean – Division Sergeant?"

"Measurements."

I stared at her. It took her a firm blink to get her eyes up from the floor, but when they struck mine it was with the same fixed scrutiny as before. As stares went, I was used to Rosamond's languid blood-shot glances, and Edwina's rigid determination not to look anyone in the eyes at all – of course I could only snatch for the feeblest words in the face of Septimus's look.

"I – I'm sorry?"

"Your measurements. For your clothes." She glared. "'Less you expect me to measure you."

Limes. I'd never even seen my measurements written down before Edwina whisked them off to the family tailor. "I – I don't – erm – I just – forgive me – I – "

She gritted her teeth. "Well. I'll see what we've got. Probably won't fit perfect, but you can take it up yourself."

Oh – quite – aside from my heretical inability to sew anything larger than a sampler being a good part of the reason why we have a family tailor –

"What? What's wrong?"

Contrition was my best option. "I – erm – I'm sorry, it – it's just – very new – "

"What is?"

Wait. The Director's door was still open.

"I – I mean – it's not – not that I – I do – want to – " (sweet nectarines, what had she said?) " – broader – you know – neighbouring – and whatnot – of course – "

A sharp frown. "You sure you know what you're getting into?"

It was quite all I could do to shake my head and brace for the worst. She regarded me a moment, trembling and pallid and more than ready to slide through the floorboard-cracks with the shame of it – and then, astonishingly, she just sighed.

"Well. Fair enough, given we're making it up as we go."

I gaped at her. I had had nothing since I entered the building but impeccable advertisements and strident sentences, assurances of confidence and capability and absolute conviction, passed down from the Director to her strange squabbling deputies. Figs – even their matching attire sang of established certainty, with its thick sensible fabrics and stylish red collars. The only thing vaguely improvisatory about the group, as far as I could presently tell, was its peculiar lodgings – and that I had simply assumed to be idiosyncratic eccentricity!

Septimus spotted my bewilderment, cleared her throat and plunged into a hasty addendum. "I mean – not everything. Just the recruitment bit. The *proper organisation* stuff. Used to chase up pig-stealers, we did – country crimes – case by case. The Director and me and Cassandra and Mr. Adelstein. And we were – we *are* – good at it. So now we've got a building, and new recruits, and job titles – still not sure about 'em, but there you go – and a town council who don't want rid of us. And as for what we do – my part'll be your part, I reckon – so – right. Look at this."

She yanked her notebook out, snapped the cover back on itself and held it up. I'd seen enough of her interactions with it to deduce that she had no intention of actually handing it to me, and as duly expected she was the one turning the pages, driving on with her elucidation all the while. I'd barely the space to keep any focus on the latter, and my perusal of the book came in wild glimpses. Some pages were thick with words, sharp-pencilled letters broken with slashes and symbols, whilst others had been given over entirely to lists or diagrams, strings of numbers and stiff sketches of what appeared to be housefronts, or more likely house-backs. A two-page spread revealed what must have been an improvised map of Dallyangle itself, complete with terse annotations. There were less architectural drawings too, though clearly meant for some practical purpose: a rough outline of the same heavy scissors the Sweetings had wielded, hemmed in by a thicket of notes. A general errands list ran a few pages long at the book's centre – one of its most ominous recent entries being *sell scythe* – and she had a page blank but for the words *Pip Property*, outlined like a frontispiece, the sharp lines scored beneath snicking holes in the paper.

"Mostly Sweetings stuff now," Septimus was explaining. "They're my main job. No one knows who they are or where they came from, but they've been causing trouble for – coming up on two and a half months. So what I'm doing – what you'd be doing – it's following any hints on where they've been, where they might go next – looks like that's Weeping Alley, if that's where they jumped you. Trying to find where they live – they've done too damned well keeping *that* secret."

She snapped the book shut. "So. That's what it is. With me. And it ain't easy. You might get mocked for it – longer it goes on, most like – but it ain't about us and our comfort, it's about protecting the town. Still – "

Sweet bergamots, but she actually smiled at me – *truly* smiled, half-grin half-snarl, a sudden flash of sharp teeth. "That's not to say there ain't a comfort in it. Our lives – the Div – it ain't like anything anyone'd expect. *I* didn't expect it. I've never had anything like it. The chances you get here are – something else."

She had real quiet to cup her words by the end of it – even the scratching of the pen had stopped. Her grin was fading, back into solemnity, though it was quite impossible to decide which of the extremes looked the more striking on her.

"I've got to warn you, though – it ain't without its dangers. You've met the Sweetings, you'll know about that. And the weather won't get any better. And the town's a bit twitchy right now. But – there ain't a dull edge to it, and the Director's got plans for us yet."

Her stare had become almost wary, the set of her jaw defiant. "Well. There you go. Now you know. That what you're after?"

Even with the dangers, and the sheer mercurial menace of her and the others, and the fact that I was undeniably the most delicate thing under this rickety roof, the prospects she thrust at me struck chords I wasn't in the least inclined to silence. Her terrifyingly unfrivolous gaze was pinching nervously at my face, trying to prise out my rationale without waiting for me to explain it – as if I knew how to explain! It was the longest someone had ever held my gaze in real earnest, without a shred of sarcasm or scorn or pity –

And perhaps it was that. Or perhaps it was the idea of what she'd described – of an existence that spiralled beyond one roof, and one stifling family, and one narrow trajectory from there to the nearest nuptials. Perhaps it was simply the sheer thrill of shaping my life to the rhythms and purposes of persons who – however much they still had to work out – were most certainly not Edwina and Rosamond.

"Oh – figs – *yes!*"

She nodded. It was almost approval! "Great. Well. That's a start."

Her encouragement set me rattling off like a music-box. "I – the whole scenario – it – it sounds – well – marvellous! So – if our work is to be essentially – erm – tracing the Sweetings through the streets – the streets in which – erm – some of Dallyangle's more affluent inhabitants – rarely venture – that would – presumably – limit the amount of time we – erm – spend in this building – receiving voluntary clients – cases – missing persons – and – whatnot?"

This time, to my unhinged delight, I got an actual grin. "Exactly! The Sweetings ain't going to leave us a visitor's card – we've got to find 'em!"

I was grinning myself, before I could bite it back. Surely this model would allow me to dodge the sisterly brigade? Surely it would prise me enough time to survive here for – at least a week?

Surely – if all I did during that week was follow Division Sergeant Septimus and frantically agree with everything she said – she wouldn't dismember me? Perhaps the fierce fervent woman with the fantastic chignon – and her colleague, who had trusted me enough to let me join – and the Director, with her formidable plans – perhaps they might all become amicable acquaintances – or – ?

Friends was too much to hope. I'd never had a friend, not since Rosamond decided to give up fulfilling that function. To have the Divisioners not utterly despise me would be enough.

"Yes! Quite! I – I can't possibly articulate how grateful I – well – I am – now – erm – I'll just fetch my greatcoat – "

Wait. My greatcoat. With the pockets.

"Pomegranates – Mordred!"

Septimus's smile vanished. "What?"

"Mordred!" I gasped again – as if this resembled a sensible explanation! "I mean – erm – nothing – nothing important – "

"Mordred?" She was frowning at me once more. "That your sweetheart?"

I flushed to my eartips. "No! Just my – erm – my pet – "

And I would have spieled off the story of the ferret, purely out of terror that she'd continue in her sweetheart assumptions if I didn't, had it not occurred to me that to mark myself out as the owner of a ferret called Mordred was to effectively carve *Nettleblack heiress* into my forehead for future reference. I spluttered to a halt, lost for any more fictitious excuses – a crimson-faced defeat which, judging by her curt nod, only seemed to confirm her suspicions.

"Well. That's fine. We ain't the police – no rules against having a sweetheart. Some of us do. The Director's got a husband."

Figs, I wanted to shriek at her, *but I've never had a sweetheart in my life! Do I look as if I'd ever manage anything of the sort?*

"I – I – erm – anyway – might I be excused – just – for my coat?"

She nodded again, quite as stiffly. "Once you've got it, we'll see about a uniform – and a bed. Six o'clock's the wake-up call tomorrow. It won't be light outside, mind. I – look, I'll just come and get you."

Six o'clock – and Lady Miltonwaters would be preparing to descend on the house, anxious to scoop me into her carriage and begin the journey to pheasant-based perdition – oh, a fig for it! A fig for all of it!

"I – quite – "

I'd almost dashed off – Septimus clearly thought me some sort of Arthurian socialite, what more was there to say? – but she caught my arm before I could disappear. She was quite as strong as she looked.

"Your name's Hyssop, ain't it?"

By this point, I couldn't entirely remember. "Oh! Me! Yes – quite – Hyssop – Henry Hyssop – "

She notched up an eyebrow. "Henry?"

I blurted the inevitable rejoinder full breaths before I could stop myself. "Well – erm – if Septimus is yours – "

A startled blink – and then she twitched an awkward smile, conceding the point. "Well. Yes. It's my only name. Came up with it myself. Now. I'll call you Henry, if you don't mind, and you'll call me what you like – so, Septimus – yes – obviously – and we'll start making you a Divisioner."

In that strange half-lit instant, much to my amazement, there was entirely nothing I wanted more. I suppose, with a second longer, I would have stammered out that very sentiment, in whatever words my nerves would let me manage –

But words of any variety were promptly thwarted by a yell from the reception-room, at a distinctly Cassandra-shaped pitch, to the flabbergasted tune of *cat – stoat – ferret – what?* The Director hurtled past us, dashing in the direction of her daughter's exclamations, the shaky floorboards trembling under the thwack of her boots. There was quite nothing I could do but let the fates – and Mordred – sprint out their terrible course.

"Whatever it is," Septimus muttered at my side, scowlingly mutinous to my pallid hysteria, "Absolutely no one can blame me for it."

It is now two-thirty in the morning, as the reception-room clock is eager to inform me, even through the otherwise sturdy wall separating it from the dormitory. I am almost – almost – too petrified to sleep. Mordred escaped disapproving scrutiny by scuttling inches, whiplashing into my greatcoat pocket just as I staggered in to witness his victory-lap. To my infinite relief, Cassandra hadn't traced the full extent of his path – and the Director apparently missed him altogether, judging from her reluctance to credit her daughter's descriptions. The younger Ballestas has since sloped away to a bed in the family home. Mordred, meanwhile, has made his own bed of my pillow – and, as he possesses the capacity to sleep for full twenty hours at a stretch, I shall invariably have to make do with the mattress beside it, which feels alarmingly reminiscent of cold porridge. The smallest variation on the inexplicable uniform is being fished out for me tomorrow. Today.

The inexplicable uniform – of the inexplicable Dallyangle Division – and – and I'm neck-deep in it even as I scribble!

The dormitory and the bed are neither spacious nor quiet. I can't see to make a soul out, but someone seems to be gnawing their bedsheets in the darkness next to me (Mordred?), whilst a flat droning snore skeins across from the opposite wall. How is one to sleep under such conditions? It's hardly as if I'm used to such disturbances – or such *cold*, gasping up through the floorboards, until you can't bear to do a thing with your feet beyond wrap them in the bedsheets and tremble! And – oh, persimmons – the last nub of the candle's just gone out, and I'm probably writing over my own writing now – but it's too freezing to stop, and too seething with sleep-noises to allow for any dozing, and I'm horribly certain my chemise hasn't dried yet –

Limes! Calm!

I have known late-night disturbances before. What else would one call Rosamond's drunken returns to the house, her shrill rattle up the banister just ahead of every other sunrise, her half-muffled giggles pricking holes in the dawn chorus? Or Edwina's late-night pacing in her study, when she keeps her boots on? Beneath all this hysteria, I *must* be exhausted. I have to be.

I have to be, because I have to sleep, because Septimus is going to wake me at six in the morning whether I've rested or not. Of course, I don't dare speculate into the future any further than this. There is a dormitory, and I'm in it, even if I can't entirely see it. There's a peculiar unit of – oh, I don't know, lady detectives? – and I seem to have joined it – and I really ought to stop asking so many questions of it, given quite how much ignorance I've already laid at its feet. There's – there's Septimus, of the handsome face and exquisite chignon – who invented her name, just as I've invented mine – and come six o'clock she'll be back with her zealous notebook in tow –

Well, then. Pageboy-haired nervous wreck I may well be, but that settles it. She's quite the only thing more compelling than the present situation, and I can't let her down. So! Henry Hyssop it is, until some sensible conclusion arises. Surely I'm perfectly capable of managing the mad little interim.

Aren't I?

Divisionary admin

DALLYANGLE DIVISION
3 MARKET SQUARE
DALLYANGLE
SURREY

RECRUIT INFORMATION

NAME. *'Henry Hyssop'* **AGE.** *One-and-twenty* **HEIGHT.** *5"7, probably*

RANK. *Apprentice* **JOINED.** *October 1893* **SALARY.** *15s p.w.*

ADDRESS (HOME). *The University of Cambridge (Girton College)*

ADDRESS (WORK). *The Dallyangle Division*

EDUCATION. *Girton College (!!)*

PREVIOUS OCCUPATION(S). *Student?*

ADDITIONAL NOTES. *Claims to be 'proficient with firearms' – credentials (at least) would suggest intelligence, even if she doesn't have a degree – some sort of stammer – uses fruit as curses (?) – ~~Javert~~ Septimus appointed as ~~governess~~ mentor*

ISSUED. *1 bed (dorm), bedlinens & spare; 2 regulation shirts; 1 split skirt; 1 uniform jacket w/ belt; 1 hat; to be issued additional jacket & skirt after two weeks' work; probably wise not to give this one a lantern until we're sure she won't drop it*

* * *

SIGNED. *Henry Hyssop*   **WITNESSED.** *Division Sergeant Cassandra Ballestas*

DATE. *29th Oct 1893*

4.

OF BICYCLES, RODENTS AND PERPLEXING COMIC OPERAS

Correspondence (of doom)

PRIVATE AND CONFIDENTIAL
Matthew Adelstein, of the Dallyangle Division
3 Pole Place
Dallyangle, Surrey
October 30th 1893

Dear Sir,

I write to your home address for utmost urgency. I have heard excellent reports of the Dallyangle Division, and I require your services on a matter of absolute discretion. I will not say more until we have spoken in person, but I believe a member of my family to be in grave danger. Please call in haste (5 Catfish Crescent; arrive on foot, use the servants' entrance, and take all precautions to ensure you are not seen by the neighbours).

Money is no object.

Yours,

Miss Edwina Nettleblack

*

Nicholas –

If you'd be kind enough to inform any callers (Division included) that I won't be returning until lunchtime – urgent business – _absolute discretion_ – I'll explain later. Of course, there is every chance you won't return from your insane expedition in time to see this note – I can but live in hope.

– M

Myself again

Monday, October 30th, 1893

All I can say to the wanton optimism of last night, in the freezing brightness of the new day, is – apparently this nightmare might be more insurmountable than I'd entirely dared to anticipate.

Figs! It was already unwieldy to begin with! The county's most half-hearted prodigal escape, a dismemberment to my ferret's name, my hair gone to be bartered on some sinister chignon-market, an impossible organisation with internal discord that I shouldn't in the least be so utterly embroiled in, my continued existence in the hands of a bewilderingly striking woman with one name and the most overzealous notebook since my own – and – and – is that not enough?

There's hardly point spluttering for it (any more than I already have), so I suppose I must stagger back to the beginning. Sort of. Six o'clock, appointed hour of my doom, now very much appointed hour of my recall to life.

Curled up shivering in the chilly bedsheets, I'd forgotten where I was. Everything was half-frozen. My chemise had stiffened into impenetrable creases where I'd notched my knees to my chest. My toes didn't feel entirely attached to my feet. A clock – a tinny clock, with a strange familiarity to its skinny chimes – trilled out the hour in some room that wasn't this one. A dash of candle-flame glimmered in the grey haze above my head, and a sharp whisper lashed down through the gloom.

"Henry?"

I blinked up, dazed. There was tentative consolation in the fact that my shadowy interlocutor couldn't possibly have been Edwina. She wouldn't use my nickname, not when she pointedly refuses to remember my name altogether.

"I – erm – good morning?"

A curt sigh, half-unnerved half-impatient. Clearly, there was an expected response, and mine wasn't it. "Well. Yes. Hello. Uniform's at the end of your bed. I need you at the desk in half an hour."

"The – wait – what do – I – ?"

Then it struck me.

"Division Sergeant Septimus?"

The flame twitched, and there she was. Towering above the bed with the lines of her face traced by her taper, she was stern-featured and solemn as those enormous women in Rossetti paintings, and thrice as handsome as the scariest of them. Her chignon hadn't dropped an inch from the whorl of last night.

"Who else," she snapped, as if my astonishment were the most unreasonable thing in the known world, "did you expect?"

Telling her how positively supernatural she looked was out of the question. She was already frowning for my open-mouthed scrutiny as it was. Confessing the truth, and curtailing all I'd signed up for last night, in the face of her exasperation, seemed equally impossible. Pears, what else could I do? Salute? Get up?

I scrabbled half out of the bed, then froze quite to the mattress. There was nothing more to my substance than the bedraggled chemise I'd spent the night in.

"You look cold," she observed awkwardly, jabbing a hand in the vague direction of my crimsoning face. "You'll need warmer drawers. It's only going to get colder, mind."

If I'd been blushing before, I was blazing as a hearth-fire now. It was, admittedly, quite efficacious for warming me up. "Oh – erm – of course – "

"Good."

She spun round, marched off across the dormitory and cupped her candle-flame to various points in the opposite wall, where drizzling tapers had been fixed in metal frames, with mirrors balanced precariously at their backs. The effect was somewhat antiquated beside the bright gaslamps in reception, but it served the purpose, scraping light over the beds. These beds looked, in the sallow gleam, like nothing so much as a plateful of scones, bedsheets and occupants lumped on top of them like unspread clotted cream – though scones would have been circular, and reassuring, and these narrow matchbox-bedframes were anything but. Around them, the room stiffened into focus: pale floorboards, narrow iron legs to the bedframes, unused beds with bare mattresses lined up beyond mine, plentiful cracks in the plaster on the walls. Not a scrap of velvet or brocade in sight, which quite shouldn't have unnerved me as much as it did. The ceiling was the most perplexing of all – a mass of gently rotting wooden beams at varying heights, some of them scorched black, others monopolised by spiders as stout as my thumbnail. What had this building been, before the Division seized hold of it? Some sort of cottage? A dairy? Figs – a *stables*?

"Two, three, four!"

Septimus and I jumped in chattering unison. All around us, grinning heads were springing out of the clotted cream, scrabbling hands flinging back the bedcovers, the sudden movement spasming the flames on the wall. Snarling tangles of plait, a bun still half-pinned in place, straggling curls of loose hair – two girls, and a rather cherubic boy – all seemingly unfazed by the cold, or the early hour, or their own bewildering occupation.

At which ominous juncture, as if to nail the insanity through my forehead, all three of these startling sirens started singing.

"A rollicking band of Divvers we,
Who, tired of our chats with Property
Are going to chase up a burglaree
By Sweetings grim and gory!"

Septimus flushed, whirled about on her heel and stalked for the door. Her retreat didn't in the least seem to stop them.

"We are not coming to buy cravats!
We're making up for our sergeant's lack!
We'll scupper the Sweetings' next attack – "

"You've made your point!" Septimus snarled, slamming herself out of the dormitory so furiously that a worrying quantity of dust splattered from the ceiling to my bedsheets. Her tormentors slumped back over their beds, sniggering up towards the trembling roof-beams. The mirrored candles shook with them, sputtering smoke.

"Flawless," one of the girls remarked, swinging sturdy stock-inged feet over her bed's end. "Fifteen minutes' rehearsal, and all! Cassandra Ballestas's a better librettist than Gilbert."

The boy snorted. "Don't tell Septimus that."

"Cass'll have the whole of *Pirates* rewritten before the year's out," the girl in the bed beside me declared magisterially. "And while she does, I'm getting dressed."

With that, my compatriots appeared to shrug off their interest in Septimus. Whilst I tottered to my feet – leapt from foot to foot, I should say, for the chill creeping up through the floorboards – they busied themselves anew with tugging their bedsheets to order, unfolding skirts and trousers and jackets from under the beds, spitting on their boot-toes to get the dirt off. I could hardly help but stare. It was sartorial viscerality like I'd never imagined, all this yanking and brushing and thumping and wrenching. The girls had corsets, grubby cord-boned things they could evidently lace without so much as glancing back over their shoulders – one of them to a startlingly narrow extent, her teeth taut in her lower lip. The boy just gave his shirt a quick slap-down before buttoning a jacket over it. The woman nearest me had a bowl of water beneath her bed for shivery morning ablutions, but she didn't look askance at the others for not bothering. She – and it spun me back to gape at the wall! – flung off her chemise altogether, in fearless scorn of the cold, and stooped naked as a nymph to grab a new one from under her pillow.

I gasped a frantic breath. In the midst of this – what – what was I – ?

But shivering stock-still was hardly going to help me, not when the others were positively festering with movement. Heart somewhere vaguely level with my gullet, I forced myself to turn, to fumble my way through my options. I had two piles of alarming fabric balanced on the end of my bed. One was my ruined outfit of the night before – with a corset, pears preserve me, which I had quite no idea how to lace, because there'd always been a maid to sort the fastenings! And a silk-panelled corset with impossible lacing would immediately scream to the room that I was the sort of individual to *have* a maid, without need to fret for self-sufficient practicalities, and – and I could hardly have them spotting that! To my other option it was, then: a stern brown-and-red clothes-heap to match everyone else's, thick and scratchy to the touch, with 'HH' brusquely back-stitched into the inside of the jacket collar. And a complicated skirt, riddled with buttons, which –

No. It wasn't a skirt. Well – it could look like one, and had done on Cassandra last night, with the front panel buttoned down – but when one snatched it up and gaped at it the truth sprang forth. It was a split skirt, cunningly disguised, which a quick fold of the front could transform into a full-blown pair of culottes.

Cranberries. Sweet, bifurcated cranberries.

And, on the subject of perturbing realisations: where was my ferret?

"Who's this?"

Much as I would have preferred it, I could hardly have gone unnoticed by the others. The girl in the bed beside me had me firmly in her scrutiny – and, mercifully, rather more garments ensconcing her than had been the case a few minutes ago. Her jacket was unbuttoned, her shirt carelessly open at the collar, her thick hair knotted in a nest of plait about her neck. Looking at her, I was rather reminded of Rosamond, or at least how Rosamond might have worn such a uniform – though this young woman was blonde to my sister's dark curls, strong-armed and ruddy where Rosamond was emaciated and pale, and possessed (as indeed all three were) with the broad bucolic accent of a pasture-grown Dallyanglian. She had a kind of hearty confidence about her – and the remnants of a summer tan, clinging to her cheekbones – that made one think of outside work. I wondered if, before this impossible employment, she'd been some sort of farmer.

"I'm – erm – the new recruit?"

This was, apparently, entirely the wrong thing to say to remain incognito in a room of Divisioners. Before I could stammer any further excuses, the other two faces had loomed over. The taller was an amazonian country girl in muddy boots and that frighteningly cinched corset, whilst the boy was a foal in human skin, with gangly brown ringlets and smudges on his jacket. Fortunately, they all appeared to be dressed. All, that is, except me.

Figs.

"Didn't know we had a new recruit," the girl with the insectine corset observed, with rather too much suspicion in her tone for my nerves to stand. "Where'd you come from? You're not the Ballestas governess snuck in to join, are you?"

"'Course she's not!" The boy flung her a sceptical glance. "The Ballestas governess looks like a spectre!"

He bobbed his head to me, clumsily polite. "Beg pardon, but you only look like half a spectre."

I made myself disentangle the uniform shirt from the pile as I held their stares, prayed they wouldn't think me appallingly rude, hoped with my last shred of sense that I'd not start putting it on backwards. "Oh – quite – well – I – I enlisted yesterday – well, in the middle of the night – as one – erm – does – "

A raucous gasp from the blonde girl tugged all eyes from me to her, for which I'll perpetually be in her debt. "Oh! Of course! She must be Septimus's new lackey!"

Lackey?

Now was, admittedly, hardly the moment to be gaping incredulously at her, especially not as she'd inexplicably decided to fling me a sunburnt smile. "Cass mentioned it last night. This little needle's supposed to be restoring Septimus to her former glory."

The boy rolled his eyes in a burst of coltish bravado. "She'll have a job there!"

My decipherer grinned at me, tossed out a hand, caught mine as I wrestled it out of the shirtsleeve and wrung it to the bone. It was horribly impolite of me to wince – I could only hope she'd not noticed.

"Welcome to the Div's Inferior Contingent! Apprentice Divisioners all in here. The second generation. The younglings. I'm Gertie Skull, that's my little brother Oliver – Ollie, you've got dust in your hair – and the bonkers tight-lacer's Millicent Musgrove, cousin by name and Skull by nature. You?"

I had to consider it for a good five seconds, and mask my panic with a wild scramble into my astonishing new split skirt (not that I dared wear it any fashion other than skirtwise). Mercifully, Oliver Skull was leaping about too, beating the remnants of ceiling from his curls.

"Me – erm – yes – Henry – Hyssop – "

"Hyssop!" Gertie Skull declared, plummeting two meaty hands onto my shoulders – and tactfully ignoring my shriek of surprise. "Good for the nerves, if you stick it in your tea. And I reckon you've been Sweetinged, eh?"

"Your haircut," Millicent Musgrove supplied hastily, for my bewilderment.

I swallowed, snagged in their stares, dangling from Gertie's fingers. "I – well – quite – "

"Poor lamb." Gertie squeezed my arm. "All the more reason to chase them down, that's what I say. Seek a penalty fifty-fold for Henry Hyssop's ringlets!"

She was singing again, the same tune as before, tugging me closer with a conspiratorial grin. "Now, Septimus may ask you if you can get us to give it a rest with the blessed G and S, but I'd better tell you straight out that it's not going to happen. As long as we've got *The Pirates of Penzance* at the Dallyangle Theatre, comic opera shall be our presiding spirit!"

I tried for a dazed nod. Was jovial conversation with one's colleagues naturally disposed to be this bizarre?

"There's – erm – a theatre in Dallyangle?"

The whole room gaped at me.

"I – mean – of course – the theatre – in Dallyangle – "

"Hard to miss," Millicent smirked. "Don't crash your cycle into it, though. Septimus still owes them some stucco."

"What? I – what – crash my – what?"

Gertie twitched up a sandy eyebrow. This was a fairly appropriate reaction to the cadaverous pallor currently stiffening me from the eyes down.

"Bicycle. That's what Septimus does her jobs on. And you're good with a cycle too, right? That's why the Director picked you to go with her?"

Marbled to the spot, it was a struggle even to shake my head. Everything was still now, too still, sepulchral-still, positively spectral in the dim light of the mirrored candles, stricken apprentices staring at me like so many gravestones.

"I – I – I don't know how to – figs! – how to do anything of the sort!"

And in Gertie Skull's answering expression, I saw my doom.

For all that I'd resolved not to antagonise Division Sergeant Septimus, this was an involuntary infuriation I'd not had the sense to envisage. The rational dress – the trousers – the split skirt – *of course!* I'd seen such outfits cartooned in Rosamond's *Punch*es, seen snide sharp engravings of women crashing bicycles and women tumbling off bicycles and women smoking cigars atop bicycle handlebars. A real bicycle (and herein lay my damnation) I'd never so much as glimpsed – for how could Edwina do otherwise than disapprove of them, and shake her tutting head over the derisive illustrations, and assure Rosamond and I that such hectic contraptions would never find their way under *her* roof? And Rosamond had sniggered, and drawled out *ond dwi'n moyn dysgu seiclo* or something else equally inflammatory – but for all her ironical professions of interest, she'd never disputed Edwina's ruling. And now here I was, resoundingly ill-equipped for the purpose, trembling in the Division Sergeant's path –

"Septimus'll flay you," Gertie whispered, hushed and awed and mystic as a monk, and it was all I could do not to burst into tears.

"What d'you mean, *leave the bicycle?*"

Humiliation at Girton barely twitched a candle to this.

Six-thirty in the reception-room, the clock sniggering for my despair, the gaslights and walls as horrendously bright as ever, the windows slowly shrugging off the dark to match them. The other three apprentices darting past to vanish through the double doors, pausing only to brush my shoulder, or pat my arm, or pinch my cheek – all as much as to say, *you're in for it now!* Septimus, palpitating with rage before the desk, about to set another ceiling crumbling. The Director, staring her down from the top of the corridor, twisting a ring of silvery keys between her fingers – the keys, I guessed, to wherever they kept the bicycles. Presumably the idea was to stop Septimus simply bolting away with them. Whether or not that would work with her present pitch of anger, I didn't dare speculate.

Where was I, in this ghastly scene? Still shivering, wretched encumbrance that I was, with the doors at my back and the sharp autumn breeze jabbing me in the shoulder-blades, heartily wishing one of the apprentices' pitying farewells would be vigorous enough to knock me straight through the floor.

"Miss Hyssop can't cycle," the Director explained, the soul of ever-so-slightly-strained patience, her pacifying smile trembling. "And you can't leave her behind."

Septimus all but spat fire. "Why can't she cycle? What's she doing with me, if she can't cycle?"

The Director sighed. "Septimus, I explained this last night – "

"You didn't tell me this! She's got no idea what she's doing – what if she gets hurt? And how'm I meant to do my job? This ain't an honour, it's more like a punishment!"

The Director's smile finally shrivelled. "Don't presume to know my mind, Division Sergeant. She won't get hurt if you look after her. And I had been meaning to trial you without the bicycle – there have been complaints about your cycling of late. You know as well as I do that the Division can't have complaints."

A smart of ruddy colour under Septimus's eyes. "What – who – ?"

"Glad you asked, Javert!"

It was Cassandra, sauntering in through the double doors. She had a ledger, leather-bound and fat, tucked under one arm, which she tossed onto the desk with *thump* enough to dust some plaster from the walls. We could only watch – the Director coldly admonishing, Septimus boiling over, my hands scraping each other to pieces with panic – as she thwacked the book open, the spine audibly cracking in the sudden quiet.

Cassandra's bony finger slid into place like a bookmark. "Cycling chaos, appendix the hundredth! September eighth, fresh-returned from her suspension – sorry, *unpaid leave* – Javert's interesting decision not to apply the brakes took out half a hearse and two funeral mutes, for which we still owe the Fitzdegus five pounds. She claims she was chasing the Sweetings, but was her desire to out-race her previous speed record also present in her mind? Who can tell! Then we have – September twenty-fifth, when Lady Miltonwaters was narrowly persuaded not to shoot at our illustrious Division Sergeant after her overzealous signalling made the lady's gig bolt. And on October sixteenth, the sevenfold genius chased Pip Property into the side of the Dallyangle Theatre – "

"You've only got Property's word for that!"

Cassandra flicked up an eyebrow. "Did you *not* cause the bicycle-sized welt in the side of the Dallyangle Theatre?"

"I – but – look – they were the one not being a sensible pedestrian –!"

The Director cleared her throat, slicing through the pair of them. "Thank you, Cassandra, you have made your point. Septimus – you have accomplished great things in the field – "

"And caused utter disasters," Cassandra muttered.

" – but your skills are making you reckless – with your own safety, as well as that of others. I cannot let you become a public menace. Not when your every misstep only gives our detractors more ammunition, and certainly not with so much at stake. Not after what you – well. I am sure I hardly need to finish that sentence."

Crimson to her hairline, Septimus visibly swallowed a snarl of retorts. She was still angry – horribly, obviously so – but something in the Director's words had yanked the anger out at the root, left it flailing in midair with nothing to ground it.

"Work on foot for the rest of the week, and take a little more care." The Director was gentler now, hooking the keys to the loop in her belt. "Then I might consider reopening the shed."

Pointed as she could manage, Cassandra slapped the ledger shut.

This was plainly the last straw. Septimus lashed about on her heel, all without dislodging a single strand of the impeccable chignon, and stalked out into the chilly morning, so swiftly I had to sprint to get through the doors before they slammed. Ahead, there was gloomy sunless sky and steaming breath and cold. At my back, cut off by the closing doors, the Director was staring intently after us, and Cassandra sat smirking behind the desk.

I wanted – but, of course, I didn't dare – to snatch Septimus by her excellent elbows, collapse to my knees and implore her to forgive me for inadvertently destroying her peace of existence. Septimus, as was only to be expected, didn't give me the chance. She set a fast pace, straight into the heart of the market square that bustled up its awnings before us. The furious set of her shoulders ahead of me, taut and broad in the brown-and-red jacket, was warning enough for me to stay quiet.

The market square was a seed-bed in the process of sprouting. It was framed on all sides by a peculiar assortment of buildings: the squat small-windowed sprawl of the Division, a glittering broad-paned shop with – figs – Nettleblack's Tinctures stacked up in the window-display, an empty tavern with a swinging chequerboard sign, a formidable butcher's with *enquire within for pies* plastered on the door, and something crape-draped and grim with the morose look of an undertaker's. Between these disparate bastions, the venders were preparing their stalls – sliding bright slabs of fruit-boxes into place, clattering the lids off pots of jellied eels, scratching chalky prices onto slate slabs, jostling us relentlessly in the doing of every task. The flicker of the street-lanterns, still lit against the miserable grey sky, dragged all the colours to the surface and made them smart – the gleaming red and green of the apples, the gaudy stripes on the awnings, the silver-gold sheen of the eels in their jelly.

Sweet plums, but need I even specify it was at that instant I realised I hadn't had breakfast?

A wiry chap in a patched apron darted backwards to survey his stall, jammed his heel down on my toe. The moment he spotted me, one could visibly trace the courtesy tumble off his lips, and the gap-toothed scorn flare up in its place.

"And we've got the Dallyangle Do-gooders! Another day of being useless, is it, ladies?"

I had barely a moment to gape at him – and at his colleagues, twisting about to investigate his sudden spleen – before Septimus snatched my arm, wrenched me away past the eel-sellers. "Come on. Ignore 'em."

Figs.

In the man's sneering remark, and the sneers of his compatriots, and Septimus's alarmingly plural glower, the full extent of my stupidity in choosing my disguise had become horrendously apparent. The Dallyangle Division – the unconventional organisation, puzzling out its status and its purpose – why I ever thought joining it would provide a place for me to *hide* – ! Everything of me was now horribly distinctive, and acknowledged for as much by every squinting pedestrian we passed. The sharp lines of the uniform, the short-cut split skirt, the burgundy cuffs and collar, the broad hat with its splaying brim – all of it striking as a theatrical costume, and bizarre as a *Punch* illustration! After that first group, there were more shoves, and more smirks, and more snide cries from behind the stalls. Septimus, storming ahead with her hat under one arm, could just about scowl the attention away, but I could hardly be expected to manage anything like the same indifference!

"Halloa, you poacher-pestering vision!"

I started fit to dislodge my hat for this new greeting, gasped the hoarse dregs of a bedevilled scream – but Septimus didn't look daunted in the least. A gorsebush-haired young man was tottering towards us through the nearest straggle of stalls, shaky-armed under the weight of an enormous wicker shopping-basket, wild grin pale in a nut-brown face. He seemed here to buy, early as it was, flinting off the freezing wind with a tangle of moth-eaten scarf, his rust-coloured greatcoat bunching at the elbows where the basket pulled at the sleeves, his trousers far stripier than the maddest of the market's awnings.

"Not on the cycle today?" he beamed, once he was close enough to notch his voice down from a shout. "Makes a change! And not the only change, I see – this a new friend of yours? Very rodent of you!"

Septimus struck up that sharp-toothed smile I'd glimpsed the night before, dipped her head to him. "Morning to you too, Nick. Need help with your basket?"

Now, I confess, I found myself frowning at him. Lemons – of course I knew I hardly had any right to do so – but I couldn't iron it off my forehead. I may have known Division Sergeant Septimus and her strange abrupt ways for all of one night, but – but – even so! I'd grown used, in that one night, to the state of affairs at the Division: that everyone else either pitied or despised her, and that I was, in a peculiar terrified way, the only one wishing her well, admiring her hair, and so forth. This was something new. This stripy-legged man with his grin and his basket – he was the first individual in Dallyangle that I'd seen address her with real joviality – and the warmth didn't seem unwelcome to her. The discovery was sour in my teeth, though I couldn't for the life of me fathom out why. All that she'd said to me last night, all that confusion over Mordred and sweethearts – was this cheerful basket-wielder *her* sweetheart? And – I – well – he looked pleasant enough, probably – and why shouldn't Septimus have a sweetheart, odd and solitary and angry as she is? – but –

"Don't you worry, it's only rodent food."

This sentiment was bizarre enough to tug me out of my head. Nick rolled his eyes, dropped to a conspiratorial mutter at her shoulder (he was shorter than her, but he still had a few inches on me), holding her gaze with his glinting hazel eyes. His hushed tones were a stage-whisper through the market's clattering, spiky and excitable in a voice that streaked the Dallyangle drawl alongside something else I couldn't place.

"Mr. Vernon Vibbrit, that agricultural cavy-photographing nitwit, thought he'd scupper me yesterday when he bought the town out of timothy hay for his guinea pigs, but I've got him now! And I woke up at five-thirty to do it! Since when've fancy rats, I ask you, ever needed anything half so lar-di-da as *timothy hay?*"

Septimus, much to my bewilderment, appeared to be nodding along.

"So Vernon Vibbrit'll be in for a shock when he deigns his way down to the market today. Rats don't *need* timothy hay, but d'you know what those pampered cavies *do* need if they're to last the winter?"

She actually smirked. Pineapples, he was definitely her sweetheart.

"Food!" Nick cried triumphantly. "And I've just bought all the food! *All the food!* Which he can now buy off me, once he's publicly recanted his rat slander! So much for your almighty guinea pigs, Vernon Vibbrit!"

By now, I was simply gaping at them both. Nick glanced past Septimus to snag my eye, burst out laughing when he saw my expression. "Hallo! This little fieldmouse knows her fancy rat from her *rattus rattus!*"

"Right! Introductions!" Septimus declared suddenly, awkwardness stiffening back into the set of her shoulders. "Nick, this is Henry, a new apprentice. I'm training her – Director's orders – and *that's* the only reason I ain't got the cycle. Henry – "

"Henry!"

I jumped. Quite understandably, I wasn't used to my name booming across the market square. "I – erm – rather – "

"Lovely, that is! And I've got a rat called Henry, too! Well – I've got a rat called pretty much everything, any name you like. I can get you a Pirate King rat, and a Frederic and Ruth to go with him!"

He threw down his basket – figs, but the cobblestones nearly burst it – and grabbed my hand between his, pounded it until my finger-bones rattled. "I'm Nick. Nick Fitzdegu. *Not* an undertaker like the rest of them, but – you might've twigged – a rat-breeder extraordinaire. D'you like rats, Henry?"

To have professed otherwise, with my hand still fettered in his, would have been reckless in the extreme. "Oh – quite – "

"Then we can be friends!" He tugged me close, closer than I'd expected, until I could gasp in the twang of tobacco on his breath. "D'you fancy buying some fancy rats, Henry?"

He was grinning at me like a lunatic – and I was quite about to combust for lack of a polite excuse!

"I – erm – "

"Not now, Nick!" Septimus snapped. He pinched her a mock-pout, squeezed my hand as he set it free, flicked me a cheery twitch of a wink. "And she couldn't even if she wanted to. You know how the Director is about rats."

He smirked, conceding. "Fine. No, I know – Henry could have the noblest of intentions, and your Director'd still think you were making her buy them to throw at Property. Reckon a rat could make a good spy, if you set them to it."

Septimus swept his basket up from the floor – only a sharp jolt of her eyebrows admitted its weight – and dumped it into his arms, decidedly less jovial than she'd been a moment ago. He'd evidently done something to displease her, though I'd not the faintest which part of his madness it was. "Right! Get on with you, Fitzdegu, I've work to do."

He scoffed, softened to a smile. "See you at Matty's, eh?"

"'Course you will," she agreed brusquely, already striding away. Nick held the smile for me the way you'd hold a door, a little distractedly, until she yelled my name back over her shoulder – and then I was gone, or he was gone, and Septimus was waiting for me at the next row of stalls.

"That ain't what I meant," she muttered, the moment I reached her, with that odd inward scowl of our first encounter. "I ain't *throwing rats* at Property – and I never spied on 'em! They've just got more help to give than they're – "

"Division Sergeant?"

Peaches. It was a risk, but I had to query. This was the umpteenth enigmatic reference to the cravat designer in so many hours. Perhaps it was that – or, figs, perhaps the revelation that I wasn't the only person in Dallyangle inclined to hold a pleasant conversation with her had spurred me on to up my game, however terrifying I would inevitably find her response.

"I – I was just – wondering – could you possibly – I mean – who is – erm – Property?"

I'd expected another of her bone-shrivelling glowers, but got a pinch of scrutiny instead, a frown both hopeful and perturbingly sceptical. "You don't know 'em? Pip Property – the cravat designer? Shop on Angle Drag?"

"I – erm – no?"

She nodded stiffly. "Well. Fair enough that I'd think it. They designed your cravat."

"I – 'they'?"

"Yes."

I glanced to her. She didn't seem inclined to elaborate – and I wasn't in the least of a mind to disagree with her. "Oh – I – I see – and they – ?"

Her teeth lashed out, sunk into her lip. "They know things. About Dallyangle. The darker side of it. And it's information we might – "

Then she stopped, her gaze skewering something over my head, off towards the outskirts of the market where it narrowed into a street. She'd been glaring, but now she brightened – not quite a smile, but a sharp straightening-up, a glint across her navy eyes. I stared at her, stunned, wondering vaguely if I'd turn my head to find the Director hastening up to us with bicycles in hand.

"Lorrie," she yelled. "Ain't you got rehearsal?"

She dodged round me before I could query any of this, bounding past a stall-front of bulging pumpkins to meet a tradesman loitering at the market's edge. Of course I darted after her. Fidgeting alone in that uniform would only have brought more shoves and sneers down on my head.

Sweet merciful persimmons. If Nick Fitzdegu with his fancy rats wasn't Septimus's sweetheart, this golden-curled street-seller surely must have been. He was tall and strong and wiry as her, with a face like a hero in a book-illustration, a tray of posies looking far too flimsy for his shabby coat. There wasn't a cravat in sight at his open collar, which I can only imagine endeared him to her.

"Call-time's not 'til this evening, Sept," he hissed. "And it's only ever principals get called this early. Probably best we don't talk too long – I start work in ten, and the Div thing's been putting off customers of late."

"Then I'll be a customer," she retorted briskly, flashing him another of her sharp smiles. "Or let 'em think I'm one. Got a flower I can hold?"

He stuck his tongue out. "Got some off-cuts you can have, if you like."

"Off-cuts! For *me!*"

"Could just give 'em to your colleague – if that's what she is?"

Cherries, they'd spotted me. Now they glanced me over in eerie unison, this dizzyingly tall pair with their stern shoulders and dashing faces. Side by side, she was easily the more compelling of the two; her hair gave her the edge. His curls were pleasant enough, but her chignon could have launched ships.

The flower-seller sighed. "You've scared her half to death already, Sept."

"She ain't that much of a sap," Septimus shot back, in what was quite possibly the wildest overestimation of my capabilities since the Division hired me in the first place. "She's my assistant, as of yesterday. If I can keep her upright long enough to get her on a cycle, she'll be more'n a match for the rest of 'em."

I gaped at her. "I – really?"

Given how much I'd derailed her routine, and how resoundingly little I'd managed to show myself worth the derailment, it was a fair question. It seemed to unnerve her, all the same. She frowned, froze, quite as if she'd forgotten her unusual argument, until the flower-seller laughed outright.

"One posy for the assistant. I assume you're planning to tell me her name?"

He juggled his flower-tray onto one arm, plucked the smallest of the bunches and tossed it to her, the flowers quivering above the hand's-width of twine that held them together. She fidgeted the posy between her fingers, clearly unsure what to do with it, his wry question whiplashing past her. I wondered – and nearly glared, for how uneasy it made me! – whether she'd proffer the bunch straight back to him, or raise it to her lips and kiss it, or clasp it against her jacket and thank him in a grinning whisper –

But she did entirely nothing of the sort.

"Hold these, would you? Make us look like his *customers?*"

She glanced up, between us, stabbed out her arm to thrust the flowers at me. The instant she'd done it, her eyes widened. Then her whole face closed, smartingly defiant, rigid with some retrospective panic. Peaches, it was quite as if she expected me to laugh for the inadvertently warm gesture, or splutter an incredulous refusal, or slap the posy to the floor!

My own face was blazing fit to scald off the breeze. Somehow, amazingly, I got a trembling hand up with my next breath – I could hardly leave her looking so inexplicably perturbed! The stems were cold on my palm, studded with droplets from where they'd been sat in water. I must have looked thrice as ridiculous as she clearly thought she had, clutching the posy as if it were poised to fling up its tendrils and strangle me.

"Well!" she declared abruptly, several long wincing moments after I'd taken the flowers, skidding between impatience and relief, "Introductions! Henry, this is Lawrence Tickering – "

Lawrence Tickering rolled his eyes. "Lorrie, please."

" – my brother!"

Brother!

"Good!" I heard myself cry. "I mean – right – yes – I see – "

She blinked at me, disconcerted. I quite couldn't blame her. "Well. Anyway. Lorrie has a new job to end all fantastic jobs, when he ain't a tailor or a flower-seller or anything else – he's in a show! *The Pirates of Penzance* at the Dallyangle Theatre! As a Pirate in Penzance!"

"Which is only chorus," he added, flushing. "I ain't trained, or anything – "

"There's no 'only' about it. He's a *tenor*. He's got *stage business*. Tell her about the chest and the life-preserver!"

Lorrie sighed. Even so – something in him was evidently warming to her latest request. "It's in Cat-Like Tread – d'you know it? The song where the pirates get ready for the burglary. With me?"

I was still somewhat mystified as to what a life-preserver was, but I could hardly admit as much with Septimus keen and impatient at his side. "Oh – erm – of course – "

"So I bring on the pirate-chest with all the burglary stuff in it – y'know, *here's your crowbar, and your centre-bit –* "

Pomegranates, he really was a tenor, the lilting lyrical kind that sailed through the drone of the Sunday hymns. It wasn't improbable that I'd heard *him* in the Sunday hymns – which was in itself a startling thought. Edwina's private pew concealed us from the bulk of the congregation, but a voice like that was far too distinctive not to strike up a recollection.

" – and then I get to be the pirate who takes the life-preserver, and it – well." He smirked. "It gets a laugh."

Septimus nodded triumphantly. "'Cause he's brilliant!"

Lorrie swatted at her. "Enough of this, you. Look – come to the stage door later, you can give me all the news then."

"And your news too, mind." She grinned, ducked in close to murmur a coda. "How's your secret sweetheart? Do I get a name yet?"

"Soon," he retorted swiftly, darting a quick glance in my direction. "When she's ready. But never mind me – I've a mort of questions for you, and *why ain't you on your bicycle*'s only the top of the pile. It ain't – ?"

"What?"

He bit his lip. The hand that had flitted her away settled along her shoulder, kneaded until her glare wavered. "It ain't the rest of 'em again, is it? Cassandra and the like? They ain't still getting at you?"

She coloured to her eyebrows. "As if I'd care, even if they – "

"And Property? Not still – y'know – "

"No," she snapped. He must have caught the warning; even I shivered. "They ain't. I'm fine. Nobody *gets at* me. It's just that I'm training Henry, and she ain't learned how to cycle yet."

Lorrie arched an eyebrow, eyes on mine – as much as to say, *is there something she's not telling me?* But – figs – as if I could answer him! As if, with her standing rigid and defensive between us, I could have stammered out all that his fraternal concern wanted to hear! It would have been quite unthinkable, even if I'd possessed half the gumption to manage the words, to confess what I'd seen: that my existence in the Division had been as good as designed to exasperate her, that Cassandra kept a ledger for totting up her misdeeds, that the contingent of apprentices hemmed her in with melodious malintent, that the Director seemed in constant despair of her continued abilities!

I swallowed. It felt vile to drop my gaze, after the pleasantries of earlier. But – she was there, and already uncomfortable – and what else could I do?

"See you later, Lorrie," she muttered, lashing about on her heel. "Better do the job before the Chorus of Police snatch it off us."

And she was gone, back at her brisk pace, out of the market square and down a narrow side-street, heedless of the puddles that splashed up her boots. I didn't dare look at Lorrie again – didn't dare do anything but dart off in her wake. After the way *that* had ended, further conversation seemed entirely out of the question.

5.

IN WHICH I BECOME UNPRECEDENTEDLY INTERESTING TO PERTURBING FACETS OF DALLYANGLE

More of my wretched self

Beyond the throbs of the church-bell, I'd very little idea of the time on that first morning. Mercifully, the breeze died back, and the air got – if not precisely warm, then at least marginally less chilly. Septimus stalked us right to the outermost edges of the town, where red-brick cottages and rickety tenements gave way to drooping trees and greying fields, swollen with rain and leaves after last night's storm, long grass tossed about in matted heaps. There was a river cupping the north-eastern border, which I'd not known about – it was just as swollen as the fields, and just as grey, and far too murky to make out the depth from the muddy towpath. On the other side of the water, a flat-capped farmhand whizzed through a seam in the fields atop a rattling bicycle, a basket on the handlebars crammed with woven sacks. Figs, but how Septimus sighed, and shook her head, and glared after him as we slogged past!

By that time – half past eleven, courtesy of the church-clock's chimes – we appeared to have woven through and around most of Dallyangle, all without sign or trace of the Sweetings. Weeping Alley had been rain-soaked back to idyllic innocence, every hint of last night's terrors washed from the back walls and the cobble-stones (to my cringing relief, I must confess; I've quite no idea how I would have explained away any bloodstained remnants of Mordred's ghoulish work). I didn't anticipate us making it to Catfish Crescent – it's on the town's uppermost bucolic perimeter, and there'd hardly be much to survey beyond a cluster of towering houses – but it was a mercy all the same when we didn't. Quite apart from the inherent horror that would have accompanied such a detour, I was consummately exhausted from all we'd walked already. My boots ground into my heels, unused to vigorous cobblestone-striding – nigh-on sprinting, to keep anywhere near Septimus. Unbuttoning the split skirt might have made it easier, but I quite hadn't the daring to stride around in unabashed culottes. It was during these panicky chases that I felt my lack of corset, and blushed relentlessly for it. Edwina had always deemed me disappointingly flat-chested (one of the many ways in which my feeble being has thwarted her), which saved me from the worst of the indignities, but my ribs and waist seemed to be quite melting out of shape without something to keep them in place. Between that and my ruined hair – oh, lemons – I must have looked more the family disgrace than ever even Rosamond had managed.

I still had the posy, though. That was something. I'd contrived a means of tucking it inside my belt, though it must have been playing horrendous havoc with its capacity to retain its petals.

Back at the Division, all was hushed and relatively serene, the heavy doors softening the clatter of the market outside. October's valiant attempt at sun was slicing through the windows, pallid with cold, leeching all the red to the surface of the wooden counter. The clock snicked at the quiet, and heat straggled up from the wood-burner. The Director had vanished into her office, but Cassandra Ballestas and Gertie Skull were sat at the desk, heads together and sniggering. It quite couldn't be about Septimus again – surely?

Well. Not entirely. The two were folding a piece of paper into a kind of improvised mechanical dove, and now – heedless of our bewildered scrutiny – they tossed it about with giddy abandon, garish at the palms with matching fingerless gloves.

Septimus, of course, stopped quite dead. "What're you doing?"

Cassandra smirked. Her hat perched on the desk, fading in the sun, speckled with dust motes. "Working. Zealously. Obviously."

"You'd talk to me about zealous work – "

"Do you need five minutes to check the definition with your Girton girl?"

Septimus was all fists and teeth. "I know what the word means!"

"Want to hear my latest *zealous* verse, then? It's in your honour!" Cassandra flipped the paper bird in her hand, bent a wing back to recite from the pencil-scrawl down the side – it was another song.

"She is the very model of a very mad Divisioner, For messing up our record the Director's not forgiven her —"

"Let's have the rest later, eh?"

It was just as well Gertie intervened, with Septimus halfway towards Cassandra already, fists poised to thwack the dove straight into the wood-burner. Gertie shot me a wink. Placating the Division Sergeants was clearly an accomplishment in which she took a bewildering amount of pride.

"If you two've really a mind to kill each other, you can do it after lunch. Unless you're taking out your rivalry on the Div mice instead?"

Septimus glared at her. "What?"

"Mice." Gertie arched an eyebrow. "Three, all dotting the corridor with their mouse guts floating free. Wouldn't know anything about that, would you, Sarge?"

Figs.

Mordred. Unsupervised. Amok.

I was inches from a visceral and ferret-based explosion when Septimus struck up an irritable retort. (This, retrospectively, was probably for the best. If the Division still thought Mordred my sweetheart, I'd have quite no sane way of explaining that he'd an intermittent habit of devouring proximate rodents.)

"I'm only just back. I ain't had time to look at any mice."

"Pretty violent *look*, if you ask me," Gertie grinned. "But you're straight back out, so you'll not have time now. The Director wants you and Hyssop to run this beast of a thing over to Mr. Adelstein, see what he makes of it."

Septimus snatched the paper dove just as Cassandra threw it, crumpled it into a carnation with the dregs of her infuriation. "This the anonymous letter?"

Cassandra rolled her eyes. "Just let Adelstein have it! Let anyone else have a case, for once!"

"Like you?" Septimus snapped. She was folding the page out of its creases, twisting her notebook from her pocket and pinning it inside the cover. "The Divisioner who writes chaff on the evidence?"

Cassandra's freckles twitched, her smirk wavering into a scowl. "I see you're still taking notes of your own, Javert. I would have thought failing to *take note* of a certain town-sized burglary odyssey would have all but killed that little book of yours. Such a shame it'll take you so long to carry your commonplace to Mr. Adelstein – think how much quicker you would have been on two wheels!"

Short of tearing the paper free and hurling it back at her – which, for several seconds, Septimus looked horrendously inclined to do – there wasn't much she could offer by way of retort, beyond a vicious look and a hasty retreat. I could only dash after her, smarting feet and all.

The square was far busier now that the sun had risen in earnest, and the purchases therein infinitely more tumultuous. Bulging hessian sacks trundled between the stalls on improvised carts, spitting cabbages and beetroots to stick between the cobblestones' teeth. There were at least two individuals obliged to wrestle with live geese, all whilst valiantly thrusting coins into their seller's peck-marked fingers. The Division's doors had kept back the full flurry of shouting, but now it churned about me tenfold: cries for eels, for poultry, for pumpkins and mangelwurzels, for cow's tongues and sorrel and parsley, for the immediate release of the geese in question. Staggering through the chaos, half-choked on far too many squab-bling earthy scents, narrowly dodging a sprawled horizontal fate at the hands of a renegade cabbage, it was the hardest it had yet been to keep Septimus in sight.

Greengages, but was this the moment to slow her down – to calm her down – to emulate Gertie Skull? Was I – *me* – supposed to placate Septimus, to brush her anger off like dirt on a greatcoat, as the other Divisioners clearly hoped I could do? Lorrie jostled into my head, eyebrow notched and hoping for reassurance. I'd already dodged away from him, in my inimitable cowardly fashion – I quite couldn't dodge away from her too!

"Erm – Division Sergeant?"

She didn't stop. With every vendor and goose in the town hollering out their produce, I doubt she heard me. I gasped an ache of a breath and hurled myself past her, tumbled into her path before she could disappear.

"I – erm – I – could I – "

"What?"

Benevolent my aim may have been, but the market was still reso-lutely determined to squash it. Septimus shook her head, strode us on again – faster, almost at a run herself, until the jostle and the yelling were behind us, and nothing more than a few placid cottages tilted close on either side.

"What'd you say?"

I gulped. "I – yes – just – I really must apologise for – you know – my inability to operate a bicycle – "

She shot me a grim look. "Can't be helped."

"Well – " – she was still driving us forward along the street, even now! – "I – I could still learn – I'll learn in my own time – "

"Your own time? How much of that d'you think you'll get?"

Lemons. This was a hole, and I was actively leaping into the abyss. I staggered through the same puddle she'd kicked up earlier, stagnant rainwater stinging at my ankles. "I – erm – I'm sure I could – find some – "

She snagged to a halt, so abruptly I stumbled into her, lashed about to glower me down. "You really don't know a thing. D'you even *care* just how much you don't know?"

"Yes!"

I'd blurted it without thinking, it seeming about the only answer that might go some vague way towards mollifying her. Then, of course, I heard myself, and even now I can't but wince. Did I care? Do I care? *Can* I care, with sheer terror leaving so little room in me for anything else?

"I – well – I know my spontaneous – manifestation – in the Division – has been – erm – somewhat unorthodox – but – "

"Unorthodox!"

She twitched as she said it, and I panicked. "Oh – as in – unusual – unprecedented – not – not something you might have expected – "

"I knew what it meant!" she snarled. Of course it shamed me quite as much as it should have. "And I know it don't even *begin* to cover all the allowances that've been made for you! You don't even care how unprecedented – and I know what that one means too, so don't you patronise me! – it is for a new Divisioner with no experience and no idea who we are to be out in the uniform at all!"

My blazing feet petrified in my boots, pinned me to the spot. I ought to have – apologised, at the very least! – but she'd frozen me quite beyond anything of the sort. I could only stare at her, my gullet twisting like a wrung-out handkerchief, too tangled in her unanswerable argument even to wish myself through the floor.

"And it ain't only unprecedented – it's dangerous for you, and it's unfair on me! What if we meet the Sweetings down an alley, and I can't protect you? What if someone else gets hurt – or burgled – or worse – because I can't get there fast enough? What about me and the rest of the Div, who had to fight for our jobs, up and against and over everyone who thought it weren't seemly we should have 'em? I *earned* my rank, and my bicycle, and my independence – and now I'm losing it, just to make room for you!"

She was so incandescently menacing – and so utterly correct on every point – that what little there was left of my nerve shattered, until every fibre of me was weak and slumped as my waist without its corset. "I – I'm sorry – I – "

"Just let me do my job," she snapped. "For all our sakes."

She whipped round and stalked off down the street. I swallowed hard – I was halfway to tears – and trudged after her, the agony in my feet crackling up my legs. The rest of the walk was as silent as the morning's had been, but for my ragged half-stitched breaths, and the rattle of my heart in my ears, and the stab of her boots over the cobblestones ahead.

Everything hurt: my limbs and my chest and my paltry pride in equal measure. I was far too queasy from the pain to notice much about our route. I had just enough wit left to register that the red-brick housefronts were getting more extravagant, growing extra floors and steep front steps, their large windows flashing with glimpses of grey sun. The shouts and squawks of the market and the main street grew fainter, gave way to soft new sounds – the drip of last night's rain from the roofs, the burble of a robin darting between cobbles and windowsills, the distant splash of the river at its muddy banks. There quite wasn't a flower to be had at any turn, for all that this street unfolded larger and neater than the dormouse cottages and tottering tenements. Flat empty gardens sat under front windows like doormats. The best by way of intriguing foliage was to be had at one house, skinny and tall with a glossy black brougham parked at its side – there were glass cases poised precariously on every windowsill, bristling full of perfect feathery ferns, raindrops studding their grey-tinted enclosures like the proverbial jewels on the tortoise.

Septimus glanced them over with a scowl. "Stupid plants. Stupid cravat designer. 'Course Pole Place is expensive, you idiot."

Sweet green figs. If anything could jolt me out of my weary misery, it was decidedly this.

"Pole Place?"

She glared back over her shoulder. "Yes. Mr. Adelstein and Nick live at the other end of it. Hurry up."

The other end – and this I remembered, just about – the other end of Pole Place led straight into Catfish Crescent! In a few steps we'd both be strangled by the wretched nettle-crest!

"I can't," I spluttered. "I'm sorry – I – "

I'd not even devised an excuse before she snatched my arm, marched us past the ferns and the front steps and the ever-more-elaborate housefronts. I gasped – not that her grip hurt me much more than sheer exhaustion already had, but she really was painfully strong. We were up the steps of the largest house in three jolting bounds, and she was rapping flakes of paint off the elegant olive-coloured door, her fingers digging in above my elbow.

"Mr. Adelstein's a detective," she muttered hastily. "He's part of the Div. Nick's his lodger. There – you've got a bit less ignorance to flaunt now."

The door sprang open, promptly transformed into a butler. He was – I quite don't know how else to describe it – at least thrice more *butler* than the sullen man Edwina employed, with a suit crisp and unyielding as a boot-scraper, and professional scorn to match. Septimus whirled about, her hands springing to notch in the small of her back – stern, and resoundingly determined to look it.

"Division Sergeant Septimus for Mr. Adelstein," she declared. "Div business."

"Of course. Do come upstairs."

The butler inclined his head to her, clipping his consonants to perfection. She stiffened; the contrast between his mock-genteel monotone and her brusque twang couldn't have been more pronounced, and he was clearly relishing it.

The door snicked shut behind us, not that the temperature changed much. Mr. Adelstein's house was a smaller, draughtier mirror of my own: the same sweeping central staircase, the same tall back window (though without the foliage-splattered stained glass), the same dizzying upward spiral of floors upon floors. His taste, admittedly, was far less gloomy than Edwina's. The floorboards were lighter in colour, curdling into Persian rugs wherever space allowed, and the walls were papered the politest shade of crimson I had never known to imagine. He didn't even need his gaslights, not when his large windows heaped in piles of cold autumn sun. Those panes alone were infinitely more pristine than every garment I presently possessed.

Upstairs became a drawing-room, stretching the length of the house, full of burgundy carpet and disconcertingly austere chaises – and, peculiarly enough, the bristling scent of tobacco. These walls were hung with more storm-ridden landscapes than it seemed feasible for one room to contain, painted thunderclouds and ragged trees looming over an assemblage of leather-topped desks. Perhaps the desks were the most startling thing: there was a veritable herd of them, lined up against every wall, covered with impeccable stacks of paper. There were maps, letters, files, huge ledgers with gilt monograms – in short, a level of nightmarish order that could not have shamed Cassandra's jumble of ledgers more if it had tried. Figs, it probably was trying.

The papers fluttered as one when Mr. Adelstein swept into the room, sharp-browed and fierce-eyed as a goshawk. It was a look (and a flawless herringbone suit, and a stern russet hair-parting) to vivisect a suspect at twenty paces. He seemed to stare me quite out of existence, without even glancing in my direction. Currently, he was endeavouring to blaze a hole straight through Septimus's forehead. Judging from her expression – stiff, unblinking, rather pale at the lips

– she wasn't precisely overjoyed to be the subject of that inquisitorial stare.

(Well – he *certainly* wasn't her sweetheart.)

He nodded coldly. "I assume this is the letter, Division Sergeant."

She fumbled for her notebook, extricated the former mechanical dove and held it out to him without bending her elbow. "Delivered to the Div yesterday."

"I see." One seamless eyebrow flicked towards his hairline. Plums, he must have drawn that hairline with a ruler. "Did it arrive with the unusual folding and the – ah – annotations?"

"Not exactly." Her teeth dashed along her lower lip, a quick uneasy twitch. "But it weren't me – Cassandra and Gertie – "

"Ah." He pinched the letter from her hand, ran two sharp fingers over it to smooth the creases. "If the contents are as vicious as the last anonymous letter to the Division, doubtless Cassandra and Gertie were unable to resist. If you'd wait?"

He'd read it twice through in a matter of seconds. Somewhere – lost amongst the canvas storms and the innumerable papers – a clock's faint ticks kept him strict to time. I watched his eyes lash across the page; they weren't pure yellow, were they? Surely it was the light?

"Yes, it's the same as the last one. The same content, the same conclusion, the same call for the Division to be disbanded. *Go back to your husbands* – evidently they didn't witness Tom Ballestas fixing your log-shed last week – *stop pretending that anyone wants you to protect them* – and ah, yes, here I am once more, *your Jewish lackey.* The Director, once again, receives the harshest criticism, if one could call these ill-articulated ramblings anything of the sort. Has she read it? Did she read the previous one?"

Septimus managed a brusque nod – only to flush, the moment she realised he was still examining the letter, and snatch for a verbal affirmative. "Both of 'em. Cassandra and Gertie were all for making sure she never found out the letters existed, but the Director was too clever for 'em."

"Indeed," Mr. Adelstein agreed absently, frowning along the page. "She's too clever for much of Dallyangle to understand or condone, and this *correspondent* of ours doesn't like it. We can only hope that this attack on the Division remains confined to letters until I discover their identity."

The alarm jostled up my ribs. The Division – the handful of peculiar individuals with whom I'd rather thrown in my lot – did he mean to suggest that they were under some kind of *attack?* But – it couldn't be – it wasn't Edwina's doing? And even if this letter was nothing to do with her, what then? If something was undermining the Division, that could well mean further investigations *into* the Division – into those who made up the Division – into those, more to the point, who made up their very characters just to hide in the Division –

"What's this?"

Mr. Adelstein, hawk-eyes on the hunt again – oh, plums, for me. Cross and across my face, as if he intended to split me in two with his stare alone.

"We have a new recruit?"

Septimus frowned, cleared her throat. "Well. Yes. My assistant."

He was still staring at me, but he spoke to her. Perhaps he'd sensed my fear, somehow deduced that it would cripple my words; perhaps he simply didn't regard me as worthy of being questioned directly. "Is this a recent development?"

"Very recent," Septimus admitted, glancing back at me with sudden wariness in her scowl. She'd caught his tone, his implications – his suspicions – it was all horribly evident on her face –

Figs, I wanted to shriek at her, *you know I couldn't have written that letter! I didn't even know who you were! You can't believe I'd want to undermine the Division!*

But hadn't she just lectured me, quite rightly, for doing precisely that? Hadn't she snarled about how much I'd upset everything with my sudden arrival – wielding my lavish education, impossible to refuse? Hadn't she already complained of how I'd stepped on the other members, and made a mockery of their self-betterment? It hardly seemed much of a leap to assume that I'd complement my disruptive activities with a spot of anonymous letter-writing.

I gasped – purely for the sheer horrendous logic of it – which only made my wretched trembling self look guiltier than ever.

"I see."

Mr. Adelstein sliced me open once more, narrow-eyed, then caught Septimus on a meaningful glare. He presumably meant to be surreptitious, but how could I be anything less than hellishly attuned to his meaning? In that glare, he was discreetly recommending that she say no more about the matter – that he'd investigate it – that she mustn't let on that I'd abruptly become the most threatening force in Dallyangle short of the Sweetings, as far as he was concerned.

"Anyway. I do have an additional message for the Director, but – well, it requires absolute discretion, and – "

At which juncture the door nigh-on fell in.

Nick Fitzdegu whirligigged into the drawing-room in bare feet, swirling papers off the desks, quite oblivious to the freezing tension he'd just catapulted into. His wiry shoulders were bristling with rats – persimmons, live rats! – dozens of scrabbling rats, blotched with brown patches or unnerving albino, clinging on for dear life to the worn linen of his shirt, skinny tails swinging. Their presence shunted his relentless exuberance into supernatural intensity, until his very appearance seemed more than enough to set the lightning crackling in the painted storms.

"Matty! I've done it! Vernon Vibbrit's already appealing to the *Rodent's Gazette!* – "

Then he crashed headlong into Mr. Adelstein's pointed stare, spasmed into a nervy giggle, dashed a lean brown hand through his hair. Not entirely to anyone's surprise, he dislodged a rat in the process.

"Ah. Aha. Sorry. Didn't realise you'd another meeting. Makes sense you'd start mocking up a search party, the way they were all on at you this morning, and – Septimus! Hallo again! And Henry too – back for rats, eh?"

"Nicholas!" Mr. Adelstein snapped. It seemed incredible that this finicky young man, whose hair and features were as meticulously tailored as his suits, could bear the chaos of Nick Fitzdegu lodging under his roof. "We established my meetings as rodent-free zones, if you would care to recall."

Nick blinked, enviably unfazed. "Timothy hay vengeance campaigns wait for no detectives, Matty."

He sauntered over to us, a satyr in stripes with faintly squeaking shoulders, snatched up the smallest of his rodent legion and proffered it to me with a jaunty grin. "Sure I can't tempt you, Henry? Not even for Henry the rat? This one's called Henry now – closest I could get to a fieldmouse, for your fieldmouse eyes, and your terribly twitchy fieldmouse smile! And you'll need another one to go with her – a lady, of course, 'less you want a whole score of them on your hands – here, what d'you think of these two together? Have a hold, go on!"

"Nicholas, this is not the time!"

Mr. Adelstein was almost at a splutter – figs, I didn't think I'd ever hear him splutter – but Septimus beat him to it, glowering Nick and his rats a full step back from me. "She already said no!"

I blushed quite through my hairline: wasn't Nick her sweetheart? And – oh, persimmons – to accept an inexplicable pair of rodents from her sweetheart, even if said acceptance was fuelled purely by abject fear – it really rather was the height of appalling manners, wasn't it?

Nick, the possessor of both a functioning voice and an unshakeable nerve, threw himself at once into salvaging the confusion. "Alright, you two! No harm done! What're we talking about in here, then? Don't worry about me, Henry, I know everything. Lodgers do, eh, Matty?"

Mr. Adelstein gritted his teeth. "Very amusing, Nicholas."

Nick winked at him. "'S it still *absolute discretion* we've got today?"

"It's the consequences of this morning," Mr. Adelstein explained irritably, nudging at his hairline, as if a strand of that slick pomade had fallen out of place (grapes, of course it hadn't). "Division Sergeant, unless you can vouch for your assistant's trustworthiness – and capacity to refrain from distracting the room by fawning over Nicholas's rodents – I suggest you have her wait outside."

My jaw quite dropped.

Pomegranates, I'd not said a word since we crossed this man's threshold! Not a word – not even a fruit! As if I wanted Nick to flail rats at me – as if I didn't know that Nick had an understanding with Septimus! And – just to compound the bewildering insult – the detective seemed infinitely *more* infuriated by my moment in the rat-breeder's orbit, than by the entire suggestion that I might be out to destroy the Division on every conceivable front!

Septimus glanced down at me. It was all there, sharp in her sharp scowl. Exasperation, impatience – and now, thanks to Mr. Adelstein, the slightest twinge of suspicion. *D'you even care just how much you don't know?*

But then she spoke, eyes on mine, her voice brusque and terse and defiantly unanswerable. "I'll vouch for Henry. I'm training her, and it ain't training if she's just stood out on the steps."

I've not the faintest what Mr. Adelstein's orderly face did. I've not the faintest whether Nick held his rats, or dropped his rats, or dipped in to nod his agreement. There was quite one thing in my known world, and it was Septimus's expression. She was still scowling, but the corner of her mouth had twisted into a grimace, a silent warning. Whatever I may have been – and she clearly wasn't sure – she'd decided to trust me, and to make me take note of it. If I betrayed her now, I'd do it in flat scorn of her stern appeal to my better nature. If I betrayed her, she'd make me feel it, and all her exasperation with the mysterious Pip Property would be nothing next to the war she'd wage on me.

"Tell them, Matty," Nick urged, years and worlds away.

Mr. Adelstein cleared his throat, and Septimus broke our stare. All at once, she was back to attention, her hands folded neat against her spine, her face as perfectly motionless as her chestnut chignon.

"I was summoned on a house call this morning by a private client."

"Two sisters," Nick added. "Just like the ballad. One dark and one fair, and both worried half out of their wits."

It was quite as if he'd thrust a rat down my throat.

Even then – it was too soon – I'd barely had half a day! –

"They were most anxious to discover the whereabouts of their sibling. She appears to have been spirited from her bedroom – at what time and to what purpose, they are at a loss to conjecture."

I gasped. They all ignored me. The story – *my* story – was far too gripping.

"Though my attentiveness to the matter of the anonymous letters remains unwavering, we ought not to pass up this new opportunity purely to fret over our own concerns. The Division, in short, has been offered this case."

If I could just – nobody was looking at me – if I could make it, alive and relatively implacable, to the end of the briefing –

"And guess whose case it is?" Nick cried delightedly. "Edwina Nettleblack, the soap baron!"

"Tincture," Mr. Adelstein muttered, seconds before my own lips twitched it.

"*Tincture* baron! Not an actual baron! But you do know the one – the heiress! That mad Welsh lot that made good on their family medicine! The Div'll be in the money if you sort her out, eh, Matty?"

Mr. Adelstein sighed. "Well, Nicholas, I can hardly deny that it would be very much in the Division's interests to attract her support, as I'm sure the Director is all too aware. Miss Edwina Nettleblack is unswervingly eager to find her sister. The missing girl is apparently rather young, likely to stumble into all manner of dangers – and she is on the verge of marrying into the nobility, as Miss Edwina was extremely keen to inform us. With the Director's permission, I shall take the lead on this case, and find the youngest Miss Nettleblack before – "

Saints, plums, and Septimus forgive me, but I couldn't. I was as truly guilty of this as I'd ever be guilty of anything – and, accordingly, my legs gave way.

For heaven knows how long, there was nothing but panic, swirling semi-conscious panic and a ghastly dearth of steady breaths. I could have been anywhere – I think I *was* anywhere, and everywhere, pinwheeling in my head from Gower to Cambridge to Catfish Crescent to the Division, strung up on the neat brown plait that had been my hair, until something cut me loose and hurled me shrieking into every place at once –

Then the panic shattered, and the dregs of it crushed themselves together like rags into paper – only they made a ceiling instead, pale and poorly plastered, with a large crack wriggling out of one corner. I was staring at that ceiling from a bed, upon which I seemed to be sprawled (persimmons!), a spindly wrought-iron thing that rattled when I twitched, its neat-made bedsheets either threadbare or knitted, the smell that clung about it thick and distinctly not human. My boots were still laced, my uniform as stiff and scratchy as ever. The posy, crushed of half its petals, was still pressed beneath my belt.

I'd not been dipping my toe in these observations for more than a moment before something brushed at my temple. There were rats, at least five of them, and they appeared to have made their own paltry bedsheets out of my cropped hair.

"Figs," I gasped, quite at a loss for how to proceed.

"Henry! Still alive?"

The rats were – just about – reassuring in the context of Nick Fitzdegu's voice, though the bed decidedly wasn't. I stared about, eyes swivelling, far too scared to move my head, and there he was: cross-legged at a desk under a dirty porthole of a window, decanting his rat food into chipped bowls with manic precision. He flung it down when he saw me gaping, skidded about on his chair to toss me a smile, snatching up a mug from beside the bowls on the desk. It had a glorious scent quite unlike any tea I had ever encountered, heady with cinnamon and cloves.

"Here you go. Food and fluids, that's what you need, and chai's nothing if not invigorating – ancestral recipe, that. And I stuck a few drops of Nettleblack's in it, just in case. Hope you don't mind the bed – bit un-gentlike, I know – but better than the floor, eh?"

I blinked. How to ask him to extricate his rats?

"I – erm – what – what happened?"

"After you collapsed? Well, we got you upstairs, and – you sort of fell asleep. Think you were asleep, at any rate. You were talking a lot. Chattering away like a right little medium!"

Now I sat up, so sharply that half the rats went flying. "I – but – what – what did I say?"

"Begging your pardon, but it was mostly nonsense." He grinned, stretched down one lanky leg and nudged a flailing rat back to its feet on the bare floorboards. "The sort of stuff that doesn't make much sense on its own. Just lots of *but you can't* and *please don't* and the like – and fruit, whole market-fuls of fruit. Bit of a thing for you, the fruit, isn't it? Or is it just hunger? Apparently you had to skip lunch. And possibly breakfast. You need to eat, you know that?"

Pineapples, but I hardly heard him. It was all back, every scrap of the terrible revelation that had knocked me senseless in the first place, shot through with a new nightmarish question: what would Septimus think? If my conscious existence had exasperated her before, how much more would my spontaneous delirium bristle at her nerves? And to have swooned in the wake of – oh, pomegranates! – what must have seemed like an utterly tangential concern – some missing heiress, nothing to do with the Division – she must think me entirely deranged!

"Septimus – she – where is she? She didn't – doesn't – is she angry with me?"

It was Nick's turn to blink. He folded the mug of chai into my palm, slid off the chair – holding my gaze all the while, as if I were yet another rodent he was endeavouring not to startle – and perched himself down on the end of the bed, lean face cupped in his hands.

"I wouldn't say *angry*. More – eh, what's the word? – when you're a bit, y'know, you don't know what to do, and you don't like it, but you're more confused than annoyed – "

"I – erm – perturbed?"

"There you go!" He smiled, snatched a tumbling rat without looking and notched it over his shoulder. "Perturbed, then. Maybe a bit guilty? She's downstairs with Matty, waiting for you – but they're not talking about you anymore, don't worry. It's the case. She's not sure the Div's got space for it – chasing the rich, bringing them back like naughty children with a Division-ful of governesses."

This was about as reassuring as anything could have been. If Septimus objected to Mr. Adelstein working for my sisters, surely that made her distinctly disinclined to aid investigations into the missing Nettleblack?

"Plums." It was a sigh, but more relief than dismay, rounded off by a voracious gingery gulp of the chai. "I – erm – I really am sorry – for – well – I didn't mean to inconvenience – "

He flapped a hand, swatted my apologies out of the air – then set that hand, quite as he'd set the rat, on my shoulder, and gave me a bolstering shake. It was just as well that I'd halved the chai; his gesture set the remnants slopping up the mug. "No harm done. No one's angry with you. Mostly people just want to feed you. You'll be alright, fieldmouse – I know Septimus might look scary as a penny dreadful, but she'll look after you – "

"Nicholas!"

There were terrified squeaks, and they were mostly mine. The detective was glowering round the door, from Nick to me to the chai in my hands, as if he could prise all the proffered comforts away from me with sheer glare alone.

"How long has she been awake?" he demanded.

Nick flashed me a quick smile, sprang off the bed to weather the storm. Plums, but I had to follow his example, even with my lungs garrotting themselves on my ribcage, plunging my face into the last of the chai by way of a brief escape. "Gently, Matty! Henry's only been back a few minutes!"

Mr. Adelstein sniffed. "I see. Clearly, she doesn't waste time."

If I'd had more nerve – if I'd had any nerve – I would have – oh, I don't know – I would have expressed my utmost incredulity, and in no uncertain terms! Yes! Whatever he was insinuating, he was about as wildly wide of the mark as it was possible for a detective to be – and quite what right did he have to be prodding me with such insinuations anyway? I saw myself in my mind, growing a good three inches and transforming into Rosamond, saw a killingly ironical smirk framed in feral curls. *Sweet pomegranates, Matty, but I've really no interest in stealing your lodger – the only one conjuring a scandal here is you!*

But I wasn't Rosamond. "I – erm – I do apologise for – the yelling – and the collapsing – quite – "

Mr. Adelstein was still glaring at me, head notched to one side. If I'd been deemed a fieldmouse, he was decidedly living up to his goshawk streak, ready to swoop down and dash me into the skies. But – that said – there was something else in his look. Something had sharpened there whilst I'd been stammering at him, something quite apart from his wary disdain.

"That's quite alright," he returned coolly. "As Nicholas might say, no harm done, Miss Harriet."

Figs. *Figs.* There it was, and there was consummately nothing I could do to keep the horror out of my face.

"Harriet? Who's that?"

Mr. Adelstein didn't drop my gaze, not even for Nick's bewilderment. He edged himself further into the tiny attic-room, round the three enormous rat-cages that littered the floor, where rodents scurried into their hay at the creak of his footfalls. Now, he was close enough for me to spot the yellow flecks in his eyes, his disapproval visibly sparking into triumph.

"Henry is an – ah – unusual name for a woman. I simply assumed it was short for Harriet."

How – how could he have – *what?* I'd been the soul of timidity for the entire duration of my acquaintance with this man, short-haired and pained-looking and as far removed from the confidence of the wealthy as it was possible to be! Had Edwina and Rosamond given him a likeness of me? Had I gasped out something in my hysteria by way of a fatal clue?

No. It wasn't even what I said – it was how I said it. My peculiar accent, too bizarre for Cassandra to place – but if you broke it down into its composite parts –

It froze me quite cadaverous. My traitorous voice cowered in my throat. Every word – however timid, however inarticulate – *every word* only confirmed his suspicions!

"Is it short for Harriet?"

I gasped a breath, made myself swallow. He had no evidence, nothing, beyond the first smartings of an idea, and a smattering of circumstances which surely – surely? – couldn't stand up on their own. But he plainly expected me to quail at the mere suggestion of his victory, to slump to the floor again, to sob myself into a frenzy and confess the lot –

"No," I heard myself declare, rather louder than I'd meant to, every word rattling back off the rat-cages. "It's just Henry."

Well – if he thought I had any intention of making it an easy triumph – !

He blinked, startled, but there wasn't time for him to retort. The same name I'd just brazenly assured him was my baptismal original was ricocheting up through the floorboards in Septimus's voice, thick with impatience. She must have caught our voices, and she clearly wanted to be away from the place.

I could second her with a vengeance on *that!*

Mr. Adelstein arched an eyebrow. Pomegranates, he recovered quickly. "Your superior has been lecturing me about the apparent foolishness of taking on the Nettleblack case. If you'll excuse me – *Henry* – I think I've heard more than enough of it for today. She's waiting for you downstairs."

There was the slightest twinge of a sneer about his ruler-sharp lips. Scurry back to *your superior*, it seemed to say, and enjoy it whilst it lasts.

But he had to step aside. Nick was there, looking unabashedly baffled, and my desperate gamble had been right. As long as I denied it, Mr. Adelstein didn't have sufficient evidence to overrule me. It set my skin prickling with terror, but I made myself dip him a – not a curtsy, which would have had far too much of *Miss Harriet* about it, but a terse bow, the sort of thing I imagined Septimus would do.

"I – erm – of course," I stammered, and sprinted through the door before I could catch his reaction. I had just enough wit left to put the mug back before I descended the stairs – decidedly empty of its brilliant contents, which doubtless he would take as my greatest insult yet.

The fear's still coiling in my chest, even now, back in the Division dormitory with my journal on one knee, and half of Dallyangle between me and Pole Place. This isn't merely a pheasant-shoot – this is a duel in earnest – and, once again, my very future seems determined to stake itself on the outcome!

Mercifully, the incessant sprinting seems to have come to an end for the evening. We spent far too much afternoon on yet more laps of Dallyangle, in which I watched and shivered whilst Septimus checked the locks on outhouses and cellars, scribbling in her notebook with vigour fit to snap the stubby pencil. She stopped us at the market to pick up bread rolls, shoved one into my hands with a wary frown: "Nick's right – you need to eat!" The sky darkened, thickening to heavy shadows between the houses, and a sharp wind knifed in from the fields. No detective dropped from the swarming clouds to ensnare me, for which I was profoundly grateful. Not that his absence helped when it came to recovering from my bout of terror; the slightest sound in the street was enough to set me twitching.

Now I feel, I confess, quite a thing apart from the curious cosiness that's sprung up around me. For the others in the dormitory – Gertie Skull and her relations and their self-declared Inferior Contingent – it's a gentle evening in familiar shades, unhampered by scheming sisters and their detective-errants. Slabs of warm thick-buttered toast, punched through with the toasting-fork, are being passed in to us from reception. Gertie is cross-legged on her bed, steadily devouring that shiny-backed copy of *Life and Limbs: a Comic Romance of the Medical School!* (She was both delighted and perturbed to discover that I'd already finished it – I am not, she insists, to tell her whether the disguised surgeon heroine chooses the rakish fellow-student or the swaggering stableboy, nor am I to reveal the fate of the doctor's missing gangrenous hand.) Oliver Skull is stood on his creaking bed, fiddling with the mirrors behind the dripping candles, to universal demands of *brighter!* – whilst insisting in a splutter that the lights can't manage it. Millicent Musgrove splays her spare split skirt over the draughty floor, digs under her bed for a ramshackle sewing-kit, applies herself to some deft repairs on the interminable buttonholes. I have a hasty glimpse of Mordred's pale head, darting out of a break in the floorboards beneath my bed, before he vanishes back to a subterranean existence I cannot even attempt to pursue. Cassandra leans round the door, smirking – "Millicent! Your young man's out front, wondering if he can squeeze in an evening stroll before night shift?"

There is something I can do, at least, something beyond hysterical scribbling. That raggedy scrap of petals survived the day at my belt. I fear Gertie would demand impossible heaps of explanation if she caught a glimpse of them – so into the journal they go, too swift to be seen, whilst the Skulls are watching Millicent leap into her button-boots. I've never been one for flower-pressing – Rosamond was the amateur botanist, in her clifftop youth – I can only hope the poor posy-remnants stay vaguely in place on the page –

Figs. Right. I'll have to finish here – no time – I'll explain properly later – but –

In short – I may well be duelling Mr. Adelstein for my life, but something rather worse has apparently just happened to Dallyangle. A decapitated head, it seems, has unexpectedly appeared onstage, in the prop-chest of *The Pirates of Penzance*.

6.

OF SEVERED HEADS IN
STRANGE PLACES

The Director's Record

October 29th 1893 (Sunday)

REPRIMANDS, &c. — Septimus, for seventh (?) attempt to involve
Pip Property in the Division's affairs. Fine of one week's pay
if situation occurs for an eighth time without <u>extremely
good reason</u>. Gertrude Skull, for another untimely visit to
the tavern next door – one shilling.

LETTER. — Will send to Matthew for examination. Contents identical to those of the previous missive. Handwriting and
sender unknown. *Mem.* – perhaps best to open the post
myself for the next few weeks, until this so-called correspondence dies down. Cassandra and Gertrude were far too
shaken for my liking when they brought the thing to my
office.

NEW RECRUIT. — Miss Henry Hyssop, with Septimus as mentor. An
unorthodox but necessary move. Number of recruits urgently
needs increasing, if we are to meet the council's demands on
time, and Miss Hyssop's education may yet prove useful. (As,
indeed, may the training process, to Septimus.)

October 30th 1893 (Monday)

MICE. — Irrelevant, perhaps, by comparison with other announce-
        ments, but worth noting that an unprecedented number of
        mice – or, the mangled remnants of mice – have appeared in
        the building. Could send Millicent (*not* Gertrude) to enquire
        whether her parents' tavern has started keeping a cat. We can
        hardly complain if the Division has inadvertently acquired a
        mouser, but the creature must at least be trained to clean up
        after itself. Cassandra claimed to have seen a monstrously
        elongated rat on the premises last night – which could
        simply be Cassandra's overactive imagination exerting itself
        once more – but I *will not* have rodents in the Division, and I
        do not especially wish to tolerate the dismembered remains
        of them either.

MATTHEW. — Letter delivered. Ensure evidence arrives intact next
        time (what on earth possessed Cassandra to scribble all over
        it, and indeed over every scrap of paper she finds?). News of
        possible case: missing Nettleblack sibling, of Nettleblack's
        Tincture family. Division involvement in the matter pres-
        ently suspended, in light of major new preoccupations (see
        below).

SEVERED HEAD AT THE DALLYANGLE THEATRE. — *Urgent.*
        Septimus and her new assistant dispatched to scene. No
        further news as yet. Real potential for advancement of the
        Division – if nothing else, it might buy us some time.

        Keturah St. Clare Ballestas, Director of the Dallyangle Division

Myself once more

More or less still Monday, October 30th, 1893

Sweet elysian pineapples. *At least they're distracted* is all I can say.

Judging by the reaction at the Division, this was the first time in everybody's collective lives (including mine) that such a thing as a severed head had turned up as a sudden and pressing concern. Within twenty seconds of the announcement, the building was a whirlwind. The Director herself strode into the dormitory, silenced the room with a stern stare and a tactical removal of the spectacles, broke the news as if she was snapping a twig. The instant she left, Gertie and Oliver scrabbled about with feral eyes and terrified grins, stockinged feet plummeting into boots, scraps of paper snatched from bedside tables to scrawl the news to their family. I seized the moment of chaos to peer through the crack in the floorboards – to check that Mordred still had *his* head attached, or perhaps that he didn't have the severed one clutched in his jaws. Beyond that, I couldn't do more than cling to my elbows as the candle-flames flickered, far too stunned to register any of it as remotely real.

Dallyangle never had anything like this. In its year of existence, the Division hadn't encountered a murder – certainly not a dismemberment. It was horrible – it was terribly exciting – it was penny-dreadful stuff – it was the meat of *Life and Limbs: A Comic Romance of the Medical School!* – it was infinitely more frightening than stolen pigs – it was practically metropolitan!

So Gertie was yelling, at any rate, as she clattered off to run the news to Mr. Adelstein, buttoning her jacket as she sprinted. Out in reception, Cassandra was scribbling a frantic entry in her ledger – no, in a notebook of her own, marbled at the covers, pressed between the ledger's pages. She didn't even glance up to snipe at Septimus as the Director gestured us past – for we were to hasten to the theatre, and retrieve all the evidence we could carry.

"Open the morgue, and make it presentable! Gertrude, make sure Mr. Adelstein gets to the scene as quickly as possible – take a bicycle – and put that ridiculous novel away! Septimus, go straight there – bring me everything you can find – hold the fort until Mr. Adelstein arrives! Cassandra, compose a dispatch for the council at once – they will need to hear this from us – "

This was the last I heard of the Director's descant – she'd stationed herself in the midst of reception, hurling her ring of keys at Oliver, yelling orders to everything that scrambled past her, the closest to uncontrolled I'd ever seen her reach – before Septimus tugged me away into the night.

The rain had held off, and the cobbles were drying. The market was a skeleton now, stripped of its awnings, a few stark limbs discernible against the leathery black sky. My feet smarted the moment I sped up, and my chemise was quite slick with sweat, but the Division's mania had crept up on me, and I wouldn't let a whit of discomfort or a scrape of freezing wind slow me down. Huddled cottages with candlelit windows flashed past like so many cats' eyes, whilst the shouts and snarls of a crowd ahead got closer and fleshier. Plums, but here I was, dashing behind Septimus, pinched alive and giddily distracted – not away from, but headlong into, the heart of the madness!

And there was the Dallyangle Theatre, throbbing like a jack-o'-lantern. I understood on the instant why my ignorance of the place had provoked such incredulity. It was far larger than I expected, the stucco façade whorled and writhing with architectural furbe-lows, lit from below by the blazing light of the foyer – for every one of the glassy front doors had been swung wide, hurling people and illumination into the street. The scene was hellishly splendid: the strange garish building with its pillars and frieze, horrendously out of place in the bucolic town, and the heaving heap of greatcoats and carriages jostling for place outside it. Septimus wrestled us through a gap in the gigs, sent a gaslit-eyed horse shying as she clambered under its head. She was yelling *Division!*, but even she could hardly fling the word high enough to soar over this chaos. It was pure wild scrabble just to get to the doors. I cried out, I fear, quite as much as anyone else in the crowd – there was an elbow sharp in my side, then a heel gouging into my toe, and an open-palmed hand rattled my teeth in my head. By the time we'd cleared the worst of the throng, I was bruised as a peach.

Right back by the stalls entrances, the foyer was at its quietest. There were pinches and scars studding the scarlet plush carpet, the remnants left by walking-sticks and high-heeled boots as the audi-ence rushed for the street. The doors ahead of us had mirrors in them, set between polished coils of wood – and for one startling moment I snagged eyes with myself, flushed and bedraggled with the crowd at my back. Pomegranates – was that truly what my cropped hair looked like?

I quite couldn't stop to calm it. We were through these doors in three smart steps, and then it was darker even than the empty market. I blinked, and rows of soft empty seats unfolded out of the gloom, down a giddy rake to the orchestra pit and the fussy proscenium of the stage. It was warm in here, close and stifling, the air crammed with sweat and half-melted wax. The footlights were still lit, twinkling faintly out of their shells, speckling weird spasms of light over a painted mansion at the back of the stage. A chest – *the* chest – sat lone and sinister centre-stage, ringed by plaster gravestones – some of them felled, one of them broken in half. As far off as they could get, a swathe of the company still lurked, lurid at the faces with greasepaint, their garish costumes huddled under shawls and blankets.

Septimus swung up onto the stage, glanced over her shoulder open-mouthed – quite as if there'd been an audience still in those musky stalls, and she was about to do nothing more bizarre than belt a few bars of song. Fortunately, the look brought me into her orbit. Before I could disgrace myself attempting to emulate her easy climb, she'd dropped to one knee and leaned over to grab my waist, dragged me up after her without even a frown for the effort.

I'd not so much as a fruit to stammer in thanks before she sprang upright and whiplashed away to the performers. Had she felt – through the jacket – my consummate lack of corset? Did she disapprove? Medlars, the thought was more than enough to squirm me to my feet.

"It's in there," one of the actors cried, swaggering forward to meet Septimus. He was shivering in a thin silk shirt, ruffled at the neckline with a froth of lace, his honey-coloured hair clasped in a creamy ribbon. "In the – wait – you're not the police! Did no one send to Gulmere for this? Dear Lord, they haven't summoned the *Division*, have they?"

"'Course I'm from the Division," Septimus snapped. "Now – you're playing Frederic, I assume – where's Lorrie? Lawrence Tickering?"

The actor blinked at her. With this lacy man in his rumpled silk and enormous boots, and Septimus in her high-buttoned jacket and trousers, they looked alarmingly like they were playing a scene themselves: the villain and the principal boy, blustering through their first confrontation. "Who?"

Septimus flushed. "He's a pirate! He has the stage business with the life-preserver! You're in scenes with him – you'd've been acting together right when this happened – so where is he?"

"Oh. *Him.*" A curling sneer from the actor – limes, he recovered quickly from a close encounter with a severed head! – and a lavish wink to go with it, shirt-cuffs flapping like moths as he folded his arms. "The pretty boy with the cockney vowels. He's outside – flirting with the management, as usual. I'm sure it must be a real perk of your job, fretting over the likes of him – " (another wretched wink) " – and if that's the fun your sort get out of joining the Dallyangle Division, I can't completely blame you for – "

"Oi! You two!"

A haggard-looking man in a faded bicorn hat stumbled out of the cluster, a plaid rug slung at his shoulders, the dregs of his false beard sweat-matted and slipping off sideways. "'Case you've forgot, Hector, there's a head in a box over there – time enough to snipe at the chorus later! And you, fellow – planning on doing your job tonight?"

Septimus whirled about, teeth flashing in a snarl – and, from his sudden pallor, it became abruptly apparent he'd only just realised she was a woman.

"I – ah – beg pardon, miss – but – "

"I ain't *miss*," she spat at him. "I'm a *Divisioner*, and I know full well what my job is, Pirate King! Right! Cast! File in!"

The remnants of the company were hardly inclined to obey her in any punctual manner, but she was already spurring them onwards – snatching the inimitable notebook from her pocket, lashing the spine back on itself, and seizing the stubby pencil that had been lodged in the folds. "I need names. Everyone in the show, everyone working backstage. Anyone who had access to that chest. Go!"

Hector rolled his eyes. "Do you mean to have us recollect the names of every audience member from memory too?"

Septimus met him head-on with a twitch of a glare. "No need to bother, Frederic. Your box office'll tell me that on the way out. Pirate King! Got an inkling what the names of your crew are?"

"I – well – " " – the man was far too abashed to refuse her this time – "I'll have a think – ah – well, you have Samuel – no, that's his char-acter – "

"Let's just start with a register, then!"

She jerked her head at me, eyes flicking to the right, where heavy drapes slumped down from the flies. "Henry – Lorrie says the pirates come on stage left in Act Two. Have a look back there. Mind you don't touch anything."

"And if you break any of the ladies' parasols," Hector added sharply, sneering me towards the wings, "Your silly little detective-club will have to pay for them!"

I doubled my pace after that, blinking like a maniac to accustom my eyes to the gloom of backstage. Within a few frantic steps I'd tripped on something. No one onstage seemed to notice; the grudging roll of names droned on undisturbed. Nectarines – of course, of *course* it was a parasol underfoot – but Hector would never know it wasn't just trampled in the panic, if I snuck out quick through that narrow little door ahead –

I gasped when I sprinted through it, and the paltry tallow-light flickered with me. The narrow door led you to an equally narrow corridor, lit only by candles cupped in hollows above head-height – and the temperature was bruisingly cold after the warm stickiness of the auditorium. Darting further in showed me why: whilst half of the corridor cricked towards the back of the stage, presumably leading to the dressing-rooms, a forked alternative took you directly to a door, and this door was flung open to the street outside. There were the rusty remnants of a lock, a gangrenous key still poking out of it, but the structure was more than flimsy enough to have caved with a shove.

Well. Peaches. This quite didn't help.

Onstage, Septimus was still holding court, having apparently gathered the lists she needed in flat defiance of the company's reticence. I edged back into the throng, as surreptitiously as I was able – she didn't look inclined to be interrupted.

"Right! We've got a head in a box. So where's the body?"

Hector and the Pirate King exchanged a stunned glance. "There – there isn't a body – there's only ever been a head – "

"But are you *sure?*"

A combination of incredulous exasperation and infectious head-mania had apparently seized Septimus tenfold, with the names in her notebook and the whole investigation spieling out before her. The excitement hurled her voice a good three crescendos closer to fortissimo, and – you could see it when she skidded round, snagged in the footlights' glimmer – struck something rather unearthly into her navy eyes. *The resident downward spiral*, Cassandra had called her – but you'd quite never think it to look at her now.

"If there's a head, there's a body somewhere. I ain't saying for definite that it's in this theatre, but it can't just've vanished, and this is the first place there is to look."

Hector gaped at her. "A corpse running amok in Dallyangle, indeed! Is this ridiculous young woman actually suggesting that we scurry off to hunt her a headless cadaver? Good Lord, she's another mad cockney!"

Septimus's answering snarl was almost certainly more charismatic than the motley group's entire operetta. "I'm asking anyone who thinks they've got useful information to come forward with it, and – you! Police! Don't think I can't see you sneaking off back there!"

A gaggle of men dislodged themselves from the shadows of the wings, their dull blue-black uniforms striking a passable imitation of the helmeted officers I'd seen trudging about Cambridge. Next to Septimus, they were so many guys and mannequins, limp and quivering in the face of her fervent sharpness.

"Look – we're not policemen – we're just bass-baritones, mostly – "

"That don't mean you can just run away!" she snapped. "And backstage ain't to be tampered with 'til Mr. Adelstein's seen it. He'll be along with more Divisioners soon, and I need you all to stay here and speak to him."

The bass-baritones flung a volley of glances to me, woebegone and beseeching. What a giddy delight it was just to shrug! I looked – and was – a far softer touch than Septimus, but her spare zeal seemed to have leapt into my veins, and it made me firmer than I'd ever yet been.

"*More* Divisioners!" Hector spluttered. "God help us! If there are more Divisioners, what are you two supposed to be doing?"

Septimus set her teeth. "We're here for the evidence. I've got the names, we'll get the ticket register – Henry, bring me the head."

Wait.

Figs.

I was perfectly content being an awestruck observer – not – why was *I* the one to have to go pearl-fishing for the thing?

"But – don't you – erm – think – "

"The head," she growled, skewering me on a javelin of a glare. "Now."

It was there in her eyes, even half-feral and glittering as they were. This was a test. *You really don't know a thing*, and now here was a chance to start remedying that. Her glower twitched; she was realising, too late, that I might turn tail and sprint away, never mind the attendant humiliation it would hurl back at her. For one shaky moment, right in the midst of her virtuosic performance, she looked every inch as awkward as she'd been that morning, inadvertently proffering me a bunch of flowers, steeling herself for me to laugh them out of her hand.

I settled my shoulders. Staggered towards the chest, with its slammed lid and splintered wood, every eye on the stage grazing my bruises. She swallowed – with the cast watching me, she had a few seconds to steady herself – and tipped forward on her boot-toes, quite as morbidly curious as the rest of them.

For my part, I felt nightmarishly light-headed. Oh – *no!* – not the best phrase, truly *not* the best phrase –

"Pomegranates!"

The company screamed for my scream. Even Septimus flinched. I reached into the chest, grabbed a bristly crop of cold greying hair – lifted – failed – shifted to a two-handed grip – tried again – it was heavy, I'd not expected that –

And there it was. A man's head, mutton-chopped and silver at the temples. Eyes shut, skin grey as the hair, face stiff but otherwise unconcerned. Not a whit of blood.

Which – wasn't that – ?

I gaped at it, quite the little public-executioner, fear fast curdling to sheer bewilderment. Granted, my experience with severed heads was about as extensive as the rest of Dallyangle's, but – surely – surely the expression ought to look more pained? Surely it ought to smell of something that wasn't quite so – so sickly, so cloying, so clinical in one's mouth? Surely there ought to be blood – or even bloodstains? Surely the decapitated remnants of a recent murder victim were supposed to look less – well – one would have to check with Nick Fitzdegu and his family of undertakers, but – less *pristine?*

Septimus had it out of my hands before I could stammer as much, tipping it up to the gleam of the footlights. A universal whimper sent the whole cast scuttling backwards. "Right! Either he ain't been beheaded here, or someone's done a job and a half of cleaning him up. Does anyone recognise him?"

Hector – and I could have hurled the head at him for it, had I still held the head, and been of a considerably braver disposition – actually rolled his dark-lashed eyes, one hand cupping his billowing shirt close to his corseted waist. "Almost a sensible question! None of us recognise it, and none of the audience did either."

Septimus scowled. "None? Are you sure? No reactions stood out? Dallyangle ain't a large town – surely someone must know – "

"Apparently not," Hector retorted briskly. "Well, you've got the head, and you've got your little list, and absolutely none of you will be missed when you finally see fit to make your exit – so is there anything else, *Divisioner*, or are you going to leave us be?"

Figs, I wanted to yell, but you shan't sneer at Septimus! Not tonight – not when she gets far too much of that from her own colleagues! Not when you've barely aided her enquiries beyond scoffing and denying things! Not when – surely – you ought to be glad of her protection until the reinforcements arrive!

Septimus blinked at him, panic spasming across her eyes. "Wait. What – where are the police chorus?"

Hector smiled nastily. "They ran into the wings when you pulled out the head with such feminine tact. They've probably gone home, costumes and all."

"What? But – they can't go out backstage – I told 'em – "

"Yes. Well, you see – if you want to order fake policemen around, you have to *be* a real policeman. That's the trick of it, sweetheart."

Septimus flushed. "Look, this ain't helping – "

"It's really very flattering that you want to play the man for us, but you're welcome to put your skirts back on whenever you like. Even our poor bumbling bass-baritones wear the trousers better than you!"

That was quite enough of such categoric untruths.

"Division Sergeant?" – and it was me, shaky-voiced, every word a physical thing to push across my tongue. "I – erm – you know best, of course – but – there's something backstage that – erm – you probably ought to have a look at – I – I might be wrong – and – well – please do correct me – if I am – "

She stared. Stark and angular on the stage's edge, knuckles taut about the head's jawline, her glare furrowed and wrong-footed. I'd overstepped – of course I had – and with the whole company watching us –

"You ain't wrong," she declared suddenly. If anything, she sounded a little surprised. "Good idea. And – there you go, cast, Mr. Adelstein's here!"

Merciless peaches. I flung a tremulous glance past her shoulder, where Gertie Skull pelted up the aisle – Gertie Skull with a herringbone suit at her back, the ruler-perfect hairline and darting yellow eyes of my detectival foe.

"As you were," Septimus called to them, stiffening out of her startled scrutiny. "I'm taking names, registers and head back to the Div. But first – Henry – backstage! Show me! Right!"

And without another glance at scornful actors, sprinting Divisioners, or (to my infinite relief) scowling detective, she thrust the head into my arms and dashed past the curtains, crunching the parasol underfoot as she went. The company's stares whipped me into a sprint, clutching the head like a sans-culotte, following her down to the brittle back door – pausing only to stumble into an errant stagehand, and send them into a fit of blue hysterics.

The crowd hadn't dispersed in the least when we emerged. If anything, it had swelled, heavy with the gruesome news. The nearby houses were seeping light, their windows spliced with silhouettes as the inhabitants craned for a better view. The air was cross-hatched with voices, frightened cries and spluttered incredulities and drawling speculation all tangling together. I wouldn't have been stunned if the whole of Dallyangle had heard of the head's appearance by now, heard of it and gasped of it and conjured a story round it over their tea – or, as this surge of people had evidently done, come out to gawp for a sight of it. Septimus was ahead of me, hacking our way through the hordes with the whole box-office register to appendix her notebook, and I had the head in the crook of my arm, masked under my hat. There didn't seem any decorous way of transporting it, other than getting it away from the seethe of bystanders as quickly as we could manage.

It quite astonishes me, in retrospect, that I could be so briskly cavalier about my grisly burden. I can only surmise that Mordred's antics with Maggie Sweeting's finger – or, quite possibly, a week spent reading *Life and Limbs* – had heightened my capacity for ghoulishness tenfold.

"And there was no blood at all?"

I twisted through the crowd to catch Septimus's words. "I – erm – not in the chest – "

"And none backstage either, by the look of it."

"Well – that back door – "

"Fair point. Could've killed him somewhere else and snuck the head in there. But who *is* he, that's the question! Maybe not all the audience could see him. Some of 'em must've, though. There's a box on the side we could check. Close up to the stage – looks like a good view. Anyone in there would've had the head and the audience both, clear as you like – "

"Sept!"

Septimus swung round. There, twisting past a cluster of sweat-hemmed gentlemen in evening-dress – tousled blond curls, greasepaint, the smudged remnants of a skull and crossbones poking out beneath rolled-up shirtsleeves – figs, it was Lorrie, still in his costume! He was hurling questions ahead of him, half-singing them to make sure they survived the distance – "Are you alright? Are you safe? Did you get it?"

Septimus grabbed his arm, shouldered the gentlemen aside and ushered him away down a side-street. The throng hadn't spread this far, and the sudden space was quite unsettling. The space – and the fact that a ruddy-haired woman in a lavish opera cloak had disentangled herself from the same knot of gentlemen to stalk silently after us, shoulder to shoulder with me. She was evidently far too well-bred to return my startled stare, her brisk little eyes like tiny hooks in Lorrie's back.

"Lorrie – God's sake – *you,* are you alright?"

Lorrie swallowed, wrenched his voice back to the wryness of this morning – albeit none too convincingly. "Well, they stopped the show, didn't they? There I was, ready to do my bit with the life-preserver, and then I get upstaged by a head."

She cupped his painted face in her hands. Of course she'd seen through that queasy bravado. "You ain't hurt?"

"Yes!" He tried for a feeble smile. Beside me, the strange woman sniffed amusedly. "Or – no – y'know what I mean. Sept, I'm fine – why'd I be hurt?"

A crisp nod. "Good. Right. Lorrie – I've got to ask – did anyone take that grand-circle box stage left? It's got the best view for the head – and the cast ain't exactly being forthcoming with their information – "

"They did." He softened to a frown, almost apologetic, lifted a shaking hand to squeeze hers. "Property had that box tonight."

She froze. "'Course they did. Well, that's a start – "

"Sept, don't. Not again. This is murder you're talking about."

"I know that!" she snapped. "I ain't saying they did it. But they'll know something. They always do."

"But – "

He clearly had more cautionary words simmering on his tongue, but she didn't give him time to drape her in them. She wrenched her eyes away from him, skewered the woman at my shoulder on a sharp worried look – brusquely inquisitive as ever, for all the expensive weight of that opera-cloak.

"Sorry, ma'am – d'you need our help?"

Lorrie gulped. "Sept – "

The woman waved a hand to quiet him. Figs, I'd been right – she must have been nobility, and practiced mistress to a fleet of servants, from that gesture alone. Beyond that, there was the heavy rich warmth of her cloak and her gown, the ruby necklace glinting at her throat, the gloves that lapped above the elbow on her arms. Dressed as she was, she would have stuck out like a peacock amongst the homely bulk of the audience. Even the gentlemen she had been with couldn't match the ostentatious brilliance of her skirts.

Even so. Her ruddy chignon was straggling rather at the ears, whilst Septimus's hair was as indomitably perfect as it had been since I met her. In that, at least, I took no small degree of comfort.

"No, Lawrence, I ought to explain myself. Doubtless this is the same sister of whom you speak so fawningly."

The woman stepped past me, closer to the pair of them, her rubies glittering more viciously than ever under the lantern-hook that sprang from the theatre wall. One of her gloved hands curled about Lorrie's arm, squeezing firmly enough to smudge his false tattoo. "My name is Miltonwaters. Lady Elvira Miltonwaters. I was in attendance at the performance tonight – I am a benefactress of this theatre, you see – you might even say, its principal patron – and I offered Lawrence my assistance upon the mass exodus. The poor boy was all alone, and clearly distressed, as you may well expect! What an ordeal for him – " – and the glove crawled up his arm, patted his cheek – " – reaching for a prop and finding such a monstrous substitution!"

Persimmons –

My arms quite gave. The head squelched away across the cobblestones. Not a single one of them appeared to notice.

"Lady Miltonwaters's been very kind," Lorrie mumbled, shooting his sister a warning look. Septimus was staring taut-faced at the older woman's fingers, now drumming lightly on the gooseflesh of her brother's bare shoulder. "Milady, you're right – this is my sister – this is Sept – Septimus."

Another gloved hand snaked out, slipping past Lorrie's chest to hang open-palmed for a handshake. Septimus ignored it. "Miss Tickering. Your face is peculiarly familiar – and far too comely for those trousers, I might add. I assure you, my dear, there is no need for you to take a man's name, nor adopt the attire of one. That you support your brother's talent is distinction enough."

"It's Division Sergeant Septimus. Not Miss Tickering. I ain't Tickering, or Miss anything. And what's Lorrie's talent to you?"

Figs – with her brother at stake she was fearless – and with *Lady Miltonwaters!* Where had she been yesterday, when I needed someone just as undaunted as a guiding example?

The lady's lip curled. "Division Sergeant?"

"Sept's in the Dallyangle Division, Milady," Lorrie blurted, forcing a wary smile. He shifted his shoulder, ever so slightly, but Lady Miltonwaters's hand moved with it, fingertips still pattering carelessly against his skin. It seemed alarmingly forward of her, especially considering that – if I recalled the blur of today aright – Lorrie was supposedly meant to have a sweetheart. (Unless *Lady Miltonwaters* was his sweetheart?) "She was one of the first recruits, too!"

"Oh."

Lady Miltonwaters arched an eyebrow, every sinew of her face sharpening with unconcealed disgust. "*That's* why I know you. The impertinent cyclist who nearly damaged my gig. Stuck with the Dallyangle Division that long, have you?"

Lorrie winced. "Milady – "

"Really, I'm astonished that any woman should choose to spend her days in such a brutish occupation. *Division*, indeed – division of what? You are not affiliated with the New Police, or the old police, or – or anything, are you? It's simply you on your own, you and your useless little rabble, as far as I can tell."

Septimus set her teeth. "The council funds us. And the Div's proved its worth."

"*Has* it? Not to me! Not when it sits back and gawps as a brace of criminals ransack my house!"

"We're chasing the Sweetings," Septimus insisted, crimsoning in the lamplight. Her gaze darted to Lorrie, back to Lady Miltonwaters, navy eyes twitching at the edges. "Every other case we've had, we've been just fine – and this one'll be the same. The Director's got it all under control – "

"The *Director!* Is that what we're expected to call your heathenish leader now? What right does an individual like that have to make our town into her personal vivisection? She may have sucked the rest of the council into her farce, but I always knew it was a mere matter of time before she forgot her lines. Dallyangle does not exist to prove true any delusional ideas she might have about women, especially not women of her complexion. I'm sure, *Miss Tickering*, if you were to think for yourself a moment, you would have to agree with me."

Lorrie's fingers spasmed, as if to grab for his sister and hold her back – but Septimus didn't move, though she was clearly quite starched with fury. Instead, she just flicked her eyes down, skimmed over the train of Lady Miltonwaters's gown, glanced up again with a steady glare. Her voice, when she spoke, was positively brittle with restraint.

"You're standing on a severed head. Milady."

And, stunned as I was that Septimus hadn't snarled Lady Miltonwaters into oblivion, I could hardly swallow my smile when the latter found the Division Sergeant's remark to be correct, and shrieked like a struck partridge.

"So!" Septimus swiped the head off the cobbles, proffered it face-first to the palpitating noblewoman. Lorrie shrank out of Lady Miltonwaters's grip at last, staring at his sister with an expression as fond as it was indignant. "Got any idea who this man is?"

For all her whaleboned solidity, I really thought Lady Miltonwaters would keel over. "Do you make a habit of thrusting severed heads at passersby, or is tonight's atrocious behaviour merely the exception to the rule?"

Septimus shrugged, dropped the head into my upturned hat. "Got to try and identify the victim, don't we?"

"Dash it, girl, you can't do so by carrying a head through the streets of Surrey! This is hardly the fifteenth century!"

(This from the woman who would have had me wooing by pheasant-shoot!)

"We'll do what we've got to, to get this case solved. And don't you worry, Milady – it'll be solved sooner than you think!"

"I suppose you had better hope so," Lady Miltonwaters returned snappishly. "For your own paltry sake."

Septimus folded her arms. "I wouldn't underestimate the Div, Milady. Even our rawest recruit's from the University of Cambridge!"

Pomegranates. She'd hurled it at her adversary in belligerent triumph, striking the aristocrat on her favoured ground, flinging a hand at me – but –

But, as she could hardly have known, having Lady Miltonwaters prick up her ears for a scrap of prestige was precisely the opposite of everything I could have desired in that jolt of a moment!

"The University of Cambridge?"

The cloak swirled about, lashed the edge of my hat. Lady Miltonwaters had turned to acknowledge me at last, and now she was far too close, heady at the neck from a bottle of scent, the weighted hem of her crimson skirts lolling across my smarting toes.

"Do you mean to tell me that this cringing hermaphrodite hails from the *University of Cambridge?*"

Septimus could retort, could glower, could wrench the noble-woman backwards over her finger and snap her prejudices to pieces – but I was far too terrified even to speak. Under her sneering stare, I quite entirely hated myself. It was everything the month at her uncle's estate would have been, in one horrendous burst of scrutiny. I could pick out what I was to her in those gleaming black eyes: milk-faced, and wormish, and raggedy as my cropped hair, and spasmodic with fear, and heartily easy to despise. With her looking at me the way she did, I could have been a thousand times more brilliant than my feeble self, and still found something to squirm for.

"I – erm – "

Her glove sprang up again, smeared with greasepaint at the fingertips, gripped my jaw and twisted my face back and forth. It was a gesture I'd watched, as Edwina stalked through her would-be housemaids and checked them over – although Edwina's amateur attempts had nothing of this pinching scorn. I'd seen how the maids' cheeks had bulged with the pressure, seen the pulses snick in their necks. None of that had warned me quite how much it would hurt.

"I was an Oxonian myself, and I don't remember anyone who looked half as appalling as you attending the varsity matches. Tell me your name, and let's see if I can place you. Or, I should say, let's see just how truthful you have been about your alma mater."

Plums. "I – "

"'Fraid there ain't time for that!"

I couldn't move my head, but the voice was Septimus's – and the grip, too, tugging at my shoulders, until Lady Miltonwaters's fingers pinioned nothing more substantial than the air before my eyes.

"We've got a head-hider to halt. Lorrie – there's still cast in the theatre – Mr. Adelstein's in with 'em – they'll be in need of you." Her eyes widened as she held Lorrie's stare, pointed with concern. He nodded, bit his lip in a remorseful grimace. "I'm sure Lady Miltonwaters's got her own way home."

"Are you?" Lady Miltonwaters cried. "It's not for you, you unsexed goblin, to dictate what your brother can and can't – "

"Night, Sept!" Lorrie yelped, scrambling past us and dashing headlong for the main street. Lady Miltonwaters thundered after him, opera-cloak flapping – but the theatre doors had swallowed him, and her well-dressed entourage tangled her up straightaway.

As soon as Septimus had made sure of Lorrie's escape, we were gone, clipping down the street and looping round clumps of houses, until we'd made it to a road where even the sound of the crowd couldn't entirely reach. The lanterns were sallower here, the darkness softer and quieter, the buildings solid cottages with neat front lawns. Some of them had candles flickering in the windows – one or two even sported carved turnips, flaming with eerie grins.

Septimus sighed, slowed our pace. Perhaps the candlelit stillness of the street appealed to her, or perhaps she'd finally noticed how much I was limping.

"Not very dutiful of me to say it – and you ain't to mention this language to Cassandra – but – that *bitch!*"

She gasped, as if the word had tugged off a scab. "Pawing at Lorrie like that – he ain't her *poor boy* – and he's got a sweetheart – God, if she'd dared it any longer I'd've – ! Well. I'd've shamed the Div, most like."

She groaned. "I'd relish it no end if the Director went right up to Milady Miltonwaters and knocked her teeth out – but she won't. There's no way we'd keep our funding if we struck an aristo with an uncle in the manor. *And* a bloody town councillor, at that. The Director'd never let me get on the wrong side of that kind of power, not even for Lorrie. Someone already wants the Div broken up, and we can't give 'em any more reason."

I swallowed, managed a feeble nod. Behind the nod, I was dili-gently eviscerating myself. Figs, but – this struggle they had, the Director and the Division, with Lady Miltonwaters and her ilk – it made a flat mockery of my twitchy little fear of socialising at the country-house! All I'd just seen – the vicious attitudes, the barbed words – *they* were the weapons to strike persons and organisations out of existence, without a pheasant-shoot in sight.

I really rather was a fool behind my bedroom walls, wasn't I?

Septimus's hand plucked at my jacket sleeve, tugged us both to a halt. She turned me about, tilted my face up to catch the wallowing rays of the nearest lantern – briskly, yes, but gently too, darting her head about to examine me, rather than contorting mine. "You're alright? She didn't hurt you?"

I gaped at her. Not eight hours ago, she'd resented every inch of my existence – yet here she was, squinting, taut with concern. Taut and close, close enough for me to catch the sheen of sweat on her temples, the pale notches in her lip where she'd bitten it.

With the darkness nestling around us, and the turnips beaming in the windows, and her eyes almost black against the dim light and the shadows, there was something astonishingly soothing about giving myself up to her scrutiny. It was something I quite couldn't have felt had it been daytime, had the street been a notch less quiet, had we not both staggered in tandem through the ghastly interlude with Lady Miltonwaters. Septimus frowned, touched a fingertip to my cheek – there must have been a mark there – as if she could smudge the redness away along with the greasepaint, narrowed her eyes when it didn't work.

"It'll fade," I heard myself stammer, my voice shatteringly bizarre in the silence. She blinked at me, then nodded; she didn't ask me how I knew that.

Then she blanched, as did I. Turnips and soft lights were all very well, but there was still a severed head in my hat.

"Right," she declared, dropping me abruptly. "Well. Come on. We'll get the head back and make a likeness of it. Any chance Girton taught you to draw?"

It seemed my irrelevant accomplishments weren't entirely super-fluous after all. Our return to the Division had been quite as feral as I'd feared – Oliver pranced about the main desk like a gangly stag, delirious for a look at the head, and Cassandra smirked above her ledger with quips at the ready. The Director had sliced through her subordinates, taut at the lips with the effort of keeping her calming smile in place, ushered me into the morgue and tugged Septimus away to her office. I'd been given another fold of toast, a scrap of flimsy paper and a broken pencil, and the others were under strict instructions not to disturb me whilst I made the all-important sketch. Mordred, having apparently decided that this ruling in no way applied to him, snuck round from the dormitory after fifteen minutes, clawed up onto my shoulder and nibbled curiously at my earlobe.

The morgue was like a house just built, or a shoe not yet worn – it smarted with its newness. The walls were plastered the palest white yet, and the floorboards had been painted to match them. There was a pallid cold slab in the middle of the room, trying very much to look like marble, which I co-opted as a desk, and a few rickety wooden chairs. That said – greengages, it's hardly as if I knew what to expect of a morgue! – but I couldn't entirely tell which part of this ashen room was supposed to store the bodies, or how it intended to preserve them once it had any to store. Perhaps the Division hadn't decided either. There was space for what I could only guess would be a grisly cabinet built for this purpose, marked on the white floor-boards in dark painted chevrons, but no cabinet as of yet.

"Not got the budget, from what I've heard. Bit of a shit morgue, eh?"

I started, pencil squiggling over the page. I had the head on the table before me, and my faltering sketch was half-finished – but Gertie Skull had sloped in, muffled in a knitted cardigan, and she'd seen my eyes drift to the empty corner.

"'Scuse my language," she added wryly. "You don't look much of a one for swearing, I'll give you that. 'Part from the fruit. Anyway. Can I get a look at the head? I've never seen a head – not seen many corpses at all, really – none of us have, 'less someone's got some dark secret I don't know about. Or an aunt in state. Alright?"

I swallowed. Weren't they all – wasn't there some sort of stricture – wasn't I not to be disturbed? Was she inclined to make off with the remnants of my toast – quite the largest evening meal I was likely to get?

"Oh – I – erm – "

She'd sauntered past me already, swung her elbows down on the not-quite-marble until she was practically nose to nose with my cadaverous subject. Her sandy plait tumbled over her shoulder to swat the head between the eyebrows – not that she particularly seemed to mind it doing so.

"Bloody hell. That's a head, that is. A real head. Thought it'd be – well – gorier – and smell more – y'know – like in *Life and Limbs* – but – it's still a *head!*"

"I – I thought the same," I admitted. She was here now, and genial as ever – I could hardly snub her! "Division Sergeant Septimus – she did too – it does seem awfully – erm – preserved – "

"And apparently it's not got a body."

She pushed up off the slab, dragged another of the spindly chairs over, leapt onto it as if she were mounting a horse. Her feet dangled either side, heavy in their woollen stockings, dusty at the soles. "So we've got a mystery! And investigation's already started – you hear a lot when you loiter in the corridors of this place. Septimus's in with the Director right now, and she must've got Ballestas senior in a good mood. Care to have a guess why?"

She wasn't mocking, but I blushed all the same. "I – I'm sorry – I – I don't know – "

An incredulous cough of a laugh. "No need to be sorry! But how about this – Septimus's done her usual, wanting to bring Pip Property in to ask about the head – and tonight the Director's not said no!"

Now I glanced up in earnest. The idea of Pip Property, complete with curious cravat-based occupation, mysterious pronouns, and windowboxes full of ferns, had become rather a household myth to me, a legend, a Division ritual – not a real person in the slightest, and certainly not one about to manifest on the doorstep. "They – what?"

"It might be almost useful this time, too! Property was there at the theatre, and could well've seen something, something worth telling us. Best-case scenario, it'll help. Worst-case, it'll be bloody good fun."

Why could I only envisage the latter?

Gertie blinked at me bemusedly, sunburnt forehead creasing to a frown. "Hang on – Hyssop – why've you got a ferret round your neck?"

Sweet cloudberries.

Mordred hadn't bitten me for a good ten minutes, and I'd grown absentmindedly used to the warmth at my collarbone. There was hardly any concealing him now, without even a gush of hair to muffle him under.

"Oh – erm – I – "

She arched an eyebrow. "You do know the Director banned rodents?"

"Ferrets aren't rodents!" I blurted. Panic spat the pencil out of my hands, skidded me round on the chair, until there was nothing between me and her smirk. "I – erm – it isn't – he's just – he has to stay with me – I can't – I – "

My voice curdled in my throat. She laughed.

"'Don't tell the Director, Gertie'?"

It was shameful in the extreme, but I could only nod weakly.

"Reckon I can manage that." She ran a hand along her plait, caught the end and pushed her fingers through it, eyeing me ponderously. Between that, and the slab beside us, and the bright gaslit walls of the morgue, she might as well have been carving me open, merrily dissecting with her feet still swinging, like the heroine of *Life and Limbs*. "He's our mouser, then. And you're his keeper. There I was, thinking you a perfect little porcelain doll – and now it turns out you're a regular rule-breaker!"

"I – erm – I'm not!" I cried, my voice and my blush back with a vengeance. "I didn't – please – I never meant to – "

"Why," she drawled, nudging my skirt with her toe, "are you still so bloody terrified? 'S not like it don't take one to know one! Keturah Ballestas's got more than her fair share of spotless lads and lasses – Septimus, before all her madness started, *she* was a case in point – and Matthew Adelstein wouldn't know misbehaving if it poked him in the eye – but we're not all machines, y'know."

This was precisely the sort of conversation Septimus would reproach me just for listening to. But the room was small, the door shut, and I'd no polite way of leaving – no way of leaving at all that didn't involve pivoting past Gertie on her tottering chair. Her stocking had left a dash of dust on my skirt. Persimmons, but if that wasn't entirely the most ominous gesture she'd made yet –

"You should come out with us one night." She'd dropped her voice, and her eyes were smirking quite as much as her lips. "The Inferior Contingent. When there's not a head to draw. Millie's dad's tavern's just round the corner. Drinking and Divving ain't exactly bedfellows, so you have to dress a bit careful – it's worth it, though, for the company! I've a friend there – well, I say *friend* – bit of a chess partner, if y'know what I mean. She's got a ferret too – bought it off me! – though the spoilsport never brings it along. Could be fun. Think about it, and let me know."

Then she dipped closer, barely skimming a whisper. "Don't tell Septimus I said any of this. Well – not like you could tell her anyway, 'less you wanted the Director to come down on that ferret of yours. Best to be careful, eh?"

In the face of which, of course, I could only amend my earlier assessment: *this* was the most ominous gesture she'd made yet, without a doubt! I couldn't speak, not even in monosyllables, with her gaze so smug and searching on mine. Whether she'd meant her languid spiel as a threat or not, it worked on my lips like a wax-seal, folded her sentences tight to the back of my throat and held them there until they set. And what did any of it mean? Why was it being murmured to me, over that freezing slab with its gruesome decoration, at whatever ragged hour of the night it was? Where was Septimus – stern, and comprehensible, and concerned with nothing more alarming than the innocent mechanics of Divisionary duty?

Gertie winked. "Make sure you get some sleep, Hyssop."

She's asleep now, at any rate. All of them are. It's as late as it was yesterday, the reception clock-chimes squirming into the small hours. The dark is monstrous, too thick to make out what my pencil's doing – there's a box of candles for general use behind the reception desk, but I quite only have nerve enough to filch one at a time. I finished the drawing – not well, I should note, though it does slightly resemble a face – but I didn't see Septimus again, before I finally gave in and tiptoed off to the dormitory. Gertie Skull, meanwhile, is a string of steady breaths in the darkness beside me, dreaming – oh, plums! – of taverns and ferrets and heaven knows what.

It's horrendously cold again – infinitely colder than it should be, inside a building with a wood-burner in it! I had to pick my way into the Division's back yard after completing the sketch, scour my hands under the icy water-pump with soap (Gertie had, in a marginally less frightening move, proffered me that) to scrape any trace of the head from my fingers, and not even the combined efforts of taper-flame and bedsheets have warmed them since. Everything else of me throbs for its own sorry reasons, relentlessly enough to distract me from the worst of my current panic. My feet are cracked and swollen, my legs quite leaden, my chest smudged with yellow where I twisted past those elbows in my ribs. Even my chemise is wretched, the delicate fabric worn to holes at my waist – unaccustomed to rough skirts and heavy belts. For this, I can only groan, as hushed as I can manage amidst the shufflings and the snores. With no money, and the sewing skills of a tardy schoolboy, and no idea where one might obtain clothes beyond the work of the family tailor, how am I supposed to replace it?

I could ask Septimus.

Figs – no, I couldn't – I'd never get the words out.

Correspondence (from the past)

<u>21st Dec, 1887</u>

Miss –

I hope you don't think this impertinent. But – after that chat we had – you said you wanted us to correspond – so – call this a start.

Most of the stuff I said already. About your parents – I'm so sorry – this must be so difficult. And I think it's brilliant that you're handling it like you are – the new servants, your sisters away and that. But you said it would be nice to talk, so if you ever want to talk – and you think you can talk to me – I'd be alright with that. No – nothing improper. Just an ear.

Also – I've sent the sample scraps you asked for. Let me know which one you want for the lining. I can mock a few options into bodices if you need to test them.

Your servant (well, your tailor),

Lawrence (Lorrie) Tickering

*

<u>16th January 1888</u>

Dear Mr. Tickering,

        I am grateful for the sentiments you express in your letter. As you say, it is of crucial importance that our correspondence remains respectable. I think I can trust you: you have not once struck up town gossip about my tailoring requests. It is foolish, perhaps, that I should care so much, but I cannot have any questions asked about my character. I am forging vital friendships in preparation for my sisters' arrival, and I must not allow such friends to suspect that I am in any way – not what they would expect me to be.

But it is hardly incriminating to confess that the last year has not been easy. The family name and fortune are counting on my abilities. I cannot doubt them, especially now that there is no one beyond me to temper my doubts.

I would appreciate the mock-ups you suggest, with the grey wool as usual. Additional payment is enclosed.

I have not signed, for safety's sake. It would perhaps be sensible either to burn this letter, or to send it back to me with your next, to which I am greatly looking forward.

*

<u>27th Jan, 1888</u>

Sounds like a plan! Mock-ups coming with this letter.

But of course I wouldn't gossip! Is that a thing tailors are meant to do? I wafted into the job by a bit of a happy accident. I've got a sister too – just the one, mind – and the old ghouls who ran our orphanage wanted to set us up with nice sensible countryside jobs – anything to get us out of London. Sept was meant to be the seamstress – they gave the Singer to her – and they wanted me out on the farms doing terrifying things with a reaper-binder – but that way round lasted all of two days. If I ever thought harvests were a bit quaint, I can't see it now. But of course Sept loves driving all those monstrous machines.

Let me know if you want me to come adjust the fit.

L. T.

*

<u>25th February 1888</u>

Mr. Tickering,

           I am delighted to report that you have done it again. The second option is exactly what I require. I have sent it back so that you might fit it to the tweed. I fear I must have tweed if I am to be deemed suitably presentable, but I cannot abide the feel of it. It is – I do not know how to explain – but it is wrong. Against my fingers, perhaps, I can bear it, but nowhere else.

I confess I would not know to point out a reaper-binder. I do not think I am supposed to carry knowledge on such things. And yet I am expected to be able to distinguish a pheasant from a grouse, which is not an easy thing to do when they are soaring high above one's head. I am also expected to know when to smile during the many, many anecdotes about pheasants and grouse that I am obliged to attend to, and I fear I am falling short in that too.

Would you come at your earliest convenience when the lining is finished? I would like to hear more of your stories about thwarting your orphanage matrons. I do not imagine I shall ever be in a position to defy anything, but it is pleasant all the same to listen to you do it.

*

<u>3rd April, 1888</u>

So – don't panic – but I wildly underestimated the amount of buttons – and the supplier's run out. The bodice is fine – completely forgot the cuffs existed – entirely my fault. There's a new tailor moved in close to you – at least I think there's tailoring involved, seems mostly like design and accessories – but I reckon if any business could point me to extra buttons! Name's Property Cravats if you want to give it a check-over.

I'll come as soon as you want – and bring stories aplenty.

L. T.

*

<u>15th April 1888</u>

Mr. Tickering,

I have made the investigations as you suggested, and I think it is the best way forward. That said – the proprietor of Property Cravats is certainly unusual, and I would not recommend involving my name in the purchase. It is not that I do not deem said proprietor capable of carrying out my requests – but I have gathered enough information to know that my friends do not approve of the individual in question, and doubts might be raised about my suitability to remain within the circle were it known that I supported their business.

I do not know why I call them my friends. I do not trust them. I know, indeed, that I would receive much the same treatment as Property Cravats, if I were for an instant to let myself slip in front of them.

You are my friend. And I am looking forward to your visit immensely.

7.

IN WHICH CRAVATS RETURN
TO MY EXISTENCE

More of myself

Definitely Tuesday and Hallowe'en now, I think (figs, I've not done these dates well, have I?)

Well. Plums. I started the day by stepping barefoot into Gertie Skull's ablutions jug, and it hasn't improved from thereon in.

I knew, at least, what to anticipate from the morning, beyond my own giddy clumsiness. Septimus didn't make the personal trip to my bedside this time – it was hardly as if I expected her to wake me every day! Gertie and the others sang me awake, tearing the curtains down and striking lucifers for the candles on the walls, sniggering between gasps of croaky patter –

"*How beautifully dull the sky,*
The chance is rising very high
That after breakfast we will see
Our sergeant strangle Property! – "

(Perhaps that was what distracted me into the jug – their relentless good cheer, and my hazy recollection of why that was, and the thought that Septimus's cravat-designing chimera might be arriving at the Division in a matter of hours, and – and then, of course, I felt the water gushing up my ankle.)

I was quick with the uniform, before my vigorous colleagues could glimpse the holes patching my chemise, and out into the streets with Septimus just as the church-bells throbbed six-thirty. I didn't dare another conversation with Gertie, beyond a smattering of stammered apologies for the jug. The smart in my feet I was ready for, although it was still plain agony keeping up with Septimus through that horrible heaving press of the market square, with its vegetable stench and the sellers' shoves. I'd not been able to manage my corset again, and my waist felt weak as damp rags. Between that, and my exhaustion, and quite how much my teeth were gritted to keep the various pains away from a cumulative scream, I was almost glad we didn't indulge in much by way of conversation.

Pomegranates, and *this* was the respite!

We were back at the Division by luncheon, back to Cassandra scribbling in her marbled notebook, fingerless gloves in and out of a thick wooden bowl. Apricots – truly, apricots, in the bowl, full to the brim – and wherever had she managed to get hold of apricots in October? She barely glanced up from her prose and her feast, just twisted about on her stool and spat another stone into the woodburner. The Director's keys were heaped beside her book, the ring looped about her wrist, presumably as some quiet gloat regarding the continued unavailability of the bicycle-shed.

"Septimus! Hyssop!"

Gertie Skull. Popping up from behind the desk, still in her knitted cardigan, ash smudging her cheek, a sliver of apricot juice snagged at the corner of her mouth. "A word?"

Septimus glared at her. "What? Is it Property? They can't *not* come, not – "

"Not Property," Gertie interrupted, edging her way round to us, fidgeting with a frayed woollen cuff. It was the closest to nervous I'd ever seen her. "It's – it's just – and you'd better promise you won't explode – "

Septimus's glare darkened. Partially for Gertie's ominous cringing, partly for Cassandra's apricot-devouring obliviousness. The younger Ballestas's pen scratched uninterrupted across the page, swift and strident, without even a tremor for the room's unease.

"Why?"

Gertie swallowed. "The head. The head in the morgue. It – "

"Yes?"

"It – it's kind of – sort of – not in the morgue anymore."

The colour went skidding up Septimus's forehead, knocked itself out on the perfect line of her chignon, tumbled down to catch in her cheeks.

"*What?*"

Finally, Cassandra glanced up. She had a mouthful of apricot, ink flecked amidst her freckles, and there was the strangest glint in her eyes – as if she were a rushlight, and Septimus's impending fury had lit her like a match.

"It went missing in the night. Maybe, Javert, if you'd not been so set on sweet-talking my mother, you'd have had the sense to stand guard over it. And don't you practically sleep in the morgue anyway?"

Septimus's jaw quite dropped. "But – who – who'd take a head – ?"

"Who, indeed!" Cassandra grimaced, twirling her pen with a mocking frown. "Not great for your case to have lost the evidence on day one, though, is it? I'm afraid it'll have to go in the Director's Record – "

"It ain't *lost!*" Septimus snarled. "It can't just creep off on its own – someone's stolen it! For all we know, you've stolen it – and you've done it to spite me, you – !"

She smarted to a halt, inches off her expletives. Cassandra's grimace widened a few teeth as she struggled.

"You – ? Finish your sentence, Javert, go on! I'm sure you had a *brace* of oaths to hand when you bungled everything last time!"

Gertie – she was rather practiced at placating remarks, wasn't she? – was across reception in three bounds, one sturdy hand on Septimus's arm as the latter started forward. "You two! Not the time! Look, *steal*'s a bit of a strong word. It's not improbable someone's just moved it. Let's have another check, shall we? Cass – you've got the keys, right?"

Before either of the Division Sergeants could snarl a protest, Gertie had a pincer-hold on both of them, marching them off down the narrow corridor in a clatter of boot-heels. Cassandra grabbed wildly for her notebook as the apprentice yanked her away, stuffing it wrist-deep in her jacket pocket. I naturally assumed Gertie meant for me to follow – and it hardly seemed gallant of me to leave Septimus alone – but the latter's voice came ricocheting back into reception not two steps into my pursuit, furious and spluttering –

"Stay at the desk, Henry! We can't leave it empty!"

I could quite picture her as she yelled it, taut against Gertie's grip, jostling with Cassandra, crushed at the sides in that tiny hallway. Limes, but her rationale made sense. With the desk unattended, Property could quite easily have dropped in, dropped straight back out, and innocently claimed there'd been no one to speak to.

(At which chary observation, I had to blink. Thinking like that did make me sound rather wonderfully like Septimus.)

The corridor was quiet now, the ruckus shuttered behind the morgue door. The ticking of the wall-clock sprang out of the sudden hush. Without the Division Sergeants' sparring, and with the other apprentices roaming the streets, the building was almost peaceful. There was – what was there? – a faint skim of rain down the window-panes, and the guttural gasps of logs collapsing in the wood-burner, and a muffled murmur which must have been the market outside, as if the market had been dropped into one of those glass fern-cases on the Pole Place windowsill. I could hear my very breaths, deeper than I was used to them, right down to my stomach without a corset to pinch them shallower.

I confess it, though it must hardly come as a surprise – I was scared. Nervous. No – *anxious* – for, aside from the head's inexplicable disappearance, nothing had happened to terrify me as yet. I just – plums, if Pip Property was coming – I just quite entirely knew that it would! And here I was, far too small for the room, with its elbow-high desk and great double doors – the last and only bastion of Division left to greet the most perturbing living legend two days of delirious work could conjure! It was all I could do to edge behind the desk, to scrabble up onto Cassandra's high stool – crab-apples, as if it would make me taller – and notch my eyes to the doors, in some vague approximation of readiness. The heat of the wood-burner scratched at my stockings. I ought to have been glad of the warmth, but I was far too close to it, and it only made the ache in my legs throb more.

And – when those doors opened – what would come through them? After last night's debacle at the stage door, my mind was bent on conjuring up keelingly horrific visions. I pictured, garish-coloured and fantastical on the wrong side of my eyes, a viciously elegant creature of Lady Miltonwaters's breed – or, perhaps, a close cousin to Hector the disdainful tenor – all glimmering jewellery, sumptuous fabrics and tiny waist – sneering and cream-complexioned – with a frill of venomous shirtfront, trailing like the ring of a death cap – or a pert feathered hat topping a cascade of hair. Then, of course, I could only imagine this shifting nightmare as wearing *my* hair, the plait Maggie and her accomplice had chopped off to sell – and, inevitably, arranging it far more exquisitely than I'd ever managed, in a padded chignon or a gushing hero's queue. And the vision would look at me just as Lady Miltonwaters and Hector had done, just as lofty and just as scornful, until that stare alone had withered me through the floor, and there wasn't a soul left to hear any testimonies –

The door twitched. I could hardly swallow my shriek.

But this slender silhouette couldn't have been the fiend of my night-mare, because there wasn't a feathered hat or gush of hair in sight. It was a gentleman, slim and wiry as a wrought-iron railing, his murky blue suit cut perfectly down his legs, his dandyish greatcoat darkened at the shoulders from the rain. His jet-black hair was sleek, cropped close to his olive skin, and arched back at the front – the sort of jaunty pomade-manipulation that Mr. Adelstein, with his finicky precision, could never have countenanced. He sauntered in, let the doors slump shut behind him, quite as if he'd weakened their substance with a nudge of his kid-gloves, and left them swooning in his wake.

"Gracious. And there I was, fearing I'd have to fend off Septimus – isn't *this* the most intriguing little alternative!"

Then I gaped. Between the voice, with its arrogant clarinet drawl – and the ever-hastening descent on the desk – he – she? – had shrugged off the mannishness of the initial impression like a second greatcoat. Now she – or he – or – pears, I could only presume, though it felt presumptuous even to presume, and it seemed with every new gesture the dandy would change my mind again – was at the desk, and leaning against it, one elbow notched on the wood.

I thought of Septimus, her refusal to call Pip Property anything but *they*. The explanation, it seemed, was lounging before me.

Wait. Did that mean I was allowed to do the same – or was this some special privilege reserved for the two of them?

"This ain't funny, Cassandra!"

Property – it *must* have been Property – twitched up a dark eyebrow. Pomegranates, but those eyebrows were positively calligraphic, sardonic rather than scornful. "And we have inimitable lavish-haired fury, hollered in from the wings, doubtless in the grip of another shattering difficulty. To think that poor roaring delight used to be the pride of the Division! Well – is this a bad time?"

I barely heard a word. My gaze – as it was inevitably going to – had dropped, down Property's sharp cheekbones with their foxing of freckles, to a starched collar knotted with the most marvellous paisley cravat. The better part of it was burgundy, with the pattern starting out in cold greyish blues – but the silk leant it a gleam that made the dark colours bright, and turned the grey silver, and – oh, cherries! – right in the midst of it, there was a stud of real silver, the shining head of a cravat-pin. I would, I confess, have cheerfully handed over quite as much of my hair as Maggie and her accomplice wanted, if the price were a cravat like that. I – persimmons – how it glimmered, even in the wan rainy light, even scraped by the garish gaslights, even twinged with the paltry glow of the wood-burner –

"Poor child, I fear it would be far beyond your wages."

I blushed, then – of course I did! – for Property had noticed my staring, and curled into a smirk. "Although, with your hair, I might just be willing to let you pay in instalments. Not these colours for you, though. Amber, perhaps, and a few slivers of green to bring out your eyes."

Sweet spinning figs, I wanted to wail, *please make it! I'll commission you! I'm a Nettleblack! We're the richest family in Dallyangle! I –*

But the thoughts snicked between my eyes, drew the blush out. I'd grown, in the last few days, accustomed to thinking of fancy things as something of an active threat to my continued existence. The fineness of my chemise was precisely what had worn the holes into it, and my rich clothes had been the draw for the Sweetings. Yet this cravat-wielder's arrival, and attire, and the studied elegance of that deliriously desirable neckwear – all of it had trembled my old sartorial zeal back into me, driven me halfway towards picturing the amber-green cravat at my throat before I could calm myself down.

Now I saw myself properly, how insane I must have looked – gawping at Property's neck like a debutante with a fashion-plate – and it sobered me in a horrible rush. And wasn't this magnificent sartorial beacon – entirely the most stylish dresser I'd ever seen! – the inexplicable plague of Septimus's existence?

"I – erm – can I help you?"

After the aforementioned hysteria, my voice hardly seemed to exist. My cravat-muse blinked – there was something almost disappointed in those heady brown eyes – but it was gone before I could squint for it, and the cool sardonicism was back in its place.

"And I thought I was to be the one helping you."

"What?"

"That's why I came here. To help you."

Figs, but this was accurate! And now – what were we supposed to do? Show our witness the empty morgue, and ask whether Property might be remotely proficient in locating severed heads?

"I – well – ma'am? – sir? – erm – we – "

Property waved a gloved hand, as if flicking a moth out of the air. "Sweet creature. It isn't *ma'am*, though it isn't really *sir* either. My name is Property – I haven't quite decided whether I shall let you call me Pip – and I've been summoned by the indomitable Keturah Ballestas to assist yet another investigation. *The* investigation, I presume, the one that's had the whole of Dallyangle on decapitated tenterhooks."

"Oh – excellent! Good to – confirm – that you are – in fact – erm – him – her – or – is it – sorry – "

"Quite alright," Property assured me wryly, curling a hand under a sharp olive chin. If it put a wall of kid-glove between me and that cravat – ! "Fancy something a little more accurate?"

"I – what?"

A keen stare, intent enough to choke my breaths in my throat. If my disposition weren't evidently the more nervous by a sprawling country mile, I would almost have called that look fearful, wavering beneath the bravado.

"Well. You may think me fanciful in the extreme, but I confess I rather prefer it when my interlocutors don't resolve too firmly on either *he* or *she*. Can you stagger in sweet Shakespeare's footsteps and manage *they?*"

I blinked. *Here* was my answer! The aptness of the request – in light of the outfit, the demeanour, the very essence of the figure in question – was indisputable. After the whiplash chaos of their first appearance, it was rather a relief to settle us down on quite the only discernible gender the cravat designer seemed to be.

"Oh – I – certainly – "

Property grinned. Of course their teeth were immaculate, neat-edged as collar-studs. "Infinitely obliged. Now, I don't remember your face – are you new?"

I managed a dazed nod. "I – I don't look – erm – out of place – do I?"

"Out of place – not at all. Distinctive – quite unpardonably, I'm afraid." Their eyes darted to the apricot-bowl, narrowing as their smirk returned. "Gracious, the Division gets more decadent by the day! You don't mind?"

They had their glove off and their fingers knuckle-deep in the bowl before I could so much as splutter a sanction. Once they'd extricated the ripest of the fruits, they glanced back to me, eyebrows aloft. "Wait. Dearest Septimus hasn't poisoned these, has she?"

Passionfruit, they weren't serious. Were they? "I – no! – "

"Ah, but you hesitated!" They twirled their hand until the apricot tipped towards me – until I could smell it, sharp and sweet and incongruous (and me hardly having eaten a thing beyond bread since I left Catfish Crescent!). "Mouth where your money is, dear child. If she will have us play-acting the Borgias in the midst of Surrey, we simply must have a pretty androgyne to expire at my feet."

"I – I can't – "

"Not even if I threw in that cravat for good measure?"

And I hadn't the faintest what I could possibly say to this – or do, in the face of this – in the face of their smile, and the tang of the apricot under my nose, and the most inexplicable conversation I'd been whirled through since discussing ferrets with Gertie Skull – other than gape at them, quite as confounded as they seemed to want me. They were waiting for an answer, all the same, though it must have been obvious I was hardly up to summoning one –

"Pip Property!"

In the instant before my scream slung me off the stool, I caught Property's eyes curling heavenwards. "Ah, maledizione! *Here* we are again."

Septimus was – quite simply – hellfire incarnate. The chignon was still defiantly impeccable, but beneath it she was glowering, her knuckles bone-pale against the corridor walls, her stare fast rivalling Mr. Adelstein's for sheer incisive dismemberment. Cassandra and Gertie and the Director – why had they all disappeared? And what – what was I supposed to do – expected to do – plums, *able* to do – in their absence?

"Leave her alone!"

I scrambled to Septimus's side, though she'd addressed herself to Property, heard the spitting hiss as my damp skirt brushed the wood-burner. Property sighed, drew their glove off the desk and slid their fingers back into it, dipping their gaze – and how Septimus would seethe for that! – to the buttons at their wrist.

"Afternoon, darling. You seem to be doing astonishingly well for yourself, I must say, with the mild exception of whatever Divisionary mishap you've committed this afternoon. Oh, don't twitch so – your little recruit's perfectly safe, and I promise I'm in no mood to upset you again – "

"Shut up!" Septimus cried, quite beyond the Director's enforced etiquette. In one stabbing stride, she'd launched herself across the room and snatched Property's wrist, tugged all the glove-buttons clean open with the movement. "And stop it with your damn fiddling!"

Property snorted, rather inexplicably, for the remark – figs, but then their voice iced over. "Take your hands off me, dear, unless you want another complaint on that pin-perfect chignon of yours."

"No – I – I need to question you!"

A wry groan. "Gracious. Do tell what I'm supposed to know this time. Given that the new crime-shaped chimera haunting Dallyangle is a decapitatory debacle *for which I have an alibi*, am I to conclude that my unconventionality has finally pushed you over the edge?"

"It's nothing to do with your bloody *unconventionality,* and you know it ain't!" Septimus blurted, the flush creeping up her neck. "And how've you got an alibi? Ticket register says you were alone!"

"How very sentient of it. *Ticket Register* will have a habit of saying that, if one's companion requests not to be written down. Never you fear, sweet sergeant, she'll be my witness if you actually want to accuse me."

Septimus swallowed, quite audibly. "I – look, I never said I wanted – "

"Well, then!" They tossed a glance past Septimus's shoulder, to where I trembled at the corridor's end. "If this is but benign Hallowe'en sport, why not vary the rigmarole, and let your sweet-haired colleague have a go at demanding my secrets? Or, better yet – shall I call for dear Director Ballestas? Terribly unfortunate for her to miss the fun, particularly the part where I request your immediate dismissal unless you let go of me *this instant.*"

I couldn't catch Septimus's face, but the chignon twitched. Plums, that was indication enough. "Well! I've got a witness too! I was provoked!"

Property laughed outright. "You certainly were, dear. But do you imagine the pride of Bedford College will take the pageboy's word for it? Don't fret – " (and this to me, with a pale-toothed grin) " – it isn't your honesty the Director will doubt, it's your nerve. How can she assume otherwise, but that you'll simply be parroting all the excuses your fearsome Division Sergeant drilled into you?"

"She can think for herself!"

"As can you." Property grinned, leaned up until their teeth were a quivering thumb's-width from Septimus's chin. "A whole gauntlet of furious thoughts pounding the inside of that frowning forehead. I wonder how many of them you've shared with your employer of late?"

Septimus hissed. "You – "

"Division Sergeant!"

The two sprang apart, quite as if they'd both been surprised in some peculiar flirtation. The Director had appeared at my shoulder, as stern as her indefatigable smile allowed, sleeve folded over sleeve in nonchalant menace. Her voice was a veritable rein to Septimus, though it hardly did anything to dampen Property's amusement. Dapper with innocence, the cravat designer simply darted their fingers down the glove-buttons, finally fastened the cuff back over their wrist.

"I can only apologise if Septimus has been giving you any trouble, Miss – or – Mr. – Property. I assure you, it's not at all the Division's intention to menace you."

Property dashed a hand over their pomaded hair, curled their lip when their kidskin fingers came away with grease at the tips. "Just Property, if you please. For future reference. But as for your question – I don't *think* the sweet sergeant was attempting to – ah – menace me. Unless she disagrees?"

"Yes!" Septimus burst out. Apples, I surmised, but it must have been pure instinct to disagree with Property, whatever the ominous consequences. "I – I mean – no – I didn't mean – I wasn't – "

"Darling, you've already dug your grave," Property drawled,

mock-weary, "It would be simply unkind of me to stand by and let you embroider a winding-sheet to go with it. Now – "

"I ain't embroidering anything!"

A sharp cackle. "And we've brought her back to *ain't!* Don't you bother to retort, or I'll make a complaint. Gracious, I'm a poet! Director Ballestas – look – I really do have things to be getting on with today, effeminately lovely as your new recruit may be – so, am I here purely to appreciate the architectural fruits of your council funding, or is there another reason?"

Septimus and I quite flushed in unison, though she had her mouth open and a retort halfway past her collar before the Director glowered her quiet.

"Very well, Property, you've had your fun. I appreciate that this quarrel between you and Septimus must be trying, but I can't allow you to insult her – "

"Can't you? So I'm to copy one of your placating smiles, and bow to the sweet sergeant's every spontaneous calumny, and never mind the havoc your Division's constant attention wreaks on my life? *Am* I to be making a complaint after all, then?"

Now we all stared at them. Unnervingly unmatched with the wicked smirk, one eyebrow arched neatly in perfect sincerity.

It was the Director's turn to flush. "I'm sure we meant no offence – "

"I'm sure you didn't. Now, what was it you all wanted from me this time? Ah, yes – *The Pirates of Penzance!*"

"Precisely." The Director swallowed, plumbing for the calming smile and not quite reaching it. At Property's side, Septimus was glaring at the floor, gnawing her lower lip to spots of blood. "As I understand from Septimus, you were perfectly positioned to witness the moment the head was discovered."

Property's other eyebrow soared up to match the raised one. "Gracious, she really is clutching at straws, isn't she?"

"We simply wish to ask you what you saw," the Director snapped, blinking the quip away. Property, unfazed, was already halfway into another pinwheeling retort when the Director cut across them, unfurling her voice until it thrummed the spiders in the roof-beams above. "Cassandra, the sketch!"

Sloeberries. It must have been horrendously apparent even to Property – pears, especially to Property – that Cassandra's imminent mocking scrutiny was all but the last humiliating straw for Septimus. She folded her arms and hunched back into her shoulders, as if to squeeze the colour out of her face, barely managing it before a rattle of steps announced the other Division Sergeant's arrival. Gertie was following her, just to intensify the gauntlet, lurking in the shadows to relish the chaos she had determined to enjoy the previous night. Much to my twitching alarm, Cassandra was brandishing the sketch I had made – the handiwork of the disastrous creature who sent three drawing-masters sprinting in disgust, a thousand times more gauche by the drizzly light of day.

"The Ballestas protégée! Mighty descendant of Freetown's finest innovator!" Property cried. Cassandra shot them a wry look, shrivelled it hastily to a loyal sneer the moment she caught her mother's eye.

"Back at the Division again, I see. We ought to make you a detective."

Property winked at her. "You've got ink on your nose, prophetess."

The remark, for all its offhand insouciance, shot Cassandra's face straight to sudden staring suspicion – only for an instant, before she slapped the sneer back into place. The Director slid the sketch from her daughter's hand, pinched her a curious frown, a question which the latter seemed not in the least inclined to answer. With Cassandra unforthcoming on her brief consternation, the Director turned away from her, and – peaches, no! – offered the travesty of a drawing to Property.

"This is the man whose head was found at the theatre. To jog your memory."

The cravat designer's expression in the face of that sketch would have been enough to hurl even a genuine artist's oeuvre on the bonfire. It was more than sufficient for curdling my innards, stinging the blush across my cheekbones, draining spare reserves of gumption out through my twisting fingers.

"I see. Well. The outline style is an interesting choice – we have a young Pre-Raphaelite in our midst! – but I must confess my memory decidedly un-jogged. Really, sweet Divisioners – flattered as I ought to be that you all deem me such a dastardly medium, I truly do not possess the capacity to pick loose the seams of this town's criminal underthings, and my ignorance on that matter is not about to change."

It was impossible to discern whether Septimus or I were more profoundly in the grip of cringing mortification. Property twirled the sketch in their gloved hand like an improvised fan, chin tilted with a puckish smile.

"But, for the sake of your poor mortal souls, I'll offer up what I *do* know. Stalwart Monsieur Ticket Register spoke brave and true: I did indeed attend that performance, and I did indeed quiver as your proverbial tête noire came wafting out of the pirate-chest – "

"Hang on!"

All eyes jerked to Septimus, as indeed did a fair number of spasming hands. The Director was already moving to draw her back –

Cassandra to assist her mother – Property to swat her with the sketch for the sudden interruption – but she wasn't making for the cravat designer. Instead, with a universal glower for the room's wariness, she stalked to the desk, grabbed the nearest ledger, flipped it to an empty page and shoved it towards me. Pointedly oblivious to Cassandra's furious stare, she jabbed a pencil into my hand.

"Note this all down."

Cassandra's mouth fell open. "But – "

"What?" Septimus snapped, skidding about to glare at her. "She knows her letters. Ain't only you who gets to write."

For a startling moment, it seemed as if Cassandra intended to thrash past her and snatch the ledger from me. Property's eyes glinted, in evident hope that she would. The Director cleared her throat, an improvised warning, striding between the two Division Sergeants to cut off their scowls.

"Septimus, Cassandra, attend to the testimony. Please continue, Property."

Property dipped the Director an ironical bow. "With relish, my sweet utopian. Where was I? Of course – quivering – quivering along with, I'm sorry to say, a goodly proportion of Dallyangle's population, and a companion in my box to keep me out of mischief. The theatre shuddered under the roars of the pirate chorus – it was presumably supposed to constitute a song – and then, under the roars of the audience, as said pirate chorus opened their chest and brandished a head to the flies. But I couldn't have planted that head in the chest – for, gracious, I'm sure at least one individual here has considered the possibility – as I spent a good two hours before curtain-up enjoying a chaotic eel-supper with that same companion of mine, who would be more than happy to vouch for my presence should the need arise. The only person who went anywhere near that chest pre-head was the one who brought it onstage for the infinitely stupid burglary scene – a sort of moth-eaten Prince Charming with golden hair and a painted tattoo. Idle speculation, but – isn't that sweet Septimus's brother?"

Across the desk, Septimus's voice cracked. I couldn't look up; my pencil was all but aflame with my frantic scribbling. "You – you'd *dare* – "

Property ignored her. "I don't know who put that head there, but I can assure you that it wasn't me. Apart from anything else, I've no need to have done it. Whoever the culprit was – and, I say it again, the only one who touched that chest was our fraternal tenor – they were clearly determined to get your attention. Dio mio, but wouldn't you all agree I've got quite enough of *that?*"

The stunned silence that followed this aria was just enough for me to scrawl in the last few details, my thumb cricked taut on the pencil – it was a veritable race against time before I snapped it. I didn't lift my gaze from the page when a few sleek steps crossed the room towards me, not until a curled hand cupped my chin and raised my head. How could I do otherwise than gasp, with the dregs of pomade on their gloves cold and slimy against my skin? Septimus gasped too – the Director must have been holding her back, with eyes or hand.

Sweet bergamots. Property's smirk was suddenly alarmingly close.

"Now, sweet Hylas, I do hope you kept up. Make sure you add a footnote for your Division Sergeant – have it stress quite how stupendously lucky she is that I'm not making another complaint."

I blinked. I hardly dared do more.

Property swirled about on one polished leather boot, sauntered back towards the doors. The rain was still beading down the windowpanes, not that it slowed their pace in the slightest. They were astonishingly at ease – more than at ease – they were *whistling*, and the tune I just about recognised. I'd had it sung at me, jaunty in Lorrie's voice, as he grinned on the market's edge, a short strange sentiment about *crowbars* and *centre-bits* and *Cat-Like Tread*.

"They won't," Septimus snarled, as the doors slammed. A slap of rain across the floor was all we got by way of retort. "They won't pin this on Lorrie. Damn it, I won't *let* 'em!"

Cassandra leant back on the desk, not without a quick scowl towards where I lurked trembling with the ledger. "Isn't this a sea-change, Javert! You usually explode with pride whenever anyone brings up your brother and his pirate-chest – "

"Cassandra, enough," the Director hissed. Her voice slumped into a sigh, long and shuddering. "No one will be jumping to any conclusions. Matthew is still compiling testimonies from the backstage workers – once we've examined them, the business should hopefully become clearer. Septimus, take the rest of the day off."

Septimus stared at her, jaw slackening. "No! Not if you're – "

"No one is going to approach your brother tonight. You have my word."

"But – the head – we have to – "

"We have to maintain control of the situation. As far as Dallyangle is concerned, the Division is dealing expertly with this unpleasant matter – but we will only be able to deal expertly with this unpleasant matter if you keep your emotions out of it. Inviting Property into another case was a mistake, and one which you will not repeat."

"But – "

"You're off-duty until tomorrow morning. That's an order, Division Sergeant."

Septimus shouldered past her and stormed down the corridor before I could even draw breath, far too swiftly for me to make out her features. Gertie followed suit in a noiseless retreat, not without a wry grimace to me before the corridor swallowed her up. I was half-inclined to drop the ledger and trace the same path. Pomegranates, I've not the faintest why – it just seemed horrendously imperative to search out Septimus's face and assure it that I hadn't been swayed by Property's spiel. But I didn't – I couldn't. Having me spasming at her heels would doubtless only shrivel her mood further.

The Director sighed again, one hand drumming an absentminded arpeggio onto the desk. *Her* face was all too clear, struck with three-fold light from the lamps and the windows and the wood-burner. She was weary, devoid of her smile, creased at the eyes with the effort of pressing something down beneath her expression. I'd quite no idea whether I ought to speak, and she seemed in no hurry to find words. Instead, she slipped off her spectacles, dashed her fingers up to massage the dents they left on her nose.

"Cassandra," she murmured eventually. Word by word, she was uncoiling, the careful poise of earlier gently put aside. "You have to stop vexing her."

Cassandra snorted. "When she stops vexing you, I will!"

"Your mockery isn't gallant," the Director returned irritably, shining her glasses on her jacket sleeve. "It is exhausting. Do as you know I would, and end it."

For a moment, Cassandra seemed on the point of retorting again – but this time, something caught it before the quip could form. She fished the ring of keys from her pocket, slipped them into her mother's hand.

"I'll do better. I'll get the head back."

It was the Director's turn to stare. "What?"

"Don't you fret, you haven't got room for any more fret," Cassandra blurted, squeezing the Director's elbow. In four rather over-cheery strides, she had crossed the room and unhooked her lantern from where it dangled on the coat-stand. "Javert can't find the head, that's all. But I will. I'll go and look tonight – have another try at the practical side. Panic not, you've still got *one* Division Sergeant who knows how to function!"

"Cassandra – are you telling me the head is missing?"

"Not after tonight, it won't be!" Cassandra had a hand on the wood of the door, grinning beneath her freckles, eyes bright and triumphant. "Really, Mother – you could have a little more faith in me!"

"Cassandra – !"

But Cassandra was gone, swirling through the double doors, sauntering into the fading rain.

The Director glanced to me, and I remembered my continued existence at roughly the same instant. I started, enough to finally snap the pencil. I could only hope that my habitual terrified stare was not poised to incriminate me for yet another contemporaneous offence.

"Do you know anything of this, Miss Hyssop?"

Words. I'd all but forgotten them.

"I – erm – well – quite – I mean – yes – sort of – "

"Where is the head?"

"Gone," I managed, strangled as a piccolo. "I – erm – I think – missing since last night – quite – "

She gritted her teeth. "And how many people know of this?"

"I – Septimus – Cassandra – Gertie – me – you – Septimus – "

"I see." Her fingers stiffened on the desk, pressed at the tips into a straining steeple. "We must make sure to keep it that way. There's no need to worry the town. With any luck, Septimus has simply misplaced it."

Property's voice sang in my head – *it isn't your honesty they'll doubt, it's your nerve* – and the phrases leapt out before I could quench them. "But – Septimus – she didn't move it – it was in the morgue – erm – when Gertie and I left – after I drew the sketch – she can't have lost it – and she was brilliant when she had it before – at the theatre – getting all the information – and – "

"Miss Hyssop." The Director uncreased herself at the eyes – the effect was startlingly stern. "Whilst I appreciate your good intentions, now is not the time for mounting the Division Sergeant's defence. I have the whole Division to protect, and my own credibility with it, until this head can be found, and preventing any further mishaps must remain my priority. Of Septimus, I can only say this – I had high hopes for her, and it is my fervent wish that she will stop laying waste to them."

I gulped, nodded. Her gaze was a warning. As far as she was concerned, there'd be no more discussion – of her strategic arrangements, of Septimus's faltering abilities, of Cassandra's parting-shot, of any of it. Not with me.

"Now." She blinked hard, and the smile flared back, brighter than the gaslamps, elegant and serene and with entirely no hint left in it that anything was amiss. "I will search the building for the head, and – wait – is that your transcription?"

The sudden whirl of topic made me jump, hastily scuff the pencil's remnants from the page, twist the ledger about in shaking hands for her to examine. "I – of Property's account – I apologise – my hand-writing isn't very – "

"*The theatre shuddered under the roars of the pirate chorus,*" she murmured, tucking her spectacles in place and squinting along my delirious cursive, " *– it was presumably supposed to constitute a song – and then, under the roars of the audience, as said pirate chorus opened their chest and brandished a head to the flies...* This transcription – this is word-for-word!"

I blushed. "I – I can write it out again – more neatly – if you – "

She waved a hand to silence me. "Cassandra can copy it into the records when she returns. She does so relish her writing. But – Miss Hyssop, I must congratulate you. Property was, as always, verbose to a fault, but you still managed to transcribe every word they said."

Now I gaped at her. I'd initially assumed her remarks to be reprimands – as remarks to me usually were. To be abruptly pressed cheek-by-jowl with unquestionable admiration was utterly baffling. She couldn't mean to praise me, surely? Not when she had been forced to strain to decipher my incurably appalling penmanship? Not when, in pure desperate panic, I had neglected to separate empty quip from useful information, and simply splurged Property's every whimsical breath onto valuable Division stationery?

"I – oh – I – "

"I shall put your drawing on the noticeboard too. Outside the main doors. Someone passing through the market square might recognise the man, and any information about his identity would be very welcome."

Figs. The ghastly sketch. Pinned up for public consumption.

But if she was right, and it could help the case –

"With Septimus off for the night, there isn't much else for you to do today." She frowned, considered. "I certainly cannot ask you to watch for the Sweetings alone. Gertrude will run the desk tonight, and Millicent and Oliver will supervise the Hallowe'en celebra-tions in the square. Take the time for yourself, and be back for work tomorrow morning."

I stared. *Time* – to scrounge a proper wash, and perhaps a new chemise –

From where? And with what non-existent money? There was always Gertie to ask, if I wasn't to disturb Septimus – but Gertie, if I became any more dependent on her goodwill than I already was, would see me feral in some forbidden tavern with her before the week was out!

It was wanton terror of the prospect that set me blurting an alternative, quick and wild enough for the Director's eyebrows to spring into her hairline –

"Might I – would it – is there – a bicycle – that I could – erm – borrow – and somewhere to practice?"

She pursed her lips. Surprised, but evidently not displeased. "I was under the impression that you could not cycle. Have you tried one before?"

"Oh – quite," I stammered, a flagrant lie for which I can only ask belated and bruised forgiveness. "I – I just want to – if I could get better at it – I mean – it might – erm – I might prove more useful to Septimus – and I'd be a very – safe cycle – cycling person – you wouldn't have any complaints – "

"Very well!" She was smiling in earnest now. "The shed's round the side – I'll unlock one for you. Don't try to cycle through the Hallowe'eners, though. Go to the towpath, where the river looks out on the farms, and do your practising there."

And here was a prospect fit to shove the last vestiges of my cravat hysteria quite out of my ears! I thought of it, and beamed for the thought, with as much delirious optimism as the situation required: if I could contrive to grasp the bicycle in a night! If I could meet Septimus, tomorrow morning, and announce that I'd done so – that we could resume our investigations on the bicycles, and that I wouldn't be inconveniencing her any more on that sore and sorry point! And there wouldn't be helpless rage then – quite the opposite! Would she smile? Would she crackle, as she'd done last night at the theatre, caught up past awkwardness on the elation of the moment?

I tumbled into a bow for the bemused Director, far more feverishly obliging than the one I'd tossed at Mr. Adelstein. Figs, but the quest had quite begun.

8.

IN WHICH DALLYANGLE BECOMES
ABRUPTLY MORE FRIGHTENING

More of my journal

O ptimism was entirely too optimistic a word. I – oh, where to start?

Bicycles are not like the engravings in periodicals. There's nothing of the neat-drawn line about them. The spokes don't glimmer beguilingly, and the handlebars certainly don't stay as balanced as they appear in pictures – in all the forced stability of pictures! Skirts don't whirl about gracefully to dodge the worst of the pedals, especially not when you're far too feeble-headed to unbutton them into culottes. Landscapes don't unfurl alongside one like a magic lantern, not even on Hallowe'en (though half the lamps in the market square had been papered with cut-out patterns to turn them into magic lanterns, until every housefront I wheeled past was positively dripping with stars and witches). Plums – no – what happens, you see, is that you *hit* the landscapes, off the side and over the handlebars, and sometimes without leaving the bicycle – as I did, several times, with one particularly fiendish weeping willow. But I ought to be grateful the willow was there at all, to stop the wretched contraption from pinwheeling into the river!

I was out grappling with that monster for what must have been hours, if the faint reprimands of the church-bells were anything to judge by. When I'd first weaved the bicycle out of its cramped little shed and through the market square, the rain had only just stopped, and Hallowe'en was busy assembling itself around me. The tradespeople were up ladders sticking paper to the lampposts, or sluicing down their stalls to replace melted ice and fish-heads with turnips and punch, or rolling rickety barrels on their ends, to crack open and tip brimful of apples and water. With this to occupy them, I'd hoped they wouldn't notice me. If anything, I had quite the opposite – the news of the vanishing head had apparently caught up with them, regardless of the Director's wishes, and left them inclined to more heckling than I'd yet encountered. Someone hooked out an ankle to trip me, scoffed derisively when the bicycle just about kept me standing.

Things hardly improved from this inauspicious beginning, even when I'd managed to heave the contraption onto the solitude of the towpath. My gasps were pale in the air before me, snagging on my eyelashes. My hands had decided to freeze to wren's talons. All my old ailments were still resoundingly in evidence, leaving me smarting and throbbing at the waist and the feet. The bicycle itself seemed determined to hinder me – lemons, the *heaviness* of it! And the *grease!* Or – I don't know – oil? – whatever it was – the black slime, that scoured my hands and uniform positively bubonic! I'd thought it best to hold the bicycle close to me whenever I wasn't sat on it, in case any more discontented souls appeared from the gathering dusk and tried to wrest it out of my fingers. The pedals, as a consequence, lashed great smirking rents in my stockings, and the wheels groaned over my toes as much as they did the muddy track. Even then, I was madly determined not to give the thing up. I couldn't shrug off the idea of Septimus's delight, hovering before me like a corpse-candle.

But it was profoundly dark now, and I'd still not grasped it. If I grasped anything, it was the handlebars, right before the front wheel buckled and sent me skittering over them. How was one supposed to balance the thing? How to get momentum, when the beast was so much stronger than me? And how to even *see* the pedals – gloom aside – around the tangled flap of my skirt?

I sat up on the bank, groaning fit to dislodge a lung, in what can only be described as the sorriest of conceivable states. My uniform was torn – right out of the seam at one shoulder – and filthy, patched with bicycle-effluvia and river-mud and brushings of bark from the willow. One of my jacket buttons had fled, like a frog, into the depths of the river. I'd left off my hat, and my hair was as much weed and willow-leaf as it was truncated curls, whilst every scrap of my skin you could get at rivalled the uniform for welts and dirt. My boots had survived – just about – but the stockings were hopeless. As, indeed, were the legs quaking inside them, and the shoulders above them. I stretched my ankles, and wrenched my collarbone up in a weary shrug, and gasped for the sudden snarl in both.

The goblinous black bicycle, one wheel ticking around in a maddening loop, lolled on the towpath beside me with all the smugness of Mordred.

"How," I spluttered – to the bats, perhaps, veering over the dark fields beyond the water – "How is a soul supposed to – how does she do it?"

I hardly needed to ask. Septimus wouldn't topple off one of these wyverns. Any crashes on her part would be perfectly managed and ferociously deliberate.

But – what was that? Why the sudden silence? Well – countryside silence, as silent as the countryside ever gets – the distant whir of the bats, and the faint suck of the river in the weeds –

The bicycle wheel had stopped spinning.

I shuddered. Without another horrendous tumble to warm me, it was colder than ever. But – beyond that – figs, yes, I was afraid, and quite understandably so. Getting snarls and kicks from a newly soured Dallyangle was ghastly enough when the Division was still within sprinting distance. But out here, on this lonely path, there'd be no defence, if some insurrectionary civilian saw fit to hammer our supposed insufficiency into me further –

Up. Up, and get the bicycle back.

I locked my arms, sickled myself over the monster, pushed. Even just walking beside the contraption was an effort, with the mud clinging to every notch in the wheels. Still – the noise was better than the quiet, and the noise only got sharper as I weaved back between the houses. Now I had cobblestones, rattling in tandem with the bicycle, and the faint thrum of the market square – faint, then louder, and louder still. Odd new smells pressed my gasps out of the air: smoking vegetables, and cheap candlewax, and heady mulled spices, and – was that pie? – *pies!* Sweet bergamots, steak and ale pies!

The street spat me into the market square, and the pie-steam nearly sent me toppling. Trestle-tables whorled around a turnip-lit stall outside the pie shop, heaving with strange flickering people, whacking their plates for a second round of food, or grabbing at the pie-trays as they sailed overhead on brawny shoulders. Millicent and Oliver stood sturdy on the other side of the crowd, draped in the light of the lanterns at their belts – supervising, as the Director had said, but mercifully training their supervision in very much the opposite direction from my staggering entrance. I softened my footfalls, for all the difference it would make – I had quite no desire for them to spot me so dishevelled. Lorrie Tickering was rather more proximate, evidently oblivious of Property's quipped denunciations, his golden hair gleaming like a votive, clambering through the tables with an armful of dinner wrapped up in a newspaper. He barely glanced anywhere near me, and he was gone in a few brisk strides down another dark street. Well – if he hadn't noticed me, and Millicent and Oliver still hadn't noticed me – if no one in the entire market had noticed me – if I simply resisted the temptation – and made a quick dash past the stall until the Division loomed out of the shadows – and it was hardly as if I had any way of paying for a pie –

Never mind the pie. Mind, instead, the two figures on the nearest trestle-table, four half-eaten crusts between them, square-jawed and strong-armed to within an inch of their lives, composed entirely of wool and waterproofs and muscle –

And one of them – the woman – was missing a finger.

Figs.

A cat-screech of a clatter, and a few barks of protest. I'd dropped the bicycle, and it had probably snagged a few skirts and legs and toes on its way to the cobbles, and now Maggie and Not-Maggie Sweeting – the former with a bloody bandage where her index finger used to be – were staring at me quite as fixedly as I was gaping at them. My cropped hair made me unmistakeable, but it wasn't just that. This time, I also boasted an equally unmistakeable lack of pockets large enough to conceal a dismembering ferret – which made me – damsonberries –

Unarmed, ripe for revenge, and a horrendously easy target.

I skidded around, gave up any gallant rescue of the fallen bicycle, and sprinted into the nearest darkness. Not towards the Division – not towards Millicent and Oliver – nothing half so sensible! There were too many people milling between me and these bastions of safety, too many punch-glasses and gleaming eyes twisting round to find me, too many fists bunching up to join in the spontaneous attack on the apprentice. Away, instead, in the direction marked out by Lorrie, down that narrow street with its sputtery lanterns and shadowy front porches. Was it this shabby cottage Lorrie had disappeared into, with the patchy grass and peeling front door? Or the tenement further along, with the cheery array of turnips jostling in the nearest window? I – surely I would have seen the cottage door open – surely –

A snarl behind me. Too close, and gaining!

I tore up the tenement steps, pummelled the door both-fisted with all the force I was capable of. Whether I was right – or not – it hardly mattered – for I could see the Sweetings striding double-speed down the middle of the street, demon-lit by every available turnip, arms bristling from the fists upwards. At their backs – they'd somehow gathered a motley handful of their fellow revellers. Some of them were still clutching the crumbling remnants of their supper.

"Why d'you run, Morfydd?" Maggie hollered. "Guilty conscience, is it?"

"Sounds about right!" someone bawled behind her – one of the handful, a bristle-bearded man I'd never exchanged glance nor word with. "Well might she look guilty – her lot can't even keep hold of a head, 's what I hear!"

They were all yelling – and there was quite nothing I could do –

"'Course they can't do the job!"

"Can't trust them to keep us safe!"

"They're worse than the police!"

At which, to my unprepared astonishment, the door opened. There wasn't time to register who'd opened it – there wasn't time for anything – there was just panic, and the frantic scrabble of my feet, as I hurled myself over the threshold in a blur of mud and delirium.

"Quite shut the door!" I heard myself shriek.

The hallway wasn't lit. As if this stopped me! In one mad blind instant I was twisting about to kick the door into its locks, grabbing for my unknown saviour to steady myself. My snatching hands tore a gasp out of the darkness, and the steadiness veered away from me, until I tumbled out of balance entirely. The door was shut – that was something – but the stony hallway floor set off every scrape and bruise in my limbs as I crashed down against it. I'd no time even to cry out before the poor door-opener toppled themselves, boots snagged on my ribs, crushing my scream in my chest.

The Sweetings – and their improvised cohort – they wouldn't break down the door – would they?

I had barely swallowed the thought when hands grabbed my shoulders, flipped me like a pillow on the cold stone floor. There wasn't breath enough in me for a yell, but the words dashed out even so –

"Please – don't listen to – they're the Sweetings – "

"Henry!"

I froze. With that voice, I could hardly do otherwise.

"Septimus?"

I couldn't blink out a thing, but I could hear her. I could feel her – scrambling to her knees and darting a tentative hand down my sleeve, where the fabric had wrenched out of the arm-socket. "What're you doing here? Are you hurt?"

No! This wasn't – my reunion with her – it couldn't happen like this, it *couldn't!* I was supposed to manifest tomorrow on a perfectly functioning bicycle, and surprise her, and cheer her Property-addled spirits! Not this confounded invalidism, not this dishevelment, not this perpetual wrecking of her equilibrium, not legitimately bringing a paltry riot to her door – not again!

A perfectly functioning bicycle. A perfectly functioning bicycle which I'd just as good as handed out to the vengeful market square. Assuming, of course, that tonight's many falls hadn't broken it before they could tear it apart – in lieu of me.

"I – erm – I – "

Her hands moved, hooked gently under my arms, lifted until the stone settled beneath my boots. "Come on. You've got legs – use 'em. Lorrie, get the Nettleblack's!"

For one nightmarish breath, the world imploded.

"What?"

"Tincture." She sounded entirely nonplussed, as well she might. "If you're injured. Thought everyone had a Nettleblack's Tincture at home. Lorrie!"

Of course. My surname was strange in her voice, less brittle, devoid of the click in its finicky T's. "Oh – I – quite – "

A jagged slash of candle appeared, bobbing down a wrought-iron banister towards us. It was her brother in the flesh, having apparently grabbed a turnip from the window by way of a nightlight. "Sept, what – ?"

"Hang on." She gave me a quick bolstering shake – plums, if only I could see her! – her voice startlingly close at my ear. If I'd dipped towards that voice, her lips would have brushed my fringe – my skin – not that I could – figs – of course not! "The Sweetings, you said. Maggie – Norman – what've they done?"

It was something of a relief to discover that Norman had a name – that my whimsical appellation was not the stuff of Dallyanglian folklore.

"I – quite – they both recognised me – but – erm – it's not just that – "

"What?"

I swallowed. It didn't stop my fingers shaking. "They – there's more than just them – I mean – I don't think – erm – that is – the others don't recognise the Sweetings – but – but there's a whole group – they're chasing me – they – they know about the missing head – and they're – not happy with the Division – "

"Ain't they!"

She jolted as she growled it, somewhere between incredulous and furious, and the motion nudged her clean across the distance I'd been so wary of. The sharp line of her nose, the scald of her cheek, the grim set of her mouth – all straight through my fringe and against my forehead – like a sting, like a burn, like heaven knows what – enough to leave a mark –

Enough to make me gasp. Enough to make me blush. Enough to jerk up my chin, swifter than a breath, to get my face a fraction closer to hers –

"Stay here," she blurted suddenly, lashing about to fumble with the door. "You'll be safe. I'll sort 'em out. Trust the Sweetings to start slandering us. Lorrie – look after her."

"What? No! – wait – you're in uniform – you can't go out there – "

But she was gone already, and the door was rattling into its locks again –

And there was Lorrie. In the weird shadows of his improvised turnip-lantern, his face was a very vignette of omniscient doom.

It was quite all I could do to splutter at him. "You – you have to go after her! She – they – she can't – they'll – "

"There's no stopping her," he snapped. "Never is. She's too damned reckless for her own good, and she won't listen to you or me say otherwise."

"But – what if – "

He glowered me silent. "Upstairs. Now."

I felt positively in custody. He'd not even brushed my shoulder as we trudged up the stairs and along the thin corridor, but he'd *directed* – voice and eyes alone – until I was over his threshold, into his sagging easy-chair with its worn crochet blanket, and grasping a tin mug of weak tea in my filthy hands. He clambered about the cramped parlour, balancing a mossy log atop his tiny grate, setting the turnip on a three-legged stool, dragging a brittle wooden chair out from the shadows.

The whole room seemed to cluster, every piece of it another moth to the fire's feeble flame. Its rough stone walls were puckered with cheap prints, and the floor was piled with drooping heaps of sheet music and fabric. What few bits of furniture there were looked uniformly rickety: a skinny Singer sewing-machine, tottering on a coltish table – and, of all things, a battered little piano, spilling song-books from its lid, squeezed between the narrow walls.

He plucked a cracked bottle of my family tincture from a shelf, balanced it beside the turnip on the stool. As far as I knew, the recipe of Nettleblack's Tincture was little more than nettle tea left to cool, but it didn't feel entirely polite to hurl this insight into his neigh-bourly gesture. I tipped a drop into my mug, as ostentatiously as I could, as if casual use of my family's fortune-making medicine was something to which I was wholeheartedly accustomed.

At least (paltry mercies) there was nowhere in this musician's cave which could have hidden a head, no surface strong enough to support the weight that had filled my hat, no gap into which it could have been thrust – not even inside that piano. Not that I thought – plums, of course not – he quite couldn't have been responsible! He loved *The Pirates of Penzance* far too much! He was more attached to his little moment with the props than I'd known it possible for a man to be – he wouldn't scupper it! He was horrified when he saw the head at the stage door! He was – he was – he was Septimus's brother!

He could be as innocent as he liked, but in that moment he was still utterly terrifying for rather different reasons. He was darting about, holding the room in precarious balance like the scraps of twine that bound his posies – and his current expression was more than enough to stiffen one's veins. Whether he was glancing in my direction, or stoking the fire, or folding himself into the other chair – he was frowning, and the frown was for me. I could imagine it in words, even if he was far too polite to snarl them: *what are you playing at?*

As if I knew how to answer him!

And as if – with the outside world tenfold more fearsome – as if I had any means of escape!

"Visiting Sept out of hours, are you?" he managed eventually, insouciance straining at the edges, hands taut on his knees.

"I – "

"Ain't as if the other Divisioners've extended her that courtesy."

I noticed the pies then, half-opened at the fireplace's edge, still sputtering webs of steam. The fire might just about keep Septimus's hot, but even so – I'd hardly meant to interrupt her at dinner. And now – now she was out in that horrible burning darkness, under the twisted shadows of the magic lanterns, facing down heaven knows what – and it was entirely my fault.

"I – well – "

"And none of 'em," Lorrie added, "'ve ever tried to kiss her before."

My mouth fell quite open.

Figs, as well it might!

"I – oh – I – "

He sighed, settled into a glare. "So if you'd think to make another game of her – if Cassandra Ballestas's put you up to it – or Pip Property's said something – Sept don't deserve it, and I ain't going to let it happen again – "

"I – I – I – wait! I wasn't!"

Lukewarm tea slopped over my knuckles. My head felt quite entirely on fire. All the while, he was still glowering at me, the eerie light driving his eyebrows sharper and sharper up his forehead.

"I – erm – I didn't – I mean – I wasn't – not consciously – nobody's put me up to anything – I – I didn't even know she was here – I just – saw you – with the pies – and – "

"Not consciously?" he echoed incredulously. "If you weren't following her here, what on earth've you been doing instead?"

"I – I was trying to – I was teaching myself – erm – to ride a bicycle – but – but I lost the bicycle – "

It was his turn to gape at me. The paltry remnants of my sentence blazed in my face, set me squirming right to the edge of the chair.

"I – I fear – the Division Sergeant will be rather – fighting off a mob – to get the bicycle back – and – I – I can only profoundly apologise – erm – for the inconvenience – "

My wretched surrender wrong-footed him. "I thought the Director'd taken Sept and you off the cycles?"

"She – she has," I admitted feebly. "But – it – it's only because I can't – erm – so if I can pick up the knack of it – "

He frowned. It didn't seem a warning anymore. "You've ragged yourself into this state just so Sept can get back to her cycling?"

"Plums! Yes! And – " (it would have been far more impressive, had I not been crimson-faced and stammering quite so much as I was) " – I – I think you can surmise from *that* – just how little I have – erm – sinister designs on your sister's existence – even if I – I keep inadvertently scuppering bits of it!"

At which, hopelessly beyond thoughts more strenuous than simply imploring my heart to remain docile in my ribcage, I tipped two inches of tea down my throat – choked – and coughed half of it straight back up again. The chair's arms rose around me like the sides of a bath, cupped me as I sank into panicky silence. I hardly dared look him in the eye.

He cleared his throat. "How d'you mean, scuppering bits of it? And – here – throw me your jacket, I'll see to the shoulder."

Now I had to stare at him, awkwardness or otherwise. "I – really?"

His face – figs, how to read it? – it wasn't one thing or the other, flickering somewhere between bemusement and wariness. He didn't entirely trust me, but the state of me rather spoke for itself.

"Really." He extended a hand across the fireplace, fingers flinting together. "Toss it."

I could only hope he'd not make out my lack of corset in that dingy firelight. If he did notice anything, he ignored it, for which I was weakly grateful. As soon as he had my jacket he was patting along the nearest shelf for a web of thread, a thimble, a bent needle. He was quick with his stitches, faster than I'd ever been, and he flicked me a wry smile when he noticed me gawping for it.

"Tailor, remember? Made all the Div uniforms, I did. And those cycling-skirts were *far* too much faff for you not to use 'em properly – you bear that in mind, alright? Now. Why're you scuppering Sept's life? From what I hear, you've already got a walkabout head busy with *that* job."

His tone had softened, more sardonic than accusatory. It was enough to confirm my faltering suspicions. Clearly no one, not even Septimus, had told him what Property had said of his proximity to the head – and I quite wasn't inclined to disrupt the pattern.

"Well – erm – I just – the Director wants her to show me how to – exist – and I don't know anything – and – I can't really do anything – and it all reflects on her – "

"Look." He leant down, tugged a stitch taut, squinting along the seam. "If the Director wants Sept in on your Div training, that can only be a good thing for both of you. The Director definitely don't think badly of my sister, no matter what you do. Made Sept a Division Sergeant in the first place, didn't she?"

"Well – yes – fair point – "

"Mrs. Ballestas – that's the kind of patron you want, that is." He grimaced. "Not like dear Lady Miltonwaters, whose idea of a mid-show pick-me-up's to send me a chocolate-pot. *Chocolate* – right before I've got to be on and doing *here's a first-rate opportunity to get married with impunity!*"

He was singing again. I could only assume the lyric was some further reference to the opera, and not a direct reiteration of Lady Miltonwaters's sentiments over the chocolate-pot. "What – what does she want? I – erm – "

"With me?" He bit his lip – and then, the thread, as he reached the end of the tear. "Don't know. But I wish Sept hadn't had to see it."

I swallowed. "Don't let her – I mean – just – be careful – she's – she could be dangerous – you heard her last night – "

A wretched sigh. "And what'm I meant to do? Stand up to her? She's patron of the theatre – the whole town might as well be her playground. And I ain't exactly good at – well, let's say, Sept got all the recklessness. But it'll be fine. I've got a sweetheart, and Miltonwaters won't risk her reputation. She'll lose interest in me, just like she did with Hector, and then she's out of my life again."

He glanced up, wary and solemn. "I'm sorry she hurt you, though."

I dipped a hasty nod. I quite couldn't tell him, but he'd solidified my conviction tenfold. Had I actually accompanied the noblewoman in question to that infernal pheasant-shoot, there would have been no escape – there had barely been enough of an escape last night.

"I – erm – I'm sorry too – for you – "

He shrugged, heavy with unconvincing bravado. "'S not all bad. I've – ah – friends who've got practice dealing with Miltonwaters. And she ain't always awful – she said she'll get me a Frederic audition!"

"Frederic?"

He flashed a sudden grin. "The lead tenor in *Pirates*. Hector won't let go of the part 'til someone wrestles him out, never mind that he can't do the time change in Beautifully Blue. And Sept – she'd love it if I got cast – she ain't been able to see the show yet – if her first time had me singing the solos – "

All in a precarious whirl, he was on his feet, flinging the mended jacket at my collarbone. He grabbed the piano lid and wrenched it up, struck a spidery chord, hummed his way into the midst of it. One stripy-socked foot sprang up onto the chair, notching him into an odd heroic pose, his hand scrabbling over his heart in euphoric dismay. It was quite the marvel he didn't knock anything over.

"Away, away! Ere I expire! I find my duty hard to do today! My heart is filled with anguish dire – it strikes me to the core! Away, away!"

He was beaming at me now. His voice had a marvellous way with the high notes. Even so (and this was very much a private thought), I still found myself rather more interested in discovering whether his sister shared his talents in this respect. Though the sentiments of that particular song might not be to her taste, the idea of her reinterpreting the brisk little excerpt Lorrie had just tossed down to me – of hearing her sing, with that same grin she'd struck up for the theatrical anecdotes – and if her brother was this good, there was more than a chance she'd be even better –

Passionfruit – Septimus!

"Your sister! – she's not yet returned – "

I believe we would have physically grappled to beat the other down the staircase, had the very voice I'd just been pondering not ricocheted up from the entrance hallway, heedless of the late hour. I gasped, and Lorrie did too: she was back. She was alright. Unharmed by that horrendous gathering outside, and clearly not perturbed by any spontaneous gesture I may have inadvertently hurled at her.

"Lorrie! I can leave a cycle in your hallway, can't I?"

She'd done as much before he could retort. A brisk volley of boots on the stairs, and then she was crashing through the doorway, flushed and only half-simmered down from a ferocious snarl –

It wasn't a flush. Dark over her skin, along the ridge of her cheekbone, there was a bruise, blotching purple in the hearth-light.

So much for *unharmed*.

Lorrie sprang out of his chair. "Sept!"

She swatted him away, wrenched the snarl into her wolfish smile. "Don't you fuss. Weren't as bad as you're imagining."

"You don't know what I'm imagining! I don't care if you're the best the Div's got – you can't keep sprinting straight into the worst of the fights!"

"Was I supposed to leave 'em to it?" she retorted. "Millicent and Oliver'd sorted most of it already. One drunk gent panicked and swung a fist, that's all. And the Sweetings'd already scarpered."

"Good," he muttered tersely. "I've had just about enough of those two. Look – are you sure you're alright? D'you need something cold on it?"

She swiped the bottle of tincture from the stool, tipped a fingernail's-width into the lid and downed it, in a sharp-elbowed swoop of defiance. "I'm fine. My face ain't the problem, anyway. All that out there – yelling at Divisioners in the street – I'll have to tell the Director. It's that head's fault. Word's out that we've lost it."

He frowned. "Thought you said it got stolen?"

"It was! Obviously! But those idiots out there won't hear of any telling that don't make the Div look useless."

"But – I mean – even if it is gone – it ain't an end-all for the case, right? Or – " – and he hesitated, gulped a nervous breath – " – for the Div?"

Figs. I'd not even thought it until he voiced it. The Dallyangle Division were quite everything my previous life hadn't been. They were competent, and capable, and purposeful – as formidable as their Director. Surely they'd continue to thrive, even without the head? Surely my sheer presence hadn't cursed them?

"'Course it ain't!" Septimus declared. "The Div ain't what those louts would've made out. And they thought they'd swipe one of our cycles, as if that'd help anything! God knows how they got it. Not a jack of 'em knew how to ride it!"

Lorrie sighed, flicked me a quick glance. He may not have given me his unalloyed trust, but he didn't seem inclined to parade my bicycle-based incompetence before his sister at this obvious juncture. I could be forlornly grateful for that, at least. I'd meant the whole endeavour as a surprise, after all, before it went so disastrously wrong. I wondered whether he'd ever seen the like before – whether anyone had ever planned Septimus a surprise, had ever dropped something delightful into her hands and cried *this is for you!*

Or – whether someone had – possibly Nick Fitzdegu – and my morbid fixation with her loneliness was just that: morbidity. The Division weren't well-disposed towards her, and those strangers tonight hadn't known her, but this surely didn't prohibit her from having *some* friends. Property, dapper hurricane though they may have been, hardly spoke for the whole of Dallyangle when they derided Septimus across reception. Perhaps – more likely – I was the solitary one, netted off in my terror and my lies.

Septimus blinked at me, the last of her account sputtering out. She seemed startled, as if she'd forgotten I was there. I quite couldn't blame her – without my Nettleblackishness to make me interesting, it's easily done.

"Ah – Henry – I – "

She hesitated, then caught herself, brisked up her usual brusqueness. "I assume you'll be wanting an escort back to the Div? Might be the safest thing."

I swallowed. She didn't want me to stay with them – of course she didn't! And why should she? They had unwrapped pies going cold, and there were only two chairs, and she'd done more than enough Divisionary dogsbodying tonight –

"And then you're coming back?" Lorrie added – to her.

That settled the matter. I scrambled back into my mended jacket. He gave me a wary smile, but not another word. Once we were out in the streets, wheeling the battered bicycle between us, the shrieks and the festivities were far too feral to allow for any conversation. There was just chaos, and apple-bobbing, and a few raucous yells that she made us ignore – and then the garish gaslight of the Division, where Gertie carved turnips behind the desk, and pouted jokingly when I didn't join her. At Septimus's insistence, Gertie tossed me an apricot – then another one – and then, eventually, a whole cracked plate of bread and cheese, produced by some camembert alchemy from behind the desk: "Cass's not yet back – so leave some for her, alright?"

Septimus glanced at my expression as I cut myself a portion, her navy eyes slackening to the widest I'd seen them. "I – right – look – you ain't skipping any more meals!"

"Quite," I managed vaguely. It was all I could do not to simply inhale bread, cheese, apricots and crockery on the spot.

The dormitory was dark, the curtains tacked up. The beds were unoccupied, and my solitary taper burned low – but slowly enough, mercifully, for me to eat my tea by. Beyond Mordred, shinnying up my bedframe to steal an edge from the cheese, it was just me. Just me – for Septimus left, almost as soon as I'd entered, flung me an awkward little nod and vanished back to her brother.

Addendum – which I can only hope emerges vaguely legible, given that it's currently chiming four in the morning and I don't dare sneak next-door for another light to scribble by – in the few paltry hours

I've been asleep, I've done nothing but dream every inch of that encounter in the stairwell. Quite how I shall face her tomorrow, I've not the conceivable faintest.

Did I want her to kiss me?

Can I want such a thing?

Figs! Get back to sleep!

Correspondence (from the past)

<u>30th October 1889</u>

Mr. Tickering – Lorrie,

You were right to suppose me nervous at our last meeting. My sisters arrive in a week. I have not seen them in an appallingly long time. They have been reluctant to visit me here, and I certainly have not had the licence to disappear to Wales. But perhaps the delay is for the best. I would not wish to subject them to the demands of society for longer than necessary – though I have no doubt they will both find those demands far easier to navigate than I. Rosamond was certainly an alarmingly popular child.

To practical matters: the pair of them will require new clothes. Whatever they wore to frolic on the beaches of Gower will be entirely inappropriate here. I will send their measurements, and I would appreciate you making enquiries (surreptitiously) with Property Cravats for accessories and decorations.

I hope your music is still proving suitably entertaining.

*

<u>14th Nov, 1889</u>

So much!!! Sept and I are saving for a piano now. We'll be able to afford it in about a thousand years – maybe. But still.

Hope your sisters' arrival is alright? I'll have a sneaky chat with Property. (Also – does this mean we should change the timing of our afternoon tea?)

*

<u>2nd December 1889</u>

I am profoundly sorry it has taken so long for me to reply. I do not know to whom to confess this – no, I do know, and it is certainly you – and I can only hope you will not think me beyond the pale for it –

I do not think I like my sisters.

No. That is not what I mean. I care for them greatly, and I will do everything to ensure their happiness – but I do not like to have them in the house. I do not like what they have made of my quiet. And I am afraid that they think the same of me – that I do not even possess the capacity to make them happy.

Let me explain.

The elder – Rosamond – has done nothing but despair since she arrived. I do not understand why she should launch into a tantrum at my recommendation that she not go walking out in a pair of our father's trousers. She was a child when he died; perhaps she cannot remember him wearing them. She sits in the garden and sobs, and when I attempt to reason with her she will snarl her replies only in Welsh, which our mother always forbade under an English roof. I have given her the attic, with its pleasant country views, but I do not think she deems it enough, and I do not know what else to do. I cannot let her simply go back to Wales – not before she is married!

The youngest is another matter. I thought her name Henrietta and addressed her as such – Rosamond calls her Henry – it transpires she is actually Harriet, but she has not corrected me. I certainly cannot admit to being such an unforgivable sibling: what will be thought of me if it is learnt that I slipped on my sister's name? But the girl is a mystery. She follows Rosamond about the house like a forlorn spaniel, and cringes away from my every attempt to instigate a conversation.

I must bring them both into society slowly. They evidently require more time to adjust than I imagined. But I am sure they will do well when they are ready.

I want you to come sooner, but I must let them settle first. Might we resume our tea-meetings in the New Year?

*

17th Feb, 1890

I'll say it again – <u>stop worrying</u>. Have you had that chat with Rosamond about the trousers? I can always make her some new ones. Sept wears trousers all the time now.

You were asking about Sept – as to an answer, I'm not sure. She doesn't know anything about you. I was thinking – maybe I could tell her you exist but not say who you are – if that makes sense? You can absolutely trust her – as much as you can trust me.

*

<u>3rd March 1890</u>

Now that my sisters are poised to enter society, I do not think it wise to name me in your disclosure to your sister, but otherwise your suggestion sounds appropriate. It is only certain individuals from whom we have anything to hide, after all. And I am glad that you have a sibling of whom you are fond, and who is fond of you in return.

I am trying to do as you suggest, and give my sisters the benefit of the doubt, but I confess I had strong words with Rosamond last night. She has apparently spent the last few years teaching her younger sister to shoot – which, admittedly, will prove useful for endearing her to the Miltonwaters set – but she has taught her so little of anything else! Henrietta cannot sew, or play an instrument, or manage a household, and she is proving even worse than I at holding a conversation. Yet she does not begrudge Rosamond for her carelessness – she seeks out her company far more readily than mine. I cannot always translate what is being said: they both speak Welsh with terrifying ease. I am not sure, moreover, that the conversations are always congenial to the purpose. Rosamond has made no secret of her dissatisfaction with the present situation, and if she does nothing but poison Henrietta with it –

I will remedy the latter. I have a mind to send Henrietta to Girton College. She might form her own circle of important friends there, and it will get her away from Rosamond's influence. As for Rosamond – in one respect, at least, I can report an improvement. She seems to have forged a friendship of her own. My friends must not discover it – it is with the proprietor of the cravat-shop – but, as far as I can tell, they have managed to galvanise Rosamond from the worst of her pining. Anything that settles her here is all to the good.

Would you come next week?

*

15th April, 1890

Do you want to come here instead? Sept's out in the days – would that be easier? I don't think we can sneak round your sisters forever – they know I exist – even if they never see me, I still send all their outfits – and sooner or later at least one of them's bound to crash in on tea.

In haste – and in hope you're alright –

_L._

9.

OF DIVISIONARY CONSTERNATION

The Director's Record

October 31st 1893 (Tuesday)

SEVERED HEAD. — *Urgent*. The most important piece of evidence yet to be housed in the Dallyangle Division has disappeared. Last recorded sighting in the morgue on eve of Monday 30th. Cassandra is currently searching the town. All Divisioners to be involved in the recovery – but *not* to be sent out simultaneously, or in any quantity that might cause alarm.
Mem. – We have witness testimony claiming Lawrence Tickering was in charge of the chest prior to and during the head's appearance. Obviously, this must be handled *carefully*.

DIVISION SERGEANT SEPTIMUS. — Altercation this morning between the aforementioned and Pip Property. Ensure Septimus is not left alone with Property in future. The Division Sergeant must not be permitted to squander her former potential on unhelpful squabbles.

MISS HYSSOP. — As discovered today, our newest recruit possesses the ability to transcribe spoken testimony with perfect accuracy and unprecedented speed. I never encountered such a trick at Bedford – is it something they teach at Girton? Her penmanship still leaves much to be desired, and Cassandra would only sulk if I were to transfer any of her writing-work to a newcomer, but – well, it is certainly worth bearing in mind.

ASSAULTS. — I had hoped not to have to document this kind of setback. But – somehow – news of the missing head is already circulating, and the consequences are being felt. Millicent Musgrove and Oliver Skull were harangued by the public in Market Square, and Septimus (off duty at the time) was struck across the face in the same quarrel. All three are recovered and resuming full service tomorrow, but – all the same. Septimus reports angry demands for the New Police.

I shan't let it come to this. We *will* find that head, and we *will* meet the council's ultimatum, and public ill-feeling *will* dissipate. It has to.

Keturah St. Clare Ballestas, Director of the Dallyangle Division

My less-than-triumphant return

Wednesday, November 1st, 1893? – or something to the gist

I ought to be glad of today's working arrangements. My duties – for the first time since my arrival – have allowed me a chance to document the day (at least, the first half of it) *during* the day, as opposed to my usual candle-gobbling scribble. But where it may yet allow me a decent night's sleep – figs, that's it! That's quite the only silver lining! It's just notched past midday, and in every other respect – well –

Plums. Well.

I gave in last night, and slept in my uniform. The wretched rag of my chemise was halfway to paper, and the temperature had tumbled in October's wake, and – the Division was already a bastion of eccentricity! Gertie Skull laughed outright to see me curled up in full-buttoned jacket, when the raw morning tapers betrayed my shivering state. She was sleeping in her cardigan, which I'd not seen her remove for at least a day – though it would quite be the pot calling the nettle black for me to disapprove. One look at my hair – there were still bits of towpath and willow contained therein – sent her swinging under the bed for her ablutions jug, thrusting it and the bowl at me with a meaningful eyebrow. I flushed to my ears as I slopped the worst of the dirt off, and she watched me amusedly: "Christ, Hyssop, you look like a bloody hedge!"

Septimus was waiting for me at the desk, picking at the burgundy fabric of her cuffs. The reception-room was quite as freezing as the dormitory, for once. Not a soul had lit the wood-burner, and the cold slunk in through the swinging doors, as Millicent and Oliver shivered past into the grey outside.

But it wasn't just the doors. One of the windowpanes had been smashed, shards of glass kicked into the corner, the jagged hole gasping in cold twinges of breeze.

There wasn't any sign of Cassandra. I was a veritable tangle of heaven knows what: relief, to get Septimus alone – and wanton fear, of what she might think of me, of what Lorrie might have said to her – and unease, to think that the entire exchange was happening in a room with a broken window – with a window that must have *been* broken, deliberately, in the vicious blur of last night. But she was pointedly ignoring the shattered glass, and I quite didn't feel I could mention it.

"Henry." She glanced me over, arched an eyebrow. "You look a wreck."

It wasn't so horribly picturesque as a *bloody hedge,* but it stung thrice-over. And this was purely based on my matted hair, the cuts and bruises splattering my face and hands, the stubborn smudges of mud on my jacket and skirt. How much more she might have said, had she known of the torn-up stockings, the emaciated chemise, the ongoing lack of corset!

I was entirely crimson, and entirely wrong-footed with regards to a response. Was I to admit, finally, that I'd no access to ready money? Was I to – as if I wanted her to know! – confess what I'd done the previous night, with the bicycle and the towpath and the interminable tumbles?

"But it ain't your fault," she added quickly, catching my horror. "You'd a mort of criminals at your back, and you took a nasty fall in Lorrie's hallway – "

(And you did too, because I knocked you over!)

" – so! I've got a plan. You're going to be staying at the desk today. Give you a chance to recover – away from the worst of the public. If you're learning about the Div, you might as well try the boring side. There won't be much going on in reception, but you can sit, and there's the fire, and – " – bewilderingly, she flushed – " – and I thought that'd be nice for you."

I gaped at her. Did she want rid of me? Was she so repulsed by the hedge-haired wreck before her that she would rather I stay here – with Cassandra, who thoroughly despised her, and wouldn't skimp to tell me as much – instead of accompanying her? And she was still banned from the bicycle-shed – which left her, what? Sallying on foot into the same throng that gave her the yellowing bruise? Dodging the town's disapproval? Facing down the Sweetings? Snatching a precarious chat with Lorrie, and a cheery flirtation with Nick Fitzdegu?

All of which she'd done, for as long as she'd worked here, before I turned up to spoil everything.

"But – but – I – erm – are you sure – you – you won't be – ?"

"I'd rather be alone."

I was ready to collapse into exhausted sobs – and stunned, I confess, by the viscerality of my reaction – until she heard herself, and her eyes widened, and a bristle of explanation jolted up her throat.

"That is – well – I – it ain't that I'd always rather be alone – just that, sometimes, I need it. It ain't a reflection on you. You've been making progress, you have, and you can make even more when you're back out tomorrow. Yes! But today, you need to rest! Clear?"

I forced a breath. *She doesn't mean it as an estimation of your worth to her, she's entirely said as much.*

"Clear – yes – quite – "

"Good." She flashed me one of her swift sharp smiles – figs! "You'll need a day to calm down, if we're trying you on the cycle soon."

"Oh – erm – of course – "

"About that." Her teeth dashed over her lip, tracing the shape of the smile. "Lorrie did mention what you were up to last night. With the cycling. And that."

Persimmons.

Words of sheer insanity sprang out before I could bite down on them.

"I – but – it was supposed to be a surprise!"

Now she stared, a stark ring of white round each navy eye. My every fidgety theory from the previous night darted about her expression. Had I been right? Had she never had a pleasant surprise prior to this (albeit profoundly botched) attempt? Or perhaps such an assumption was wildly off-key. Perhaps there had been surprises, and each of them had been ghastly, and the last thing she ever wanted was another round of tactless wretches crashing bicycles in her name –

"Right," she managed, collar twitching as she swallowed. "I see. I – yes. Well. Good. I mean – idea. Good idea. The cycling. But you don't have to – I mean – I'm glad you did – but – "

She cleared her throat. "But with all that's happened, safest you don't go off on your own to do it. We'll get the cycles back soon enough – I'm working on it. I'll teach you then. Alright?"

Peaches – what?

But I'd – the whole affair had been a disaster – and – yet here I was, struck slack-jawed in front of a hopeful modulation –

"I – yes – alright," I stammered, words taut as a string of stitches. "Yes!"

She nodded. "That's a job for later, then. Right! Today! I'm off, but first – here's breakfast, if you've a mind to eat. No – I *insist* you eat. Here!"

She flung a hand out, and a marvellous scent swirled up to grasp hold of me. Fresh-wrapped in crisp market packaging, she'd managed to obtain a bacon roll – a *warm* bacon roll, seeping its warmth through my fingers. I lifted a fingertip from the paper, and the sheen of melted butter glistened on my skin.

Quite abruptly, I wanted to sob again.

"Right!" she declared. "Yes! Eat, and I'll see you later!"

I managed an astonished smile, and then she was gone, striding out through the double doors into a sullen rainy morning.

The doors had barely swung once before Cassandra appeared in them, too bleary-eyed and scarf-muffled to notice Septimus departing, a brace of logs jostling under one arm. Quite of an instinct, I whipped the bacon roll behind my back. If Cassandra guessed that her rival had obtained it for me, there would doubtless be sardonical consequences.

But she didn't seem of a mood to notice. I could have pranced across the room twirling the roll atop my head (in a hypothetical world in which I possessed the capacity to express unfettered exuberance), and she still might not have noticed. There were weary shadows bruising her brown skin, smudging her freckles and hollowing her eyes. When she eventually spotted me – after she'd all but staggered into me – that tired stare shot wide with suspicion.

"Why are you still here? I don't care what Javert thinks – no one said you could filch my job!"

I swallowed. "I – erm – I'm supposed to be helping – at the desk – "

"Helping?"

She scoured her eyes with the fingers on her free hand, where they showed inkstained and nail-bitten above her fingerless gloves. "Like you did yesterday? When you sprint-scribbled like a demon just to show me up?"

"I – that wasn't – no! I – I'm sorry – I didn't mean to – I – "

She was still glowering. Persimmons, what would mollify her?

"I don't have to – to write anything more – I don't think the Director would want me to – after she saw my handwriting – "

"Spare me the humility, Hyssop," she snapped. "Mother can't get enough of your *unprecedented speed* – she's put it in the Record. But – look – "

She tipped towards me, lanky and scowling and profoundly aflame beneath her exhausted edges, dipped her voice to a shaky mutter. "*I'm* the writer at the Division. I do it, and I'm good at it, and as far as Mother's concerned that's all there is to it. So you find something else to be incongruously good at. Draw the pictures, crash the cycles, whatever – but *not* the writing. Got it?"

It was all I could do to meet her glare, to scrape words from my trembling thoughts and stammer them out to her satisfaction. "I – quite – of course – "

Her whole stack of logs came tumbling down into my spare arm with half a second's warning. "Good. I'll have you on burner duty, then. Get a fire going – and mind you keep the ash off my papers. It'll smoke like anything, but you try keeping the wood dried out in weather like this. Why is it so cold in here?"

I managed a feeble nod to the sharp-toothed remnants of the windowpane. "Oh – erm – there's been – discontent expressed – "

She stared at it, eyebrows pinching in alarm. "About the head?"

I was almost grateful. At least this was a problem against which we could stand in some kind of alliance. "I – I think so – well – in point of fact, yes – did – did you find it last night?"

For a moment, there was stark silence. Staring into this unwelcome development gave me Cassandra, blinking at me as if I'd just hoisted up the logs and struck her in the chest with them. Only for that moment, before she swallowed hard, and her reply faltered out.

"No. I thought I – no."

Her eyes narrowed, skittering away from mine. "Got the same treatment as everyone else, didn't I? Lots of angry civilians, and not a scrap of missing evidence. But I thought everything would simmer down by this morning. The town can't have forgotten all that we've done for them, even if Javert's done nothing but fail them for months – "

She set her teeth. "If we get any more of this, it's her fault, not mine. Now – have you ever made a fire before?"

"I – "

"Scrape out the ash first," Gertie Skull called suddenly, sauntering out of the dormitory with *Life and Limbs* bookmarked in her fingers, her bushy plait burrowing in a knitted snood. "There's more logs out front when you need them. Oh, and check the burner for dead mice before you light it. I had one in each of my shoes this morning. Don't know why no one'll tell me where we're keeping this Div cat!" – and, sainted medlars, she winked at me with enough conspiratorial relish to freeze every ounce of my blood.

Cassandra rolled her eyes. "Much as I don't want to puncture your joy – there's no cat. Think about it. Would Mother really put up with anything half so chaotic as a pet?"

"'Long as there's mice, there's hope, eh? Also, Cass – meant to ask last night, but you were out – what's the next bit of the new lyrics? *When I sally forth to make cravats, I await the sergeant's next attack* – what?"

"I – oh." Cassandra affected an insouciant smirk, though there was hardly any sinew to it. "I haven't found the rhyme yet. Give me time."

Gertie threaded past me, brushed a half-knitted hand along Cassandra's sleeve, dropped her voice a notch. I dashed round the desk to kneel at the wood-burner, scrabbling the logs into a hasty stack beside it. I could still hear their every word, though the market was louder than the usual morning hush, the babble wriggling unfettered through the hole in the window – but in this position it would at least appear as if I was trying not to eavesdrop. (More to the point, it would also be possible for me to sneakily wolf the bacon roll.)

"You alright, Cass? You look bloody ghastly."

I pinned my gaze to the wood-burner, freezing cold and feathery with ash, snatched a tentative bite of my glorious breakfast. The roll promptly knocked me into ravenous delirium. I couldn't eat it slowly, not for fruit nor worlds.

"When am I ever not alright?" Cassandra retorted briskly, striding to the desk. Gaunt over my head, she unbuttoned her cape, unpinned her hat, untangled her bright mauve scarf until it sat on the counter in a bulging heap. "I just had a grim night. If I *look* anything, that's why."

"You were hunting for the head, weren't you? Did you – "

"No! Can you all just stop asking? I didn't find the head!"

She'd essentially shouted it. Gertie's voice, when it came back to her, was quite as bewildered as could be expected. I'd finished my roll, and in its absence I was more than at leave to share her confusion. "Cass?"

Cassandra sighed. "Sorry. Anyway. Hyssop – are you this slack with Javert? Get the fire up, now!"

All that shivering effort with Gertie Skull's ablutions jug quite went for nothing. By the time I'd scraped the ash (mercifully no dead mice), and crammed in the spindliest logs, and torn up my roll's wrapping for kindling, and dropped lucifer after lucifer into the damp heap, I was stiff with dust to my elbows, and grey patches smarted in my skirt. The fire, fortunately for my blackened fingernails, was finally blazing, enough for Cassandra to stop glaring at me.

Not that she'd been able to do so in any sustained manner throughout the morning. As soon as Gertie sauntered in search of a kettle, Cassandra darted round the desk, scrabbled through the drawers under the counter, yanked out fistfuls of loose pages and folded them inside the cover of her marbled notebook. She was away down the corridor at a hasty trot the moment she'd finished with the desk, reappearing with yet more paper crammed between the book's covers. Only once the notebook was back in her pocket did she seem at all satisfied. Now, she was curled on her stool with her scarf back on, sipping morosely at her belated tea, whilst Gertie swung on the other chair and gulped down more of *Life and Limbs*.

My job, it seemed, was to crouch beside the wood-burner like a skivvy (we'd run out of chairs), picking splinters off the last unburnt log to make more kindling. My eyes streamed – from the smoke, and from the ever-thickening nudge of heat – though it was a feeble relief to feel the burner waking up. Gertie had had trouble enough heating the water for Cassandra's tea, and our servings were still simmering in the kettle. Until it boiled, there was little to do but stare out the sullen flames.

Septimus – where would she be now? Still in the market square, chatting to Lorrie about his Frederic audition and his mysterious sweetheart? Stalking out to Pole Place for a rodent-based rendez-vous with Nick Fitzdegu? Squelching along the towpath, wondering what could have gashed such rents in the willow's trunk? Ahead of the snarls and derision? Safe?

"The hell?"

Gertie sprang off her chair, scrambling round the desk, clutching the novel like a miniature glaive. "Alright! *This* time I'll give it to them – "

"Gertie!"

As Cassandra had leapt from her stool too, I stumbled upright from my ashy cave. Pears, but only then did their frantic exchange make sense. There was a pale envelope jutting through the broken windowpane – Gertie was wrestling the double doors open – Cassandra was racing to grab the letter – it could only have been another of *those* letters. The anonymous letters accumulating in Mr. Adelstein's desks. The missives demanding the disbanding of the Division.

"Gertie, wait!"

Cassandra snatched Gertie's arm before she could fling the doors wide, clutching the envelope in her other hand. "You don't know who might be out there – it's not safe!"

Gertie twisted free, dashed around her to squint through the broken window. The world subsided for a minute to her furious gasping breaths, spliced through with the crisp ticks of the clock – before she slumped into a groan, and whacked the windowsill open-palmed.

"Nothing but the bloody market. Could've been any of them!"

"I'll check what it says," Cassandra declared, cracking the seal with her thumb. "More than one of us should go, if you think we ought to search. We could get Hyssop to stay with the desk. The one moment in my life I need Javert's menace and she's nowhere to be – "

She trailed off. Her face spasmed, eyes lashing over the letter. Bewilderment, fear, panic – in short, every twitch an expression with which I'd long been familiar, all squirming for supremacy. Without warning, she clenched her hand into a shaking fist, crumpled the paper to pulp inside it.

"Cass – "

"Yes," she blurted dazedly, gaze swimming up to Gertie's. "Yes, it – another letter. Same as last time. Nothing new – and I don't want Mother seeing it. Best not to mention it at all, I think."

She stalked across the room. For one terrifying moment, I thought she meant to confront me with it – but then her stare veered downwards, past my skirts to where the wood-burner blazed, its door still swinging wide from the last damp log. I saw her plan on the instant, and – for all that she frightened me – gaped at her incredulously. I couldn't pretend to any expertise in Divisionary matters, and I'd irritated everyone under this roof far too much already, but – surely burning the letter hardly solved the problem? Surely Septimus would want it, to deliver to Mr. Adelstein, to provide yet more distraction for the detective before he delved too thoroughly into my case? Surely –

Cassandra shouldered me aside, veered round me and stooped to the wood-burner. Short of open confrontation, there didn't seem any way of delaying her –

"Cass, spin round and say hallo to your ma, why don't you?"

Gertie Skull had hollered it, a perfect yelp of warning. Cassandra whirled about, springing to her feet, thrusting the letter towards the burner as she went. "Mother!"

Heart distinctly higher than my ribcage, I twitched my eyes down. Figs, she'd botched the throw. A snowball of letter shivered at my feet, fluttering in the draught. Seconds, Henry, *seconds* –

I kicked it. It skittered under the burner, out of sight.

"Cassandra? Is something amiss?"

Cassandra forced a strained smirk. "No! All fine here! Did you want something?"

The Director blinked at her distractedly, spectacles dangling from her ear. "I – no. I thought I heard the front doors, that's all. Your father was of a mind to drop in – but clearly he has decided to listen to me and keep his distance."

Cassandra stared. "He – what?"

"Just a precaution," her mother explained smoothly, pasting on her serene smile. "Tom has been fretting over the Division of late, and expressed a wish to manifest today for some – I quote – *moral support*."

"And – you told Dad not to come?"

The Director's smile twitched. "Public feeling towards the Division is – ah – a little fractious at the moment, as I am sure you must be aware. Tom's apothecary is thriving, and Johannes is so enjoying his studies with Adelaide, and I don't wish our present misfortunes to compromise either of those things – "

"By having the rest of our family publicly associate with us?" Cassandra finished indignantly. "Mother, that ship sailed years ago! It's hardly as if the town's brimming with Black families – and, in case you hadn't noticed, you're just a bit notorious – Dallyangle's not exactly going to forget who is and isn't married to Keturah Ballestas! Or who her children are, for that matter!"

"*Director* Ballestas in here, if you would, Cassandra," she murmured. "I simply meant that, until this head has been retrieved, we might have to be more careful. For their safety. But I am sure our caution need only be temporary. The town was fractious before we caught our first poachers, and they changed their minds swiftly enough after that. And Johannes has his governess to keep him occupied – Adelaide is more than capable of shielding him from any difficulties we may have to deal with. What we must concentrate on is stopping the Sweetings, and finding that head – as quickly as we can."

Cassandra gaped at her. Her eyes were slack and wide, her hands gripping the nearest ledger in taut-knuckled fists. "But – surely – "

"Surely, this is not a topic appropriate for this setting," the Director retorted crisply. "Well, then – you're quite certain we have had no visitors?"

Cassandra, in a staggeringly unusual occurrence, seemed entirely devoid of words – so much that Gertie was obliged to leap in, to patter vague excuses in her stead. Whilst Gertie held her mother distracted, Cassandra's gaze darted back down, behind her skirts to the wood-burner and its splayed door. I wasn't sure whether she'd be able to glimpse the lack of charred letter atop the logs, but dropped to my knees even so, set my elbow to the door and pushed it shut. She frowned at me. It was all I could do to pinch my face to a terrified smile, to gesture at the slow-boiling kettle by way of a flimsy ruse.

"So all's been quiet," Gertie prattled cheerily. I couldn't see her or the Director whilst crouched over the wood-burner, but the former's ongoing spiel was sufficiently absorbing to drag Cassandra's eyes away from me. "Just been sat with a novel, we have – "

"What novel?"

A rustle at the desk. Gertie must have been waving *Life and Limbs* at her. Cassandra hissed, a spasm of wordless caution, not that her colleague seemed to heed it. "Same one as usual, ma'am! Nothing too taxing, just a bit of romance and severed limbs – "

The Director's voice was a dagger. "I do not think it wise for you all to be wasting the Division's time with that idiotic book. Especially not when the drivel makes light of *severed limbs*, in the face of our present – "

Thwack over my head. I nearly toppled into the wood-burner.

Footsteps, several of them, smacking over the floorboards.

Figs – whatever it was – I decidedly wasn't standing up to meet it!

I ought to defend myself, and insist in no uncertain terms that my reluctance to emerge from behind the desk wasn't driven purely by cowardice. The panicky patter approaching from the front doors didn't match Septimus's stride, and there were more than enough Divisioners stood up to handle any disaster. The Director et al hardly needed my staring incompetence to solve their problems. Besides – as long as they all remained absorbed in these new arrivals, it gave me quite the impeccable moment to thrust a sooty arm under the wood-burner (wincing as my bare hand brushed the scorching metal) and extricate the crumpled letter. For want of any more intelligent hiding-place, I simply shoved the paper into my pocket.

"Adelaide?" The Director's tone was puzzled, still trying to slip out of its last sharp edges. "Is something wrong at the house? Who are your companions?"

"Begging your pardon, Mrs. Ballestas – Cassie – but it's this gentleman and lady here you ought to be worrying about. What did you say, madam – someone had snatched your purse?"

Even with the burner's heat scraping at my face, I shivered. This new voice had a chill to it that outmatched the breeze through the broken window, icy and level and light as a lyric soprano. There was an accent, the faintest thing, too faint to decipher, almost flattened away. It was the sort of voice that could – not so much shatter glass, as turn things to glass, freeze them in their tracks and leave them trapped like an insect in amber.

Not getting up was my most sensible idea yet. If this Adelaide was the Ballestas family governess, I could quite only imagine the terror of the bedtime stories for Cassandra's younger brother.

"Calm yourself," the Director managed, note-perfect professional at last. "You did right, Adelaide, to bring them here. Sir – madam – as you may be aware, this is the Dallyangle Division, and I am its Director. We exist to provide protection suited to this town's particular needs. If you could just tell me what happened – "

"*You!*"

This sudden shriek must have been from the visitor – the purse-less lady. There was a man's voice sharp at her heels, stiffening into a growl –

"You, girl, you said you were taking us somewhere that could help!"

Adelaide's icicle voice cut through the air again. "I thought the Dallyangle Division could assist you, sir. Do you not agree?"

"No!" the be-thieved woman snapped, without hesitation. "No, I do not! This motley group have done nothing to stop the burglaries – and they can't even keep hold of a man's remains!"

The Director's voice scrambled up in retort, over a snarl of protest from the beleaguered couple. "I assure you both, the only thing hindering investigations into your stolen belongings is your lack of confidence in my Division's abilities – "

"Is she blaming *us?*" the man spluttered. "Do you want us to find that head and catch your killer for you, while you're at it?"

"I want a policeman," the woman declared, her voice fading as the footsteps rattled the floorboards once more. Limes, the two of them were leaving. "The constable who patrols through Gulmere. I want him. We can be there in twenty minutes if we take the carriage!"

The Director sounded quite as incredulous as we all must have felt. "But – madam – what on earth would be the point in going twenty minutes to a different village, on the off-chance that a constable might be – "

"It's gone too far!"

Cherries, the purse-thwarted woman wasn't wrong! The debacle seemed to have sprung out of nowhere, to have escalated at the same horrendously swift rate!

"We've had to have New Women, lady thises and lady thats, lady professors and lady bicyclists and lady inspectors – but not lady *directors!* Not to protect us! It might have started as a novelty, but the joke has more than worn off! So yes, *madam,* I will go to Gulmere – because your people haven't done anything useful for months, and now you can't even manage your job! Perhaps it isn't meant to be your job at all!"

And the slam of the doors came smarting up through the floorboards before the Director could stop it, jolting a cindered log to pieces in the grate.

I gasped a steadying breath, uncurled my fingers from my elbows. If the words alone had frozen me to a huddle of panic, I could only imagine what they must have done to everyone who had been at the same height as them.

"I'm sorry, ma'am," Adelaide murmured into the sudden silence. I flinched – I hadn't realised the governess had lingered. "I didn't know they were of an opinion with the rest of the town – "

"That is not the case!"

The Director's voice struck the room with exasperation enough to make us all jump, every gaslamp and flame decidedly included.

Cassandra's hands were clenched behind her back, smarting at the knuckles, inkstained fingertips burrowing into her palms. She was staring fixedly towards that icy voice, her features pinched somewhere between a glare and a plea. The kettle began to shriek, a knife of steam jerking up above the desk.

"Enough of this. We have other things to be getting on with."

Word by word, the Director was ironing her tone back to composure. "Adelaide – you have your duties and my son to attend to. Gertrude – see to the kettle, put that poisonous novel down and – and concentrate on your job. There is not time, under present circumstances, for you and Cassandra to be frittering your energies away on such frivolous brain-rot. Now, is there anything else that requires sorting?"

Gertie kicked me. I took the hint, skittered upright. "I – erm – "

"Oh – Miss Hyssop."

The Director swallowed. Her golden eyes darted over me, took in my pallid terror with strained frustration. Perhaps she'd wanted to meet a stern steady gaze, unfazed determination, unbroken resolution. Something, in short, more akin to Septimus.

"Just – ah – fetch us more logs, please."

Outside the doors was a thicket of rain. Icy, yes, stinging down the back of my collar, setting my eyelashes fluttering like fractious moths, worming into my pocket to soften the creases of the stolen letter – but driving great cracks through the dust on my sleeves, until the beginnings of the brown fabric emerged again. It was probably the closest I was ever going to get to a bath. I closed my eyes, tipped my head back and let it drench me. My teeth rattled with the chill, whilst sodden tails of fringe pressed themselves to my forehead, and slaps of wind stiffened my skin.

I'd find the log-shed in a moment. After the Director's despairing look, I imagined I had as long as I wanted to fulfil my paltry task – as long as felt productive. She'd set Cassandra and Gertie to a similarly assiduous purpose as I scurried out of the doors, ordering both to copy things into various ledgers. Simple jobs, easy jobs, just so that we could feel we were *doing* jobs.

Perhaps it isn't meant to be your job at all!

Passionfruit, but I missed Septimus.

Then my eyelids twinged, through the lashing of the rain, enough to smart my eyes open. Something – what? Something to jolt me out of my slack daze – something that hadn't touched me, but – even so –

I was being watched. Gaze straight as a steady pistol-shot across the square, through dripping awnings and puckered umbrellas and the geese-ridden clamour of the market-traders. A pale young woman, maybe ten of Septimus's strides away from me, skewering the Division in a freezing stare.

I blinked at her. She didn't disappear. If this was Adelaide the governess, she quite matched that unnerving icy voice I had just heard, with her silver-blonde bun, the dull grey shimmer of her gown, and her unwavering scrutiny. Unless, of course, the girl was simply a ghost – a possibility which I confess I couldn't entirely dismiss. But if she was Adelaide, then what – I don't know! – did she expect me to run and fetch the Director? Was there *more* to say, after the nightmare she'd just instigated? And if that was the case, why didn't she wave – speak – anything?

10.

IN WHICH MR. ADELSTEIN TURNS
THE PROVERBIAL SCREW

Casebook of Matthew Adelstein
(translated from his frighteningly meticulous code)

Pertaining to the Nettleblack affair

Harriet (*not* Henrietta) Morfydd Hyssop Nettleblack, missing since Oct 29th. Youngest heir to the Nettleblack fortune (see appendix: 'Nettleblack's Tincture'). Twenty-one years of age, pallid skin, brown hair, green eyes, sickly-looking. Welsh, and most likely trying to hide it, if the cut-glass accent of her eldest sister is anything to judge from. Motivation for running away presently unknown.

Still in Dallyangle – and disguised as a member of my own Division!

I know I don't possess a case compelling enough to make a positive identification. Yet, granted, I'm not without evidence. A new Divisioner enlists on Oct 29th, calling herself *Henry Hyssop*, matching the physical description provided by Edwina Nettleblack and the family portrait (minus most of the hair). She collapses upon discovering that Harriet Nettleblack is being pursued. She cowers behind Division Sergeant Septimus (prone to poor judgment with short-haired androgynous types), cosies up with the other Divisioners, and fawns over Nicholas, as if to seize upon my allies and prevent them from indulging my suspicions. The latter seems, infuriatingly, to have had some effect.

It makes sense for the youngest Nettleblack to choose the Division as her hiding-place. We are the only means of locating missing persons the town possesses, unless it wishes to overcome its antipathy towards the police and involve the section-house with the man on the Gulmere beat – and we are also woefully short on new recruits. If this renegade Miss Nettleblack doesn't wish to be found – and that much is evident – what better plan than to conceal herself amidst the very people who will be charged with finding her? If she were not so vexingly disruptive, I could almost admire her for the scheme.

But accosting her outright would be unwise. The Division's other members – particularly the younger ones – might be unwilling to give her up, a sentimental attachment which could prove fatal for us if left unchecked. The Division's reputation has been shaken enough in the past two months. If Edwina Nettleblack, the heiress with the household name, were to accuse us of hiding her sister – or, worse, leading her astray from her familial obligations – it could cause all manner of additional problems. The business of the Sweetings – and now, the missing head – has unhinged our standing with the town and its council already. I will not have Dallyangle's wealthiest family sticking their oar in to destroy us.

If only the wretched girl had hidden herself somewhere – *anywhere* – else!

But to the practicalities. I must find some way to extricate 'Henry Hyssop' from her maddeningly effective place in our throat. I need to sever any ties of affection she has cultivated amongst our members, to force her out of the Division – and *then*, only then, will we be suitably positioned to 'discover' her.

If it were to be posited, say, that the girl had inveigled herself into the Division with the express purpose of tearing us apart – were, indeed, one and the same person as and/or an accomplice of the author of the anonymous letters – she could be cut from the Division, exposed by the Division, and brought back to Catfish Crescent by the Division to be curtailed by her grateful sister-guardian – all, I imagine, within the same day.

This plan is *not* as insane as it may initially appear:

Firstly, I have no evidence that Harriet Nettleblack didn't write those letters, or isn't acquainted with the perpetrator. The sudden desire of an unworldly heiress to join our Division is certainly bizarre enough to merit suspicion. If I pursue her for the letters, I might either catch the culprit or eliminate a suspect. (It does admittedly seem odd that she would want to destroy the very organisation currently concealing her from her sister, but who's to say there isn't some larger scheme of which this is but the beginning?)

Secondly, the slightest hint – even if ultimately untrue – that the aforementioned prodigal is part of a conspiracy against the Division should be enough to destroy any burgeoning friendships she might have formed with our members.

Thirdly, Miss Nettleblack the elder is determined to keep her sister's flit as quiet as possible, at least within her own social circle. This mania for secrecy works to our advantage, particularly when my plan for extrication relies on her sister appearing at best malicious and at worst insane. Even if I turn out to be wrong about the youngest Nettleblack and the letters, there will still be an heiress engaged in a vigorous campaign to ensure that no one in Dallyangle hears a thing about it. Thus, the Division are saved the poor publicity of another major mistake.

Fourthly – to press on the previous point – if Miss Nettleblack the elder ends this affair by owing a debt of tight-lipped gratitude to the Division for the return of her sister, I will have secured us an ally of potentially seismic influence. It's more than about time we gathered some of *those*. Something, at any rate, to counter the sway of that pernicious council-member Lady Miltonwaters.

Fifthly – yes, Nicholas, I *do* ponder my moves thoroughly! – even if I'm wrong and Dallyangle does hear of it, it will give the true culprit(s) behind the letters a burst of confidence in my supposed ineptitude, and induce them to make a cripplingly exposing mistake of their own. Harriet Nettleblack moves from suspect to bait, and everything irons out accordingly.

(And at some point in all of this, presumably, the rest of the Division recover the missing head, and finally apprehend the ever-elusive Sweetings, thus shoring up our reputation against any further tangles.)

Impeccable!

And now Nicholas is blinking at me amazedly. I concede, there was perhaps overzealous force in my triumphant flinging-down of the pen.

To resume, and develop! The Director has far too much to juggle at present to be pulled into my scheme (if she would share more of it with the rest of us, perhaps it might be otherwise, but that's a rant for a different page). But I do need a field-agent in the Division building, someone to help me 'investigate' Nettleblack straight out of her disguise. And who better than her immediate superior? Division Sergeant Septimus has a character much in need of salvaging after she permitted those burglaries, and she has already proved herself incapable where the Sweetings are concerned – so why not offer her this instead? The Director, when she does get to hear of it, will surely thank me for giving her former protégée the chance to redeem herself. It certainly would be a coup for the Division's fallen star to regain her brilliance, having exposed the dangerous inveigler masquerading as her assistant.

In summation. The Division will be saved from another potential threat. The Director, even if she remains too preoccupied with her administrative secrets to spot the plan in action, will ultimately have cause to be grateful to me. Septimus will emerge with her abilities restored. Miss Nettleblack the elder may find herself supporting the Division more than she could have anticipated – and her original exorbitant offer of payment to us can still stand, meaning that my share of said payment can still stand, meaning that the crumbling monstrosity that is Nicholas's rat-attic ceiling can still stand, and finally be repaired in earnest!

Nicholas, meanwhile, has retired to said appalling excuse for an attic with a pronounced smirk and an armful of rats. Apparently my jubilant antics with the pen are making them jump.

Pertaining to other affairs

Wrote to Ma and Ta to inform them of the severed head situation. I don't want them to fret, but equally I would rather they heard of it from me. Doubtless they'll insist I leave the bulk of this one to the Director and her strong-arms. I can't imagine either of them remaining especially calm at the thought of me dashing about with decapitated limbs. If anything, they would much prefer my present situation. Whilst protecting Dallyangle remains the Division's business, protecting the Division has become my business – at least where that pesky heiress is concerned.

But I haven't told them of the Nettleblack affair, nor its potential aftermath. They'd be proud, but they'd also turn up unannounced to supervise the work on the attic. It was difficult enough finding an excuse last time they noticed something – I must tell Nicholas to stop smoking tobacco in the house, if the scent can truly permeate a letter to the extent that it did.

Despite the staggering precedent of his family, he seems convinced that mine would respond in a more welcome fashion. It's patently useless to explain to him that his father and sister never thought much of his prospects to begin with, and *still* forced him out. How much more damning could my parents be with me, the prodigy, the impossible infant they moved worlds to have? They acclaim me to everyone they meet – to their entire village. I can hardly take one step in Gulmere without being besieged by fawning neighbours, anxious to discover what Moira and David's brilliant son has been up to.

But Ma and Ta *certainly* wouldn't relish having to tell their entire village about Nicholas, in any capacity.

Speaking of Nicholas, he's going to crash straight through the ceiling in a moment. I've warned him about trying to lift those cages on his own. He could come out with me today, for the next instalment in the Nettleblack proceedings – better that than leave him to poke more holes in our house. Besides, it's raining. He can walk close at my shoulder, and my hand can rest on his, and it'll all be perfectly decorous to the rest of Dallyangle as long as we're sharing an umbrella. Small mercies, amidst this ghastly weather!

My journal, continued

November 1st, escalating

And of course it only got worse! I was rather battling Mr. Adelstein for my continued existence before this head debacle took over, wasn't I?

Ah, yes! That's quite how the second half of my day's been, parcelled up in one dreaded name, forcing itself into my sole safe location! As far as my paltry Dallyanglian geography was concerned, Pole Place was the area to fear and avoid, where the Adelstein desks bristled against the storm-laden walls and the Adelstein detective papered his house with schemes to prise me out. Pole Place – but not the *Division!* Not the reception-room, with its valiant wood-burner! Why did he have to come here – and after the morning we had just endured? Why couldn't he stay shuttered up in his desk-palace and leave me be – and, more to the point, leave the one place where I felt almost akin to comfortable without a sharpness to its gaslamps, a tang on its air, an ominous creak to its every rickety floorboard?

Well. He couldn't. And he isn't remorseful in the slightest.

Where did I break off? Adelaide – the governess – frozen in her freezing stare. She was so fixated on the Division, she appeared to have quite forgotten the market-goers weaving about her. Her unshawled shoulders didn't even look to be shivering, though it was as cold as it was wet, and stray slivers of sodden silver hair were steadily flattening themselves to her pale face. The damp geese gave her a nervous berth. A few impatient elbows crooked towards her, irritated customers trying to shift her from where she blocked an intersection in the stalls. I wasn't close enough to be sure, but I'd a horrible suspicion that Adelaide didn't blink for them.

Had she blinked at all? Why was she still watching us?

I edged for the log-shed – was it the log-shed? – a sodden wooden structure with logs in it, crouched close to the front of our building, a little shorter than my shoulders, water driving in rivets off its metal roof. It was something to duck behind, at least. Not that I was cowering – she was certainly unnerving enough to hide from, but I also had to duck to fetch the logs. Obviously that was my principal impetus – if the movement also happened to take me out of her sight, that was but happy coincidence –

Oh, pomegranates. Retrospectively – of course I was hiding!

Once I had the logs, I didn't wait. She was still there, still watching. I'd not nerve enough to meet her gaze again, but I could feel it, the same cold twinging that had first prised my eyes open. She stared, and she didn't stop staring, until I had both double doors closed at my back.

After that, I had the best respite I could have snatched, crouching beside the wood-burner with the moss and ash and smoke. The clock made a valiant attempt to out-tick the splash of the market – and indeed the rain, clattering on the windows and puddling on the floor beneath the broken glass, as if the missing pane had simply melted over the boards. The wood-burner heaved, struggling through the green weight of the damp wood, until the logs burst and snapped. There were a few more hours of this peculiarly raucous peace, and a merciful absence of furious civilians, before Cassandra flung Gertie and I an additional boon – not without a swift look down the corridor, to ensure her mother was ensconced in her office.

"Any things you've got to make the time go faster, you might as well grab them now. No one's likely to come knocking after that."

I twitched for her gloomy tone, met Gertie's glum scowl with a grimace of my own – but I still ran for my journal. Let Cassandra see that I had no interest in poaching her writerly position – that I had scribbling enough of my own, without stealing any of hers! I had various tentative excuses prepared to meet any enquiries about what I was writing (the most outlandish being that Henry Hyssop dabbled in penning epistolary fiction), not that anyone had yet asked. Time sprinted when I wrote. Septimus would be back, quite before I even knew it.

Cassandra arched an eyebrow to see me with a notebook, but a cursory glance at my spasmodic handwriting gave her shape enough to tell I wasn't scrawling anything official. Her most twitchy look she reserved for Gertie, who had belligerently resurrected her copy of *Life and Limbs*, albeit with the book poised for shoving under the desk if the Director re-emerged.

"I thought you'd be throwing that in the burner, after earlier."

Gertie shrugged. "Done my jobs already, haven't I? If your ma wants me out doing anything else, she can tell me. 'Til then, I'll have my comfort-reading. Dr Stoker's just found out it was Laura who operated on his walkabout hand, and he is *not* pleased. It doesn't want you to put it down, this book – once you're sucked in, that's it. You've just got to keep at it."

Cassandra blinked. Then, beneath her splatter of freckles – of all things – she flushed. "You don't think it's frivolous brain-rot, then?"

"*Life and Limbs*?" Gertie snorted. "I mean – I can see why your mother would, but – I love it! D'you want to borrow it when I'm done? Assuming you can sneak it into your house, that is."

"I could do," Cassandra allowed, tweaking up a wry smile. "Mother's right on one thing, though – I don't know if it's a bit too *spirit of the age*-ish, with all the missing body parts."

Then some new thought slapped her out of her brief good-humour, her smile and blush shrivelling as one. "You don't think – the Head-Hider – "

Gertie frowned. "What? That they read the novel and got ideas?"

Cassandra shivered, her gaze twisting away from the book. "No, you're right, it sounds insane. Of course that's not the case."

"I mean – it's as sensible as any other – "

"No, it's not!"

Cassandra sighed, slackened her voice. "And Mother would never credit it. She hates that novel more than anyone. Let's just – not say anything about it. No point going mad with speculation. And – Hyssop! Any reason why the fire's choking?"

She wasn't wrong. I'd tumbled into my writing – Adelaide the governess required far too much nightmarish description – and the wood-burner beside me had crumpled into its grille. "Oh – I – erm – sorry – "

"One job, Hyssop," she muttered. "Get more logs and fix it."

More logs. Outside.

"I – but – "

Cassandra flung me another glare. "Do you have a problem with that?"

Persimmons. *I've quite no mind to go outside until I can be sure your family's petrifying governess is no longer staring a curse onto the building?*

But the clock had trilled all manner of hours. She'd be gone. Surely.

"I – no – I'll just – put this away – "

She nodded tetchily, turned back to Gertie. I stumbled to my feet, legs snarling for the sudden movement, scuttled into the dormitory as the two of them resumed their fractious critique of the novel. The lights were doused, and the dim grey room was freezing, its cold striking all the more keenly for how closely I had just been curled with the wood-burner. My journal took up its usual hiding-place, tucked beneath the underside of the pillowcase. Whilst I was there, I snatched the moment to check on Mordred – heaped under the loose floorboard beside my bed, snuffling gently, his pale fur mercifully not quite as bloodstained as I had feared. The longer I took in here, the more I delayed any second sally out to the log-shed, and the better chance I had of not encountering –

"Hyssop!"

I ran. Swift across reception and through the double doors, my breaths taut in the top of my throat. There was the rain again, slapping my fringe back – the cold slipping down my neck – the log-shed – and beyond it – but I'd not meant to actually look at the market! If I didn't look, she couldn't be there!

I dredged a desperate gasp. This was absurd. What concern was it of mine, whether or not an inexplicable governess with a voice like a poisoned needle happened to be loitering amidst the market's clamour?

Something else jolted into view. Two figures, emerging from the thicket of stalls, a tangle of legs under a glossy black umbrella. These two plainly had no time to stare. They were already clear of the market, barrelling through the bedraggled customers, catching their ankles when they nearly tripped on a sodden-feathered goose, almost upon us –

The legs under the umbrella – the rusty greatcoat and stripy trousers – I knew them – and that could only mean the neat dark herringbone beside them –

And after *that*, of all things –

I quite didn't think. I just flung myself away from the doors. The log-shed was large enough to duck behind. I'd not be seen here, not unless they turned right round. Did that make this my third crouched concealment of the morning? It was all I could do to pray it wouldn't portend something half as unsettling as the others.

The sodden moss-scent crept under my teeth. It was unnerving in the extreme, to smell this much of a forest in the midst of the market square. The approaching voices untangled themselves from the hubbub behind them, the footsteps rapping ever closer on the slippery cobbles –

Figs, I'd been right.

"Matty, for God's sake – !"

"It was never a serious *idea*. I didn't even write it down. I merely objected to your over-liberal use of our dwindling spice supply on that little – Nicholas! If you could refrain from lowering the umbrella every other stride?"

"It was a maniac idea," Nick Fitzdegu huffed. They'd stopped, outside the building, the other side of the log-shed. "'Course I won't poison her chai!"

I gasped. A snatch of moss – hopefully moss – dashed against my lips.

Mr. Adelstein sighed. "I was not in earnest. You know that I would never compromise the Division – "

"And I don't see why you think Henry is!"

A slap of water on the metal roof. One of them must have jolted the umbrella, sent the rain dashing off at a sharp angle.

"I explained this to you at great length, Nicholas! If you'd care to recollect! She isn't *Henry,* she is Harriet Nettleblack, and she may well be planning to break apart my entire organisation!"

Plums.

Nick snorted. "I've told you, you've not got any proof."

"You saw how she reacted to the news of her own disappearance! And you've seen the engraving of that gauche family portrait – "

"But what if it's not her? And what if she's innocent, whoever she is? You'd be disgraced, the Div'd chuck you out – or do a Septimus on you – and all this, 'cause you didn't want to show your fieldmouse the hand before you picked her up!"

Mr. Adelstein groaned. "Nicholas, if you could refrain from making yourself understood exclusively through rodent terminology – "

The moss – almost certainly more insect than moss now – twitched at my face again, and I quite broke. I've not the faintest what possessed me – whether it was a frantic desire to curtail their conversation, a reflexive retreat from whatever crawled amidst the logs, or some paltry scrap of pugnacious instinct – but it sent me scrabbling out of the shed, hands and knees and a tangle of skirts, until I was back on my feet and staring my persecutor clean in the yellowing eye. Nick didn't believe him, he had not a tangible shred of evidence for his claims, and – and –

And I forgot all my sudden self-assurance the moment he struck up his goshawk glare. What on earth was I doing? Septimus was nowhere in sight nor sound. I was alone, devoid of even my ferret by means of defence. No one in the Division would have nerve or patience left to come to my aid. Appealing to the public was out of the question. Most alarmingly of all – I had no conceivable way of denying just how much I'd overheard –

"Henry!" Nick gasped, crimsoning right up to his battered fedora.

Mr. Adelstein ignored him. He leant across the log-shed roof, greatcoat fastidiously sickled to keep it above the sodden metal, dropped his voice to a murmur and held that murmur sharp to my throat.

"If you confess now, Miss Nettleblack, I can assure you that this shan't become any more unpleasant than it already is."

I gulped. "I – I don't know – erm – what you mean – and you don't know what's happened here – it's already unpleasant – quite without your intervention – "

"You refer, I suppose, to the hole in the window?"

An idea snatched at my sleeves. If anything in the world could distract this man from his pursuit of me – and, more to the point, could dispel whatever bizarre suspicions he had about my intentions towards the Division – it was the very same something I had just extricated from the wood-burner –

"I – erm – and this letter! Look! Someone – this was – pushed through the window – this morning – "

I dragged the damp page from my pocket. He snatched it without blinking, flattened it against his lapel, pinched it in a cursory glance. His eyebrow arched, meticulously derisive.

"Of all your efforts to confound me, I must confess this the strangest one yet."

"I – what?"

"'*Quickly, Laura! To the operating theatre! Dr Stoker has arrived, still searching for his missing limb, and he wishes to lend a hand with an amputation! In heaven's name, he has but one hand left to lend!*'"

He glowered up from the paper, his voice pinning back into place after the mock-agitation of his quotation. "If you really thought to distract me from your case by copying out a page of *Life and Limbs: a Comic Romance of the Medical School* – "

I gaped at him. "What? It – no – it's a letter like the last one – attacking the Division – "

His yellow eyes narrowed, exasperation tipping into incredulity. "I can read, Miss Nettleblack, and I promise you it is nothing of the sort."

He flipped the paper in his hand, jerked it level with my gaze. The paltry moment of scrutiny he offered me was enough. I wasn't staring at mysterious, Division-eviscerating vitriol – I wasn't even staring at a letter. The page before me was filled to its edges with a novelist's spiralling prose, speech-marks cutting it up into dialogue, a fictional scene with fancifully-named characters. A scene I recognised.

Sweet persimmons, he was right. It was the operation from *Life and Limbs*.

"I – but – what?"

He ignored me, tugged the paper away, folded it into his breast pocket. "Now, where were we?"

"Matty, enough," Nick pleaded, tugging at his companion's sleeve. "Let the fieldmouse be."

Without even glancing at him, Mr. Adelstein stepped neatly out of his grip, skirted the log-shed until we were both on the same side, pinned between the shed and the building in a narrow strait of cobblestones. He still had hold of the umbrella, and he cast it over the pair of us. The rain vanished – the sky vanished – quite all vanished, beyond his glower, and the flapping ebony canvas above him, and his clipped words in their relentless mutter.

"Whether you prove to be the culprit behind the letters – the *real* letters – remains to be seen. On the one hand – why would you want our Division disbanded, when it provides you with such a convenient hiding-place?"

"I – I really don't – erm – understand – "

He sliced his free hand through the air, cutting me off. "On the other – you arrive unexpectedly at the Division, no doubt begging to be hired. Your fingers are constantly black with ink. You deliberately position yourself to disrupt our proceedings – "

"I – I don't! I've quite no intention of disrupting anything! I – if – if anyone's disrupting the Division – at present – it's you! – with these – these unfounded allegations – about me!"

His thin lips slid apart in a snarl. Perhaps he hadn't anticipated that the accusation could topple back towards him. "That's absurd."

"Is it?" – and I quite couldn't stop – "I don't think so! You – you have no proof I've done anything – and you – you don't know who I am – or anything about me – and – I – I'm – just – this is my job! I have quite as much right to it as you – and I quite shouldn't have to – to defend it – against – this! You! Quite!"

He gritted his teeth. "If that truly is the case, I look forward to being proved wrong. It can be an intellectual exercise, analysing whatever innocent explanations you invent for your superiors."

"You – what?"

But he hadn't any words left for me. He shouldered past, umbrella and all, and then the doors were thrashing in his wake.

Nick was at my side, mittened hands dashing over my shoulders, proffering the dampest attempt at an apologetic smile I'd ever glimpsed. "He doesn't mean it – he's just under a bit of pressure – all of the Div are – seeing threats and Nettleblacks in every shadow – "

It wouldn't be enough just to stare at him. If I didn't do better – if I didn't summon something vaguely resembling bewildered composure – or even more incredulity – I would be lost. Nick would hesitate, his eyes would narrow, and he'd gather every scrap of what Mr. Adelstein had so easily spotted.

Words! Any words! Hurl them forthwith!

"I – I don't know what – I mean – what Mr. Adelstein thinks he's doing – !"

I forced myself double at the knees, bent to the shed, scooped the nearest logs into my arms. Pomegranates, but so much for my newly clean sleeves! "Now is an extremely – bad time – this morning has been difficult enough already – and he quite isn't helping – "

"No, he'll help, he will! He only wants what's best for the Div!" He'd dropped to a stripy knee, and now he was tugging at the logs in my hands. "Look – give those here – I'll carry them in. Least I can do."

"Oh – no – really – I'm quite fine – besides – I – I fear you might be disappointed – if you follow Mr. Adelstein inside – "

He blinked. "Come again?"

"Well – erm – if you've come to visit Septimus – she – she's still out – "

"Hyssop!"

I flew to my feet, wrenched the logs from Nick with wanton force I'd not imagined myself capable of possessing. Gertie Skull had stuck her head out into the rain, *Life and Limbs* crooked open above her by way of a makeshift umbrella, and she was grimacing fit to knock the very droplets off-course.

"You'd better come in, Hyssop. The detective's here."

Mr. Adelstein was quite as systematic as his uncannily neat hairline. I could do nothing beyond slump before the wood-burner, smarting from face to limbs (with rage, or fear, or pain, or all three?), and simply *listen,* as he worked his way through the whole Division from the Director downwards. He – I can't call it *chatted,* it was far too quietly fierce – but he consulted with her first. He'd not yet deduced the culprit behind the defamatory letters, he told her, but he thought it might be someone within the Division – a disaffected member – or perhaps even a suspicious new recruit. If she didn't mind – figs, *if,* it was always *if* with his talon-rapping sentences! – he would need to examine the records?

The Director was all taut agreement, tight-faced with shock and incredulity, evidently still struck by the chaos of the morning. And so Cassandra slid off her stool and stalked down the corridor to heap ledgers off her shelves, brought them back one at a time whilst Mr. Adelstein tapped his sopping leather shoe with maddening impatience. She glowered as she did it (evidently oblivious to the fact that his insinuations weren't aimed at her!), kept her own papers stuffed in her pocket, stomped away to her office once he had the bulk of the books. Nick, hovering helpless Nick, was dispatched back to Pole Place, balancing the umbrella against his shoulder, too many ledgers stacked in his trembling arms.

With Cassandra gone, and the Director watching anxiously, Mr. Adelstein started on Gertie Skull. Was there anything she'd seen, any strange behaviour? Anyone rifling without permission through the Division's paperwork? Any suspicious writing or materials thereof, flitting about the building?

Fortunately for me, he hadn't reckoned on – well, on Gertie Skull. She knocked his every question off-kilter with a quip, a snort, a scathing roll of her soil-brown eyes. *If you think one of us'd ever write those letters*, she snapped, *you're even madder than Septimus!* The retort earned her a crisp reprimand from the Director, but as far as I was concerned it was chivalry incarnate.

At which horrendous juncture, Mr. Adelstein determined to search the place.

The dormitory – my journal – Mordred –

Surely he wouldn't try there – surely?

A cursory glance about reception, a sigh for the puddling footsteps drying on the floorboards, a token frown for the limp tablespoon of mouse under the bench – and then he was halfway towards the dormitory door. Gertie sprang into his path, cast a stare of desperate appeal to the Director: detective or no, that room was the only place the Division apprentices got any respite – she couldn't let him upend it!

The Director nodded tersely. "Gertrude makes a valid point this time, Matthew. When Division Apprentices Musgrove and Skull return, I will confer with all of the dormitory's occupants. Your logic is purely speculative at present, and not something I wish to alienate my recruits over."

After *that* resounding refusal, a rather sullen Mr. Adelstein folded himself down on the bench, neat as uncut pages, and settled down to wait. Figs – for what? What more could there be? The Director had explicitly refused to let him conduct any further searches – and she was still nearby, setting down a bucket to catch the water under the smashed windowpane. Gertie Skull was on fervent alert, watching him from Cassandra's stool. I was doing much the same, though it was fast stiffening the room to the same horrible chill as the dormitory – but I quite couldn't turn back to coax the wood-burner, not as long as he was sitting there. He was darting impatient glances at his pocketwatch, or glowering at the bucket, or shivering in his damp suit as the cold crept in – doing everything but making a graceful exit and leaving me be. Surely he didn't plan to wait out Millicent and Oliver?

The doors slapped together, a sputter of fresh rain lashing over the floorboards. Septimus – at last! – she was back, soaked to the bone, lithe as an eel in her red-and-brown uniform. She'd actually slipped on her hat, for once, though she doffed it awkwardly the moment she caught Mr. Adelstein rising from the bench. (Even so – emerging from the hat, the chignon was still perfect, in its fierce unshakeable way.)

"Has something happened?" she demanded, tugging her notebook from her pocket. "You ain't usually – "

"Indeed." He cleared his throat. "If you'd care to lead the way to your office, Division Sergeant, I'm afraid I require a word."

She blinked, eyes flitting to the Director. "I – I ain't – "

"You haven't done anything this time, Septimus," the Director returned wearily. "Matthew is just pursuing an investigation."

"Right. 'Course." Septimus glanced at me. "Henry – "

"Just you," Mr. Adelstein interrupted briskly, already striding across to the corridor. "No need for the apprentice. If you would?"

I saw her scowl – she quite must have seen me blanch – but by then he was gone, and there was nothing for her to do except follow him, notebook flat to her palm. The Director watched them go, then retreated to her office, shaking her head. Between the rattling of the rain, and the splash of the bucket, and the relentless clock, and the hiss of the logs as they coughed out desperate rasps of smoke, even the sound of their footsteps was lost.

The meaning wasn't. The pale plastered walls, the rain-splattered floorboards, the precarious gaslights, brightening as the windowpanes darkened and slickened – all of it was clustering at my eyes, pressing fit to smother me, until I could hardly feel my fingers shaking on the desk. He was going to tell her who I was. He hadn't yet – when he said *Nettleblack* aloud, I'd sense it – but he would. I could quite picture her stare, the shocked colour under her eyes. Then, of course, that stare would curdle into a snarl – for hadn't she helped me, hadn't she done over and above what ought to be expected of her, only for me to lie to her face?

"No need for the apprentice, my arse," Gertie Skull muttered suddenly. If anything could jolt me from my horrible stupor, it was this – close at my ear, half-infuriated, half-wicked, like Oberon and Puck all at once. I started round, and wasn't surprised in the least to see her smirking, tilted on her stool to put only a few paltry inches between her nose and mine. "Down the corridor with you, Hyssop, it might not be a long chat."

My mouth fell open. "You – erm – you don't mean – ?"

"Go!" she hissed impatiently, shoving me round the desk. "You want to learn anything in the Div, you learn it by listening. Whatever he's up to, it's no good, and Septimus'll want your help. She doesn't even know what happened this morning – she needs you!"

I flushed – passionfruit, Gertie knew precisely what to say, didn't she? – but her sentiments pushed me the rest of the way, down the unlit shadows of the corridor, my hands scrabbling along the freezing wall to keep me steady. I'd not the faintest which door led to the right office. The Director's door was first – then there was Cassandra's room, with its broken gaslights –

There! Voices! Pressed close to the door, straining over the clatter of the rain on the roof, shivering with the sudden lack of wood-burner, I lifted a trembling hand and bit down on it.

"One of the *Div?*"

Mr. Adelstein's voice was a very adagio of melancholy warning. "I'm afraid so. I've taken some ledgers to conduct preliminary examinations – but I fear that simply combing the records might not be enough."

She caught his implication instantly. Of course she did!

"What d'you want me to do?"

He sighed. My surname, my sister's search, all balanced on his teeth –

"This isn't a detail I've any intention of burdening the Director with, unless I turn out to be correct, so there's no need for you to make a note of it. But – just in case – I want you to keep an eye on your assistant. I have reason to suspect that she has a hand in the anonymous letters."

What?

Septimus voiced it quite as I thought it, just about drowning my bewildered gasp. "Mr. Adelstein, I can't believe – "

"If you'd hear me out," he insisted. "There's something odd about her, and I'd be astounded if you hadn't noticed it. Do you never catch yourself wondering why she seems so desperate to remain in the Division, yet so determined to unhinge the Division's affairs? She talked her way past Cassandra – not, I imagine, a difficult task – despite lacking any of the qualities necessary for the job, which has undermined your entry requirements. She's deprived you of your bicycle, crippling the competence of your work pursuing the Sweetings. She stages theatrical swoons in my house, delaying the communication of vital information between myself and the rest of us. She clearly knows nothing about the practicalities of the Division, and doesn't seem inclined to learn. You must have noticed – well, at least *some* of this?"

Figs. *Figs.* He couldn't – he *couldn't* take it, and he couldn't twist it, and –

He could. He was. She'd gone silent, and he didn't stop.

"And yet, as I'm sure you've observed, there are some things she *can* do. For one, she can certainly write. Her hands are always smudged with the evidence of it."

"But – that's just where she was transcribing the other day – "

"Are you sure it's only that? Can you be certain that she isn't penning anything else? The Director has refused to allow a search of the dormitory – for drafts, blotting-paper, writing materials, anything – but you – "

You! You quite leave her out of this!

I gulped, jammed my fist down on my tongue to stifle the sound. No – it wasn't a gulp – it was a sob, or the wretched beginnings of one, and those were freezing tears stinging at my face.

"No!" Septimus snapped. "Henry ain't writing those letters!"

"With all due respect, Division Sergeant," he interjected smoothly, "This would hardly be the first instance in which you ignored an alarmingly obvious fact until someone else pointed it out to you."

"This ain't like that!" she snarled, smarting through the deadening darkness of the corridor. "And even if it was – which I don't believe – I'm a *Divisioner,* Mr. Adelstein, not a spy, and I ain't got time to be – "

"You're an investigator, though, are you not? And the Division is, to speak plainly, greatly in need of a successful investigation. If you could locate what your assistant is writing – "

"I've told you – she ain't!"

He raised his voice a notch. "*If* you were to search, and find nothing, and the Director never had to learn of my mistake, I assure you I'd share in your relief. But if you *do* find something – well. In that regrettable instance, you know where I am, and you know what duty would dictate of you."

I thought, half-delirious and horrified as I was, of Lorrie in his socks on the previous night, one leg up on the chair, hollering out that song. *Away, away! Ere I expire! I find my duty hard to do today!* I thought – and it was the bitterest thought yet – how I'd idly wondered what Septimus would sound like, singing that same refrain. I'd wanted to hear her do it.

I'd cursed this whole situation into existence!

And I couldn't even deny his claims, not credibly, not without confessing the truth. Either way, it would shatter Septimus's precarious faith in me. I would be a mendacious stranger with a cowardly streak far too deep-set for trust – or a criminal out to destroy her beleaguered livelihood – and it wouldn't just be her recoiling from the discovery. The Director, Cassandra, Gertie – all of them – they would join their detective in believing the worst of me –

Two warm hands at my elbows made me start. If I'd not been gnawing at my fist, I would have screamed away my eavesdropping.

"Come on," Gertie breathed in my ear. One hand became an arm, braced around my shoulders, absorbing every judder of my sobs. "Come away, now. Quiet as you can."

She waited until we were back in reception, and then she spun me about, quite as you'd twirl flowers in a vase, and clamped my head into her shoulder. I did nothing more articulate than weep. Her worn cardigan, her neck, the bristle of her plait – woodsmoke clung to the lot of it, smarting at my eyes, until I could hardly tell whether or not I was still deliberately crying. Even if I could have managed one of my wretched half-sentences, I didn't dare conjure an excuse, nor an explanation. Fortunately, she didn't ask.

I only vaguely registered the fact that she moved me. She scooped me up, and then we were in the dormitory, right at the side of my bed. Calloused hands brushed my buttons open, eased my jacket off my shoulders, patted down a heavy lambswool blanket in its place, stepped back from my bedside to let me curl up. Gertie's voice murmured over my head, brushing away someone's enquiries with brisk assurances that I'd be alright, that it was just a fit of the morbs, that this morning was probably to blame, that she'd look after me.

Figs – and she'd given me a lambswool blanket.

She quite couldn't have known, but even so. I'd had a similar blanket back in Wales, for the dregs of autumn when it rained relentlessly, and the storms thwacked Rosamond's sunflowers against the drawing-room windowpanes.

I was crumpled over on my side, and knit-palmed fingers were sliding through my fringe, nudging the damp hair out of my eyes – and I was a child, exhausted with sobs, and Rosamond's voice was murmuring *cer di i gysgu nawr, chwaerlet* – and I was asleep quite before I knew it.

Well. I'm awake now, and restored to one-and-twenty with its attendant bruises, and I seem to have been left alone. Of course, I've been writing, nestled under the blanket. Pomegranates, but Mr. Adelstein shan't have my journal too! He may be trying his consummate hardest to take everything else from me, but if he thinks I'll curtail the one stalwart exercise of my life – if he thinks I can't be more careful – then I'll prove him entirely wrong. I can try and hide the journal more thoroughly. It's far too large to squeeze into my pocket, or I'd emulate Septimus and Cassandra's notebook-methodologies – but if Gertie and the rest of us hold firm, we can keep him out of the dormitory, and I can devise some feasible alternative. I can – oh, I don't know – but as long as I can stumble just ahead of his grasp, I can and will make sure to do it.

The Director's Record

November 1st 1893 (Wednesday)

MISSING HEAD. — *Urgent.* No leads, no discoveries, and no further
    developments.

VANDALISM. — Before six o'clock this morning, a brick was thrown
    through the window of the Division's reception. There
    is every possibility it could have been an unrelated event
    (drunken Hallowe'en disorder?), but in the wake of today a
    more ominous possibility seems likely.

MATTHEW'S LATEST SCHEME. — The aforementioned visited
    the Division, searched as much of it as was deemed appro-
    priate, took most of the ledgers for further examination, and
    conducted a private interview with Septimus. As I under-
    stand it, the visit concerned Matthew's investigation into the
    perpetrator of the anonymous letters – he seems convinced
    that it could be a member of the Division. Tact is needed here.
    I must not let his investigation sow discord amongst the
    other Divisioners, but I must also not be seen to be curtailing
    a perfectly reasonable examination. However abhorrent his
    theory may be, if there is any – *any* – truth in it, we must know
    quickly. The deadline for the Sweetings is approaching, even
    if I am the only one aware of it, and we cannot have internal
    strife disrupting our ability to meet it.
    Mem. – when is an appropriate time to begin informing
    everyone of the deadline? Perhaps, in view of the present
    circumstances, it is best to give them a few more days. Once
    the head is recovered, and our management of that affair is
    back on track – and that *cannot* take longer than a few more
    days – then it will be time to start disseminating such infor-
    mation. There is no need to worry the others unnecessarily.

MATTHEW, PART TWO. — Might be worth reminding him that we
    do not have the staff nor the wherewithal to get involved in
    Miss Edwina Nettleblack's family affair. His work with the
    witness testimonies from the Dallyangle Theatre is taking
    far longer than it should, and I suspect the temptation of

this Nettleblack business is to blame. (In the future, such cases might fall within our remit, but for the moment missing remains and violent burglars must take priority over thwarted aristocratic marriages.)

ADELAIDE. — Unnerving incident in reception today, in which the well-intentioned but overzealous actions of my son's governess caused a discouraging scene with two members of the public. Some enthusiastic publicity, or reiteration of council endorsement, might be useful in the near future, to address these absurd concerns. Yet it is, of course, important to ensure that the community feels able to hold us to the high standards on which we pride ourselves. Which leaves us – me –

Which leaves one course of action. We must find the head, and meet the deadline. No one in Dallyangle can accuse us of failing if we simply *don't*.

Keturah St. Clare Ballestas, Director of the Dallyangle Division

11.

MAE GEN I BROBLEM

My journal, ascending to new madness

Later (heaven even knows when)

Figs. Plums. Passionfruit. *Everything!*

I quite don't know what to say. I don't know how to phrase it.

Am I a despicable human being, a terrible sibling – or something else entirely – something that's not just a sensation – something that has *words* to it – something – ?

Sweet peaches, but just let them try to flatten me now!

I confess it began ominously. I snapped off the last entry at the sound of chatter by the door, thrust everything journal-related inside my pillowcase and curled up into feigned sleep. A few breaths later, knitted palms were nudging me back to life – and there was Gertie, with Millicent and Oliver gargoyling out from either shoulder, staring down at me in the most unnerving manner.

"How're you feeling, Hyssop?"

I swallowed. What would make them less inclined to probe for an explanation? "I – erm – adequate – quite – "

"There's a bit more colour to her," Millicent remarked knowingly, one rough thumb brushing down my cheek. "She'll be fine, Gertie. It'll do her good."

"I – what – what will – ?"

Gertie cupped my shoulders, tugged gently until I was sat upright – and then swerved, rather too abruptly, into a crafty grin. "What I told you before. It's been a ghastly day for the Inferior Contingent, and we need a night out."

And the terror, the panic, the half-delirious hysteria – all of it came ricocheting back. I gaped at her – of course I did – I could hardly breathe! I had never – I didn't even know what such a thing as a *night out* entailed – and going with them would invariably mean encountering people outside the relative safety of these walls – and Maggie and Norman Sweeting were resoundingly still at large – !

"I can't," I managed to gasp.

Gertie's grin didn't drop a tooth. "You can. Septimus won't find out. Swap your jacket for that greatcoat of yours – and get that cravat back on, too! – and no one'll even know you're Div. Just one drink in Checkley's. You might enjoy it."

"You *will* enjoy it," Oliver insisted, with the sprightly glee of a choirboy mid-solo. "Pour yourself some pirate sherry! Only wish I could come too – I've got Sweetings lookout tonight, worse luck – so you have to go, Hyssop! Go in my place!"

I saw, then, what I'd been far too dazed to notice before. Gertie and Millicent were out of their uniforms – not precisely *disguised*, but certainly not dressed in any way that screamed out their occupation. Millicent had traded her split skirt for a yellow stuff gown, belted with a jaunty necktie to show off her tight-laced waist. Gertie's plait wobbled in a bushy whorl on the top of her head, flaunting the crochet collar she'd pinned to her work-shirt – though her skirt was a gregarious blue check, the very picture of a harvest party. They looked, in sum total, like nothing I'd ever imagined – wild-coloured, and sure-footed, and resoundingly determined to wring all the enjoyment they could get out of the drab rainy night.

I bit my lip. There was no getting out of this.

Much to my surprise, they didn't sneak us a path across reception. I'd – rather naively, I suppose – not imagined there to *be* another route out of the Division, unless they meant to wrestle the back yard gate. But of course they had their secret exit: an old door at the back of the dormitory, too stiff to move much in either direction, but wedged open enough to wriggle through. It did at least explain why it was always so horrendously cold in that room. Not that this new know-ledge felt like much of a triumph, as the lashing rain slapped my fringe across my eyebrows, and my greatcoat sponged up the wet of the storm for the second time in a week.

But our destination was close – a stout brick building with six sturdy sides, one of the many lining the market square. Squinting against the downpour, I couldn't distinguish much by way of architectural decoration – and in the first stunned moments of sudden warmth, and yowling din, and the heady burn of a strange sour smell on the air, I'd not the faintest what it was they'd tugged me into. It was only when Millicent drove us through a knot of cackling rustic youths, thwacked a brazen tattoo onto a stained wooden counter in the centre of the chaos, and a frothing tankard sprang across the wood into her waiting fist, that it made any feeble degree of sense.

It was the *tavern*.

Millicent nudged me, flashed a terrifying crooked-toothed grin. "Panic not, Hyssop! My parents own this place, and everything's on the house for dearest daughter and her friends. No one'll bother us here!"

I managed a delirious nod. My hands scrabbled up, as if clinging to my greatcoat collar would salvage my alarm, even in the midst of the churning crowd. Edwina was in my veins, pressed close – closer than the throng around me, closer than Gertie at my elbow and the bar against my arm and Millicent's stiff petticoats digging into my side. I could quite imagine the reprimands she would have summoned for me: *you cannot be seen in such a place! Debauching yourself and the distinguished match I would have made for you! Even your feckless wastrel of a sister never showed lack of judgment enough to cross the threshold of a tavern –*

I gritted my teeth, and my sister's imaginary tirade sputtered to nothing. Edwina wasn't here. Edwina hadn't outlasted the day I'd just had.

And – *hectic purgatorial figs* – Rosamond quite *had* shown lack of judgment enough to cross the threshold of a tavern, because she was standing not three feet in front of me.

The room wasn't a giddying blur anymore. It was clear and specific as the set-piece of a nightmare, clustering up on my eyelids. Queasy tallow-candles dangled overhead in their green glass lanterns, pasting a weird verdant glow over hordes of grinning faces, the smell dripping down from them quite curdlingly vile. The six dark-painted walls were studded with doors, branching off to shadowy corners, every scrap of free space pockmarked with photographs: of the market, of an enormous Skull-featured family stood atop a cart of hay, of Lady Miltonwaters in a riding-habit with a pheasant under her arm. Panels of frosted glass flashed into view through a tangle of limbs, sheltering tables and booths, patterned over with fish-hooks and clumsy acanthus leaves. The bar stood firm at the centre of it all, hellishly sticky to the touch, blasting that sour smothering scent past elbows and shawls and lapels. People clustered about it – quite dismembered by the dim light and the bustle – jostling, laughing, gesturing with strange thick-handled tankards, jabbing me in the ribs without noticing I was there to be jabbed.

And – there – loose-haired and laughing in the midst of the crowd, draped in a gown tacked from the folds of her Morris fabric, clutching a tankard in two brittle hands, was none other than my infernal, unhelpful, inexplicable, immensely inebriated elder sister.

"Rosa!" Gertie yelled, writhing past me.

But – what – how – Rosamond – how could she – *Gertie Skull* – ?

"Nos da! And who might you be, fair stranger?"

My mouth toppled open. It was my sister's voice, unmistakeably my sister's voice, brimful of more drunken exuberance than I'd ever heard.

Gertie beamed, jolting out a hand to steady her. "The hell've you been drinking, Rosa? It's me! Gertie? Gertie Skull?"

"*Is* it?"

Rosamond blinked, wallowing deep in a vacant smirk, one skinny arm swinging over Gertie's crocheted collarbone. "You are but shadow, shade and spirits to these sparkling eyes, but I'll believe you. Well, then! What fresh madness from the Division? You've lost a head, I hear – how very careless of you!"

Fresh madness – but – wait – that would mean –

I had barely enough time to skitter through the thought before Gertie's untankarded arm loped back through the crush and snagged me at my shoulder. Then – figs, and thank heaven I'd the presence of mind not to articulate *figs* – she slung me forward like a catapult, sent me careering into Rosamond. For one floating instant, the tavern was gone, and there was just the sharp tang of her sweat, the snarl of wild ebony curls at the edges of my face.

I wanted to cling. She smelled revolting, and her heartbeat was rattling like a stone in a jewel-box, but – even so! It was still Rosamond!

She didn't let me hold on for long. In hindsight, it was probably a mercy, however cruel it felt. Her arm slipped off Gertie's neck, turned into a slick hand at my cheek, tipping my head up to the ghastly green of the stinking lantern above. She laughed, a flash of sallow teeth, porcelain-white at one corner where she'd knocked out a canine and had it replaced – but Henry Hyssop the Division Apprentice wouldn't know to notice that –

"Gertie," she declared, "Your new friend's a peach. No – a lychee. Don't mind if I devour her too, do you?"

Every word lurched against the next. I confess, I'm only half-certain this was what she actually said.

Blurry at my lashes' edge, Gertie blinked. "I – what?"

Rosamond winked at me, glittering green eyes almost black with squinting. At least – I assume she meant to wink at me – her giddy gaze was predominantly trained on my left eyebrow. Regardless of her aim, it was more camaraderie than I'd had from her since Wales. But – and this was eerie in the extreme – it wasn't to me. Not to Henry Nettleblack. Whatever she'd been drinking, it had left her entirely unable to spot a shred of her sibling in my horrified gape. It was somehow both convenient and agonising in the same unnerving moment.

"Penglog!" she yelled, hurling her stare vaguely in Gertie's direction. "You! Who *is* the lychee?"

Gertie swallowed warily. She quite wasn't relishing this tumultuous incarnation of Rosamond any more than I was. "New recruit, Rosa. Henry Hyssop. Ah – Hyssop – I did want to introduce you, but it looks like Rosa's a bit gone tonight – go find Millie, will you? I'll deal with – "

"No!" Rosamond hollered, hands clenching on my shoulders. She was staring at my eyebrow again, her eyes roiling inside the pupils. "I'm fine, Gertie. Da iawn. Bendigedig. Bendi-bloody-gedig. You go away. Get liquor for the lychee! Put a round on my tab, will you?"

Gertie gaped at her. "I – but – no, Rosa, look, I'm not – "

With a great shuddering effort, Rosamond stiffened to her normal height, pinched Gertie in a glassy glare. For three terrifying breaths, sucked in sharp through her nose, she was Edwina to the life: green-eyed, haughty, implacable, unquestionable. "Diolch, Gertie."

Gertie shrank back, alarmingly cowed, her blush a strange bruise-colour in the green lantern's glow. Before she disappeared, her fingers dug into my elbow: "Shout if you need us. Won't be long. Alright?"

"I – erm – " – but the crowd already had her.

Rosamond was grinning at me now, twirling one finger lazily on the top of my shoulder-blade. "If she brings you ale, don't drink it. These Musgroves are monster brewers. It'll spin your curly head off."

Like yours? I wanted to blurt. Either that, or burst into tears.

"I – erm – what have you been – ?"

"Drinking?" she smirked, plummeting her head onto my shoulder. "Precisely that, and rather a lot of it. Not to worry – I'm used to the stuff. Did the death's-head say your name was Henry? I had a sister called Henry, you know."

And do you miss her? Do you even notice her absence?

"Henry!" She groaned. "You don't want to hurt Henry, do you? Who hurt her? *You* did! Not you, lychee, someone else. *Not* a subject for tonight! – "

Her legs skidded under her, slung her weight down from my collar. It was all I could do to grab her before she dragged us both to the murky floor.

"Rosamond – careful!"

And then, of course, I could have consummately dismembered myself, because at no point in this horrendous exchange had anyone given me her unabbreviated name.

But she didn't seem to notice. She was looking up at me in a way that seemed liable to set me on fire.

"You've heard of me! It's all true, I promise. Cymraes ydw i! Rwy'n dod o Fro Gŵyr yn wreiddiol, ac rwy'n gweld ishe gatre. Ond rwy'n mwynhau – ah, but you don't understand, do you, poor sais?"

I gritted my teeth. *I know you're Welsh, and I know you're from Gower, because you lived there with me for seventeen years before Surrey unhinged you!*

But – rwy'n mwynhau – rwy'n mwynhau what? What would have been the end of that sentence? What was it she enjoyed?

She tugged a clumsy hand round to my cravat, too-hot fingertips glancing on my throat – then, sliding down, to delve into the knot and wrench it loose. Mulberries, what was she doing?

"Poor sais with a pretty face. Fancy a game of chess?"

What?

"I – I'm sorry?"

She giggled. It sounded like a knife-sharpener.

"Rosamond, I – " – she wouldn't go mad, not even intoxicated, I quite wouldn't let her – "I must inform you quite – erm – plainly that – erm – that there is no chessboard present – in this tavern – "

"What?" My cravat was limp at my throat, pruning with creases where the knot had held it. In another breath, it wasn't limp in the slightest, as she laced her fingers through the ends, dragged downwards until it went taut. "Not chess – *chess!* Gertie's mad nickname for it! I thought all you Div youths called it that!"

"Really – I – I haven't the faintest what you – "

She sighed. "Oh, dear. Lychee annwyl – to the point – would you mind it awfully if I took it upon myself to kiss you?"

And my jaw quite plummeted out of existence.

"Rosamond?"

Her arm twisted round my waist, pulled her close enough for me to catch the tang of her breath, the heady smell in her curls. She was sneering, and the sneer was petrifyingly self-assured. No – more than that – it was *knowing,* despite her supreme obliviousness as to my identity, and whatever it *knew* it positively revelled in.

"You know what I mean! Look at you, you miniature sapphist!"

I could hardly move. It was clammily dawning on me quite how little I knew of my sister.

"Well?"

Sloeberries, *do* something!

"Rosamond! Listen to me – or recognise me – or – at least – recognise the cravat! You – you must – you must know – dy chwaer di ydw is – os gweli di'n dda – plîs – "

"Hyssop!"

Was this better, or worse? It was Gertie, either way, flushed and furious and thoroughly devoid of tankards, ploughing through the throng to rip Rosamond away from me like a spoilt bookpage.

Rosamond blinked at her, dazed. "I thought I told you to get drinks?"

"Why?" Gertie spat, shouldering me behind her. "So you can sneak away from me and fling chess at someone else? Hyssop – are you alright?"

There weren't words. "I – erm – no – I – "

Rosamond flapped a hand at me, an ungainly shush. She was staring at Gertie's hairline, her sharp face a livid greenish mixture of amusement and pity.

"Oh, bach. You really didn't imagine you were the only one?"

Around us, not a conscious human creature had noticed the mustering row. Millicent had vanished, rippling into the crowd. The green lights kept sputtering. A new brace of elbows jabbed into my spine.

"Outside," Gertie snarled, and had a fist round Rosamond's arm before either of us could protest. The path she shoved through the horde was just clean enough to dart in the wake of, if I was quick – and I had to be quick – what else could I have done?

Well. Ran away, I suppose, back to the Division whilst Gertie was distracted. Flatly denied it to have been my sister at all, whatever I may have yelled in my much-neglected mother tongue. Hidden from the lot of them thereafter, in case Rosamond happened to remember the wretch with the cravat –

But I could hardly go into hiding a second time over! And with her in this state – and turning on Gertie – I couldn't just leave them to it!

The rain slapped the thoughts quite out of my skull. Gertie led us to the market square, empty and skeletal under the massive cloud-curdled sky. Huge puddles had swallowed up the bulk of the cobblestones, drowning the bare awnings at their bases, simmering as yet more rain shattered and seethed on their surfaces. Behind us, the tavern was boisterous as ever, though the windows were far too small for anyone to have watched us, and the light barely cast far enough to illuminate our group. Rosamond was a sticklike shadow, twisting out of Gertie's grip. Gertie was all plough-shouldered snarl. I was beyond any feigned indifference, my teeth rattling in my head, rainwater gushing down my greatcoat lapels.

"Explain!" Gertie cried, her voice cracking. "I thought – thought we'd – "

Rosamond scoffed, lurching about in a lopsided pirouette. "What? That we'd sworn an exclusive partnership? That I planned to marry you, and do right by you – ha! – and get spoony with you and the turnips in a Dallyanglian bwthyn?"

Gertie froze. Rosamond staggered closer – she was the shorter, chin jutting upwards – her drawl slurring between ironical and haughty. She was drunk as a wasp in summer, and quite as inclined to sting.

"I swore nothing. I won't. Why are you keening at me for that, anyway? Look at yourself before you blame me! How did you ever think so nobly of me in the first place? You don't understand half of what I say. You don't even know my surname. So scurry back to your personal public-house – and find someone else to spoon with – and stop trying to plight yourself to me, you sentimental idiot!"

"Rosamond – stop!"

The words scraped up my throat, threw me between the two of them. "Please – I – you – you can't treat Gertie like this!"

My sister rolled her eyes, nearly toppled with the gesture. "What *now?* I said chess, you said no – da iawn. No chess. That's it."

"I – but – that – that's quite not it!"

I spun, snatched for Gertie's sleeve. I could barely make her out, beyond the shifting shape and the raggedy breaths. "I – erm – Gertie, don't – don't listen to her – you quite don't deserve this – she – I don't know – she doesn't mean it – "

"You've known her twenty seconds," Gertie hissed, twisting out of my hand, "And clearly she doesn't want to know us. Look – come back inside, Hyssop – Millie'll be looking for us – "

A crumpled yelp behind me dragged my head about. Rosamond hit the cobblestones in a slosh of sopping fabric, pallid fingers groping through a puddle, limp wrists sagging bare into the muddy water. She coughed, a searing snarling thing that struck her shoulder-blades taut to the back of her dress.

Lemons.

"I – I'm sorry," I stammered, and sprinted to her.

By the time I had her head up, Gertie was gone, slamming the tavern door until the sodden wood trembled. Rosamond rocked in my arms, gasping for breath, bony talon-hands clinging to my wrist as I strained against her slumping weight.

I'd quite no plan, other than a shivering conviction that she mustn't recognise me. Getting her to her feet, back inside the tavern, giving her over to someone – who? – who'd know what best to do with her –

And Gertie Skull would rightly despise me for it. And Rosamond certainly wouldn't thank me. Because – as she'd made appallingly plain – Rosamond didn't give figs, lemons or lychees for anyone's peace of mind, let alone mine – not even now, as I struggled for a footing in the freezing puddles –

She arched her back, buckled at the waist, and vomited over my boots.

"Henry!"

Figs. *Figs.* The worst is absolutely not so long as one can shout a fruit at it.

"What – I – thought you weren't well – and who – ?"

Weak in my arms, Rosamond giggled.

And I snapped. I couldn't see Septimus's face, silhouetted against the light from the Division's windows, but the thought of that impeccable chignon braving the weather just to watch me slump under the most giddy-headed traitor of a sister I'd not truly known I had – it – it was entirely too much to bear.

"Division Sergeant! I'm apprehending this woman for – erm – something!"

I'd be utterly stunned if the sentiment didn't astonish them both.

12.

IN WHICH, A REVELATION

More of myself

For full five minutes in the wake of my improvisation, all was flashes and starts. Rosamond's popping eyes, her snigger of surprise. Septimus, unquestioning, spiralling past me to help hold her up. The harsh gaslights of the Division, and Cassandra's gasping bewilderment at the main desk. The yelling – the feral, interminable yelling, fit to wake the town, slapping at the plastered walls until they trembled –

"You can't *arrest* people in Checkley's! Everything's legal in Checkley's!"

"This ain't an arrest! If I don't hold you up you'll fall over!"

Then the Director's bleary-eyed head, popping out of her office with her spectacles swinging from one ear, utterly exhausted and very much looking it. "Septimus, what on earth – ?"

And Cassandra, a final dazed caveat: "Don't worry, Mother, it isn't Property."

What else was there? A bruising stagger down the unlit hallway to the third door – the same door outside which I had stood a matter of hours ago, listening to Mr. Adelstein unfurling his scheme. The murky darkness of the room beyond – "Henry, the lights!" The giddy realisation that this must have been Septimus's office – though I could barely make out the furnishings, beyond the squat little window and the solitary chair that Rosamond had slumped into, her gown dribbling off her sharp shoulders.

If I lit too many lamps, Septimus would notice my lack of uniform. Either that, or Rosamond would snatch enough light to make out my face properly, and my traitorous identity with it, assuming anything about the last few minutes had even slightly sobered her. Dim lighting it was, then. It was only half-affectation; my hands were shaking too much to manage more than one gaslight.

"Right!" Septimus declared, still largely in shadow, tugging her notebook from her pocket. "Henry – which case is it – Head-Hider or Sweetings – or is she just drunk? What's she done?"

"I might throw the same question at you!" Rosamond snarled. It was a curious thing to hear her really angry again – to hear that languid honeyed voice catch, and smart, and spasm with bewildered rage. "Not even the sodding seduction was illegal! And it wouldn't have been illegal even if your lychee did fancy it – which she didn't – so there's a beginning and an end to the whole stori ddiflas! And you couldn't arrest me even if I was doing something illegal – which I'm *not* – because in case you've all forgotten, you are not the police!"

I dropped my hands. There was quite no hope of brighter light now. Septimus's answering splutter almost felled the very lamp from the wall.

"You – seduction – *what?*"

Rosamond snorted. "Scandalous, disreputable, frowned upon, yes – but illegal? For me – or her – or even you – ha! Just call it a passionate friendship!"

Septimus skidded across the room, stooped before the chair until she had my sister pinioned on a ferocious glare. "You ain't making any sense. Reckon that makes it drunk. In need of an escort home. Henry – yes?"

Home? "I – erm – well – I – "

Another spindly giggle from Rosamond. "Excellent witness, isn't she?"

Septimus flicked a glance up at me. "Henry – you brought her in – 's that what you meant?"

Spat out in her voice, the words finally skewered me.

You brought her in.

Pomegranates – one spasming moment – what had I *done?* And if she was escorted home – and Edwina punished her – every scrap of it would be my fault – assuming Edwina didn't glimpse me on the threshold, handing her over –

"No!" I blurted. "I – I mean – yes – I mean – not quite – erm – "

"What?"

Utterly devoid of credible excuse, I simply toppled into further insanity. "I – I wasn't – please – Division Sergeant – don't hurt her!"

Septimus gaped at me. I quite can't imagine how she'd a shred of patience left. "Henry. Why'd you bring her here?"

"I – I – "

"To get my attention, by the look of it!"

Rosamond slung forward in her chair, grinning wildly between the two of us, her porcelain tooth startlingly white through the gloom. Edge by glinting edge, she was starting to sober up.

"Well, lychee annwyl, now you've got it! And you, Division Sergeant – *sweet* sergeant, is it? Of course! Naturally furious, twitchy about seductions, losing all ability to do her job – are you the dashing young Septimus of whom I've heard such titillating stories?"

My jaw quite dropped.

How – since when – what had *Rosamond* heard about Septimus? And why in the name of every passionfruit in existence hadn't Rosamond ever told me any of it? Not the lurid gossip, of course – just a hint, any hint, that such a person as Septimus existed, and resided in Dallyangle, and was available to meet –

(As if I would have had sufficient nerve to approach Septimus of my own volition!)

Septimus, meanwhile, had the spine of her notebook in a veritable chokehold. "I – I don't know what you think you – "

Rosamond tossed back her head and laughed. "Everything! I've heard *everything* about you – and I believe it! You can't even decide why I'm in your Division, for heaven's sake! Such a lovely palaver you've put on for me tonight, you and your cariad over there – wyt ti'n hoffi'r merched â gwallt byr? Ond nid merch yw fy nghariad – "

I got about one word in three, and it flung me off the figurative clifftops once again. The next voice cramming the poky room was mine, unaccountably shrill, pinwheeling past a horrified Septimus –

"Stop it! You – you're doing it deliberately – and I quite won't let you weaponise your Welsh against her!"

If I could have wrestled the words back out of the air, I would have leapt to it the instant I'd stopped yelling them. Septimus had twisted around on one knee to stare at me, her eyebrows nudging at her chignon, evidently far too unnerved by my abrupt ascent into articulate sentences to manage any of her own. Beyond her, cadaverous in the shadows of the one sputtering gaslight, Rosamond's face had gone slack – hollow astonished eyes, slanting eyebrows, parted lips.

"Gwell a gwell," she breathed. "Bugger me with a teapot."

Figs. Sweet, plentiful, uncharted figs.

I opened my mouth – and it was all gone. There weren't words. At least, there were quite none I was in any position to say.

Don't give me away – or *now does everything make sense?* – or *I'll not send you back in shame to Edwina, I promise, just please make sure Septimus doesn't find out who I am* –

All of my options were equally impossible – and entirely the only sentiments I could think of!

Rosamond smirked. Her rage had simmered away, left her back in her usual ironical state, tenfold headier with ammunition and tipsiness. She flicked her gaze – so languidly! – from me to Septimus and back again, stiffened an eyebrow into a teasing arch, crossed one leg over the other on her spindly seat. In the dingy lighting, with her drenched curls and fast-disintegrating frock, she looked far more akin to an underworld goddess than anything remotely nineteenth-century, which she must have been unreasonably pleased about.

"I'll be on my way, then, bach."

Septimus jolted from her daze. "You can't just – "

"Gad dy gleber, you," Rosamond tossed at her, beaming. "Os gwelwch yn dda, chwaerlet?"

I'd throttle her. I'd quite entirely throttle her.

"So," Rosamond continued brightly, "Let's sort out some of this confusion, shall we? I'm not the – what are they calling it, the Head-Hider? – nor the Sweetings' incestuous love-child, and I don't even know what other demons are besieging you. But I *am* Miss Rosamond Nettleblack, and I do mean *those* Nettleblacks. The ones with the tincture, and the money enough to buy you out of your very building should you in any way inconvenience me further. Or wasn't the Welsh enough of a clue?"

Septimus froze like a stopped clock.

Rosamond, insufferable to the points of her bramblebush hair, promptly tipped forward on the chair and dashed a sharp kiss to her cheek.

"I can always inform my family," she added cheerily, over Septimus's startled cry, "that this was all a terribly stupid mistake. Oh, my sister'd be most forgiving – that's my eldest sister, Edwina Nettleblack, bit of a casual tyrant, you may have heard of her – as long as you let me saunter out of your lovely doors without noting down that I was ever here, and most *definitely* without dumping me on her doorstep like a naughty child. Otherwise, I'll – what is it, again, that thing you Divisioners fear like the plague? – I'll make a complaint. To my neighbour Lady Miltonwaters and the rest of the town council. They're the ones who fund you, aren't they?"

I dared the slightest of hasty glances to Septimus's face. Bergamots, it was as horrendous as I'd feared. Her navy eyes had shot wide – with fear, panic, humiliation, all at once. She must have been crimson; the shadows were darkening across her cheekbones. Her sharp certainty, her glowering defensiveness – Rosamond had flayed it off, every last bit of it, and left her as horribly helpless as I'd ever seen her.

Rosamond sniggered into the silence. "Let me leave, now, there's a merch dda. The Nettleblacks will be *so* very grateful."

She kicked to her feet before either of us could argue further. The sooner she was gone, the better – but – of course that was only half of my thoughts! Of course I was also choking back a frantic urge to spring into Rosamond's path, to inform her she – she – I don't know – she couldn't leave yet, not until she'd – *apologised*, at the very least! To Septimus – to Gertie – to the Division itself!

If she'd not prised me out of my words – if I had some guarantee she wouldn't dash straight to Edwina and tell her everything in smug revenge – if –

"Chwaerlet?"

Sweet Jacobean blackcurrants, what *more* did she want?

"Cer di i'r dafarn heno – ac fe ddwa i. Mewn awr. Os nad wyt ti am i fi siarad â dy chwaer?"

It was hardly pretence just to gape at her. To hurl that much Welsh at me, brazen as anything, right across Septimus's flabbergasted glare – and –

What had she actually said?

Septimus opened the door, stony-voiced. "There. My – well – my apologies, Miss Nettleblack."

"Ardderchog! Which, in your furious layman terms, means *excellent*, and isn't spelt a whit like it sounds!"

Cer di – go – you, and then I – going – going where? *Dafarn?* And the last part – something about speaking to our sister – was it a threat? Why, after years of paying not a scrap of attention to me, had she suddenly chosen this moment to bind us back together – to involve herself in the life over which she had flung up all future responsibility?

Think! Think, and don't look thoughtful! *Dafarn* didn't mean *home*, and she'd just used *Division* to describe us here, so it could hardly be this building. If she was asking me to go there, it had to be somewhere I knew my way to – it had to be somewhere she knew I knew the way to –

Dafarn. Of course. Not twenty minutes since I'd narrowly escaped, and already she wanted to drive me back into that tavern.

"What the hell was that about?"

I hadn't time even to gasp. Rosamond had vanished – Septimus had snapped – and now there was nothing in the known and gloam-lit world but the latter's face, puce and snarling and terrifyingly close to my own.

"She ain't anything to do with our cases! Her family's the richest in Dallyangle – she could've had Miltonwaters and the council and the whole of Catfish Crescent on us! Are you *trying* to humiliate me now?"

"No! I – I just – "

"Why didn't you say anything once you'd brought her in? Why wouldn't you tell me what she'd done?"

For quite the same reason I can't tell you now! "I – erm – "

"And of course I wasn't going to *hurt* her! If that's what you think of us – "

"It's not – it was just – I – "

She stared at me, trembling with rage, but my words quite wouldn't form. Her eyes narrowed, waiting – then skidded down away from my face –

"Where's your uniform?"

She had the eyes of an owl, of course, and now that the dim lights had failed me I had absolutely no line of defence.

"I – I'm sorry – I didn't – it was supposed to not – erm – look like a uniform – because – erm – "

"'Cause you were sneaking into Checkley's, is that it?"

She sounded so unabashedly – well, hurt – that I'd half a mind to cry *no!*, in flat defiance of the fact that I'd just been doing precisely that. "I – I – "

"You can't just swan off to Musgrove's pub! You do realise the Director's a teetotaller? That she's banned drinking on Div time?"

Pomegranates.

"I – " – and my voice was rising, twisting, skeining to a yell – "I didn't – I wasn't – and I thought I – I thought I could – "

"Did the Director even give you time off tonight?"

I gasped for breath, and my feet keeled away from me, sent me stumbling back against the freezing wall. "I – erm – I don't know – I don't think – "

"God's sake, Henry!" she snarled. "How'm I supposed to help you? You say you're ill, and then you run off – and – and then you – I thought you cared about the job! I thought you cared a lot more than this!"

"I – I do!"

Her gaze skewered me to the wall. "It don't look like it."

The truth. As much of the truth as you can give her. *Now.*

I flattened my hands against the plaster, pressed into the cold until my fingers smarted. "I – well – look – earlier – I was upset – and – erm – some of the others – they thought going out would – would cheer me – " (but don't get Gertie and her contingent dismissed whilst you're at it!) " – and they had the time off – erm – and I assumed I did too – "

"What? Why were you upset?"

192

It was through my teeth before I could stop it. "Because I quite heard Mr. Adelstein telling you to spy on me!"

Now she paled, flayed to blank shock.

"He – erm – he said it was your duty! He thinks that I – I – I wrote those letters – the letters I've barely even seen!"

In two stabbing strides, she'd closed our distance again. You could have balanced a pencil between our collarbones, though both of us were gasping far too much to hold anything steady. I was still clinging to the wall. She peered at me, the same narrow-eyed stare I'd woken up to in reception – slack-jawed, and mystified, and slipping in and out of a scowl.

"Did you write the letters?" she blurted suddenly. Then she flushed, as if it hadn't in the least been what she'd meant to say.

"No!" – and it was rather louder than I'd intended.

She blinked. It eased her eyes loose from their squinting scrutiny, left them wide and wrong-footed, half out of exasperation and not entirely sure where they were headed next. Her mouth was still open, her lips bitten red. Her chignon had, amazingly, stayed put, eerily perfect above the ruddy disorder of her face.

She must have been agonising, all the while, whether or not to believe me.

"You ain't dismissed," she muttered abruptly, her dark navy gaze veering up into my hairline. "Obviously it was all a mistake. Yes. I should tell the Director – you might get fined – she's taken a shilling off Gertie for sneaking out before – but then we'll hear no more about it."

A shilling. I'd never thought in shillings – halfway out of my house, I'd crammed fifty pounds into my pocket without registering it an especially hefty sum – but now, even this slighter fraction seemed an impossible demand. A shilling – when my clothes were falling apart – and I hadn't washed properly for days – and I'd barely eaten – and I'd not a soul to blame but myself –

"I – I – I don't have anything," I spluttered, and my legs quite gave out.

It happened in pieces. My hands skidded off the wall. The floor, too dark to be anything other than a vague shadow, lunged up at me. It wasn't like my last faint, where the world had snapped shut like a book – this time I saw it all. She flung out a panicky arm and snagged me in it. My limp legs twirled on their ankles. We were skidding about, my weight hooked in her elbow, and then I was slung down in the chair, gasping great nauseous breaths into my knees. Her hands darted along my shoulders, eased me upright, wrenched at the stud of my penny-collar until it sprang open. My cravat was loose from where Rosamond had toyed with it – just as well, for my chest was already tightening, my panic bunching under my ribs.

"Henry?" – and she was panicking herself, albeit not quite to my visceral extent, her voice taut and low. "What is it? What – ?"

"I quite can't breathe," I rasped, which must have sounded a consummate lie, given the rate at which I was trying to swallow down all the air in the room. I knew what this was. I'd had such episodes before, shuttered in my bedroom – trembling in Edwina's study – sprinting out of supervisions in Girton's red-brick offices. I knew further panicking only made the physical sensations worse – but – but if I didn't pay this wretched impossible fine – which I couldn't – what other option did that leave her but to dismiss me? – and what other option did that leave me? – and if she threw me out, I'd quite never see her again –

And then I was crying out, sickled over the chair, clutching at my shirt to steady my heartbeat –

"I *can't!*"

She scrabbled at me until she had my face in her hands, her eyes wide and her voice shaking. "Look – I shouldn't've snapped – you don't have to have the ready money – the fine'll just come out of your wages – and that's if you even get one – you might not! – "

There – that ought to calm you – that ought to be enough –

"Is there someone I can get for you?" she demanded desperately. "Family – sibling – or – your sweetheart?"

I gulped an enormous shuddering breath. "I – I don't – don't have – there's no sweetheart – I've never – "

She frowned. "I thought you'd a chap – or – I don't know! – that you and Nick'd – "

Nick? "But – but he's – Nick and you – aren't you – ?"

"Me?" Her jaw quite dropped, her fingers trembling on my cheekbones. "What? No, I – I ain't got anyone!"

And I've written it now, so it must be true.

Septimus does not *have a sweetheart.*

Passionfruit, but I could write it over – and over – and over!

But, so as not to abandon me amidst my gasping struggles, I'll content myself with just the single iteration on this occasion. Back in her office, the sheer giddy astonishment had shocked the worst of the tightness out of my chest, left me slumping into Septimus's hands as my nerves untangled themselves. My breaths stretched, relaxed, until the air was positively rattling down my gullet. It was – and I could have wept for pure gratitude – it was easing off.

Then I could dare to breathe through my nose again, and register what my stare had been scalding into. Septimus, swallowing with relief as my gasps burned themselves away, navy gaze flicking from my eyes to my mouth and back again.

"Are you alright?" she murmured faintly.

I'd not colour enough to blush, but the sentiment was much the same. "I – I – erm – sorry – I – I didn't mean for – this happens some-times – I – "

"You don't have to apologise! It ain't – I mean – 'long as you're fine!"

I twitched at my features – I had to, she looked so wretched – until they shivered into something vaguely akin to a smile. She bit her lip, too dazed to nod. Her hands – her fingers –

They were still at my face, and they were still trembling. Her thumb brushed down my cheek, light as a lock of hair, the tip of her nail notching gently to the edge of my lips.

Would you mind it awfully if I took it upon myself to kiss you?

And that was it, and it truly was quite that simple. I didn't want her to have a sweetheart. I wanted to *be* her sweetheart. I wanted – and, figs, it was fierce enough almost to lift my own hands – to slip my fingers into her chignon, and ease the pins out, and kiss her bitten lips as her hair tumbled over our shoulders.

I snatched a frantic breath, and nearly swallowed her thumb.

It startled her back – it startled me back – and then she was straightening up, brushing at her sleeves for something to do with her hands. "Right. Yes. Well. Good to see you looking better. That'll be it for tonight – in – y'know – Div stuff. For you. Yes. Yes – ah – rest. Yes! Rest. I'll get back out there. Meant to be on Sweetings lookout tonight. But you stay – get dry – get warm. Yes. I – I'll expect you at the desk tomorrow. Usual time. Back to normal. Yes. I – yes – good night!"

And I barely had nerve left to stammer a pleasantry before she'd spun on her heel and sprinted away, headlong down the corridor, until the shadows had submerged her.

I ran. Straight through the dormitory and out the other side – as soon as I was sure I could stand, as soon as I heard the double doors slam. A dazed glance round the darkened dorm gave me bare windows, streetlamps, the sleeping ferret on my pillow, the smudgy silhouette of Septimus vanishing into the roads beyond the market. I kept my footfalls, as much as I could, to a hasty hysterical tiptoe, veering wildly to dodge the worst of the cracks in the floorboards. There wasn't a human soul left to loiter in the room, but even so – I didn't think I'd survive being caught sneaking out to the tavern again.

No. I wasn't doing anything of the sort. I was slipping quietly through the dormitory's back door to get some air in the wake of my attack, and if Rosamond was still lingering out there she would have to come to me.

The rain had pattered itself out. The market square was sodden as a bathtub, more puddles than pathways, deserted now that Septimus had disappeared. A streak of fox prised itself from the butcher's threshold and splashed through the awnings, skittering away when it spotted me staggering out into the cold. The tavern – Checkley's – was a greenish smudge in the gloom, ringed with mist, considerably quieter than it had been in the dreadful frenzy of earlier. I stared at it, at the faint shapes shifting behind the tinted windows. I'd quite no intention of going inside again, but – would she know to glance out of the door? She had said she would wait there, and in her favourite language. Was it too much to hope that the drunken delirium hadn't sucked the recollection out of her?

"Nos da."

I gasped. Rosamond peeled herself from the nearest tavern wall, shivering in her thin fabric, a brittle glass of water notched in her hand. She was staring me out, with more fixed determination than she'd shown for years, her lazy smirk almost an afterthought under her gleaming eyes. It wasn't in the least hostility, though. Between us, we must have come bearing enough apologies to uproot every cobblestone in the square – unspoken apologies, all of them, simmering between our stares. At least, mine certainly were.

But I'd more than a mind to talk of something else. *Fancy a game of chess,* she'd drawled at me earlier. She quite couldn't condemn me. Clementines – feral and trembling as I was, it seemed perfectly logical to indulge the hopeful suspicion that she might actually be pleased – that, for the first time since leaving Wales, she might find some part of my present existence worth her attention –

"Rosamond, I – erm – I – I'm – erm – infatuated – with Division Sergeant Septimus."

She squinted at me. "Chwaerlet fach, that much is obvious! I don't see why you had to run away for it, though."

Obvious?

"What? – no! – I – I ran away because of Lady Miltonwaters – "

"Eddie's benevolent overlord?" She grinned. "What, did you bewitch her too? I never thought her the type, but – "

"*No!* She wanted to trap me in an estate and – and – offer me up to pheasant-hungry suitors! And you – you didn't want to help me!"

She rolled her eyes – the movement nearly toppled her – and let her smile fade, tipped a dash of water down her throat. "Eddie wouldn't have listened to me, bach, even if I'd been English and a thousand times less disreputable. Ein chwaer wants nothing more than to shove a sister into the aristocracy – if she needs it that much, she should just do it herself. But she might yet have to now. I take it you're not planning on coming back?"

She'd snatched the words quite through my teeth. I opened my mouth, even so, more to gape at her than answer her. I'd expected – cranberries, I don't know – threats, entreaties? She didn't want to writhe in the midst of Edwina's scheming any more than I did. Surely she'd want me to return, if only so there could be another shoulder to share the burden with!

Sallow against the darkening windows, she arched an eyebrow, watched my confusion with mild bemusement. Bemusement – and more shivering, until her teeth chattered against her glass. The square was quiet enough for me to catch the sound, shrill and insistent over the cobblestones between us.

It was her teeth that tugged me out of my stupor. Out under that gaping sky, with a tavern behind her and my new bright certainty throbbing in my gullet, it seemed the most natural thing in the world for me to dart up to her, unbutton my greatcoat and drape it over her shoulders.

"Rosamond – you – you're freezing! – I – look – shall we find somewhere more sheltered? – "

She blinked at me. I'd quite wrong-footed her. The greatcoat soaked up her black hair, left her face pallid and sharp and naked in the gloom.

"Rosamond?"

Her lip curled in a hasty smile. "Chwaerlet! This is the wrong way round, isn't it? I used to drape things about you, as a quivering infant."

To which, of course, I could only swallow – it was either swallow or burst into tears. I thought, involuntarily, of my sodden-faced slumber in the lambswool blanket, of the voice I'd conjured to accompany it: *cer di i gysgu nawr*. And now I had Rosamond – close, and attentive, and softer-voiced – as if my imagination had summoned the very sentiments out of her. Of course, she was still the Rosamond of 1893, with her gaunt face and her bloodshot eyes – I can hardly say that the moment prised her decadence from her like a glove – but there was something new in her features, and it wasn't entirely the languid disdain to which I had grown so smartingly accustomed.

She sighed, lifted one cold hand and pushed my fringe back. "Fear not. No colder than Rhossili in winter, eh? Shelter, though – *that* I can resoundingly agree to, if we can make one of these benches a bit less sodden. Care to attempt it?"

It might have been a dream, one of the hazy wistful dreams that lingered in the minutes after I'd woken. There we were, tipping the worst of the water off one of Checkley's outside benches – I had insisted upon the most surreptitious positioning their outdoor seating could offer, all too wary of yet more unexpected Septimian visibility – and perching on it, her knee sharp against mine through the chaotic tumble of her skirts, my greatcoat lolling from her shoulders. She was quite my sister, and quite someone else, in entirely the same instant.

"You cut your hair," she observed, almost hesitantly.

The smile twitched out of me before I could stop it. "I – erm – more or less. Not very well."

She tilted her head, quick as a magpie, to catch my eye, grinned right to her porcelain tooth the moment she had it. "I liked it, at any rate! That would have been quite the lark, wouldn't it, if I'd really chessed you all unknowing?"

"No it quite would not!"

She sniggered. "Septimus would never have forgiven me. Division Sergeant Septimus – ti a hi – you never did make things easy for yourself, did you?"

"What?" I felt myself frowning; I'd quite forgotten to ask. "You – erm – how do you know – have you met her before?"

She winked. "I haven't seduced her, if that's what you're asking. Only heard things. Next time we meet, I might actually be sober enough to tell you them."

"I – erm – next time?"

"Oh, yes." One sallow hand curled around my knee, rapped a jaunty minuet into the damp fabric of my skirt. "I knew I had a sister, bach, and I knew I practically raised her – but I had no idea I was raising anything half so exciting as a quaint little sapphist! And if you're really going to spend the rest of your life hiding from Eddie, well – when else am I going to see you, if not clandestinely?"

I swallowed. "You – erm – you quite didn't want to see me before – "

She sighed, grimaced – then flinched it away, raised up a teasing smirk instead. "The whims of a decadent, eh? The moment I can't see you, I suddenly want to! Seize the moment whilst we've still got it, and all that, even if it's just a matter of days. And you've only had that murderous ferret for Nettleblackian company – you must be in need of some variety. You're *definitely* going to need me, the way you're going. Getting an ody out of ody hi'n dy licio di is only going to be the beginning of it, if it's Septimus you're after – "

I ought to have pressed her – all well and good of me to conjecture this retrospectively, but even so! – on her first admission. The *whims of a decadent* was so much nonsense. There was something else perturbing her – some strange new threat haunting *seize the moment* and *a matter of days*, and if I'd turned the conversation back to it she may have given it to me. But – was it selfish to want to drive the conversation *on,* instead of backwards? Was it wrong to feel that warmth still scorching in my throat – and grasp towards it – and let the ominous secrets alone to be untangled another night?

"I – erm – I'm quite not after anyone! I just – she – she's very – as I said! – and when she – every time she touches my face I – erm – I just want to kiss her – "

"Every time?" she echoed, eyebrows soaring. "Fond of the caresses, is she?"

I crimsoned quite to my eartips. There'd be no stopping her now.

So I told her the lot. I've not the faintest how I managed to stammer half of it, and by the time I'd finished the sky was more grey than black, but I took all that I knew, and I gave it as much faltering voice as I was able. How it was to dart along beside Septimus, staring at her peculiar jumble of confidence and insecurity, brusqueness and gentleness. That first speech she'd given me, notebook in hand, her bright fierce excitement about being a Divisioner. Those flowers, proffered to me by accident, just around the corner from where we were sat. The way she looked onstage at the Dallyangle Theatre, outdazzling the performers and demanding the records, swaggering about in her trousers like the hero of some grand baroque opera. Her fingers on my cheek, trying to thumb away where Lady Miltonwaters had hurt me. The close darkness of Lorrie's hallway, her lips glancing against my fringe. That stunned, smiling offer to teach me how to cycle. The endless agonies of watching Nick Fitzdegu, and Mr. Adelstein, and even Lorrie himself, to make sure that none of them could claim to be her sweetheart. And, latest and most brilliant – the discovery that she wasn't stepping out with anyone – and the revelation that had followed it – and the truth of me, steadying my spine like my abandoned corset, put into words that I could understand.

Rosamond wasn't precisely a decorous listener. She snorted, and sniggered ("You were worried about the *men?*"), and sipped her water with sardonical intent. Once or twice she pinched my cheek, or squeezed my knee where she had it caught under her fingers. Even so – I'm inclined to think she was the best and only listener there could have been, on that frantic night. If she'd been grave, or disapproving, I quite don't know what might have happened to me. I was too fragile, too raw, to defend anything of my feelings – but, with her, I didn't have to. She clapped me on the shoulder when it was done, declared her ultimatum: I must make sure to sneak out and see her again soon, as surreptitiously as was necessary, and she would furnish me with her best advice.

Then the sky was grey in earnest, and she was drifting off across the square, her shoulders stark and bony again without my greatcoat to warm them. Then I was scrambling as softly as I could through the narrow back door, past heaped blankets and snoring bodies until I reached my bed. Now, it must be – figs, far too close to next morning's call-time – this morning's – at my feeble guess between chimes, somewhere vaguely approaching four o'clock?

I'm quite too delirious to sleep, but I ought to. Apart from anything else, if I sleep I might dream of Septimus.

And what of her? Too early to say – in every sense – but – across reception, in her office – perhaps with her hair loose – is it entirely audacious to wonder whether she might be thinking of me?

13.

IN WHICH RODENTS
DO NOT HELP MATTERS

Correspondence (from the past)

<u>*4th Dec, 1890*</u>

Edwina – can I ask you something? Thought it might be easier if I don't ask in person – there's no pressure – just all the time you need if you want to answer.

*

<u>20th January 1891</u>

Of course.

*

<u>*3rd March, 1891*</u>

What do you think of me?

*

16th April 1891

I esteem you more greatly than anyone I have ever known. Your good sense, kindness and tact is unmatched – certainly by comparison with mine – and our friendship is a bright spot amidst these bleak years. I do not know if that answers your question?

*

20th May, 1891

I'm not sure I've got good enough words for saying it too – but I feel the same! Everything you said! Your forthrightness – your drive – how much you care – your – just everything that's you, I suppose – I can't tell you how glad I am you wanted to start corresponding. And then start having tea. And then do both. And – all of it!

But there are things I want to check. You don't mind that I'm a tailor? That I grew up in an orphanage? That I've got no idea about this fortune stuff you have to deal with?

*

17th July 1891

I do not understand in what sense I am supposed to 'mind' these things. I can hardly not be conscious of our differences, but I do not see why they should alter my opinion of you. I concede that the persons with whom I am obliged to ingratiate myself may feel differently on the matter, and that I must proceed with caution – but, if I have learned nothing else from these years of toadying, it is that I am far less alike to them than even I suspected.

*

9th Nov, 1891

When you say you want to proceed with caution – what do you mean?

*

8th December 1891

I mean that, for all that I may struggle to decipher the social mores of those people, I cannot alienate them entirely yet – only, mind you, for the sake of my sisters. It was our parents' dearest wish that our family should marry up, and I do not want to be the reason the girls' opportunities are spoilt. Why should I deny them their prestige, their fine things, their good matches?

Although I fear any matches I could have made for Rosamond have been all but destroyed.

*

7th March, 1892

So – what? You think we're just going to have to – keep each other secret? What's the plan? I want Sept to meet you as soon as it's not going to strangle your reputation. I want – don't know if it's selfish, but – I want not to meet your sisters – definitely not Rosamond, because then we'd only end up with the family tailor yelling at her for wrecking all of your plans. But then if they're marrying up, I'm probably not going to meet them, am I?

And I want to wait. For you. I mean – as long as you need for juggling everything. I want to help you scheme us out of this tangle.

('Us'?)

*

4th April 1892

Us.

You are right to suppose that a plan has occurred to me – circumstances under which we will both be free to own our friendship. I fear it cannot be as immediate as I would like, but nor is it a vague and distant prospect. I shall explain:

Once my sisters are married, I am free to choose my company where I see fit. I am perfectly prepared to distance myself from Rosamond and Henrietta as much as is required to protect their reputations – a movement which will not be difficult, considering that the pair of them are determined to keep me at a distance as it is. I cannot imagine any aristocrat would go through the humiliation and hassle of a divorce simply because the estranged sister of his wife acknowledged her friendship with a tailor. And now that the law has changed, my sisters would have full control of their finances even after their marriages.

But at present, I am far too afraid to give my sisters financial control of anything. Rosamond has utterly destroyed her reputation, her health, and quite possibly her sanity. She would have destroyed her inheritance had I not kept it from her – she has burnt through enough of my money as it is. She has lost me my London circle – she all but lost me the friendship of Lady Miltonwaters. I am afraid that, if I attempt to push her further down the path towards matrimony, it will do nothing but harm Henrietta's chances.

And – in Henrietta's chances – there lies our hope. Henrietta has so far remained out of the disastrous proceedings. She can succeed where Rosamond has failed. And when she does, it will leave me free to meet your sister, and leave us free to do as we wish.

*

13th May, 1892

Sounds like a plan to me!

Also – I'm glad we've got the plan. For that – and for you – and for everything. I want to start on the endearments – but they all sound insane when you write them down. It feels almost like heckling to call you 'darling' on paper – and you're definitely not a 'pet'.

*

1st Aug, 1892

News – news – news – and it can't wait – do you want to know something fun?

*

<u>5th August 1892</u>

I would like that very much. Tell me everything.

*

<u>15th Aug, 1892</u>

Sept's not farmhanding after this harvest's done. She's got a new job!!!!

You know – you might not know – there's livestock going missing from the Skull farm? So some fancy woman's coming in to stop the thefts – and Sept's one of her employees! Well. At the moment it's just her and the woman's daughter and this gentleman from Pole Place, but still! Mrs. Ballestas – her husband's the apothecary – the Black family from London – Sept can't stop raving about her. They're a proper detective gang. Sort of. Except they're not part of the police. Or they – it's – Sept explains it better – Mrs. Ballestas wants it to be different – and the missing livestock's their first case, see if they can do it. And Mrs. Ballestas is paying Sept <u>fifteen shillings a week</u> – just as a starter salary!!!

We'll get that piano in... maybe less than a hundred years now?

*

<u>26th September 1892</u>

As I said: one day I will pass on my congratulations to your sister in person. I am only vaguely aware of what Mrs. Ballestas proposes to do. I confess I was sceptical – certainly Lady Miltonwaters does not think at all well of the idea. A body of watchmen – watchwomen – both? – that are not the police (nor apparently sanctioned by the police), created from the mind of one woman? But they seem to have done wonders, if the news reports are to be believed. Is it true that the town council is proposing to fund them? Lady Miltonwaters would never allow it, but the rest of them may yet out-vote her.

And on another matter: are you still saving for the pianoforte? Is there any way that I might tip you towards the necessary amount? What use is a family fortune, if not to obtain your sisters excellent marriages and your sweetheart an excellent musical instrument?

<u>14th Dec, 1892</u>

In haste – piano update –

The Ballestases are selling their old one. Panic not – Sept's offered to pay in instalments out of her salary – obviously I'll pay half what she's paying them.

*

21st December 1892

Lorrie, this is madness. I insist you let me at least contribute!

If you do not wish to take my money in the form of Christmas charity, I have provided an alternative, in the form of Lady Miltonwaters's finest evening gown (attached). You may note that the hem is damaged. This is my doing. I have promised to atone for my clumsiness by paying for the repairs. I would be obliged, therefore, if you would mend it at your earliest convenience – you will find advance payment in the envelope pinned to the sleeve.

Now – one way or the other – will you *please* purchase the pianoforte you have so desperately wanted for the last half-decade?

*

<u>11th Jan, 1893</u>

<u>You. Gem.</u>

Come to Eelpike Lane as soon as you can – I'm singing the thanks to you myself. My lodgings are all but empty, I should say – Sept's moving out. The Division's been given that old stables by the market, and she gets a room there. I'll miss her – not that I'm telling her, obviously. You should see her – she's never been so happy.

And you should also come and see a certain mighty musical instrument...!!!

Casebook of Matthew Adelstein

Pertaining to the Nettleblack affair

Oh, she will insist on making this a long game, won't she?

I can't be sure of Septimus. Ordinarily, she'll snatch at anything that might protect the Division – especially after her bizarre lapse of judgment two months ago – but her concession to her assistant's *suspicious* nature was begrudging at best. Will she search the dormitory for me? Best to assume the negative, and proceed accordingly.

And Harriet Nettleblack herself! Infinitely steelier (and infinitely more insane) than you'd imagine, this one! Not even the threat of discrediting her with Septimus appears to have dented her exasperating resolve to remain incognito. One could almost admire her for it, if the situation with the Division's reputation were not so precarious. Nicholas, soft-hearted and soft-headed as ever, suggested that we actually put that situation to her, in the deluded hope that her natural kindness will prevail, and she'll hand herself in for the sake of my dilapidated Division. Natural kindness! If Nettleblack cares for anyone besides Septimus, it's exclusively herself, and certainly not the sisters to whom she'd have to return. What, one wonders, can be so peculiarly appalling about this wretched family?

Fortunately, if Nicholas provides the softness in our partnership, I've never failed to provide the sense. I have devised an alternative means of searching the dormitory. It can't possibly offend Gertie Skull and her horde of relations, and it doesn't rely on Septimus, Nettleblack, the Director – or anyone, in fact, bar Nicholas. He's uneasy about it – of course he is – but he'll do it. As I told him last night, the Division is far too much at stake to indulge his scruples. He has been superficially acquainted with Nettleblack for all of fifteen minutes, whilst he and I – well – does five years count for so little?

I confess I came a shade too close to mournful discontent.

He diffused the unpleasantness as he usually does. I should have known better than to hurl that last remark at him. I'd recovered my composure sufficiently to apologise for it, but he'd already forgiven me by then, and sat stroking my hair for the next ten minutes. I had to tell him to stroke away from the parting again. I suspect he does the opposite deliberately – he has a ridiculous investment in disordering my hair.

But this hardly pertains to the Nettleblack affair anymore, does it?

I really ought to have demarcated this section, with all due chagrin, as 'pertaining to the most incongruously exciting thing to happen to Nicholas Shamil Fitzdegu since, apparently, anything whatsoever to do with me'. But Nicholas has seen my writing, asked for a translation, kissed my nearest eyebrow and told me not to be absurd (I paraphrase), and so it shall stand as it is.

I have been utterly beleaguered with tasks this week. There were the names of the Dallyangle Theatre's ticket register to consider, courtesy of Septimus, and the ensuing raft of interviews with everyone vaguely suspicious. This pursuit has been in equal parts useless and unpleasant – particularly with that idiot tenor playing the opera's lead, who offered nothing of any substance and spent the better part of the discussion attempting to shrivel me under a stone with his stare.

I was all too eager to throw over this fruitless work for an examination of the Division's ledgers, until I remembered that additional piece of paper collected the same day – the prose copied from *Life and Limbs*, that ridiculous romance novel so beloved of my partner. Having entirely forgotten both it and its odd attendant episode with the youngest Nettleblack, I determined to retrieve and examine the thing immediately. Nicholas was all too delighted to scramble in pursuit of the novel – *his* novel, I should say, seeing as he is the one feverishly intent on reading a chapter to me every night – so that I might compare the transcription with the printed version. But why should Nettleblack have tried to pretend the draft page was an anonymous letter?

More curiously still, the transcription turned out not to be a transcription at all. The punctuation was different, a few extra lines sat squeezed into the dialogue, and the crucial injury to be operated on had been scrawled over and amended three times, each new idea more lurid than the last. Nicholas gaped over my shoulder, every inch a tourist at an exhibition.

"Really!" he murmured, in unfeigned awe. "Can't believe Dr Stoker was only going to lose a thumb! The walkabout gangrenous hand's so iconic!"

I glanced up sharply. Need I remind him (as I did indeed remind him) that this bizarrely edited copying was the work of a mad heiress out to flummox me away from her patently obvious trail?

He snorted. "Even I don't believe *that*."

A point which, admittedly, I had to concede. Surely even 'Henry Hyssop' would have had the sense to write something even half the shape of a vicious letter?

Nicholas's hand scuttled into my hair, plucked gently at my scalp. "Is he doing it? Is Matty changing his mind?"

"I'll compare the handwriting," I snapped. I had every Division recruitment form crammed into those ledgers; Nettleblack would have been obliged to sign her name. "As she handed the paper directly to me, and no one else even mentioned that there had been another letter, I – there!"

Initially, idiotically, I almost smirked. The writing on 'Henry Hyssop's' form and that of the novel extract looked an impeccable, idiosyncratic match.

Nicholas gaped. "Henry wrote *Life and Limbs?*"

Wait. No. Too swift and too neat. The writing was a match, but the words – worshipful Nettleblack would never have referred to Septimus as a 'governess' or 'Javert' – and the additional signature at the conclusion –

Ah.

"It isn't her," I managed dazedly. "She only signs it. The bulk of the writing is Cassandra's."

"*Cassandra Ballestas* wrote *Life and Limbs?*"

Now Nicholas was all but shrieking. I stared at him warily.

"Is that – important?"

"Matty!" he cried, tugging me up from my chair and swinging us wildly about the drawing-room. I was not precisely of a mood to be swung wildly about the drawing-room, but his elation was too disconcerting to let me protest. "It's *brilliant!* You work with my favourite writer! I know the mysterious identity of the *Life and Limbs* literary lion! And you've solved the case!"

This was rather too far, and certainly too much alliteration. "If you'd kindly recall that this isn't the case? This isn't even a case! It's – I don't know – it's just the Director's daughter and her alternative pastimes – "

"*Just?* It's a whole novel! It's already sold out to its third edition!"

I rolled my eyes. "If she had written a novel about the indefatigable success of the Dallyangle Division, it would have been infinitely more useful to us."

Nicholas snatched for *Life and Limbs* on the chaise, still lost in his whirling celebratory world. "D'you think she'll sign it for me?"

"She has published it anonymously, if it truly is her work," I pointed out. "That would seem to suggest that she doesn't wish to take up the mantle of celebrity."

(Which did beg the question of whether the Director herself was aware of her child's sally into splattering fiction and silly novels?)

"I could be sneaky!" Nicholas insisted. "When we go to do the

Nettleblack thing – I'll be helping you carry all the Div ledgers back anyway – so I'll just – have the book with me too – just in case – "

Adorable fool. "Well. I suppose I can hardly stop you."

At which he kissed me and called me a darling, a tactic which was more than conducive to ensuring my indulgence. Beyond granting Nicholas a private autograph session, and internally congratulating Cassandra for a concealed work-ethic I had never imagined her possessing – and, I suppose, raising an eyebrow for her peculiar imagination – I didn't see what else I could *do* with the information. It was entirely possible Cassandra had confided her secret to Nettleblack – the latter is, after all, quite the receptacle for secrets. Though she clearly has no respect for anyone's privacy but her own.

Pertaining to other matters

No reply from Ma and Ta as yet. Probably for the best. It seems sensible to frame the whole case for them in retrospect: *yes, everything is perfectly well with the Division again, no need to fret about that. Oh, and there was a spot of business for Edwina Nettleblack – yes, those Nettleblacks – for which we were very handsomely paid. The fee's already gone on crucial repairs for the house – no, you can't visit yet – the repairs are still in progress – I'll visit you in Gulmere, as I always do.* Then the repairs can be in progress until at least the winter of 1894.

If it were only a matter of keeping Nicholas out of the house for a week whilst they dropped in! Lawrence Tickering and his apartment could surely be enlisted for Nicholas's temporary residence – Nicholas and he have always been cordial. It would all be perfectly fine (not that I much like the thought of leaving Nicholas to the strong-armed gentleness of an extraordinarily handsome lyric tenor), except that – it wouldn't. Nicholas *is* the house, as much as I am. Only a narcissistic fool like Nettleblack could believe that he actually sleeps in that attic. I have his knitwear and his blankets tumbling off every surface outside of the receiving rooms, including our four-poster, even if all of that must be carefully rearranged each morning before the butler arrives for the day. You can't go five steps in any direction without dislodging a rat from somewhere. *Life and Limbs*, soon to be autographed (strange day it's been), follows us both around the house, broken-spined over chaise-arms and side-tables. And – most unshakeably of all – his tobacco. I ought to encourage him to break the habit, but the scent has become impossibly comforting.

Nicholas has reappeared in the doorway, still beaming with his new brace of secrets. Might he prevail upon me (I paraphrase him)

– he wants a second eye to proofread his latest piece for the Rodent's Gazette? And now he smirks; he wonders what I can possibly still be writing. And now –

And now, on penalty of having my hair stroked in a counter-productive direction forevermore, I'm instructed to inform my casebook that Matty Adelstein (he insists I don't paraphrase the nickname) shan't be working after-hours tonight, not if Nicholas Fitzdegu can help it. Very well, then – the rodent-charming siren's going to switch from kissing to nibbling my ear in a moment – let the rest wait until tomorrow.

***Septimus's notebook (kept in a shorthand which she assures me is
entirely of her own invention)***

I've got to do it.

It ain't for Mr. Adelstein. Short of me coming up against one of
those letters in Henry's handwriting, he's not to know this ever
happened. Yes. No? No. It's for me. For my own – conclusion. I was
about to say benefit, but what's it to me if she turns out a traitor? I
didn't pick her. I just did the best I could with the orders I got given
– and that's as far as my responsibility goes. Yes?

Well! Why should I get invested?

Beyond protecting the Div, of course.

And – because it's Henry.

And it's just a precaution to actually search her things. She said it
weren't true. She said it, and then I thought I'd killed her just getting
that confession. And Adelstein might be the detective, but he didn't
see her then. She was stiff as a corpse, and she couldn't breathe, and
all the colour'd gone out of her lips. You couldn't feign that. You
couldn't.

So that's all it is. Making sure.

The Div's hushed as a church. Usually is at five-thirty in the morning
– even the Director's not in yet. Never even had to train myself to
wake up at this hour. I caught the knack of it when I was about seven
years old (seven-ish) – more or less six-and-twenty now and I ain't
lost it yet. If I could manage an early rise, it gave me a mort of time
to sneak over to the boys' block and pick my way to Lorrie for a chat,
before any of the matrons woke to stop me.

I snatch for my uniform the moment I'm off the mattress. Easy
enough when you sleep under your office desk. (Lorrie thinks I've got
a room to live in at the Div – in a way, he ain't wrong.) Only one taper
lit this morning – Henry had the right of it keeping the lights dim
last night. No point wasting resources. It's fuel we'll need now, not a
glut of light. Everything's cold, cold and getting colder. My papers're
stiff with chilly damp. Paperweighting on top of 'em, my notebook's
pages curl between their covers, like they're huddling for warmth. The
inkwell's frozen solid, glossy and heavy as a pebble. There must be a
way to stop it doing that. Just – maybe not this side of December.

Hair. There I've got to pause, though the urge to dash across
reception and have done with it sets my fingers shaking on my jacket

buttons. The whole Div'd notice if I let my chignon slip. Besides –
why should I let it slip? There's naught amiss with me. Out of the
plait, down my back for one hundred strokes, up in the pins – clockwork. Penniless orphans don't tend to get hair like a fashion-plate.
Not that I own any fashion-plates – and I ain't about to start wearing
that sort of stuff either. But it's like jamming on a helmet when
you trick your hair up fancy. Armour, more or less. No one's getting
through that to peer at your thoughts, or guess who you are, or sneer
at what you've been ('less they're Cassandra, and they've got all your
records in their books). Point is, it's good hair, and I know what to do
with it, and there's a mort of bolstering in the routine of it. And as
long as I'm flaunting it, the Sweetings ain't won. They'd give limbs
to get hold of it. They've tried.

And they got Henry's hair. It ain't the first time since meeting her
I've wondered about it, but even so: what was she *doing*, wandering
round the streets at midnight, done up in those mad expensive
clothes, the ripest target you've ever seen?

My teeth're in my lip. Before six-thirty's struck, I may yet get an
answer.

'Course I want an answer! It's my job, ain't it?

The dormitory's all bare floorboards, and the floorboards creak like
anything. Not usual I'm in here trying *not* to wake 'em up. I won't be
doing that 'til six, and the reception clock's still wobbling on five-
fifty. The candles're out, and the drapes – bit too fancy a word, when
they're really just spoilt bolts – are still tacked up over the windows,
but there's enough freezing gloom through their moth-holes to
squint by. And I've got my taper, though my shivering hand won't
stay still with it, and the wax keeps dribbling onto my knuckles.

I'm glad I never slept in here. Far too much like – well – like the one
in the orphanage, with those plain plastered walls and wrought-iron
bedposts. Gertie Skull's got her lambswool blanket, though – and I
can't say I ain't glad of the texture. Without that softness, it'd be too
easy to picture a matron lurking at the end of the room. *And what
d'you think you're doing out of bed at this hour, you sullen little wretch?*

There's a weird smell on the air. Spiky. Musky. The sort of thing
you'd slap a name on straightaway if you knew what the name was.
The room was a stable once, so it ain't improbable a bit of its old
scent's crept up from the cracks in the floor –

And then these thoughts parcel themselves up and drop back
into their box, because I'm stood over Henry's bed, and it's that first
morning of her all over again.

There's my gasp, sharp and cold on my teeth.

I tug in my lip and bite down hard, 'til I can trust myself to breathe silently. It's just – she looks like a kind of sprite when she's asleep, all the more so when you see her by shaky candlelight. She's curled up like one of my bookpages, her squirrel-brown hair tangling into her pale face. If I dipped my free hand and touched her – just there, where her cheekbone starts under her eyes – it'd be like bringing a sculpture to life. I flush to think it, but I want to. When you touch her, all you can feel's her heartbeat, rising frantic to the surface of her skin.

I touched her there last night, didn't I? And she stared at me with those darting green eyes. And I damn near fell into 'em.

'Course that only makes me colour more.

She'd laugh, if she could see me. If she could hear what's in my head. She'd take in my admiration – though that word can't hold the half of it – and she'd cut it in two with a shrill little giggle, and she'd not be the first. Or she'd just run, scramble out of the Div like a rabbit – when you want to see 'em, but you snap a twig with your foot, and they skitter away from your clumsiness before you can get close.

Wouldn't she?

She twists onto her back. She's sleeping in her shirt now. Can't blame her. Shirts get issued with the uniforms, proper warm collarless things. This one's sallow next to Henry's skin. She's so pallid she's almost blue, like a starling's egg. Her, and the shirt, and the bedsheets – so many shades of pale, but only one of 'em's got a pulse, flickering in her neck –

But that ain't pale, that hard-edged lump jutting out from inside the pillowcase, where her head just was. I slide my spare hand under the linen, ease it out, hold it up to the taper. It's a book, thick-spined and heavy, dark foresty green at the covers, inkblots on the page-edges.

I'm a Divisioner, not a spy, I'd said. But here I am, sneaking round and staring out a notebook thrice the size of mine. Turning the thing in my hand. More terrified of it than I'd like to admit.

It's a proper investment, too. The sort of thing you'd get if you'd a mind to write a lot. It must've cost a fair bit. Leather-bound, soft – so soft it's at my cheek – get it down, damn you! Open it!

Scores and scores of tiny letters inside, in thick seamless ink or scratchy pencil. I lift it close again, raise the candle, squint hard. I know my letters, whatever Cassandra'd smirk – but this writing's nothing like the neat dull hand we all got taught. Here's dates, every so often, topping some of the pages. A journal? Lot of effort, to keep a journal here – and these entries are pages and pages long, the sort of page-span you can grab and hold stiff between finger and thumb.

I'm frantic. More frantic than I'd like. Slapping the pages over with my thumb, skimming the cramped little paragraphs. There must be a word – a sentence – anything – something I can make out.

There! Splayed on a half-empty page, finishing off an entry. The book topples open of its own accord. There's the faded dregs of a flower, sunk into the paper like a cranefly's wings. No – it's more than one flower. It's the paltry bundle of Lorrie's off-cuts, the one I ended up throwing at her. I wince every time I remember that, for her shock, for how stupid I must've looked –

But she's kept 'em, even so.

Does it twitch me to a smile? Alright – fine – yes, it does.

But – that ain't all of it. There's a thicket of words around the flowers, then the thicket breaks off, and the next sentence starts out clear on the creamy paper.

In short – I may well be duelling Mr. Adelstein for my life, but –

Half a snarl behind me, Gertie Skull clears her throat.

I spin. I'm too deep in Henry's writing not to be startled, and too startled not to show it. Gertie's sat up against her metal headboard, looking a mort more morose than usual. Knees curled to her chest, eyes red, lashes sticky and clumped. It scares me – as much as her having seen any of this – that I didn't hear her move, not even a creak of the bedframe.

I try to swallow again, just get bile. She – she! – has her lips pursed with disapproval, as if she's got any right to disapprove of me.

The blood scratches in my face. She's got every right, damn it.

"Put it back," she whispers – she's soft-voiced, but steely at the edges – "and I won't tell her. Don't, and I'll tell the Director."

My mouth drops open. *She'll* tell – when all she ever does is break the rules – !

But she'd still do it. And the Director'd not look kindly on me scheming with Mr. Adelstein without consulting her. And Henry'd find out.

And if this gets back to Adelstein, he'll make Henry leave.

Assuming she ain't run for the hills already.

I grit my teeth. I want to snatch Gertie's plait and throttle her with it. I want none of this to ever've happened. I want to be back in my office, or out on a bicycle, not stood here getting scolded –

"Quick now, Sarge," Gertie adds. "Don't want to wake her."

I'm too furious to speak. The journal snaps shut in my hand, louder than I'd meant it to. Then it's back where it was, and I'm storming for the door, the taper blown clean out, with Gertie's eyes jabbing me in the neck. I slam it, hard. They can wake up now, for all I care!

Henry ain't against the Div. She said so. She'd not lie.

Then why's she duelling Mr. Adelstein for her life?

Staggering away from the dormitory door, I can't think of anything else. Not that thinking about *this* sharpens it into any sense. Might be easier to concentrate in my office, maybe. Yes. That's the place to lay the thoughts out, flatten 'em into neat rows until everything comes clearer. Back to the office, then, before anyone sees. Before Gertie Skull changes her mind and chases you for an explanation. Before Henry wakes up.

There's a hiss on the air, a sudden snag of breath. It catches my feet and pins me to the spot, however suspicious that must look. There's someone in reception where there weren't just now, and they're watching me. *She's* watching me. Cassandra, early at her desk. Still in her cape, and that mad long scarf Gertie knitted for her. Five hundred snipes in her head for me, no doubt. Staring.

No. Wait. Sobbing.

What?

If she can gape at me, I can do it to her. She's turned on the gaslights, lit herself up for scrutiny in the doing. Her hat's only just come off, and her hair's not yet settled, thickety curls damp and stuck to her freckles. Damp with tears, same as her eyelashes. Deep brown eyes, nothing of her mother's gold, wide with shock. Shaking hands. Not a word in her parted lips.

Say something? Give her space?

"You alright?" I manage feebly.

'Course it's only after I say it that I spot how stupid it is. She knows it too. She blinks, sniffs, rolls her eyes like each pupil's got a weight to it.

"With those deductive skills, Javert, you could be Matthew Adelstein."

Fine. You don't want my friendly. You never do. "I was just trying to help."

She groans. Hands up to scrub at her eyes, to push the wet curls away. "Of course you were. So perfectly perfect, even when you're not perfect."

"What?" – and it's as much a genuine question as it is something snappish to say. She's the last person in the Div to think well of me. Ain't she always said so?

"That's what you are, isn't it?" she mutters. Her voice prickles, spasming off another sob. "Mother plucks you out of some farmer's harvest and you do everything right, and she's never stopped relishing it. Oh, of course it was a productive idea to cultivate Septimus – " – she's smoothing her words now, a genteel sham of the

216

Director – " " – and she's the walking proof, all the proof of *Keturah St. Clare Ballestas*'s genius that her own daughter never gets to be! And even when you wreck everything and turn the town against us – she still brings you back! She still believes in you!"

I blink at her. I don't know what else to do. Henry's duelling Mr. Adelstein, and now Cassandra's yelling at me, too furious to stick to mockery. Every edge of the Div, toppling inwards, like someone's thwacked a house of cards.

"I – look, I don't – I ain't proof of anyone's – "

"She won't do that for me, though," she snaps. There's a bleak smirk to it, and it ain't directed at me. "I'm a Ballestas. I'm not allowed to get it wrong."

No more mysteries this morning. I frown, jut her the question as gently as I can manage – "When'd you ever get it wrong?"

"I haven't!" She's at a shout, inkstained hands crumpling to fists. "And even if I had, I'd deal with it!"

Between my slam and her scream, of course we've got the Div paying attention. There's a scuffling behind the dormitory door – that'll be Gertie, skidding over to eavesdrop. Worse than that's the scrape of the doors behind me – the front doors – and the slap of cold across my shoulders. I've no choice but to turn. The Director's a stark figure against the misty gloom, hollow under the eyes, glowering between Cassandra and me with a look that'd chasten the Sweetings.

"I do hope that this is a productive discussion," the Director declares, prodding at our sudden stiff silence. "Not another unhelpful slanging-match."

I wince. Getting caught arguing with Cassandra's only slightly better than getting caught spying on Henry's journal. Even so – she started it. She can damn well explain it. Spinning some fancy words, she'll like that.

"It's fine, Mother." Not her fanciest, but there ain't a scrap of sob left in her voice. "Everything's fine. Javert was just – I mean, God knows what Javert was doing – "

"What are you doing, Septimus?"

God's sake!

I dart Cassandra a glare, and I get one back. "Nothing. Just waking up the Div."

"I see." The Director glances from Cassandra to me, narrow-eyed above her spectacles. Whatever she's worked out, she ain't letting on. "Very well. Take Miss Hyssop and concentrate on searching the towpath today. Once we've checked every bit of the bank for the head, we can start dredging the river."

I nod. Safest option. Back behind the desk, Cassandra twitches. Her ink-spattered fingers tip to nails on the wood.

"And – Cassandra, are you sure nothing is wrong?"

She'll have to say it now. Whatever it is. If she's done something, the Director'll get it out of her. I'm watching her too, mind simmering a few theories. Has she wrecked the ledgers? Bought us the secret mouse-destroying animal? Written some mocking lyrics about Mr. Adelstein on the paperwork he's currently reading? Broken some bit of the building (everyone's done that) and hoped no one'd notice?

But she's fixing herself into a taut painful smile. Straight up through her spine, perfect corset posture, bracing herself.

"Of course nothing's wrong. Not for a Ballestas, eh?"

The Director frowns. A tight little glance at me. I drop my gaze fast. She must think my evasiveness's something you catch if you talk to me, that I've gone and infected her daughter with it.

If she brings me and my secret into this – *now*, of all mornings – with Henry to face at half past –

"Well." The Director clears her throat, and I risk a glimpse. She's looking at Cassandra, and her voice's brisk. "Good. Tell Gertrude that she's to go out with Millicent and her brother, would you?"

Cassandra nods, frightened and quick. For a moment, we're all outstaring the floor. The Director sighs, stalks straight through the silence. Past us both, down the corridor, into her office. Everything I should've just done.

But I can't pretend I didn't see any of it. Even if it's bloody Cassandra.

"You ain't telling her, then?" I mutter.

Cassandra arches an eyebrow. Now her mother's gone, the fear's crumbling off her face. "Familiar strategy, isn't it?"

'Course there's no way I can answer that.

"Thought so," she hisses. Already she's shoving past me. Every word flung back over her shoulder, sharper and sharper. She's fixing herself, ready for the day, and I'm the whetstone. "Now, if you'll excuse me from the impromptu interrogation, Javert, there are logs that need fetching, things that need scribbling, and generally everything in the world that needs doing except talking to you."

And she's gone, stomping out to the log-shed, before I've got a retort.

Half an hour later, and the Div looks a bit closer to normal. I stalked outside the moment Cassandra got back in, grabbed the earliest of the market-stalls, bartered for breakfast as long as I could stretch it out. It's busier in reception when I come back – and everyone's got their usual faces pinned in place. Cassandra's stoking the wood-burner like her life's fastened to its grate. No one looks aslant when I drop the dead taper behind the desk. It ain't raining – that's something – but there's frost on the windowpanes, and it's slippery at the door if you ain't careful. The apprentices – Gertie, Millicent, Oliver, all but Henry – go skidding into the doorframe, grabbing for a hold, yelling when the hinges catch their fingers. Odd-coloured fingers, stiff with the cold. Their faces're much the same. Mine must be too.

And Henry's. She's never known the Div in a better season. Late spring, when we moved in, that's when the building stops feeling cold, and high summer gets the thick old walls on our side, keeps us shady and serene while the market melts. That said – it ain't just seasons. She picked the worst week in our history to join up, between the weather and the cases and the public and all the wretched subterfuge. I'm stunned she ain't walked out yet, even if she's never known the place any different.

And – alright, yes. I'm impressed. Everything we've chucked at her – everything I've done – and she's still here. Turns up every morning, regular as you like. Sneaks off like a maniac on a mission and tries to guess her way round a bicycle. Sticks at it. Sticks with me.

Sort of.

"Septimus?"

Henry shivers across reception, her hair curling odd at the ears, her face wincing in a nervous smile. Her skin's exactly the colour of Mr. Adelstein's best china, the stuff Nick says he ain't allowed to touch without a carpet under him –

Mr. Adelstein. Him that she's duelling for her life.

"Morning," I manage, a bit too stiffly, chucking a bacon roll at her. She blinks. Worried little eyebrows creased in the middle. She must think I'm upset with her about last night. "Trust you slept well."

Why won't it come out right? Why do I sound so bloody stern?

"Oh – I – erm – quite – "

Her favourite word. I swallow, though it ain't a natural one, and it makes my throat scream. If that forces my voice softer, so much the better. "Well. Yes. Good. Shall we?"

She nods. Then just stares. Wide-eyed, intent, like she's waiting. She's right to force it out of me, however much I smart for it. I can't pretend last night didn't happen, and she's my assistant – I'm the one that's meant to bring it up.

"I hope you're feeling better," I hear myself stammer. "After – well. Hard night. Didn't mean to – y'know. Yes. Sorry. For – yes. All of it. Yes."

"Oh!" She blushes, in that quick elegant way of hers, straight across the cheekbones. Drops her gaze, too – which is good. Gives me a moment to scowl back some self-control. "I – no – of course – I – erm – I didn't mean to – either – "

Then she glances up again. Pulse twitching in her throat, where it starts out over the red collar. Expectant – she don't know what to say next, so she's deferring to me. As if I know any better than her!

"That's settled, then!" I declare, brisk as you like. Keturah Ballestas to the life, I must be – nice crisp endings for weird conversations. I'm lying through my teeth, but if she stares at me like that for much longer I'll end up just as speechless as her. "Right! We're looking for a head on the towpath today! Yes!"

We don't talk much on the job. Ain't like we usually do, when it's too cold to keep your thoughts straight. The big exception'd been – and we're back there now, the very street, where the latticed windows hang close overhead and the puddles've frozen between the cobblestones – that row on the way to Mr. Adelstein's. Well. We ain't repeating that today. I steer us away from Pole Place, out onto the towpath. Set us to tracing footprints and peering down the riverbank – anywhere you could chuck a head if you'd a mind to get rid of it. Something's churned up the muddy path, and the chill's stiffened the streaks and bruises in place. The mud don't even dent when you step on it. The river's more sluggish than normal, crusting frosty at the edges. Soon enough, it'll just be ice. The sky's beaten the river to it – it's already the colour that ice'll be, low-hanging and solid, a sky to crack your head on.

All the while, I can't wrestle my mind off that journal. *I may well be duelling Mr. Adelstein for my life* – and if she's duelling the detective, I'm on her side. Why's it that I don't even hesitate before I know that? Adelstein ain't a villain. He's part of the Div. The Director ain't got much by way of male allies – so we need to keep him. He's good at his job, too. Never known him to be wrong before, not so wrong that every keen edge of me yells out to stop him.

But he *is*. And if he is – what then? Henry's definitely writing something, and it's definitely against him. She didn't write any of those letters, but there is something she ain't telling me, and –

And what if I find it out, and it's worse even than the letters, and it don't change a thing of my feelings? What if she's the most callous criminal the town's ever known, and I'm still desperate to keep her in the Div – and teach her cycling – and touch her cheek?

I wouldn't be. Not then. Not if it were that bad. Case in point – it'd be like Property. Did it before and I can do it again. Easy enough to switch to hate, when they don't give you another choice.

"Figs!"

I skid about. It's like Henry's thrown the word round my neck, tugged it taut and the air out with it. Where the hell are we? How long's it been? How've I lost track – again? –

The market square. It's just the market square. We're back. Late-morning – there's the church chimes over my shoulder thwacking it out – and trade's in full swing. Jellied eels ain't selling today – it's too cold for 'em. Frost on the awnings, greying the colours. All the bright colours of the vegetables shoved under hessian covers. Queues round the block for hot pies, the shop door the only warm spot in the square. Geese escaping, sacking wrapped round their webbed feet.

Lorrie's corner's empty, but for a heap of discarded wooden boxes. What?

There's a knot in my gullet. I dart my head about, as if looking'll drag Lorrie back to his usual haunt, but my every twitch only tugs the knot tighter. I ain't even the only one looking. That's his boss twisting through the crowd, grabbing at elbows, frowning and asking.

But we haven't – the Director promised me we wouldn't. No one's done anything about Property's stupid claims. He ain't a proper suspect for the Head-Hider, not really –

But – whatever Cassandra's done, whatever she's not telling us – what if it's – what if she's gone for him?

Plan, damn it! You've got time! Get to his flat. Henry won't mind. Check on him. Could be anything else. Could be perfectly innocent. Some weird-timed meeting with his sweetheart, maybe. Or he's just overslept –

What's Henry playing at?

I've already started us three stabbing paces towards Lorrie's, but she ain't moved. She's frozen as the puddles, her porcelain face fast fading the same greyish colour.

Lorrie – but I can't leave her in this state. Follow her gaze instead. Ahead of it, there's the Ballestas governess, that corpselike girl straight out of a ghost story. She's loitering by the Div doors – there *again?* Don't she eat? – watching us 'til her eerie green eyes just about gleam. But – no – it ain't her Henry's spotted. It's the doors themselves. Still swinging, like someone's just strode through 'em.

Mr. Adelstein. It has to be.

Keep Henry away from him, then. Go to Lorrie's with her.

But if he's come to try searching a second time – and he finds that journal – and he makes out more of it than I could –

"Time to go back," I hear myself blurt. Then I'm shouldering head-long through the market, through geese and shawls and shivers. At my elbow, Henry's sprinting to keep up.

Through the swinging doors, the Div's a riot. All the commotion's melted the frost. It's hot now, unexpectedly so. Cassandra's got the burner throbbing away, and left it open-doored to blaze while she holds the fort. When I stride in, she's stood up behind the desk, fists balled tight on the wood, Gertie's present-scarf still dangling from her neck, a giant stack of ledgers tottering beside her. Our ledgers, all the ones Mr. Adelstein borrowed. Adelstein himself's in the middle of the room, standing stiff and stupefied as a wax doll. Nick's by his shoulder, with a good twenty rats in his basket.

Henry's at my side. Don't have to look at her to know she's on edge. Light at my ear, there's the terrified gasp of her breath.

"I told you, and Mother's told you – there's no need to search the place again!" Cassandra's snapping. She's flushed under her freckles, and it ain't just the wood-burner's warmth. "You've already gone through our paperwork!"

Nick flings her a feeble grin, fumbling in his basket for something. Some book, smaller than the ledgers, though he can't get it out quick enough to flash its spine, not with half the rats of a mind to gnaw it. "Speaking of paperwork, actually – Cassandra – I've got your – I mean, I was wondering if you – "

"Later, Nicholas!" Mr. Adelstein sets his teeth. "Cassandra, I do not require any more paperwork. I simply wish to search the dormitory. I assume permission has been obtained from its inhabitants?"

"No it ain't!"

I've blurted it before I can think. Adelstein darts his head around like he's caught a scent, and then he's glowering me out. It's impatient, exasperated, smacks of our conversation. *Duty.* I was meant to've spared him this.

"Septimus?"

I jerk my chin up. Defiant as I can get it. I never said I'd do anything for him.

"Mr. Adelstein. Can't believe you've got us agreeing, but Cassandra's right. No more searching the Div."

Mr. Adelstein wrings out a sigh. This time, his glare's almost petulant. He knows I'm stalling, he must do. Over his head, I grab Cassandra's eyes, shove my whole plan into a frantic stare –

Do what we did earlier. Raise our voices. Draw out the Director.

"I'm afraid this is an urgent matter," Adelstein snaps. "Surely the apprentices will understand."

"The Division Sergeants don't," Cassandra retorts, lifting her voice to stage-pitch. "You haven't even explained what you're looking for."

She's right. He ain't so much as looked at Henry. If he'd not told me he was after her – if she'd not told me, out of her journal – you'd be hard-pressed to guess it from his face.

"If you tell us," Cassandra adds, all but a shout, "We can help! Or perhaps the Director – in fact, I'll call her now – "

He pinches me on another scowl. "There's no need to call your mother, Cassandra. Division Sergeant Septimus is perfectly aware of my business, and doubtless more than happy to explain it to you."

God's sake! If he meant to divide and conquer us, he's done it! 'Course saying *that* – that way round, and her rank left off – that'll be the very thing to sling her straight back into hating me!

And she's glowering across my face now. So much for an alliance. All our vague plan, all that unshouted shout for the Director, dripping discarded from her every word. "Oh. Well. If you really do know everything, do *deign* to enlighten me, Javert."

I stiffen my shoulders. Voice – quick – steady it out. New plan.

Wait. That works!

"Mr. Adelstein asked me to search the dormitory yesterday. He wants suspicious writing – "

"Anything written down, in fact," Mr. Adelstein interrupts, "However innocuous it may seem. Or anything hidden, out of the ordinary – "

"There isn't any suspicious writing!" Cassandra bursts out furiously. "I told you, you've seen all the writing! There's nothing else here!"

"Look – Mr. Adelstein – shall I just check now?" Before I end up wringing his neck, or before Cassandra ends up wringing mine. "You can wait here. I'll do a once-over. Does that work?"

Cassandra's got a mind to kill me with a glare. I can see her snarls from earlier smarting back onto her face. *So perfectly perfect!*

But Adelstein frowns. He's got no clue what I'm thinking. Good.

Then – swift as anything – he pinches Nick a look, a nod. Nick blanches. It turns his skin grey as the windows.

"An admirable compromise," Mr. Adelstein declares, clasping his hands together. "Mr. Fitzdegu and I shall remain here for as long as it takes – "

Now, only now, he pretends to notice Henry. "And your assistant. She'll wait, too. Hyssop, is it?"

They're all looking at her, so I risk it too. She's shivering, thin hands clinging to her elbows. The ink starts out on her fingertips. There's anger in her face beside the fear, there in the sharp line of her mouth.

Don't worry, I want to hiss at her. *I'll hide the journal. He won't get you.*

'Course I can't say a thing.

"Quite," she hurls back at him. Little dagger of a word.

Right.

I stalk past 'em all, slide the door open. The dormitory drapes are down, the candles out, the light stale and turgid. Not a problem. I can close the door behind me. Then it's just me, and the journal, and getting it somewhere Adelstein can't see it. But what if Henry's moved it? What if he does something to Henry, when I'm in the dorm, and I ain't there to stop him? What if the Director turns up while I'm flat-out disobeying her? What if Cassandra calls her in to spite me?

I glance back. I'd meant to look at Henry – though what I'd planned to do with my face I can't say – but there's something else to stare at. Mr. Adelstein – he's nudging Nick hard in the ribs – and then the rats are plummeting out of his basket, squeaking as they scrabble to the floor. Nick starts forward – sweeps with his arms, like he's planning to pick 'em up – but it only drives 'em forward, scurrying over my boots, 'til they've furzed into the dormitory like so many mothballs.

"I'll get the rats!" Nick cries, staged as you like, and dives head-long past me. Slams the door at his back. Vanishes.

Bloody coward!

Henry gasps, but Cassandra's quicker. "Adelstein! He can't just – "

Mr. Adelstein straightens his tie. It didn't even need straightening.

"If you wish to go and assist him in collecting up those tempestuous rodents, you're at perfect liberty to do so. I wouldn't want any of his rats tearing holes in *my* clothes, but perhaps you think yourself and your uniform of a stronger constitution."

"You landlord for the rats, don't you?" Cassandra snarls. "You planned this! Haven't you done enough already, with your searches and your ledger-snatching? Can't you just out and *say* it – or leave me alone?"

"Cassandra!"

Damn it. It's the Director, minutes too late to fit any plan. Her office door wallops shut behind her, and then she's scowling us out. Freezing-stared. Enough to smother all the heat of the burner.

"That," – and her voice's as deadly as her gold eyes – "is hardly an acceptable tone to take with the Division's detective."

"He's searching the dormitory!" Cassandra blurts. Fear's clearly snuck up on her, but she's not burnt through her fury yet. "After you told him not to!"

The Director flicks her gaze to Mr. Adelstein. He's still watching the dormitory door, as slack and complacent as he'll ever look, waiting. Waiting for Nick to find the journal.

"Matthew, what is the meaning of – ?"

Then there's a shriek – and ain't it a *shriek* to kill all shrieks!

It sets the dormitory door rattling, bursts out from under the frame like swept dust. We start – Adelstein and the Director and Cassandra and me – and skid about, as if the door's about to give us an answer. Behind it – not just shrieks, but crashes – groans – the bedframes dragged about, scraping on the floorboards – weird little yowls – squeaks – and Nick's voice atop the lot, yelling like a lunatic –

Henry. She's the only one of us not to jump. She's frozen in place. And she don't look even slightly astonished, just – despairing.

"Sweet plums," she whispers dazedly. "I – oh – not again – "

The door thwacks the very plaster off the wall. It's a volley – of Nick, bloodied and half-deranged, scooping up rats, stepping on rats, rats clinging to his shoulders and his shirtsleeves and his stripy trousers. Beyond Nick, there's blood – more blood – splattered on the floor round Henry's bed. One dead rat's sprawled on the sheets. No. Not so much *dead* as *torn limb from limb* – it's just bits of rat now, fur and tail and innards. Lording over its pieces, there's – there it goes – leaping off the bedframe – one pale shivering sprint – out down the aisle – out towards us –

The little killer hurtles straight into Henry's arms. It's a ferret. A white ferret, bloody-furred, red at the eyes. Snarling. All teeth.

Henry blinks up at us helplessly.

This'd be Adelstein's moment, if he wanted to take it. He could dash into the dormitory – he knows which bed it is now – while we're distracted. He could snatch the journal and hide it in his great-coat. He could be out before we noticed him go in.

He doesn't. He clasps an arm round Nick's shoulders, and he yells spitting blue murder up into the Director's flabbergasted face.

"What the devil do you mean by keeping beasts like that in the Division, Ballestas? Nicholas could have been killed!"

She swallows. I'd defy even her to calm down this situation. "Well – "

"Persimmons!" Henry cries. "I – you – there was quite no – he couldn't have *died!* The ferret – he just – he doesn't – he means well – he's never – erm – he's not done anything – well – anything worse to a human than biting off a finger!"

"A *finger?*"

Mr. Adelstein's livid – livider than the rat's guts – shunting Nick behind him. "And you countenance this, Director?"

Quick as patter, the Director's gaze whirls about to me. "Septimus?"

It'd be stage-perfect if I turned to Henry now, spluttered out *Hyssop?*

I can't. There's only one thing I can say, and even that sticks in my throat.

"I – I didn't know!"

"I'm resigning," Mr. Adelstein blurts. *Is* it Mr. Adelstein? This ain't like him, this slick-haired changeling with Nick gasping in his arms. He ain't impetuous. I've never known him make a snap decision. Never – *never* – seen him get angry. What the hell's done this to him? "As of today. You can find your persecutor on your own – you can hunt down the Head-Hider on your own – all of it! I come here to help you – and I'm insulted, threatened, obstructed, whilst trying to complete an investigation expressly designed to protect this organisation – and now that stammering slattern's familiar tries to slaughter my lodger and his rats!"

The Director's jaw drops. Pure sympathy, my own goes with it.

"Matthew, I – I can assure you that no offence was meant, and – and – " – she, Keturah Ballestas, *she's* scrabbling – " – and I must offer you my profound apologies for the – "

"You can't just quit!"

It's Cassandra, sprinting round from the desk, leaping to the Director's side. Fastest I've ever seen her move.

"Mother's done everything for you! You were a country boy playing at Sherlock Holmes before she took you on! And this isn't her fault – it isn't anyone's fault – so don't you shout at her!"

"I would reflect on your own ingratitude before you snarl at mine, Cassandra," Mr. Adelstein spits. "I presume you haven't told your impeccable mother about your penchant for publishing sordid *comic romances?*"

It strikes Cassandra like a slap. The Director's twisting about, dazed, staring – and her daughter's all but slumping to the floor. "I – I – "

He ignores her. "Nicholas, we must get you back to our house at once. You're hurt – the blood – your hand – "

Nick gasps a snivelling breath. "It's nothing, Matty – Henry – "

Henry starts. She thinks – fair enough – that he means her. But it ain't that. Nick's gazing back into the dormitory, back to where those bits of rat are strewn over her bed, with a look that'd keep a man in mourning for a decade.

The bloody *rat!*

Mr. Adelstein gives him a gentle nudge, and he sprints back in before any of us can stop him. He wraps up his rat in the top bedsheet – right nerve he's got, to take it! – and drips out like a mute. Past us, too shaken to look at us, out into the cold. Adelstein fires back one last filthy look, and then he's gone too.

"My office," the Director snarls into the silence. "All of you. Now."

No one starts. No one knows where to start, and I can't stand it. Most times I've been in this room, glaring over this desk with my hands folded at my back, I've always known how to begin. Sometimes it's a new plan for chasing something up. Sometimes it's about the bicycle. Sometimes Mr. Adelstein's sent a message, and I'm delivering it. Back before the last two months, it was congratulations, promotions, cycling proficiency, you name it. Don't matter which. There's always an opening. Even if I'm fighting a dressing-down, there's always an opening.

But Mr. Adelstein's gone. It's like someone's killed him. It don't seem real.

And Henry's still clutching that ferret, trembling at my side.

And Cassandra's at my other shoulder, frozen stiff.

And the Director's sat, steepled fingers, waiting.

There ain't even a clock in here to tick out the silence. The Director keeps her room bare, but for the desk and the paperwork and her Bedford College certificate framed on the plaster above her head. It's effective – you can never tell what she's thinking from this blank-walled canvas. The only other thing of her she's got here is a photograph of her husband and son, and that's on the desk facing her.

No. That ain't right. The only thing of her – the whole *place* is her. Her idea. Her innovation. Her plastered walls and sputtery gaslights, her converted rooms, her half-finished morgue, her Divisioners.

She clears her throat. That ain't right either. I always start, after she's gestured me to, and I never have to think for my first sentence.

But she ain't even talking to me.

"Cassandra. Would you care to explain what Matthew meant by his remark?"

All the stiffness gives. Cassandra's at a desperate gabble, heaping words on words.

"I was going to tell you, Mother – I just hadn't worked out how to explain it – but there's no need to fret, the novel's anonymous – it won't undermine you, or any of your projects, it was just – is just – "

The Director nods curtly. "Is it *Life and Limbs?*"

Cassandra winces. The name sounds a curse, the way her mother murmurs it. "I – yes, but as I said – "

"I told you."

"I know, I – "

"I told you when you were Johannes's age that such poisonous pursuits were not worth your time – and yet you deliberately chose not only to continue writing frivolous novels, but to publish them for all the world to laugh at. Do you wish to humiliate the Division out of credibility, with your ridiculous narrative about *gangrenous hands* and *romance in the medical school?* Are you pleased with yourself, now that your stupid tale of missing limbs seems to have found a counterpart in the very case that is threatening to unhinge us? Everything you do has a consequence – has the potential for change, for betterment – but I can see no potential in this. It's a waste of your talents, and I did not expect it of you."

I've never heard Cassandra so measly-voiced, when she finally replies. All her words shrivelled down to a shaky stammer. She can't stand me, and I'm no better with her, but – I can't not pity her, listening to this.

"My name isn't on it. And there's nothing about the Division in it. It isn't even set in Dallyangle. I – I'm sorry I didn't – I just thought – and how could I know the Head-Hider would – ?"

Her mother lifts a sharp hand, cuts her off. "Not a word of it leaves this room. That goes for all three of you. No one is to discover the book's authorship, and nothing more is to be said about it. Now, Cassandra, to today's behaviour – the way you spoke to Matthew – "

Cassandra gapes. "I was defending you!"

"I do not require defending," the Director snaps, steepling her fingers again. "If I *require* anything, it is an end to this constant and disruptive battling amongst my Divisioners. And you, Division Sergeant Septimus – " – and she won't even look at me – " – am I to believe that you have spent your time instructing Miss Hyssop in the ways of the Division, and yet have somehow remained ignorant of her – her pet?"

Her *pet*. Henry said as much, didn't she, when we first met? And I'd thought she meant a sweetheart. Last night, I'd been giddy with guilty relief, when she told me she didn't have a sweetheart.

I want to strangle myself.

"How much have you been attending to your assignment?" the Director demands. "I didn't arrange it simply for Cassandra's amusement – you do realise that? I wanted to give you a chance to prove yourself again. I wanted to see how capable you were at inspiring new recruits."

Henry's stammering something gallant. "Please – I – I have been – erm – inspired – Septimus – she's done a marvellous job – I – "

"If I wanted your opinion, Miss Hyssop, I would have asked for it."

'Course Henry flinches. Something in it sparks me at the throat.

"Look – Henry's better positioned than anyone to tell you what – "

"Not than anyone," the Director corrects tersely. Her fingers crumple in on themselves, a steeple collapsed. "*I* am best positioned to assess your capabilities, Septimus – because, unlike your assistant, I have invested considerable time and energy into discerning what best serves Dallyangle and its Division."

I flare. "And I haven't? I've been here from the start – I – "

"You have derived your ideals from me! I gave them to you, and I cannot lay the blame for them anywhere other than on myself! Do you mean to insult me by telling me that you have no idea – that you have never even thought about – how much I have had to risk in this enterprise?"

It knocks the retorts out of me like a blow. I'm so used to her self-control, to glossy spectacles and careful sentences and smiles that keep everything back. *Everything.* Not just irritation, but anger – and hurt – and danger – and even fear – all that's smarting in her words now.

"I need you to understand," she gasps out. "All of you. If the Division falls – a silly novelist here, a poisonous letter there, a detective walking out with two cases still unsolved – I fall with it. Septimus – you can find other employment. Miss Hyssop could return to Girton. Cassandra – well, you have your *novel*, don't you? You can all do as my fellow-students did, and say that I misled you, with my radical ways and my utopian thinking and whatever other platitudes you wish to deploy. But I can't – don't you see? – I can't say that I misled myself!"

"The Division won't fall," Cassandra blurts. She's frightened as I am, and she sounds it. "You won't let it – and we won't let it! And Adelstein will come back, once he realises what he's – "

The Director slaps her hands together, knots her fingers furiously. "I am not infallible, Cassandra! I cannot wish these outcomes into being! I need your support – all of you – I thought I had it!"

We're all struck out of words now. The Director's snatching steadying breaths, her knuckles stark and trembling. Cassandra won't look anywhere but her feet, shoulders taut, swallowing hard. Henry's a terrified ghost, clutching the ferret in her arms. I – I don't know what I am –

But the Director ain't finished.

"You are, at least, right in one respect. Matthew will come back – but only if he thinks there has been suitable recompense for today's events, which can be easily arranged. Miss Hyssop, as soon as this meeting is concluded, you will get rid of that ferret. If I ever see it – or any more dead mice – in this Division again, you will be out of your job."

Henry ducks her head, fumbles a shivering nod.

"Cassandra – the case is yours."

What?

Cassandra glances up, shocked as me. "Mother?"

"The Head-Hider," the Director clarifies coldly. All that composure's flooding back, draping her like a cloak. "If there is the slightest chance that your ill-advised fiction played a part in inspiring this lunatic, it is your responsibility to put it right. From now on, you will be leading the investigation. Septimus – if you discover anything relating to this case, you are to pass it directly to Cassandra. You will continue with your pursuit of the Sweetings – on foot."

I'm spluttering before I can stop. "But – I can't just ignore evidence! If you want the case solved you won't even think about it – "

I can hardly hear my words for Cassandra, stammering panic at the same time. Not that she's got anything to panic about. Ain't she always out for some way to impress? Why wouldn't she grab this chance both-handed as well?

"Mother, I didn't mean I should – I mean, obviously I want – but not this case – please – give me the Sweetings, give me anything else, but not the Head-Hider – "

The cloak drops.

"How many times," the Director yells – really yells, 'til the room's made of nothing but her voice, and that voice's cracked and smarting more than she's ever shown it under this roof – "do I have to tell you both that *I know how to run my Division?*"

I – *I* – don't dare a word. I can barely move. Her voice seeps down my throat, chokes me. From the frozen silence, Cassandra and Henry must be the same.

"Out," the Director hisses. Her eyes tumble back to her hands. I don't wait.

It's hushed as the morning again. The whole Div must have heard us. Cassandra don't linger to make sure. When we're all in the corridor, she's only got half a second to catch my gaze – and not a single word to offer, any more than I have – before she shoulders past and sprints away. You can hear her sobs between every crashing footstep, right across reception. The double doors slam.

If she's got the Head-Hider case and a mort of things to prove – or make up for – or both – what's to stop her following the only lead we've got? What's to stop her chasing Lorrie?

Lorrie, who wasn't at his post this morning. Lorrie, who might as well be missing. I didn't go back to check on him. Anything could've happened to him. Worse may well happen now.

I should've gone to him. Warned him. I had the choice, and I went running after Henry's cause like an idiot. An idiot who'd never been besotted with a dangerous schemer. An idiot who'd never learned.

"Septimus?"

Henry's followed me down the corridor. Hovering at my office door, too polite to chase me in. The ferret's another shade of pale to set her off. Terrified eyes, green as a thicket. All her apology, all her concern, glittering in 'em.

Apology! Yes! This is her fault! I was an idiot to defend her – but she's just as bad, with her secrets – with everything that sent Adelstein after her in the first place! And even now – she don't even look ashamed – just scared, always scared, too scared for anything else to leave much of a mark. She ain't ashamed. Wasn't it her who brought that ferret here in the first place? And she's had chance upon chance to tell me – really tell me –

But obviously I ain't to be trusted with anything! Not the truth of her – not even my own damned feelings for her!

"The hell were you thinking?" I snarl. "What – why – *why* is he after you? Why won't he stop? What've you done?"

Her shock's painful, her sudden flash of incredulity even more so. "I – what? I – I thought you – you said – I thought you believed me – "

"I thought you'd explained!"

And I know – and I can't say it – but how can I forget what's in her journal? How'm I supposed to ignore the way she looks at Adelstein, like he's the very apocalypse in herringbone? What do I do about the ferret – and all that's just been wrenched off my shoulders – and everything I know – and everything I don't – ?

I wish I'd not gone to the dormitory. I wish I'd never seen the damn journal. I wish I'd just – I don't know, waited! Trusted! Call it what you like!

"I – I – I did!" she cries. "I told you – that he was wrong! I haven't done anything! I – you – was my word quite not enough?"

She's right. Oh, God, she's right.

"Henry – "

She tugs her shoulders taut. "Division Sergeant – I – I can't apologise sufficiently – for – for everything – but now – "

Now? She can't. She can't resign too. Please – *please* don't let her resign –

"Now – I – I'm going – erm – to – to deal – with my ferret."

"Wait – "

But she runs, round on her heel and out down the corridor.

Now it's just me, back in my office, back where I started. Except it ain't. I don't sit at the desk and pin my hair now. I press my forehead to the door and gasp for breath. It's a nightmare, and if I breathe deep enough it'll make it stop. Or it'll push it away. Keep it beyond the door.

I can't even leave my notebook sprawled open for Henry to find. Can't swap our poses of this morning. My book might explain – if I dared explain – even in writing – especially now –

But it's in my shorthand. And there's too much of a risk someone else'll find it, if I leave it beyond my office. And it'll be a miracle if she ever sneaks into my office.

It'll be a miracle if she ever comes back to the Div.

Well. There you go. Notebook or no notebook, journal or no journal, secrets or no secrets. She might've just been laughing at you before, but she's got more than right to despise you now.

14.

OF FAMILIAL COMPLICATIONS

November 2nd 1893 (Thursday)

MISSING HEAD. — Nothing. I can earmark it as *urgent*, and it doesn't
make the slightest bit of difference.

REPRIMANDS, &c. — Where to begin?

Cassandra. I cannot reprimand her in a Divisionary capacity
for her deceit, but that does not mean I cannot feel it. How
could she be so thoughtless? I never raised her to callous flip-
pancy, to flights of useless and unhelpful fancy – to become
the sort of woman who would write a *novel* about idiotic
young men making a mockery of a medical school! To *glam-
ourise* that kind of unfeeling carelessness, the prejudices
deep-set in a system – to joke, within the pages of a popular
and insidiously influential work, about the barriers which
keep her own sex – her own race – from the opportunities
afforded to an endless string of privileged fools!

Have I not done enough to stop her from adopting such
ideas? Has the Division itself not shown her that institutions
should not be maintained if they are no longer useful – no – if
they are actively *harmful?*

And it has had consequences! Dear God, it has had
consequences! Am I to believe that the Head-Hider's modus
operandi is a matter of coincidence, a mere month after the
thing's publication?

The Division only holds together as long as we consciously reject the very world-order enshrined in Cassandra's book. Why did she feel the need to channel her thoughts – her potential – into the ventriloquized thoughts and minds of rich white men? How could she pinch her own voice to nothing for the sake of someone else's crude humour? How could my own child give a killer ideas?

Well. She will no longer be able to do so now. I have appointed her as lead investigator on the Head-Hider case, a position which will not only demand all of her energies, but channel them back in a productive direction. She must be the one to fix this. It is far too much to hope that the novel be withdrawn from circulation, but we can at least ensure that Cassandra's name is never publicly associated with it. Let the readers see what they will doubtless assume about its authorship, and let Cassandra find the Head-Hider, and let that be an end to the whole affair.

Next:

Septimus. Cautioned – or reprimanded – I fear I lost my temper too much to preserve the distinction – and sent back to the Sweetings' case, now that Cassandra has control of the Head-Hider. I know that Septimus has struggled with the Sweetings before – but Cassandra will hardly do any better against them – and surely separating the two Divisioners, restricting their focuses to one case each, can only help to enhance their concentration and get both solved more quickly?

And Septimus will apply herself (and stop allowing her fancies about Pip Property to unhinge her) to the task of apprehending the Sweetings. I have lost my chance to extract an explanation from her for what happened two months ago – and that I must allow, for I chose not to dismiss her – but if she were only to stop them *this* time, her faltering abilities might finally settle themselves back to their original promise.

Is it me? Am I the problem? Why are they all constantly compelled to keep secrets from me?

Returning to official matters. Miss Hyssop – final reprimand – keeping a ferret in the building and permitting it to attack Matthew's lodger. Possibly the only Divisionary problem accompanied by an easy solution. Miss Hyssop will remove the ferret, Matthew will be informed of it, and he can then be convinced to return.

Surely.

THE DEADLINE. — Monday 6th November is almost upon us, and the Sweetings have not been found, but I will not start worrying yet. We still have the weekend.

RESIGNATIONS. — Officially, Matthew, but I plan to persuade him otherwise. I will write to him tomorrow. At least he brought our ledgers back *before* launching into his pose of defiance.

And Miss Hyssop? She seems to have vanished. It has been hours, and she has left no word with anyone. It surely can't take this long to get rid of a ferret. Does she intend to return? Have I lost her too?

Keturah St. Clare Ballestas, Director of the Dallyangle Division

My own wretched self

The rest of that day (what is that day? November? Figs, something cold and ominous)

Things have happened. And I don't entirely know how to feel about them. But one thing, at least, has been made alarmingly clear tonight: I *cannot* let myself be found. Quite ever again. Quite.

I sprinted from the Division half-distracted, clutching my unrepent-ant ferret, a conversation abandoned in pieces at my back. I've not the faintest what possessed me to flee. The Director's orders, and her truly withering expression. The thought that Septimus still harboured the ghastly suspicions Mr. Adelstein had laced her with. The fact that I had quite no way of defending myself against them. Eventually, just the realisation – as per my usual modus operandi – that all I could do was run.

Run – and banish the ferret. I could have cheerfully throttled Mordred for all he'd wrought, but he did defend me when I first faced the Sweetings, and I was hardly cold-blooded enough to throw him in the river. The only option left to me was to somehow return him to my sisters – without the Division ever discovering it, or Edwina and Rosamond discovering me. There wasn't time to arrange a clandestine meeting, to get Rosamond on her own. There was only Catfish Crescent and the house – and, peaches, I hadn't worked out the feasibilities of turning up on my threshold with short hair and a Divisioner's uniform – but that was a matter for a mind far steadier than mine was at that moment!

The whole sprint was distinctly unpleasant. The market was closing up as I crashed through, empty boxes clattering together on every side, late buyers rolling their eyes and their taunts as one when they saw me dash past. The main street that splices Pole Place from the market was abristle with carts and carriages, the horses clinking and kicking like huge clockwork monsters, mud-splattered fetlocks making every effort to stamp my feet flat, drivers bellowing me out of their paths. My throat was tightening again, until I had to stagger to a halt in Pole Place, clutching at the nearest smooth-bricked housefront to keep myself upright. Mordred slung heavy on my shoulders, a strange shock of warmth around my collar. It was almost dark already, and coming on to rain, icy droplets spitting through my fringe. My face was far damper than the sky had yet managed – but that was my own wretched fault.

Septimus smarted on the wrong side of my eyes. I wanted to remember her softer look, the gentle brush of her fingers at my cheekbones. Now, I could only think of her last expression – her last words – how I'd spun away from them and scuttled out of the Division. Recalling that, it was all I could do not to collapse into sobs, there and then in the middle of Mr. Adelstein's street.

I swallowed, rescued a hand from the housefront and dashed the knuckles over my eyes. A heavy-caped lamplighter was trudging towards me, ladder shunted under their arm, crooking to a halt at every lamppost to flicker the street into light – far more light, I confess, than I entirely wanted. I closed my eyes to be rid of them, hurled my head into the only plan I had left. Get Mordred back to my sisters – greengages, if I could just manage that – *that* would be a start! And then I'd return to Septimus and the others, I'd be Divisioner incarnate, I'd stay composed and sensible and not scupper a single remaining thing about anyone's existence, and that would be that. It had to be possible – it had to!

"Quite," I gasped, and shoved myself up off the housefront.

It was the first time I'd been back in Catfish Crescent since I ran away. Figs, but I was fiendishly glad of the gathering darkness. The lamplighter would have to finish Pole Place before they reached us – for now, at least, I had the comfort of dusk. I stumbled past Lady Miltonwaters's house, glowering ours out, the bay windows open-curtained and garish with innumerable beeswax candles. The throw of the light caught on our front door, on the nettle-encrusted crest that preened above it, on the glossy green paint of our window-frames and the verdant Corinthian pillars which ostensibly held up the porch. All of my family's gauche ambitions, flaunting out of the architecture, to what seemed – after a week in the Division's spartan corridors – an absurdly vulgar extent. Three floors above, tottering against the mouldering sky, the attic window was open.

Rosamond was in residence. Perhaps – perhaps I'd be lucky – perhaps just Rosamond –

"Rosamond Pleasant Myfanwy Earlyfate!"

This particular terror was visceral, as it ever was, and it had me plummeting to my knees straightaway. I'd been stumbling up the garden path in a trance – so dazed by the crest, the green, the attic, that I'd not thought to study the nearest ground-floor window. It was open, rain pattering off the panes at a jaunty angle, and – an astonishing change in itself – the curtains were stretched wide. Wide enough – peaches, more to the point! – to reveal the tweed silhouette, the gold chignon with its sharp grey streaks.

Edwina, watching the street with terrifyingly keen scrutiny – and only the gloom and the tardy lamplighter had stopped her from spotting me!

Heedless of the front lawn and the drooping remnants of Rosamond's plants, I scrabbled on my knees until I was curled up beneath the window. I could only pray Lady Miltonwaters wasn't inclined to examine the Nettleblack housefront with any especial urgency. Rosamond's drawl drifted down from the attic window, stretched and gaspy at the edges.

"Eddie! Not now! I – I'm – playing chess!"

Edwina sounded quite understandably incredulous. "By yourself?"

A groan from the eaves. "Wyt ti ishe rhywbeth?"

"You are perfectly aware that I cannot understand you! Come down at once!"

I was far too thrown to move – certainly far too thrown to get up and dare the door-knocker. Why had they opened the curtains – plums, no, opened the *windows?* What could have possessed them to start paying attention to the rest of the Dallyanglian world, at the most inconvenient juncture conceivable?

Unless, of course, they had done it to better spy me out.

About which possibility, I confess, I had quite no idea how to feel.

"Right then, Eddie."

That was Rosamond's voice in the front room, close and nonchalant, not entirely as punctual as Edwina would have preferred. "If you truly, actually, first-time-in-your-life want my opinion – one, you must be desperate, and two, you won't like it. I say let Henry be. She's just doing what I should have done years ago. Always used to think chwaerlet fach'd surpass me – chwarae teg iddi hi, she's definitely done it now!"

"I do not know what you mean," Edwina returned icily. "And I do not think it appropriate that you wish to abandon our sister to whatever terrible fate must be keeping her from us. Have you not considered that she might have fallen into danger?"

Rosamond sniggered. "I can bet you she's fallen into something, alright."

If I'd not been so close-pressed to the house, I would have groaned. Was it too much to hope Rosamond would at least *pretend* to be ignorant of my whereabouts?

"If you are making light of this, it is in very poor taste," Edwina snapped. "I should have expected nothing better from you. I had assumed that your initial show of concern was not a pretence – but, as usual, I am forced to conclude otherwise."

"I just don't think she's in danger! At least I *did* show concern, which is more than you ever deign to do – "

"I am doing everything I can to rescue her!" – and, to my surprise, there was the slightest of cracks slicing through Edwina's voice. "Mr. Adelstein and the Division will find her. I have been personally assured of the Division's capabilities, and I am sure they will be able to return her safely to us."

Another snigger. "Who assured you? The Division?"

"As a matter of fact, no. But I trust the Division, and so far their discretion has been invaluable. I have told Lady Miltonwaters that our sister is merely unwell – I will not have the lady blame Henrietta – and that she will take up the invitation when she is recovered. Lady Miltonwaters has delayed her own departure to wait on Henrietta's presence. She will not leave Dallyangle for her uncle's estate until our sister is ready to accompany her. I have made sure of it."

"You really think Miltonwaters is going to wait on you – again?"

Edwina hissed through her teeth. "I am aware that your behaviour has made the situation more fraught than it needed to be. But you will not repeat that performance when our sister is saved. You will undo whatever poison you have poured in her ear, and draw her attention to the tremendous opportunity she has to secure herself a marriage of which her parents would be proud. Your negligence and malice has made her life a misery – to say nothing of the problems it has caused for me – but I will not let you spoil this for her too."

Pomegranates.

It quite wasn't real. She hadn't even got my name right.

I blinked, sputtering raindrops down my face. The blink was a comfort – the raindrops too. This bruised little sprite crouched in the storm with a ferret wasn't Miss Harriet (or even Henrietta) Nettleblack. I was Henry Hyssop, through and through, with my own terrifying problems. Edwina's tangle of marriage and nobility and familial expectations quite didn't pertain to me now.

But – and I pressed my hands to my mouth, forced the gasps down my throat as they threatened to snatch my chest from me – but what would I be if they found me? Rosamond would do anything, say anything, for an easier life under Edwina's rule – she'd already proved as much –

"I'm not spoiling anything."

It was Rosamond, her hazy drawl sharpened to a knifepoint. "I don't get to tell Henry how to exist, and neither do you. I never said a thing to her about your plans. If she doesn't like your idea, that's chwaerlet fach thinking for herself."

Of course Edwina didn't crumple. Her words petrified as she pressed them together, as if she could turn them to stone and pile them atop Rosamond's defiance. "You will do as I say, or – "

"Or what? You'll cut me off?"

My eldest sister's voice could have snapped a twig. "*No*. You are better than your spite, and I will not give up on you, for all that you have done to us."

"I haven't *done* anything to you! And neither has Henry, unless you count the pair of us refusing to let you control our every waking breaths! Just accept it, Eddie – you've lost her. You never had her. Mae wedi mynd, mae'n hapus, fe fydd hi'n well iddi hi – ah, but you've forgotten all your Welsh! The point is – you won't find her, your pet detective and his mad Division can't find her, and if you think I'm going to help – "

"I did not expect it. You have never helped me with anything."

"And you've never wondered why?"

They were both close at the window, Rosamond almost shrill. If I'd leant out, looked up – but – figs, I didn't dare.

"You left us alone for years! You swept off to England, and then you took us out of our home and brought us here and never let us go back – and now you resent us for – for what? What did you expect?"

"I did not expect the pair of you to despise me!" Edwina cried. "I have scraped to the aristocracy for years just to get you a chance! Our parents wanted nothing more than for one of us to make a brilliant match. It is the only way any Nettleblack descendants will ever have a title. And Mother and Father beg me to do it in the only will they had time to make – to secure us the renown that a century's hard graft ought to have deserved!"

She cleared her throat, pushed on. "I do not understand, Rosamond. I thought you would both be delighted with such a prospect. Is it not the happy conclusion for so many heroines? But you deliberately disgraced yourself, and now Henrietta is gone – "

"Because she doesn't want to get married!"

"But she has to!"

Edwina had yelled it, but it wasn't her usual curdling intimidation. Limes – there was something frantic in her voice, writhing just under the surface.

"She has to do it now – quickly – before – "

"Why don't *you* do it?"

A snatch of a pause. Rosamond drove into it, every word a shove of the needle.

"Why don't you marry? You know every sodding aristocrat in Christendom. You're your own perfect ideal. You clearly don't believe Henry and I are up to the job. So – do it, Edwina! Marry into the nobility! Give our parents what they wanted and let them look down and smile for it! There's nothing stopping you!"

"No," Edwina blurted. For one bewildering instant, she wasn't furious in the least – just scrabbling and desperate, unmistakeably desperate. "I cannot do that. I need – I have to – "

"To what?" Rosamond twisted her voice, a sharp imitation of our sister. "What could be more important to you than *securing us our renown*, eh? Or maybe you know – though you'd never admit it – what a stupid idea the whole thing is!"

"No – I – I – "

Then Edwina caught herself. Caught the words, where they sputtered out in unabashed panic, and polished them until every syllable gleamed with menace.

"I cannot leave you both to your own devices, Rosamond, because the fact of the matter is that you will not survive on your own. Henrietta is entirely ignorant of the world, you do not seem to understand the consequences of spending money – and there are others who wish to claim that money, who could worm you out of your position the moment they spotted your weakness."

Rosamond's retort was all sneer. "Unless you think a revenant can track its way from Worm's Head to Dallyangle, I don't think Dead and Dastardly Uncle Rhys is going to be bothering us any time soon – "

"Of course I do not think that. I was referring to Rhys's daughter. I obtained Adelaide Danadlenddu a respectable post with Lady Miltonwaters some years ago, but with Rhys as her father I doubt she will remain content with that. Our parents were able to prevent Rhys from taking our fortune, but you and Henrietta do not have their expertise."

"Danadlenddu?" Rosamond echoed, rolling the word with infinitely more ease than Edwina's clipped voice could manage. "She's using our Welsh surname?"

"I advised her not to anglicise it. I did not think it would be appropriate to have a maid in Lady Miltonwaters's house calling herself Adelaide Nettleblack."

"So – " – and Rosamond sounded quite as sceptical as I felt – "You're worried that some lady's maid cousin of ours is going to somehow steal our family fortune if you don't hawk-watch us into marriages, and for that reason you absolutely cannot touch the aristocracy yourself. You do realise, Eddie, that even *I* can see not a scrap of that makes any sense?"

Edwina's mutter was close at the window, low and trembling under Rosamond's bewildered drawl. The rush of the gutter and the thickening rain tugged me a fraction closer to the pane, straining to catch the words. "I just want one of you to take the chance. Whilst you still have it. Before I take it away from you."

"What?" Rosamond's voice skidded upwards, too startled to snap. "Eddie, we *want* you to take it away!"

"You do not know what you ask for. You do not understand."

"Only because you've never explained – "

"And it is far too late for you to ask me *now!*"

I yelped straight through my hands. Edwina's sudden shout battered it away.

"I have wasted years of my life pretending that I see the world as these people do – as *any* other people do! I have held back from everything I want for myself, and I have done it for you! But as long as I hold this position, I have a duty to fulfil, and I must see it through first. So you will talk with Henrietta when she is safely recovered, and you will take back your years of manipulation, and there will be no more discussion of me until our sister has the perfect future our parents envisioned for her. Now get out of my sight!"

Horrified as I was, I could certainly obey her last order, and I did so before anything else could ricochet out of that drawing-room. I scrambled, hands and knees, as far away from the housefront as I could get, until the sodden grass gave way to slick cobblestones, and my boots kicked free from my tangle of mossy skirts. I leapt to my feet – my mind a terrifying blank – beyond the smarting insistence that I should run – until there was a world, a veritable world, between me and every future Edwina could ever possibly strangle me with –

"Wait a moment!"

Peaches – *no!*

I'd not even time to cry out before something snatched my shoulder, spun me round, pinched to hold me there.

15.

IN WHICH I PROBABLY DON'T
IMPROVE THE SITUATION

Myself, spiralling onwards

A slick raincoat – a sodden hat – kid-gloves, soaked through –
"It is you! That nervous little creature from the Division!
Gracious, I thought I wasn't all the way to madness yet!"

The cravat. That silver pin, shining brighter and sharper as
the lamplighter approached us. Above it – the starched collar,
the deep olive skin, the dark brushstroke eyebrows, the swoop of
cropped ebony hair, the whiskey-coloured eyes with their sardonic
bemusement.

"Property," I gasped, quite devoid of anything remotely civil.

Pip Property flicked up their free hand, touched their dripping
fedora to me. "I'm afraid you've got the wrong house, sweet youth.
That was the Nettleblack residence, in all its ghastly green glory – *my*
abode is round the corner. Ferns in the window boxes. You can't miss
it. Though what sweet Septimus hopes to achieve by sending such a
poor shivering thing to spy on me in a rainstorm, I can only dread to
imagine."

Plums, let them think it! As they were currently stood, they
blocked any sightline from my sisters' drawing-room window – an
unexpected perk that was fast becoming a desperate imperative,
with that reaper-robed lamplighter drawing nearer. Although – if
they suspected Septimus had sent me, there was the horrendous
possibility that they'd march me back across the market square to
make that threatened complaint – still with the ferret about my neck

– straight to my dismissal, when I needed the Division more than I'd ever yet done –

"You seem to have acquired a fur collar," they added lightly. Their hand swept from their hat to my throat, brushed against Mordred's coat – then leapt back, astonished, the moment he snarled. "And it's alive!"

I pinched myself into a nervous smile. It was all I could think of: composure, politeness, the sort of behaviour that would leave them resoundingly disinclined to drag me off in disgrace. "I – erm – yes – this is Mordred – "

"Mordred!" They grinned. "And every bit as ferocious, I'm sure. But – look, sweet Hylas, this is insanity, to stand here and chat until the storm makes ribbons of us. I insist that you either go home or come to my house, at least until the rain stops."

It was such a giddying whiplash that my jaw quite dropped. "I – what?"

"Gracious, I'd no idea the prospect was such a repulsive one!" A sharp serif of a laugh. "There is no obligation, I assure you. If the Division beckons, I'll simply bid you a damp good night."

I swallowed. My mind was tipped on a bewildered diagonal, but I knew full well what was expected of me. Calm agreement, decorous farewells, a swift retreat. Words, then – there had to be words – they were watching me, smirking with such offhand ease –

But I couldn't go back yet. Not with Mordred. And nothing in the known and conscious world could have induced me to take him anywhere near the Nettleblack house a second time.

Scalding, impertinent, insane, the solution toppled into my head.

"Well – actually – you – you wouldn't be inclined to – erm – adopt a ferret – would you?"

I could only surmise that, in some flabbergasting fashion, my madness struck home. Property didn't respond – not in words, at any rate – just spun me round, one hand on my shoulder, and walked me away. I didn't dare glance back to watch Catfish Crescent vanish into the downpour. It was a remarkably short distance round the corner to their house. Figs, to think that it had always been here, ferns and all, and I had never even noticed it!

Past the slick sodden fern-cases and up the steps, and – plums. Property's – well, property – was quite as astonishing as I expected. Granted, it wasn't as lavish as ours, or even Mr. Adelstein's. The corridors were much narrower, the staircase banisters more brittle, the structure devoid of a sprawling back window. Every scrap of furnishing was at least a decade out of date; even the lights were just a cluster of tapers backed by mirrors, much the same as those in the Division's dormitory. Even so – every wall, every ceiling, every crevice wide enough to hold a pattern – peaches, everything of the entire entrance-hall! – was slathered in a dizzying forest of mock-up design sketches, powdery chalks and stiff-papered watercolours, glinting as Property struck more and more of the hallway candles. Rococo flower-trails, like a flattened-out fan. Wide-eyed birds, cousins to Rosamond's Morris fabric, squabbling over chalked-in blackberries. Curt revolutionary stripes on a jaunty diagonal. A burst of green carnations, scattered across the page like crumpled hand-kerchiefs. Diamonds of red and yellow, their colours set with perfect seams. Heavy-skirted figures in dark top hats, striding through a roiling landscape in porcelain blue and white. Flouncing acanthus and swirling string foliage, whirling about tiny snails with their horns spread wide. Drops of paisley – the very paisley they were wearing – though their current cravat was bright with new colours, heady purple and bronze.

Quite the most unnerving part of it was that I had seen some of these patterns before. It was like staring out my own cravat drawer! But I'd never heard of *Pip Property the androgynous designer*, not before the Division. The cravats came with no name attached, only a small storm-grey label studded with a single paisley. Perhaps Rosamond had stripped the details from them – every one had been a present from her, the only affectionate England-bound gestures she had seen fit to extend until the dregs of last night –

"See anything you like?"

I started. Property strode into my reverie with a smirk, shelling their raingear onto a coat-stand as well-carved as it was antiquated. Pomegranates – and here I was, unshelled, dripping storm onto their plum carpet!

"I – erm – well – it's very striking – "

They laughed. "There is a logic to it, I promise. Nothing but order and harmony in the world of Pip Property – oh, gracious, I've tram-pled the post."

They pivoted past me, pinching their gloves off, snatched up a rain-mottled envelope from its crumpled sprawl on the doormat. I had half a second's glimpse before they tipped their scrutiny to it. The stationery was thick and shiny as butter, far finer than anything I'd seen even Edwina receive, and the blotched lettering was elegant as a certificate. Even so – for all the exquisite penmanship, the name was wrong – I quite couldn't imagine Property ever wishing to call themselves *Signorina Properzia* –

Then I gasped. Their smirk had tightened to a stiff grimace, and they were tearing the unopened letter to fingernail squares, until all that was left of it lay heaped on their palms like salt. When there were no more rips to make in the fragments, they stalked down the hallway and vanished through a door – though they returned, empty-handed, a moment later, with the hisses and snaps of a newly-lit fire echoing at their back. They closed their eyes, sliding through a long steadying breath, then met my stare with a thin smile.

"With apologies to the parchmentier," they declared. Their every word was a rung, clutched at and clung to until their voice was back at its usual ironical drawl. "Now. You. Did I mishear that porcelain voice of yours, or did you just express a charmingly desperate desire to bequeath me that ferret?"

If any string of sentiments could thwack me back to the present disaster –

"Yes! I – well – I didn't – I – it turns out that – that – pets aren't permitted – at the Division – and I – I wasn't entirely sure – "

They sketched out the rest of my sentence for me, with the same sure-tipped skill as the designs on the walls. "You weren't entirely sure what to do with the poor creature, besides drown it in the distinctly unpoetical River Angle?"

"Well – erm – quite – "

They nodded, mock-serious. "And we can't have you leaning over any bodies of water, not when the nymphs would spirit you away. Very well! If you wish to make me this staggeringly generous gift, what can I do but – " – and their olive hand glanced across their cravat, nudged them into a wry bow – " – humbly accept?"

I flushed, warm under my eyes. I'd not the faintest what to do with my face, besides gape at them – and try not to let myself smile – and smile, regardless.

"And now," they added, with a sudden grin, "I'm obliged to give you something in return. Fear not – I've the very thing!"

This knocked my smile quite off. "Oh – I – I don't – I – "

"No, I insist!" Their fingers slipped through mine, swiftly enough to gasp the last of my objections away. "Close your eyes and follow me. It'll be a delightful surprise."

For one terrifying breath, I could barely move. Septimus would be horrified – or expect considerably more caution – from someone who wasn't her, at any rate. She clearly hadn't wavered in her convictions about the dangers Property might wield access to – and there were evidently secrets in their life, things that merited immediate paper-tearing destruction – and I'd already entered their home and proffered them my ferret, I quite had to draw the line –

They squeezed my hand. And – I don't know! – I've no idea what it was that crawled up my neck and settled my nerve – but I tipped my eyes shut, and they led me onwards.

For – well, as long as that corridor must have lasted – all of my world was faltering footsteps, and the heady scents of pomade and cologne, and the slippery press of carpet under my boots (carpet was a strange luxury, of late!). It was so quiet, the same country hush of my own house, soft and strange on the ears after so many days cheek by goose with the market. There was something startlingly soothing in it all, I must confess. I'd not entirely shaken the thought that they were about to unleash something ominous – but I was already in their house, in their hands, far too helpless to fight. The horrible impetus of decision, of panic, of staggering one step ahead of the rest of Dallyangle – it was gone, just for that moment. The next move, whatever it was, wouldn't have to be mine. Let the pen – just for a paragraph or so – fall into the hands of this elegant enigma, and give me the instant to slacken and breathe!

"And emerge," they murmured. Under my feet, the carpet gave out.

I hadn't managed any fixed expectations, but – a *bathroom?* A claw-foot tub, with a monogrammed towel swooning over the side? A floor of veiny marble, and walls painted to match, and naked candles flickering in bronze holders? Venetian blinds, slim and antique and lowered over the window, twitching with the slap of rain on the other side of the panes?

I admit, rather ashamedly, that the spectacle rendered me hysterical.

"Sweet – merciful – plentiful – "

Property laughed, slipped out of my hand and sauntered past. One insouciant wrist-flick – that was it – and then – taps – running water – *hot water* –

"I do hope you don't think I mean to insult you," they remarked, "but you really are in terrible need of a bath."

Dignity? A fig for it!

"You – you really – and you don't – I mean – erm – I don't want to impose – "

"Of course it isn't an imposition! I spent not wisely but too well on this room, and I shan't have it go to waste! Now, you must do as you wish – under those candles, that's a cabinet, you'll find all manner of apothecary delights in there – and I'll take your ferret through to the drawing-room. We'll be bosom compatriots on the hour, if I don't lose limbs to him first. Come along, you little beast!"

They sprang off the bath and plucked Mordred from my neck. Astonishingly, he didn't even snarl, but hung limp in their hands, their brazen confidence having over-mastered him to an unprecedented degree. Property draped him round their collar like a second cravat, flicked his head gently to settle him in place, and glanced back to me with a jubilant smirk.

"Just hurl the clothes into the corridor. The carpet will manage. Andiamo!"

Sweet persimmons.

The moment they sauntered off with the ferret, it was all I could do not to pirouette a spontaneous gigue around the steaming bathtub. I dashed for the cabinet, and only beamed the more: the fragrant concoctions in their cut-glass bottles would quite have out-jewelled a jewel-box. Red – blue – purple – yellow! No – they're not words enough – scarlet, then – carmine – ultramarine – teal – violet – amethyst – gold – saffron – and absolutely none of them even slightly resembled Nettleblack's Tincture! And the labels had been dyed to match, recipe incantations written close in sloping hands, in more languages and penmanships than I entirely recognised. In the end, I chose on colour, picked out the yellow bottles *(per Maria Giuditta, dal tuo caro padre* jostled close with *Persia 1880s, probably)* and lined them up on the bath-side like a row of autumnal shrubs – then snatched the towels with a yelp before the rising water soaked them through. A drop from the nearest jewel under the taps, and I had froth in abundance. The lavish madness of it actually made me giggle, as the bubbles skittered up to catch on my fringe.

Possessed as I was, it wasn't as uncomfortable as I would have expected to shed my clothes in that strange room. I thought only of getting them out into the corridor before the bath overflowed. The wretched chemise, more a spider's-web than a functioning garment, went last. I didn't dare look down; my scrawniness and bruises would only have shattered the incongruous idyll.

I've not the faintest how long I stayed in that bath. By the time I emerged, the rain outside had stopped, and I rivalled the floor for sheer pale cleanness, my finger-ends crumpled like weak paper, my hair dripping some delightful yellow scent down my neck. I'd left nothing of my clothes to crawl back into, but there was a dressing-gown swinging on the door, glorious burgundy silk. Retrospectively, I'm astounded by my audacity, but I'd no qualms about plucking it down and appropriating it.

I opened the door – imagining that the corridor would be empty – but Property had returned, lounging in shirtsleeves, tossing up a delighted cackle when they saw me. The heaps of my uniform were resoundingly absent.

"Rosy-cheeked and halfway to a Fragonard already! Do forgive my intrusion, Hylas, I've recalled the other half of my gift to you. The ferret's content, the clothes are drying, the snail's on the thorn – and *I'm* going to fix your hair!"

Rosy-cheeked quite didn't cover it. I glimpsed, in their chivalrous amusement, precisely how much of an abominable Rosamondian decadent I must have looked – impertinent enough to flaunt their own dressing-gown at them! – and flushed right down to my collar-bone. It was all I could do to manage some flailing stammer –

"I – but – I – what?"

They strolled past me, eased the plug out of the bath, swept up the towels where they'd tumbled – then dropped, cross-legged, to a dry corner of the floor, patted the marble beside them. They were twirling a pair of silver scissors, wrought into metal ivy at the top of the handles, catching the flickers of the candlelight.

"Your hair. It maddens all my aesthetic sensibilities. Who the devil did you employ to cut it like that? The finish is completely uneven, the concessions to your fringe sporadic at best – "

Their gentle scorn hooked it out of me, too fast and too truthful to stop. "It wasn't – erm – I didn't – it was never properly cut – the Sweetings just stole it – "

"*Stole* it?" Their eyebrows soared up, two perfect pen-flourishes. "You? Oh, my sweet creature, I'm so very sorry. Look – I shall make it up to you forthwith – let me at least neaten it out for you? I won't crop you as short as me, I promise. Unless you want me to."

One trembling step – then another – then I was on my knees at their side, my hands pinching creases into their dressing-gown, my nerves fluttering on my tongue, some sour mixture of fear and – guilt, though for what I couldn't say – smarting in my throat. "Oh – I – well – erm – if – just – "

Property watched me flounder, something curiously akin to concern creasing between their calligraphic eyebrows. "What is it?"

And their voice was so soft, cupping my spluttering words – and their eyes still struck in that blend of irony and goodwill – that for a moment I saw Rosamond, crouching beside me on the cliffs, come to tease out my panic and put all to rights. For one frightening instant, I could have tumbled into their arms and wept.

I swallowed hard. "Oh – erm – nothing – please continue – "

They darted me a quick smile. "As you wish, Hylas."

I summoned a shaky nod, and they raised the scissors, the sudden chill of the blades glancing at my forehead. "So – I take it the bath was a success! Excellent choice of poisons you've lined it with. Quite right of you to gravitate towards the grandfatherly stuff!"

I blinked at them. I couldn't let myself speak yet, but I confess I was grateful. If the conversation hadn't tipped back into lighter topics, I'm not entirely sure my resolve not to cry would have held out much longer.

"I stole all of it," they continued airily, scissors flashing at the corner of my eye, "from my mother. Dio mio, the crime of the century – take heed, Dallyangle Division! But she has the ca' in Venice, and the globetrotting padre, which makes it infinitely easier for her to replenish her supplies. Besides, that woman has an awful lot to answer for – *Properzia,* for a start! – and delectable bath concoctions are the only benevolent answer I'm likely to get."

They poured such simmering revulsion into the name that I felt myself wincing in sympathy. Had they not been acutely conscious of my having seen that letter prior to its destruction, I highly doubt they would have mentioned the appellation at all. It was at my teeth to tell them I'd changed my name too, but I quite couldn't risk it – not when any hint that *Henry* originated as an abbreviation might summon a vengeful Mr. Adelstein.

"Oh – erm – yes – well – I – I much prefer Pip – "

"Of course you do." They rolled their eyes. "As did Father. My family name being Property, and my Christian name Properzia – thanks to the twisted humour of mamma carissima – my infant tongue decidedly didn't want to make very much of either of them, and to shorten the lot to Prop would only have brought indisputable mockery down on my head. So I borrowed Pip, and came to be called Pip. Dallyangle's unsolicited answer to the Public Universal Friend, but with fewer sermons and more cravats."

I smiled. "Well – erm – you ought to – erm – entangle yourself with a convict post-haste – let them bequeath you a fortune – erm – that you can only take up as long as you always keep the name Pip – "

Their laugh brushed my fringe back, sent the blunt edge of the scissors pinwheeling to the nape of my neck. It was the first time in my known recollection that I'd managed anything remotely akin to wit – certainly wit that someone else had acknowledged, and been amused by. If I was struck now, it was with pure astonished delight!

"And the Divisioner knows her Dickens! In all sincerity, though – if you do happen to know anyone willing and able to bequeath me a fortune, you must direct them to my doorstep forthwith."

I gave them my shaky attempt at a wry grimace. All I could offer in that respect was my eldest sister, and Edwina didn't even let her own siblings touch the fortune – they'd have quite no luck with her.

"Very well, Mona Lisa." They sighed, snipped a few more curls from my jawline. "What a little mystery you are. I can't decide whether poor

Septimus would be more inclined to resent you or worship you."

Septimus.

It snatched me up like a faint. Septimus – her smarting hurt, her desperation, her helpless bewildered stare. Her hand brushing at my cheek. Her fingers, fidgeting on her notebook – now I was imagining, inventing the whole sorry picture – as she hovered by the wood-burner and waited for me to come back.

Olives – what if she thought I wasn't coming back?

"I suspect the latter," Property added. They were smirking, rather more wickedly than before, their eyes glinting like a decanter. "You're very charming, and the sweet sergeant is surprisingly susceptible to being charmed. I made a pretty good go of it myself, back before she decided I was a denizen of the most bucolic criminal underworld known to England."

It was dizzying meeting them on their own ground, where strange scalding flirtations and slippery genders simply *were*, and *had been*, and *could be* – and could be talked about, in fond sardonic tones, without a shred of hesitation. The scissors brushed under my ear, a sudden glint of cold.

"You don't think me villainous, do you?"

The abrupt query quite wrong-footed me. "I – what?"

"Me." They swallowed, perched up their eyebrows, a little nervously. "I don't know what Septimus plans to devise for me, or what deliciously sharp terms she may have eviscerated my character in, but I – I am not a villain, Hylas. Infuriating as the Division can be, I would like to help them. I just rather lack the means to do it in the way they expect."

I nodded dazedly. "Oh – of course – yes – and – no – I – I mean – you're not – villainous – you just – erm – talk very fast – "

Mercifully, they laughed, eyes wide with bemused surprise. "Oddly enough, I have been told. But – thank you, all the same. And if I ever can do something to your advantage, I'll be sure to let you know."

They swept the scissors away with a flourish. "Done! Never mind a thousand ships – with that hair, Division Sergeants aplenty will throw over golden fleeces for you. Now, I would detain you longer, but I fear I have arrangements and ferrets to be getting on with. Let's see if that uniform of yours is wearable again, shall we?"

They swirled up off the floor, caught my elbow and lifted me with them, spun me to face one of the marble-painted walls. Except – quinces – golden-seamed in the midst of the paint, there was a mirror, old and bruised and cloudy-edged from the steam – and blinking out from the centre of that mirror –

Was that *me?*

Fading bruises. Stark bones, staring eyes. Hair – short – shining with water – trimmed to frame a sharp jawline, a high pale forehead with a curling fringe to it. That figure looked like nothing so much as Burne-Jones's Demophoön – like they ought to have a Phyllis, springing out of an almond tree to clasp hold of them. Unquestioningly, unequivocally, they would have sent my eldest sister into fits. But in that one startling moment, they didn't in the least frighten me.

"Which reminds me," Property remarked, disappearing out of the glass behind me, "I'm afraid I threw your chemise on the fire. Don't squeak at me, Hylas, you know as well as I do that it was unsalvageable."

And all my hubris quite fell off, as the mirror-face's stare promptly spasmed into a grimace of appropriately *unsalvageable* horror.

I spent the better part of the trudge back to the Division simply holding myself together – quite literally! The loss of my corset had been bizarre, but the absence of the chemise was nothing short of perturbing. My shirt buttons were a freezing line of nails down my chest – nails, or crude metal stitches, as if Property had prised me open and botched the job of fastening me up again. Was this how it felt for Rosamond, lounging about in her Morris fabric? Was it noticeable, to the few scowling passersby I darted away from? Was it the provocation for the spitting, and the dark looks, and the sudden shove that knocked me breathless against the tincture-laden windowpanes of Mr. Ballestas's apothecary?

I clung to the window until the pane almost warmed against my forehead, gasped my way to a more sensible rationale. It was far more likely that this was more of the general animosity towards anything in a Division uniform, the same sharpening mistrust that had heckled me and bruised Septimus and sent those civilians sprinting out of our reception. Peaches, but that felt infinitely worse than a gaggle of objections to my increasingly irrational dress.

The Director was at the desk when I stumbled through the doors, sickled awkwardly over the side to fish out a spare inkwell. She sprang upright, delved instinctively for her taut smile – then remembered, presumably, quite how much I'd disgraced myself, and simmered to a neutral stare instead.

"You've been gone for a while, Miss Hyssop."

"I – erm – sorry – "

"Some of us," she added coolly, with the slightest twitch of her head to the corridor, "have been rather in doubt as to the question of your return."

I gaped at her. I'd feared the same, but to have someone else eke it into words and fling it at my head was more alarming than my own hysterical speculations. "What? But – I – of course I – "

"You left no word indicating as much." She sighed, her voice dipping like a candle-flame. "After the events of earlier, you would not have been without precedent for an abrupt escape. With all of the cases still unsolved, and Matthew's resignation – "

"I'm quite not leaving!"

It was a giddyingly impossible promise for me to make, and I knew it – but not enough to keep it back. Not in that darkening room with its dimmed gaslights and dying wood-burner, and the wind plucking at the jagged glass in the broken window. Not with the Director too quietly wretched to conceal the danger of our situation. Not with Septimus shuttered in her office, thinking the building a sinking ship, and me already vanished into the night. Not with all the louche liveliness of Property's patterned house still sprawled in my mind, striking a horrendous contrast with the drab desperation flickering before me now.

"I've – the ferret – he's gone – and I'm – I can't apologise copiously enough – and – and I'd very much like to stay – if you'll still have me – and that's quite that!"

The Director arched an eyebrow. She had evidently not been expecting words, least of all that many of them. I'd not had her scrutinise me so intently since the damp haze of my first arrival – since then, she had been more interested in my transcription than my face – and it smarted me crimson. I may have tidied my appearance more thoroughly than ever before, but would that matter to her? What was she looking for? Resolve? Trustworthiness? Or – ?

She pushed off the desk, slid towards me on two seamless strides, clamped my shoulder steady. "As you say. I'll let Septimus know. And you have a place here, as long as you wish us well. It certainly wouldn't hurt, if you wished us well. Remember that. After all – "

– and – was that – a flash of a wink in one golden eye, close enough to blur at my temple? –

" – Matthew hasn't found you yet."

Greengages.

She rolled her eyes to see my jaw drop, whisked about on her heel. "I do hope I shan't end up regretting that. Good night, Miss Hyssop."

To which I can only append with a feeble scrawl of – not even of *how* (for it was hardly an improbable deduction for someone of her capabilities to make), but simply – why? Why say that – and walk away? Why not collar me on the instant, and solve a case, and snatch back the attendant credibility?

Either she's too kind, or she's too clever, and there's some elaborate forward-thinking I'm too frazzled and delirious to puzzle out. Or – or she's both.

She wouldn't tell Septimus – would she?

And – on that topic – what am *I* to tell Septimus – of my haircut, my absent ferret, my disappearance?

Oh, cranberries – tomorrow! If it were only possible to compel my thoughts into imitating the Director – and stepping back from the frenzy – and sauntering away into the shadows – and leaving me be!

16.

IN WHICH INCONGRUOUS ELATION
IS THE ORDER OF THE DAY

Casebook of Matthew Adelstein

Pertaining to the Nettleblack affair

This is war.

So the truanting wretch thinks she can counter my efforts by striking at *Nicholas* – at Nicholas's *rats* – at Nicholas's entire rat-breeding business! As if she hasn't doomed herself infinitely more by doing so! Her murderous creature-weapon is the missing link (hadn't thought of *that*, had you, Nettleblack?): the elder sisters have also lost what Edwina Nettleblack refers to as an ermine, and it's been gone since the night of the youngest sister's departure. I can only surmise that calling the beastly ferret what it is was far too common-place for the insufferable family to cope with. They must all be so *singular*, mustn't they, these wealthy ladies with their eccentricities?

So! 'Henry Hyssop' has a ferret, as well as more than a trace of a Welsh accent, and a suspicious past itinerary, and a face the very shadow of the family portrait! Septimus has clearly reprised her idiocy and thrown her lot in with the mustelid-toting madwoman, everyone sharing that hideous dormitory with her must have known about the ferret – and Keturah Ballestas, who should have known better than all of them, simply sat back and let the subterfuge run wild!

Very well. I am at liberty to dispense with my previous concerns viz. preserving the Division's reputation. If the Division does not want my help, so be it. If Edwina Nettleblack chooses to shatter the place, well – they can hardly say I didn't try to prevent it, until they left me with no other choice!

I shall write to Miss Nettleblack the elder at once. An amended version of my previous notes on the case will suffice for evidence, provided any mention of Nicholas is taken out. I won't highlight the Division's behaviour (I suppose I owe them that), but neither will I conceal their failure to report the dangerous heiress lurking in their midst. I'll also be firmly advising Miss Edwina to have her so-called ermine taken out and strangled forthwith.

I would call on her straightaway, but I can't leave Nicholas alone. The damned ferret bit him – I could strangle it myself! – and he refuses to so much as bandage the wound until his decimated rodents are afforded some retrospective dignity. He's in our back garden, damp in the downpour, holding a spontaneous funeral for the slaughtered rat. His past and future professions colliding, as they never should have had to. I told him I'd join him before the hour struck (it was the only way I could get him to consent to having his injury looked at), so I'll have to be quick.

His injury – that *she* gave him, just to thwart me – and the rain lashing down on him in the garden – and his bite still not tended to –

Right. *Right.* I shall gather up every bottle of Nettleblack's Tincture in the house, and I shall line them up on the banisters and push them off one by one, and – then, perhaps, I shall be calm enough to write a sensible letter.

Addendum

Something of a change of plan. Post came as I was smashing the bottles. It can't wait.

First, a letter from my erstwhile Director. Dire straits, will I come back, and so forth. I shan't. Ballestas hasn't even had the presence of mind to dismiss the little imposter. Instead, she's removed Septimus from the Division's most important case and hurled her desk-bound daughter into the field instead – why? To make some sort of point? As if this will ameliorate anything! The present strain must be warping her judgment.

(Not that anything of the sort is warping mine.)

But – more pressingly – Ma and Ta.

They want to come. *Here.*

They're only twenty minutes away in Gulmere. They could arrive at any moment. Most maddeningly of all, they haven't given a reason.

How am I supposed to dissuade them, without a reason?

And there must be a reason. It could be nothing more sinister than Saturday, and Shabbat Mevarchim, and summoning me to the service. But then – why would they not *specify?* And why come to me?

Edwina Nettleblack shall have to wait. I must tell my parents that the Division is in crisis, and that I simply cannot host a family visit. But – if I tell them I've resigned, they are bound to ask why, and I can hardly confess I did so out of spite over a dead rat and a distraught rat-breeder –

And that wasn't all of my motivation, was it? It was something far more sensible than that.

Wasn't it?

Right, never mind. I'll have to tell them I've completed the case, and that the attic building-work has already started.

But then, if they miss my letter, or turn up regardless –

No. I must tell Nicholas to write to Lawrence Tickering. That was my plan, for his alternative accommodation – just in case –

But I as good as threw Tickering's sister off the Head-Hider case! And Nicholas's rats were instrumental in the skirmish! Why would he help us, after that?

And how can I even think of making Nicholas do anything, when his ferret-ravaged forearm is still resoundingly unattended to?

Damn it! Damn all of it!

Addendum to the addendum

I'll go to Gulmere myself. Tomorrow. It is *not* in panic: if it is Shabbat they mean, I will have to be there on Saturday regardless. There is absolutely no need for them to come here. If worst comes to worst, I'll tell them that I am still affiliated with the Division, and that in the present climate I fear for their safety in Dallyangle.

Is that too drastic?

No. Mrs. Ballestas was right about one thing in her frantic little correspondence: the Division is certainly dancing with its own demise now.

Myself, rather stunned

Sweet rampant figs I have absolutely no idea what day it is

I must be a target in earnest. Mr. Adelstein, newly resigned, hasn't anything to do with himself but hunt me down. And I feel far too much like one of those wooden targets I used to shoot through, up on the Pobbles cliffs with Rosamond. She'd tug me out of our nettle-wrought gate, insist on carrying my pistols in their gleaming box – *Eddie said to give you useful skills, bach!* – and prop up the targets, rough boards left over from her filthy-nailed attempt to build a garden shed. I'd been petrified by the very idea of wielding a weapon (and I can only imagine the sentiments of our steward), but even my trembling nerves didn't alter the fact that the shots went precisely where I intended them to, every time, until I could pattern out a *H* and an *N* in so many bullet-holes –

But did I truly have to begin this entry with a dissertation on my most incongruous accomplishment?

The morning's weather was as inauspicious as I'd come to expect. The rain struck in a deluge, slapping against the windows, too dark to see beyond the splatters it left on the panes. My new, ratless bedsheets quite hadn't warmed from a night of sleeping in them, and with the dormitory back door still propped open I doubted their chances of ever managing it – though someone had at least stuffed a bucket into the door's gap to catch the churning downpour. Millicent and Oliver lit the mirrored candles against the gloom, strange and solemn and subdued with not a scrap of song, every other breath a darting squint to Gertie's bed. Gertie was awake, and more or less dressed (in that she'd slept in her clothes), but she sat hunched and glowering on the edge of the mattress, draped in the yellow folds of her lambswool blanket, a bright heap of reproach.

She was avoiding my gaze, as she'd done yesterday. Calloused fingers pushed through the ends of her drooping plait.

Well. Plums. Yesterday, I had been desperate to dash into reception and meet Septimus, too flustered by that prospect to strike up a conversation with anyone else. The guilt twinged in my throat, set me blurting into the stiff silence –

"I – erm – Gertie?"

She started, a tremor beneath the blanket, but she raised her eyes.

There wasn't a scrap of a smile on that raw-lidded face, muddied to shadows in the murky room, and her voice was quite as flat and guarded as I'd feared.

"Hyssop."

A scuffle on the floor tugged my gaze away, as if Mordred had snuck back in for another snarling brawl. Millicent and Oliver were hurrying towards the door, catching every creak in the boards with their boots, pausing only to flick a brace of eyebrows to where Gertie sat. What were they thinking? What did they imagine I planned to inflict on her?

There was nothing to do but begin, regardless. "So – I – erm – about – when – what happened – erm – at – at Checkley's – "

"That wasn't so hard, was it?" she muttered, scraping me with a pitying look. Her words were terse, fragile, balancing shakily on each other's edges. "Look, Hyssop – it was my mistake, alright? I thought you were – more like me."

"I – I'm sorry?"

She shrugged. The blanket slipped, trickling to her elbows, stray skeins clinging to her cardigan sleeves. "'S not your fault. It was a bit of a reckless guess."

"I – what? I – I mean – erm – not – but – just – "

"Stop panicking, will you?" she snapped. "I only ever meant it friendly with you. I'm not going to try and woo you, or anything – "

"Gertie!"

I dropped to my knees, and the draught clambered through the fabric of my skirt. If it brought her face closer, gave her the chance to squint through the candle-mirrored gloom and stare me out in earnest –

"If you think that I – that – that I'm in any way – erm – repulsed by your – erm – inclinations – or that I'm not like you – I – you – you quite couldn't be further from the point!"

Finally, her face slackened. Shock plucked at her eyes, tipped her forward on the mattress to whisper at me. "You – what?"

Infinitely overdue, a scrap of blazing certainty sprinted across my forehead. *Tell her.* Not everything, of course – just – a sketch, perhaps, of that quiet resolve I'd glimpsed in Property's mirror. Strung between the new-trimmed folds of my haircut, surely I could manage enough to reassure her of my sentiments, my sympathy, the wild untruth of her worst-case scenario. She couldn't think I despised her. She quite wouldn't.

I needed the word. Rosamond's word, of two days and a lifetime ago, when I had Septimus's fingers at my cheek and the first pangs of that certainty in my teeth and not a dismembering ferret in sight –

"Sapphist!"

I hadn't entirely meant to shriek it. The heat shot up my neck in flat defiance of the freezing room, lashed about my face, dragged my eyes from Gertie's to wilt amidst the rickety floorboards. She was gaping at me, unabashed and deservedly so.

"I – I don't know if that's – but – if that's what it – erm – means – to – to – "

"To be sweet on women?"

"Yes!" I cried – lemons, and she jumped again. "I – that is – I mean – I – that's what I am – yes. Most definitely. Yes. Quite."

A tentative glance up, shaky with my gasps, gave me Gertie's open-mouthed astonishment. I quite couldn't blame her. She hadn't in the least asked for spontaneous confessions, and she didn't seem remotely steady on how to respond to them. Her half-gloved fingers slumped on her knees, tumbled down from her plait.

A hopeless coda was my final gambit. "So – please don't worry – about that – I'm only sorry that my – erm – that Rosamond was so ghastly to you – "

"It was no more than I deserved."

She sniffed, curled her fingers to bulky fists.

But – what?

"She was right, wasn't she?" Gertie added darkly. "I didn't even know it was Rosa*mond*. And she told me right at the start I wouldn't be her sweetheart. S'pose I was so flattered I didn't even care. Sharp pretty girl like her, meeting me flirt for flirt – I'd've taken anything – "

She caught my bewilderment, flushed, yanked her gaze down to her hands. "Should've known she'd change her mind. And I still had a week of her – a week of being someone's actual priority – which is more'n I ever thought I'd get. That's something, right?"

I'd not the faintest what to say. My very silence seemed more than answer for her. Without another glance to me, she dragged herself to her feet, twisted past me to stand at the bed's end, slapped her hands down her cardigan to beat the wool out of its bunching. I started when the clock struck, chiming through the walls, making a sharp straining tune of half past six.

Gertie sighed, hauled on her boots. Her voice shook, faltering under the sentences, as she trudged for the door. "Sounds even worse when you put it in words. Bloody hell, I was an idiot. Well – "

"No you quite were not!"

A fig for that clock and the ensuing tardiness. I all but toppled straight into her, scrambling off the floor with half my skirt snagged in my boot, grabbing for her cardigan sleeve – and tugging her about, once I had it, until she finally met my eyes. Amazingly, she let me do it.

"I – I know Rosamond – and – this is what she does! She changes on a whim – suddenly you'll go from – favoured to irrelevant – just like that – and you won't know why – and if she has a reason, she won't tell you – "

I swallowed, shoved the words over it. Quite no time to think on that now.

"But – please – don't take what she does as – erm – reflective – you mustn't believe that it indicates any inadequacy in you!"

She blinked at me. "She did it to you too?"

"I – well – sort of – "

It was as close as I dared. The point still stood.

"But – anyway – you – you're quite marvellous – and you've been nothing but welcoming to me – and I – I'm immensely grateful for it – and I'm sorry I've never said as much – and that I didn't – that I left you there – and – and – "

And, as I was bound to do the moment I noticed how many words I'd spoken, I lost the rest of it. She didn't seem to register the strangeness of the ending, even so. It was her turn to jut out a hand, to squeeze my shoulder under the swoop of my sleeve, her face tweaking into the shaky fetch of a smile. Not her habitual grin, nowhere near, but – something entirely different, halfway into a startling shyness.

"You're alright, Hyssop," she murmured. "Thanks for that."

"Oh – I – erm – of course – I'm just sorry it wasn't sooner – I – "

She flapped at me, spreading the smile tooth by tooth, until I bit back the last shivering monosyllables. "Don't go stepping on it, now. You've got the right of it. I never hated me and mine before, and I'm not about to let her make me start. 'Cause you know what, Hyssop? I *am* quite marvellous. And I won't forget it again."

I smiled. There wasn't more to say – she had plainly been wrapping the words about herself, with only half a thought to addressing me.

"Right, then! Another day!"

And if she felt rather more equipped to trample it than she had ten minutes ago – well, to borrow her phrase, that was *something*, wasn't it?

She was already sauntering for the door, snuffing every candle she passed. "Coming? Time to fix a Division Sergeant apiece for us, I reckon!"

Then she turned back, hooked up an eyebrow I can quite only describe as a gossip in its own right. "In fact – at a guess – bit of a labour of love for you, is it?"

Figs. Of course I flushed, at roughly the same instant as my every waking thought skidded out of shape.

Septimus. Being sweet on Septimus. And my last conversation with Septimus, as horrified memory was all too eager to remind me, had been hacked to pieces on far too much incredulous yelling for my nerves to stand. I – *I'd* been the one yelling at her – I'd been the one scurrying away without a sensible conclusion –

"Oh – erm – quite!"

She smirked. "Called it."

(I suppose it was only right that Gertie struck my consternation back into me. She quite wouldn't have been Gertie Skull if she'd not utterly confounded me at least once before breakfast.)

Septimus was waiting for me, carefully ignoring Cassandra's red-eyed stare behind the desk, just as thoroughly as Cassandra was carefully ignoring her. Septimus – of course she did – looked as brusque and as sharp and as handsome as ever: her chignon belligerently neat, her jaw set, her scowl notched sharp above her navy eyes. I got the tersest of twitchy glances, a jerk of a nod. I wondered – rather nervously – whether she meant to reprimand me for my paltry lateness, but she offered not even the shadow of a word. I had barely opened my mouth to flail for a feeble good-morning before she'd set the doors thrashing, kicking the rain in to splatter the floor. From her spot at the desk, one hand already cupped round Cassandra's elbow, Gertie tossed a wry well-wish of a smile in my wake.

The market was a sad huddle, half-deserted, rain skidding down the awnings to pool round the stalls. The incorrigible geese had been broken at last, and now clustered together under whatever shelter they could barge into, stamping their sacking-wrapped feet in horrible frustration. The tradespeople were much the same, crammed under their awnings, glowering for the slim pickings and the lack of custom. Even the bread rolls were damp, smartingly cold and devoid of bacon, crumpling to pale moss as we ate them in silence. The lanes were all puddle, with the odd cobblestone lurking at a strange angle underwater, to snag my boot-toe and send me skittering. When we snatched glimpses of the river, it was champing its banks almost to bursting.

I recognised, after a suitably miserable trudge of time, what we were actually doing. These paths were, to the turn and the letter, the same ones we used to take – these houses the same locks she used to check – these juts towards the congealing towpath the same ones we had scrutinised, before the Head-Hider upended everything. She had, in short, committed herself with grim resignation to the Director's orders, and restricted our activities entirely to the old shapes of the Sweetings pursuit. Judging from her pained expression, she meant the slog as a punishment – but for her, not me. Though she still hadn't proffered a word, her stride was measured, easy to match, careful not to leave me behind.

And – small mercies! – once we'd cleared the market, there wasn't a single foolhardy soul out in the downpour to harass us.

"Ah – Henry?"

She'd stopped us halfway down a street, vaguely recognisable around her sodden hat: it was the lane that dashed to Lorrie's lodgings, with its drenched turnips and jostle of red-brick houses. Sullen half-light was fringing the peeling windowsills of the relevant tenement, and tracing the cracked edges on the front steps, the pale plaster streaked with a greasy smudge that could only have been the work of the rescued bicycle. She stared at the marks, teeth tugging at her lip, then dragged her eyes across to mine.

Figs.

"I – erm – yes?"

"Mind if I go in?" She nodded stiffly to the door, raindrops jolting off her hat-brim. "Ain't heard anything from Lorrie for a day. Got to check he's alright, that Cassandra ain't given him any trouble. I mean – I know he can handle himself – and he's probably fine – but still."

I gulped the last of my bread. I had been consuming it as slowly as I could, simply for something reassuring to do. "I – of – of course – "

"Right." She swallowed, though she'd run out of roll hours back. "And – look. I – about yesterday. I didn't – I never – it weren't fair, for me to snap at you."

Now I stared. "I – "

"I just don't – ain't an excuse, I know – but you say one thing, and Adelstein says another, and something like that happens, and then – "

The words plummeted between us like stones. No – like rain, like the rain that hadn't stopped in the least – patching our uniforms, drowning our boots, welling cold between our fingers.

"Henry – I – I'm sorry."

She bolted it out, flinched the moment she'd done it. One stern blink fixed her gaze on mine, but her fingers snagged each other – twisted at the deep red of her belt, at the jacket pocket where she was presently keeping her notebook, each movement the very pattern of discomfort.

"You don't have to like me now. I ain't – I only – I wanted you to know."

"I – what – why would I not like you?"

Her eyes twitched, widened before she could narrow them. "What?"

Another second and the fear would throttle me. Words – quick – outmatch it!

"I quite can't – I mean – yesterday was carnage on every possible side – but – that was yesterday – and – well – of course I don't – I mean – it's done – isn't it?"

"That ain't all of it."

A cringe of a gasp from her. It clenched at my throat.

"I know you've a secret. I've got more evidence for *that* than I have on any of our cases! Adelstein thinks it's that you want to wreck the Div from the inside. He's given me reason after reason to believe him. And if I'd said something about it yesterday – told the Director what he thought – probably would've saved my own neck – but – I can't! I don't believe him! You'll laugh at me, but – I trust you! I don't know what you are – what you want from us – but – but – "

She stopped. Right at the heart of it – as if this wouldn't be more than enough to shatter my nerves to pieces! It was happening – so much of what Mr. Adelstein had threatened, so much of what I had feared – this was it, playing out, in the rain, in the street!

But there was the rain, and the street, and the splash of the drops into the puddles, and the rattle of a gutter overhead, and her wrenching anxious breaths, and – and me. Me. Neck-deep in the disaster, and I was still here, and Dallyangle drizzled on with bewildering indifference, and –

And she'd stopped. She didn't believe him. Brilliantly, gallantly mad she may well have been, but she *trusted* me.

If I'd been braver, I would have quite unabashedly kissed her on the instant.

"Quite," I stammered instead. "And – I – erm – you're not wrong – no! – I mean – you are – no – *he* is – oh, figs – let me just – one moment – "

She nodded, too taut for a speck of colour in her face, beyond the staring blue of her eyes. I grabbed my elbows, pressed out a gasp.

"I – well. I – it – the secret – it's – it's nothing to do with the Division. It's – it's something I want to run from – and – it's – "

To say it would have made it real. To say it would have noosed her into my danger, and brought Edwina's rage down on her head (to say nothing of Mr. Adelstein's), and compromised her beyond even the Director's tolerance. And to say it in a street – when she needed her nerve, her concentration – when I'd already shoved her off-balance far too many times –

"It's mine. No – erm – no threat to anyone but me. And – I certainly won't let it be a threat to the Division!"

She frowned. "It ain't – "

"What?"

Her words, when they came, were positively gangly with fear, jutted out at me like that posy of flowers.

"It ain't something I can help with?"

I could quite only gape at her.

"Police!"

Was it entirely reasonable of me to desire nothing so much in the known and conscious world as to strangle the utterer of that cry?

Septimus was gone in a lash of raindrops, smacking the puddles off the cobblestones with her battered riding-boots, and there was nothing for it but to chase her. All she'd just said – all I'd not had time to answer – I could feel it parcelling up in my mind, sliding out of sight, the opportunity folding away. Now, everything was a matter of horrendous corporeality. My sodden feet were splintering as I dashed down the street, my skirts leaden around my legs, my gasps rattling the shirt-buttons against my chest.

The yeller had skidded out of that dour establishment on the market's edge, its large windows muffled with ebony drapes, a peeling black sign slung low over the door. Septimus had thrown herself across the threshold without glancing up, but I was limping and wretched enough to manage a bit of bleary scrutiny. As the fading white paint informed us in full florid copperplate, we were entering *Fitzdegu and Daughter, Undertakers: Funerals in the Most Splendid English Style.*

Oh, mellifluous ironical peaches! Were yet more Fitzdegus quite what I needed at that giddying juncture?

Three paces ahead, Septimus had already gathered up Fitzdegu and Daughter in the flesh. Both of them were wide-eyed and wraith-like with Nick's almond skin, but infinitely neater in every respect, sleek as ravens in their jet-black work-clothes, too glossy at the fabric to be real mourning. They were the stricken images of the daguerreotype on the mauve wallpaper behind them – though the family portrait had another figure, all but their shoulder torn away vigorously enough to feather the paper's edge, and I couldn't recognise Nick in any of the faces. The daughter – Nick's sister? – had her hands braced under her father's elbows, her skinny arms starting out through slate-grey sleeve garters.

"Dallyangle don't have police," Septimus flung at her, ruddy from the sprint. "It's got us. We're from the Division – what's the problem?"

Miss Fitzdegu stiffened to a glare. "Oh. Well. Sit down, Papaji, I'll show them – it's just Mrs. Ballestas's women – but if you two can get rid of it, at least –"

The father slumped gasping into his waiting-room chair, and then Miss Fitzdegu was urging us through a crape-covered door. *This* was a morgue, the very thing the Division hadn't yet managed. Stark white at the walls, crisp and chemical at the nose, with empty niches presumably awaiting cadavers, and a marble-topped table splayed at its centre, and –

And, balanced precariously in the middle of the table, a severed head.

The head.

Precisely as preserved as it had been in the pirate-chest.

"Figs!"

Septimus whirled about, grabbed Miss Fitzdegu by the shoulders. "Entrances in and out of here – how many?"

"I – ah – just one – but we haven't seen anything. We were both out the back this morning – we could hardly leave the coffins to be ruined by the rain – "

"That'll be it." It took a visible jolt, but Septimus notched her voice down, prised her hands away, flipped the notebook out of her pocket. "Miss – look – here's the thing – that head – it's the same head what went missing from the Division."

Miss Fitzdegu flushed. "Well, *we* didn't steal it from you, if that's what you're suggesting! And are you not going to do anything about the break-in? Some insolent stranger waltzed straight into our private establishment and left a head there – never mind whose head! They have not reserved use of our morgue! Does your useless *Division* have anything to say about that?"

There was actually an idea tugging at my sleeve –

"You – erm – do you not know whose head it is, miss?"

She glared at me. Genial good-humour, it seemed, was not a Fitzdegu family trait. "I don't like the tone of this – "

"Persimmons!" I yelled at her. Much to my dazed elation, it had precisely the desired effect: she was evidently far too bewildered to recall the rest of her reprimand. "Miss Fitzdegu! I quite don't ask it to accuse you! It's just – you're an undertaker – you know about the – erm – recently deceased – "

"I *know* this head is not one of ours!" she snapped incredulously. "Look at him! He's been dead and embalmed for at least a week!"

Septimus's voice was a mirror to my own. *"Embalmed?"*

Miss Fitzdegu arched an eyebrow. "Is that not obvious?"

Then she gasped – I suppose it was startling – as Septimus sprinted past, tore her hat off and scooped the head into it, tossed it to me with what must have looked like far too much practice. I grabbed my own hat, slammed it down on top of the head, until we had our evidence firmly secured between the two of them. There'd be no chancing it this time!

"Right! Miss Fitzdegu – we'll send someone round to see about the break-in – but first – "

Septimus flung me a scorch of a glance, and it was quite as if she'd hurled the rest of her sentence straight through my forehead. First, the head had to be returned to the Division before it disappeared again – even if it wasn't her case, even if Cassandra made her pay for it.

"You can't walk off with that head!" Miss Fitzdegu burst out. "Not after you lost it! You can't be trusted with it! Just go and get us the police!"

Kumquats, but if ever a sentence were calculated to galvanise us both –

Septimus plunged for the morgue door, swept Miss Fitzdegu aside with the most decorous of shoves: a sneaky shunt of the elbow as she pocketed her notebook. Mr. Fitzdegu senior hadn't time to look up from his chair before we ricocheted past – certainly not enough time to register the indignant spluttering of his daughter. She wouldn't chase us, would she? Not out of the shop?

The rain struck me square through the fringe, blurred the market square to bedraggled stripy shimmers. Septimus's voice, half a snarl, glanced over my hair – "Round the back, before she makes a scene!" – and then we were plunging through a narrow lane that skittered along the side of the building, cutting a seam in the shops, kicking the puddles to pieces. The flurry of the main street was just about visible up ahead, carriages rattling across the slim gap that marked the end of the lane, though we still had a fair amount of sprint to go before we reached it. Septimus was right to tug us onto the detour – Miss Fitzdegu's protests were all too audible, enough to have started another sopping mob had we sprinted across the market square –

Something snagged me at the neck, lurching out from a sheltered doorway with an elbow-grip fit to shatter a teapot. I was still clutching the head; I'd quite no hands to stop it. My legs buckled, crumpled me backwards, out of the puddles and off the lane. I cried out – sweet pomegranates, of course I did! – and it skidded Septimus about, struck her face to furious horror –

"Don't do anything rash this time, dearie," Maggie growled past my ear. A freezing jab at my temple – cold, metallic, impossible to cringe away from with her arm around my throat. I, of all people, knew precisely what it was. "'Less you want Morfydd's brains to fill one of those hats."

17.

OF PANIC

My horrendous account resumed

Was it rather missing the point, in that appalling instant, to be cursing myself tenfold? I've no idea how I could have dodged Maggie's grip – but having to stare at Septimus, in all her incredulous terror, with a pistol pressed to my head, felt like quite the most unforgivable ineptitude I'd yet inflicted on her.

"We're being followed," Septimus blurted. She was still in the middle of the lane, even if I wasn't – Maggie had tugged me under a front porch, out of the downpour that hammered on the close-pressed roof above us. "They'll catch up with us any moment now."

"No, they won't."

It wasn't just Maggie. The second growl wasn't so much a growl as a physical thing, a miasma of sound and breath like stale bread, jostling at my other shoulder. "'S only idiots like you roaming the streets in weather like this. And you think we wouldn't wait 'til we had you alone?"

Septimus's eyes were flicking between the two of them, her fingers bunched into panicky fists. "Market's just down the street. Angle Drag's out the other end. If I yell, they'll hear it."

Maggie's arm tightened around my neck, the slick waterproof fabric sliming at my jaw. The clogging smell of the waxed material would have been quite enough to buckle my legs, if everything else about the situation hadn't already done so. "And if I shoot, like as not they'll hear that too. Only one who won't hear anything's Morfydd here. So go on, Divisioner – scream for the police!"

Septimus twitched. Her mouth opened, the slightest nervous fraction, until her gaze skidded down and hit mine. But – what could she do?

Maggie swung me about, and I caught a drizzly glimpse of her compatriot – glowering in his waterproofs, raw-skinned and bristling and miry at the boots – before he shoved the door ahead of us, shunting it open to fetid gloom and damp wood. He glanced back over my head with a terse snarl – he'd lost more teeth than I remembered, and the remaining ones were vigorously cracked. "Follow on, you. Mind you don't trip – Maggie's a bit light-fingered with our new toy."

The stairwell they dragged us up was in a positively corpselike state. Rain dripped from the roof to pool at the foot of the stairs, the light came in fits and starts through filthy little windows, and the flimsy wooden stairs groaned for our every step. There were doors studding our route, but the shuddering downpour made it impossible to pick out any sounds behind them – not that either of us would have dared yell for help, not with that pistol shunted so close to my temple. The Sweetings took us to the very top, across a skinny landing fungal with mouse droppings, until we'd crossed the threshold into a bare-boarded attic, sagging like a tent at the roof-beams. There were no skylights in here, and we would have been in slatted darkness had it not been for a trio of rushlights suspended from one of the beams, casting a shaky sallow glow over the floorboards. The lights had been crammed into a flimsy globe of glass and metal, dangling from a chain above our heads – distinctly recognisable, in both look and ghastly smell, as a fitting that ought to have been the property of Checkley's Tavern.

Norman kicked the door shut, shoved Septimus to the far side of the room. Her expression should have incinerated the nineteen-fingered siblings past all pistol-holding comprehension – as furious as it was frightened, her fists still clenched. But the room was entirely devoid of furniture, but for the stolen lamp, and there quite wasn't anything she could seize upon by way of an improvised weapon. Norman plainly knew as much; he was already ignoring her, dipping over the bundle of hats in my hands and flicking the top one to the floor. Waxy and stiff, an edge of embalmed jawline jutted up at us.

"Bloody hell!" Maggie muttered. "Two and a half for our troubles, eh?"

Norman dashed a finger over the head's scalp, shook his head dismissively at the short-clipped cut. "Don't need this. Can't get anything off it."

"Not to worry," Maggie retorted wryly. "You keep hold of your extra head, Morfydd – there's not much he'll be doing to help you. From what I hear, there's not much he's been doing to help any of you Divisioners."

She twisted me round to face her, her hand bunched at the back of my collar. The sight of her was quite as petrifying as could be reasonably expected. She loomed over me in the trembling rushlight, a ram-shouldered woman in hideously sensible storm-attire, sneering down with a grisly look half-vengeful, half-vindicated. I expected some gloating speech – but she swung her pistol up between my eyes, clutched in three calloused fingers'-worth of nightmarishly inexpert grip. Even with her clumsy hold, she didn't need any skill to make a shot at this range.

"Figs!" I gasped, quite involuntarily. "Don't hold it like that! You'll set it off!"

The spectacle of me spluttering something vaguely articulate under these circumstances was apparently enough to astonish them all. Maggie's eyebrows staggered up her head, wefting through strands of sodden greasy fringe. Norman struck off an exasperated snort. Septimus, sickle-backed under the drooping roof at the edge of my eyeline, simply gaped at me.

"Who says," Maggie spat dazedly, "I don't want to set it off?"

Sweet clementines! If I'd known she had no idea how to hold the thing –

Actually, I'm not sure. Would that have made it better or worse?

"You – you clearly don't! – because – if – if it were your aim to kill us – why would you not have – erm – already done so? – so you must want something – "

She rammed the pistol under my chin. I was far too terrified to think – beyond the smarting truth of her hand, and the position she presently held it in – merciful greengages, if she'd not taken her finger from the trigger –

"That's enough from you." Her narrowed eyes flicked to Septimus. "Your little friend's not wrong though. There is something we want. Thought we'd have another crack at it now we've got this lovely pistol."

Septimus glanced to me – blanched – forced a vicious sneer. "Meaning what?"

Maggie grinned. "What d'you think? You got away too easy, didn't you?"

"The first time," Norman added sourly. "But there'll be no one rushing in to protect you here."

The blood shot back to Septimus's face, bruised it stark purple.

"But – last time – you said – "

Maggie flinted a few sparks of laughter. "*We* didn't say anything! Reckon that was them feeling sorry for you. All that stuff about not needing so much brown hair. Morfydd's got brown hair, and that sold just fine!"

"And we can't cut yours off in the street." Norman stalked across the mouldering floorboards, and – *figs* – shoved his hand claw-fisted into Septimus's chignon. "Not with these knots. You'll have to keep still."

Septimus promptly did exactly the opposite: twisting in his grip until she could glare straight back at him, snarling as the movement tugged at her scalp. "And what if I don't?"

Maggie tossed me a look that was almost wry. "Doesn't love you very much, does she?"

My chin jolted another horrible fraction, jabbing my eyes up to the lamp hanging above our heads. She had the pistol under my jaw like a fish-hook.

"If you don't give up that lovely hair of yours, we'll start breaking bits off this one. Owes me a finger, she does. But look who's got the proper weapon now!"

Cranberries. I suppose Mordred did count as a *proper weapon*, with his indefatigable mauling-streak. Even so – if there had been some way of summoning Property here with my ferret in hand, bristle-toothed and ready to confound the Sweetings once more, I would have seized upon it both-fisted –

Blurring at my lashes' edge, Septimus froze.

"That's it!" Maggie crowed. "Wasn't so hard, was it? Better for everyone, this is – no bosses, no blows, just you and us and the ferret girl for luck. Oh, and this!" – with another sharp jab of the pistol against my skin – "Best investment hair can buy, this! Makes everything so much more efficient, eh?"

Before anyone could unhinge Maggie's last ghastly question, Norman was yanking the pins from Septimus's hair, flinging them away to skitter between the floorboards – wrenching the chignon in the wrong direction, until her gritted teeth collapsed into a yelp of pain –

And I quite entirely forgot to fear for myself.

My hands flew at the pistol, clean through Maggie's shoddy grip, hooked at the fingertips and tugged. Maggie was quite too stunned not to let me get away with it. I had to throw down the head to manage the movement, but that was the least of my concerns. Everyone else was moving too – Septimus shoving into Norman, sharp shoulder jutting out, trying to knock him sprawling –

And then we were facing each other.

Figs.

I had the pistol, and a far better idea of what to do with it than Maggie had heretofore demonstrated. But the Sweetings – they had Septimus. Norman had hauled her about, still clutching her hair, and now the pair of them ducked behind her by way of a shield.

Septimus could only stare at me, straggles of collapsing chignon clotting to her forehead, more petrified than I could entirely bear.

"Put it down, I would," Maggie jeered. Norman's fist clenched, dragged Septimus's head back. "Put it down and run, before we change our minds."

"Or don't," Norman growled. "Shoot your sham sergeant if you want – won't be many who'll miss her. Just don't get blood in the hair."

Septimus gasped, half-breath half-sob.

But the Sweetings were larger than her. Burly elbows and muscle-taut sleeves poked out past Septimus's shoulders, and the crowns of their heads jutted above hers. The air here was utterly still – for once, no wind to contend with. In pure technicalities, I could have made the shot – but, sweet bergamots, of course I couldn't! – not when there had to be an alternative –

The attic floor sloped under my feet, creaking and uneven – uneven as the gorse-prickled grass atop the Pobbles cliffs. The wooden target stood propped on the bushes before me, wanting only the last shot to spell out my initials. Rosamond was at my shoulder, watching and marvelling. *Eddie said to give you useful skills, bach!*

I held Septimus's terrified gaze a moment longer – and I led it up. Directly above them, where the glass-hemmed lamp wobbled on its chain.

Then I fired.

I quite can't write it without trembling, without a jolting desire to snatch the ablutions bowl and retch into it – but I aimed straight through the chain – and – just as Septimus jerked her arms up to shield her head – the entire rushlight contraption came plummeting down on them in a scald of flame and fat and metal – and shattered to pieces on the floorboards.

The lamp hit Norman square on the crown, and he tumbled backwards, lost his hold on Septimus with an astonished snarl. Maggie got the lash of the chain, and the scorch of melted tallow-fat. Shards of glass sprang at them all from the floor. The universal howls rattled my teeth in my head, struck my voice to a horrified yelp.

"I – I'm so sorry – I – "

Norman staggered towards me, crunching through the broken glass, wrenching the pistol from my fingers with force enough to hurl me sideways. Another moment, and he would have snatched my wrists. With a blazing bruise on his head and glass in his forearms and burning tallow streaking down his hands, he quite would have throttled me –

I ducked past him, grabbed Septimus at the arm. She was stumbling, wild-eyed, shaken enough to let me drag her at considerable speed – out of the door, onto the rickety landing – where the steps buckled inwards as we clattered down them, and the rain puddled at the bottom of the stairwell – and the doors on the stairs creaked as their inhabitants shunted them open –

The banister shattered to quills a foot ahead of my hand. Every door on the staircase promptly slammed shut. Two floors above us, Norman roared in exasperation, raised the pistol to take aim again –

"*Go!*" I shrieked at Septimus, slammed the door behind us and shoved her headfirst into the street.

After two gunshots, there was no way we could expect bucolic placidity outside that door. Heads in ragged lace caps popped out of every nearby window, swivelling for a sight of the disturbance, or ducked back inside lest the next shot take aim at them. Voices struck and caught and babbled; the doors across the lane shuddered as those behind them fiddled with the locks. The rain, skidding off slated roofs, churned to a filthy stream in the gutter. A small crowd was massing in spite of the downpour, gesturing towards us in frightened bewilderment.

I couldn't stop, not even for the frantic demands that were already clustering about our shoulders. I clung onto Septimus and pulled her into a sprint – straight down the lane, round a break of a bend, past sodden red-brick housefronts and banging shutters and a startled flurry of men rolling a barrel –

Septimus lurched to a halt, staggered as I toppled backwards into her. Here were the old houses gutted to tenements, the first frill of cottages, the turnips rotting on the windowsills. We were outside Lorrie's apartment again, and it was quite impossible to judge which of us looked the more profoundly hag-ridden.

No. It was her. A shard of the glass had caught her at the temple, and the blood was seeping down her face in truly horrendous quantities.

"Stay here," she gasped, marching me up Lorrie's front steps. "I've got to stop 'em – if they've got a gun they'll be killing people next – "

"You're quite doing nothing of the sort! They'll kill *you!*"

She snatched for my fist, prised it from her arm. "I ain't letting 'em win! I can't! They'll just get worse – and if all I ever do is run – "

"You never run!" I cried. "You're entirely the bravest person I know – but I quite won't let you go and get shot – "

"*Let* me! It ain't your choice! We've as good as given 'em the head if I don't – "

"Septimus! Hyssop!"

We whirled as one. Two figures crashed over the cobblestones towards us, swift-kindled panic blazing in their faces. One of them coltish and gangly, trailing wild brown curls – the other clutching her cinched waist, struggling to gasp for breath –

Nectarines – Oliver and Millicent?

"Where in hell've you been?" Millicent spluttered, before she'd even reached us. "What's happened? We heard – "

"There was a gunshot," Oliver hollered behind her. "Heard it from the market square. What – " – from the sudden horror on his features, he must have spotted the state of Septimus's hair, or quite possibly the prolific smears of blood on her face – " – what happened to you?"

Septimus glared at them, shoving loose chestnut skeins behind her ears. Her fingers smarted red where they had grazed the cut at her temple. Not that the realisation seemed to provoke her to anything more sensible than a sharp grit of her teeth. "Nothing. I'm fine. I've got it under control. Take Henry back to the Div and keep her safe."

Oliver's jaw dropped. "But – what about you?"

"I said I'm fine!" she snapped, her voice spasming. "Tell the Director I've gone for the head – and the Sweetings – and this time I ain't leaving 'em to do their worst – "

"*No!*"

They all whirled as one, a brace of wide eyes. I quite hadn't meant to yell at such a voracious pitch – but when the alternative stood as it did –

"The Sweetings – erm – they have a gun! You cannot possibly go back and face them on your own! Not even to retrieve the head! You may value your life at a thread – but I quite do not – so – so – I insist that you muster more of the Division to support you – and – quite!"

Septimus gaped at me – struck from her impulse, just for a moment. It was all the opening Millicent and Oliver required. Before I could attempt another sentence, the two of them had grabbed an arm apiece, pinned Septimus between them, skidded her about and barrelled away down the street.

"Septimus, you can't fight a gun!"

"Since when'd the Sweetings get a *gun?*"

"And you're hurt – have you seen your face?"

"We'll get the others – but you're in no fit state to come!"

"Back to the Director with you, now!"

If there were jeers and snarls as we careered across the market square, I didn't notice them, and I don't imagine the others did either. Septimus twisted away from Millicent and Oliver as soon as we hit the market, but – a tiny mercy – she didn't try to turn back, just reached up to neaten as much errant hair as the remaining pins could manage. Inside the Division – starting out in fierce pallid colours with the gaslights blazing, far brighter than the attic's gloom – Cassandra and Gertie sprung up from the desk in slack-faced horror, pens tumbling from their hands to pool ink on the ledger.

"Get the Nettleblack's!" Millicent bellowed at them. Spontaneous pistol-wielding aside, it was still enough to make me jump. "And get the Director! The Sweetings've got a gun and they've shot Septimus!"

Septimus flung her an incredulous glance, opened her mouth for a raft of corrections – but the Director was already bursting from her office, fear sparking in her golden eyes, beyond even a vestige of her old serenity. "They – *what?*"

"I ain't shot," Septimus managed to blurt. Cassandra was frozen in place, whilst Gertie scrambled around in the desk-drawers for a tincture-bottle. "It's worse – it – there ain't time for this – "

The Director snatched her at the elbows, tugged her forward into the gaslight, ran a shaking hand down her cheek. "You are alive. You are safe. Everything else can be worked out from that crucial start-ing-point. But you – your face – you are hurt – "

"So she can't go back out there," Millicent insisted. "Tell her, Director!"

Septimus all but screamed with exasperation. "No! God's sake, listen to me! Yes, the Sweetings're armed – but it ain't just that! I know I'm off the case, but – we found it. We found the missing head."

Cassandra jolted on the spot. A sharp hiss scraped past her teeth.

"We've got to go back – quick – it's where they jumped us – come on – "

Persimmons.

Septimus spun on her heel and crashed back through the doors before soul alive could protest. I'd quite no intention of watching her sprint to her doom alone – a sentiment I apparently shared with almost everyone in the room! Gertie, Millicent, Oliver – even the Director herself – all but Cassandra hurtled parallel in Septimus's wake – skidding across the market square, round the corners, the same route in reverse, another ghastly lap in this nightmare of sprinting and smarting and hammering one's feet to numbed oblivion –

But I can't in the faintest understand what we found.

The front door swayed on its hinges. The attic floor and the wooden stairs were speckled with tallow and blood and mud-splattered footsteps, right out into the street, and the Sweetings were long gone. The attic itself – it – well – it wasn't entirely empty. Our hats were stacked, neat as teacups on saucers, in the corner of the room – soaked through, but spotless, and with neither tallow, blood nor mud anywhere near them.

The head itself was quite nowhere to be seen.

Now, everything has slipped into silence, but for the patter of the rain on the windows. Still, eerie, country silence. I'd not thought such a thing as silence could will itself back to existence, after that.

Septimus gave the Director as full a report as she was able: that we had rediscovered the head in the undertakers', that we'd been on our way back with it when the Sweetings set upon us with their newfound weapon, that the Sweetings had dismissed the idea of taking the head for themselves – and, now, that it had disappeared into hands that likely weren't theirs. I wasn't consulted, wasn't called upon to do anything other than lean against the wall outside the office and steady my breaths. After a while, their voices dipped too low for me to follow, and I'm not fully sure I didn't slide into a doze, propped up by the wall and the gloom as I was. I jolted back when Septimus emerged, her face scrubbed of blood, sipping at a tinctured mug with the Director at her shoulder, and all was softened tones and anxious frowns as the clock rattled out three-thirty. We were to rest, and we weren't to leave the Division until at least the next morning, and – and this largely to Septimus, with a meaningful eyebrow – everything else would be taken care of. The enigmatic sentiment seemed to satisfy Septimus, as much as anything could in the wake of that day; she slunk back to her office without further protest, both hands already plucking at the chaos of pins in her hair.

For my own part – well. I struck a guess on my way to the dormitory, and it worked: there was a fist's-worth of cheese and three slices of bread left under the desk, and a shaken Cassandra professed to have no appetite for it. Once I'd devoured the plate, I glanced over my bed's edge – Gertie had left her jug and bowl when she and the others had headed out, with a scrap of paper poking over the rim: *feel free, Hyssop*. It seemed a logical extension to carry the jug to the back door of the dormitory, fill it from the bucket until it was brimming with rainwater. Then – I was the only one in the room, and far too jittery to care much for decorum – I pinned the drapes over the windows, gasped out of my boots and stockings, poured the first round of jug into the bowl and plunged myself ankle-deep, clinging to the bedframe as the water squeezed my swollen feet. Once they'd stopped smarting – two changes of water later – I twisted free of my sodden clothes, draped them over the bedpost to dry, and crawled into the only things I had left: my old shirtwaist, creased like a carnation, the mud-hemmed skirt I'd left the house in, and the greatcoat, buttoned to my chin. I didn't bother wrestling with the penny-collar; my cravat I wrapped round my neck like a scarf. I was still shivering, my feet bare – and I'd no other shoes or stockings – was it too much to borrow Gertie's blanket too?

"Henry?"

A blister of candle-flame edged towards me through the beds (I'd not noticed how dark it had become), flickered into Septimus. She was lean and neat in her shirt and trousers, her hair so impeccably swept up you would never have guessed anything had dislodged it. All the same – the candle in her hand wasn't entirely steady, quivering against the thickening gloom.

"I – erm – sorry – I – I haven't any other clothes – "

"Neither've I," she admitted. The candle veered towards my bed, a gesture stiff with nerves. "Not here, anyway. But – look – we need to talk. D'you want to sit?"

After all we'd seen and known in the last few hours, her tone was absurdly formal, enough to twitch me into a startled smile. She stared, to see that, then darted her gaze away. Plums, she must have thought I was mocking her.

"I – of course – sorry, it was just – today's been – "

There quite wasn't a sentence for it.

I perched on the bed first, tucked my feet beneath my skirts, felt the mattress contract as she dropped down beside me. The candle, in its tin holder, she'd balanced on Gertie's bed, and its light was paltry at best. For a few shaky breaths, there wasn't anything beyond darkness, and the sheeny beeswax smell of the taper, and the sudden warmth of her leg sliding against mine.

I flushed to my hairline, gripped the bedsheets to keep myself still. If I had twitched my leg, she would have moved.

Figs, let her not move.

"You saved my life," she muttered suddenly, tremulous as the candle-flame. "They'd've killed us both if you'd not dropped the light on 'em."

It caught in my throat, thickened, left me inches from a brace of sobs. The words fluttered against my teeth: *of course I saved your life! I place tremendous value on your life! I'm entirely infatuated with you, whatever you may think of me!*

"The Director ain't sure what to do," she continued, more brusquely. "There's no precedent for it in the Div – shooting with a criminal's pistol, even if you weren't shooting it at 'em. With the head gone again, though, and the two of 'em still out there with that gun, I reckon it's the least of her worries."

Now I froze. "You – you don't think she'll dismiss me – "

"Not if I've anything to say about it." Her voice was low, fervent, clumsy with its own sincerity. "I'm your defence, and I've told her as much – and I'll tell anyone else needs hearing, too. You had the pistol, and you could've got yourself out. You only stayed and fired 'cause of me. You ain't going anywhere, Henry, I swear it."

I gulped – she must have noticed I was blinking off tears – and managed a feeble nod. If I had only – anything, more, than a feeble nod! I wanted to latch my arms about her and kiss my thanks into her forehead – to plunge my face into her collarbone and gasp her in – to turn her towards me, and press our brows together, and hold her close until her hands stopped trembling –

"About Maggie," she murmured, ducking her head to peer under my fringe. "Why'd she call you Morfydd? And when'd she lose her finger?"

This, at least, I could answer. "Oh – I – my ferret dismembered her – erm – and I gave a false name – when she took my hair – "

She seemed more assured than surprised. "That bit I did know. The hair, I mean, not the – dismembering. Well – I suppose – 'least that ferret was good for something!"

We both smiled then, the sort of smile that has a faint sound to it. Her gaze snagged mine and stayed there, until I'd entirely abandoned my capacity for blinking – until I blushed, to find myself still staring, staring and managing it – and enjoying it, far too much. "Well – quite!"

She swallowed. Her smile was shrinking, turning her bitten lips to one sharp line. "I – look – what the Sweetings were saying to me – I owe you my life, so I definitely owe you an explanation. And it ain't so different from what happened to you – I mean, more or less. But they tried to steal the hair off me once before, and they very nearly got it. I was – I'd been – "

Her face twitched. By some startling force of will, she didn't drop her gaze.

"I'd been tricked. I thought I was heading out to meet someone – to do – well – never mind what, something else – but it was all a set-up so the Sweetings could jump me. And I know it ain't the worst thing by a long stretch, losing a bit of hair. Cut it all off in the orphanage, didn't they? It weren't that, that got to me. It was – I don't know, the humiliation. The fact I thought I was safe. More'n that – I'd a job, I'd prospects, I'd my chosen name, I thought I had – never mind – anyway. Turns out I weren't safe. I was just an idiot with her guard down. And I'd've been that again today – and worse – if you'd not been there."

"Oh – you – please – you're quite not an idiot – "

"No, I am." She sighed. "Lorrie and the Director both've said I'm too reckless, and they ain't wrong. I would've gone straight back in there today if you'd not made me think about it. And not just to get the head, either. It's – when they – last time – I assume someone's told you this? Cassandra, most like?"

I shook my head. It brought her out in a startled frown.

"Oh. Right. Well. Wasn't just me got hurt last time. The Sweetings went for me first, and I fought 'em, and they won, but then they – well. They left me to bruise and took stuff from other people instead. Burgled three houses that night, one of 'em Lady Miltonwaters's. I was the only Divisioner out – the only one who could've raised the alarm – and I – I was – point is, I didn't. I didn't stop 'em. And no one's ever forgiven me for it. And I – I've not forgiven me either."

I opened my mouth – and I quite couldn't speak. And I needed to speak. It didn't have to be a triumph of eloquence – just enough for her to know that I didn't mind – *didn't mind?* – no – that I was honoured to have her share such things with me – that her confidence was already lodged between my ribs, and I had every intention of keeping it there – and that her self-hatred was entirely misplaced – and –

"Quite!"

What?

"I mean – erm – not – not quite, but – also – I – I don't – I mean – I do – thank you – yes! – "

I swallowed. *Thank you,* that was it. "Thank you – erm – for telling me."

She blinked, wide-eyed, managed a nervous nod.

"And – about – what you said – you quite mustn't blame yourself. You – you couldn't know what they would do – and no one could expect you to fight them single-handedly – erm – especially not – if – if they had already attacked you – and how could you recover swiftly enough to – to prevent those burglaries? – and – "

The words were there, flickering in my throat, oddly-arranged as ever. She was watching me silently, waiting for me to sort them out.

"And I know – erm – I know what it – I mean – how it feels – to think yourself a disappointment – and have the world agree with you – and – I – it – it quite doesn't help anything. Particularly when – you – you aren't a disappointment in the slightest! – and you never give up – even when it's a scenario in which you can't possibly be expected to emerge triumphant – so – yes – quite. Please don't think it. I – I don't think it – of you, I mean. Not at all. Quite."

For a moment, we could only stare at each other. I'd run out of intelligible sentiments, and she didn't seem able to summon any. She dashed her teeth over her lip, then prised them away and summoned a faint smile, dazed and lopsided under glinting navy eyes.

"Thanks. I – yes. Well. Right. Yes."

She cleared her throat, one hand smudging hastily at her eyelashes. "Right! I was going to say – tomorrow, I'm going to drop in on Lorrie. Properly, this time. The head-hiding – it's deliberate, we've seen as much today. Someone's toying with the Div, and giving it, and stealing it back – and whoever they are, they ain't him. So I – I'll not be long, no longer than it takes to check he's alright. That no one's hassling him, or calling him a suspect, or anything. You don't have to come with me – but in case you were wondering what – "

"Of course I'll come with you!"

I blurted it with desperation enough to set me squirming, straight into all manner of stammered appendices. "I mean – if – only – not if you don't want me to – or – if I'd be in the way – erm – or – if you'd rather I – I don't know – "

"Then come with me." A twinge of a smile. "If you want to."

"I – I – if you want me to!"

She shot me a wry look. The smile was settling in earnest now.

"Well. Alright. Yes. And – I'll talk to the Director about it tonight – so – if she says yes and you've a mind to it, we can cycle there. Quick lesson-on-the-job. Reckon it'll be a lot harder for anyone to jump us if we're scorching at speed. What d'you think?"

And – whether it was her smile, or her undeniable affirmative, or her valiant determination to fix my cycling ineptitude, or the darkness around us, or – passionfruit, heaven knows what – something unseen plucked at my sleeve, more a kind of delicate certainty than any especial boldness. I edged my fingers into the gloom, a tremulous inch above the fabric at her thigh, until I felt the sharp knuckles of her hand where it rested on her leg – where she wasn't tugging it away – where her fingers twitched, ever so slightly, as mine slipped between them. Her eyes were wide and frozen on mine, and I'd quite not the faintest what my face must have been doing. If she moved – if she started back – if she left –

She blinked hard, plunged her gaze down into the shadows where our hands must have been. For one terrifying moment, she didn't move – didn't glance at me again, though my breaths were painfully audible, and my heartbeat shook my very eyelashes. Then – soft, but not so soft as to be imagined – her thumb brushed the length of my little finger, settled itself just at the knuckle.

I trembled.

We must have sat like that, as motionless as our shaky breathing allowed us to be, for full five minutes without daring to move. Everything was fragile, far too easy to shatter – but – at the same time – everything was calmer, and quieter, and steadier, than either of us could ever have imagined it would be. She curled up her fingers, folded them over mine in a careful clasp – and, eventually, we both conceded to believing we weren't about to let go. The candle-wick plunged itself into the wax and sputtered itself out. There weren't words. There was just the dark, and in the midst of it her hand and mine – and my every sense, and thought, and feeling, resting there between her fingers.

Our hold only broke when the silence did. There was a slam of doors and smatter of voices out in reception – Millicent and Oliver, chattering to Cassandra of unsuccessful searches and dismal weather, as the clock chimed some uncountable hour under their words – and it smarted us both to our feet. I couldn't make out Septimus's face, but her hand squeezed mine before it vanished, before a soft clatter accompanied her grab for the guttered candle, before her shadow slipped into the aisle and sprinted away through the door.

And – sweet figs – I know I've everything in this hectic village world to fret for – I know I ought to be worrying about the disappearing head, and the malign intent behind it – and the Sweetings, with their descent into overboldness and dangerous weaponry – and Mr. Adelstein, hovering above me like an owl about to strike – and Edwina, and aristocratic marriages, and all the horrors of my old life – but I quite shan't. Not tonight. Not when I can wind my fingers round the hand she just held and press it to the sharp edges of my collarbone. I can't answer for what I'll dream of, if I dream once this entry's concluded, but – I'm certain to the very marrow on the question of what I'll think about, until the warmth and the comfort and the calm of it tips me into sleep.

18.

IN WHICH SCHEMES ARE THWARTED

The Director's Record

November 3rd 1893 (Friday)

MISSING HEAD. — It's a ploy. A deliberate ploy, someone unknown and malicious out to humiliate the Division – until the town loses confidence in our abilities, until those of us with more susceptible dispositions (I must refer to Matthew, and – though I hope not – Cassandra) concede to their self-doubt – until the criminals already taunting us grow bold enough to threaten our lives – until everything I have unhinged myself to create no longer exists, and can never exist again for the strength of its very failure. And they – whoever *they* are – actually believe that this insane scheme can succeed. That I won't stop them. That I won't do whatever is required to ensure that the Division outlives them – outlives me, if necessary.

But the old vicious letters have dried up – they don't attack me directly anymore. They aim at my recruits. And I could sacrifice myself, if I were sure the manoeuvre would be worth it – but how would I protect the others then? And can I justify sacrificing them too?

MATTHEW. — Wrote. No reply. Will write again. We all have a duty to this Division, and I won't have him shirking his out of inexplicable spite.

THE SWEETINGS. — A dangerous and frightening development. Maggie Sweeting and her brother have somehow managed to obtain a firearm – which they have already attempted to use against members of the Division in broad daylight. Septimus and Miss Hyssop were set upon by the pair, threatened at gunpoint, and only escaped by the latter briefly obtaining the pistol and firing at the furnishings. Unfortunately, she did not manage to keep hold of the gun, and as far as we know the Sweetings are still haunting the town with their weapon. A search of the garret hideout to which they took the Divisioners gave us little more than a stolen lamp, and I doubt the Sweetings will return to the location now that they know it has been compromised. Once again, we are back at square one, and we only have a matter of days.

Septimus is most insistent that Miss Hyssop's shot was unavoidable, life-saving, and purposefully aimed to avoid causing fatal injury. If I had time and resources to spare for a thorough examination of the circumstances, I would. Not that I doubt Septimus's word – it is alarmingly probable that the Sweetings would have used the pistol on my Divisioners had Miss Hyssop not acted as she did. Yet, on principle, I can't condone arming Division recruits with something so lethal – if we are to maintain the standards to which I originally determined we would adhere –

This shall be a matter for after the head. After the deadline. After the Sweetings have been dealt with – for it is essential that they *are* dealt with, all the more so now that they seem to be expressing murderous intent. The pair must be taking advantage of our present position (see below), attempting to compete with the Head-Hider's ghoulish notoriety and secure their former place as Dallyangle's greatest criminal threat.

And we need Henry Hyssop. She is more of an asset than I ever dared to hope, and she might prove herself incalculably useful.

THE DEADLINE. — Outrage, indignation and fear are all well and good, yet they do not alter the fact that the Division is in indisputable peril. We have three days to finish the matter of the Sweetings. Their case is already a major priority, now more than ever before – because we have been too lax. We must end it, before it ends us.

I will have to start informing the Division of the deadline tomorrow. Just the Division Sergeants for the moment, I think. Meagre though it may be, we still have three days, and I do not wish to frighten the apprentices out of doing their jobs effectively. I can't answer for what the news will do to Septimus and Cassandra, but they need to know. If nothing else, it might help shock Cassandra into some kind of productive work-ethic.

What, then – for to face it, momentarily, on paper, is far better than fearing it in silence – what would be our next move, were we to miss the deadline – were our funding to be withdrawn, and the Division disbanded? What will happen to my Divisioners? What will happen to me? Do I commence a campaign for our return – will anyone credit me? Or do I give it all up as a failed endeavour – a desperate, selfish hobby-horse – that has run its course, done some good, and been quietly strangled before it could start doing harm?

No. Of course not. To think like that is to shrug myself off in the process. *We still have three days*, and this maudlin self-reflection is not serving anyone. I have practicalities to address. Let us turn to those.

RESOURCES, OR THE LACK THEREOF. — I had not initially deemed it a problem that the Division's numbers were increasing rather slowly. Recruiting members in our piecemeal fashion allows us to fully acquaint each new Divisioner with our modus operandi, without the need for formalised training – which, at present, we are not in a feasible position to consider. Of course, every member of the Division is valued and able. And, as we have proved, strength of numbers is not a pre-requisite for protecting this town. Our first assignment was a triumph with only four of us on the case.

But when we are faced with *two* unprecedented and deadly threats to Dallyangle – simultaneously – and there are just seven of us to combat them, our scanty numbers start to work against us.

I thought I had solved this matter, settled it as one case per Division Sergeant. But if Septimus, our most resilient and experienced member, cannot best the Sweetings singlehandedly, I cannot send her out to look for them without support from other Divisioners, support which must extend beyond what Miss Hyssop alone can provide. And then – if I have to divert everyone except Cassandra into the Sweetings' case – who will look for the head? And how are we to catch our head-hiding persecutor off-guard if only one person – who *also* has to manage the desk and field any incoming enquiries, and who may yet have to take on Matthew's position if he does not return – is conducting a search?

And Cassandra must lead the Head-Hider investigation. I cannot go back on that now. For her sake. She needs clarity and consistency, a fixed purpose, something to which she can pin her abilities, something to hone her from her lackadaisical carelessness and –

But does that make *sense?* Does it serve Dallyangle? I cannot stake the town on my daughter's reform –

And Septimus did manage to find the head, before the Sweetings attacked her –

But if I turn back to Septimus, and I set aside Cassandra's paltry efforts to give credit where it is actually due – childish though it undoubtedly is, my daughter will never forgive me –

And I cannot lose her entirely, however close I may have come –

Enough.

It is two in the morning, and you are no longer making any sense. This is an official record of the Division's affairs, not a place for your hysterical ramblings. You will return to your home, and get some sleep, and then tomorrow a clear arrangement of resources will manifest itself. It always does.

It has to.

Keturah St. Clare Ballestas, Director of the Dallyangle Division

Casebook of Matthew Adelstein

Pertaining to the Nettleblack affair, and to that wretched Division with which I intend to have nothing further to do

Arrived back from Gulmere this afternoon (mercifully, nothing amiss with Ma and Ta, beyond concern for my safety) to yet another missive from a certain Director who shall remain nameless. As if I intend to respond to her now! The Division is at least proving useful in one respect. According to Ma, the hamlets are ablaze with rumours of Divisionary incompetence – and thus my excuse, this time, has been readily accepted. No parental visits to Dallyangle until the business dies down. Never mind that Nicholas and I aren't part of the business anymore!

The real business is putting an end to Nettleblack's prodigal dalliance. I've sent the letter to her eldest sister – it can only be a matter of time.

Nicholas doesn't know I've done it. He would have attempted to persuade me out of it, like the kindly beloved he is. When Edwina Nettleblack's reply comes, that will be the moment to tell him – once it's happened, and past, and there's nothing left to jar on his sentimentality. I have far too much of Nicholas's irrepressible generosity to be managing already. He's developed the infuriating habit of relocating the Director's letters, and leaving them between the pages of my casebook, or in the pockets of my jackets, or wherever else he thinks I might happen upon them. He doesn't even resent the Division for the loss of his rat.

I sometimes wonder if he resents his family. If, indeed, he ever gives in to such an unsavoury thing as resentment.

He's perched on the chaise, awaiting our evening meal in quintessential Nicholas fashion: by balancing a rat on his knee, and wafting a carrot at it, and endeavouring to educate it by means of the vegetable. He's left off his waistcoat. I ought to fetch him a cardigan, he'll be cold.

And now he glances up to meet me. "What are you staring at?"

Your ridiculous antics with the rodent, I've told him, mock-peremptory. Followed by a brusque appraisal of his chances of success in training the creature to jump for the carrot, and a gentle suggestion that he really must ensconce himself in a dressing-gown, at the very least. I'll have the butler bring one down for him – and then, with nothing to do but wait for Edwina Nettleblack, it might be advisable to send the butler away until the dinner hour –

Idiot! Idiotic saccharine scribblings on dressing-gowns and rats! Has the ghastly affair turned me into a diarist, all blushes and blotched ink? Am I fated to be nothing better than that little demon Henry Nettleblack? – nothing better than her unworthy adversary? – than – oh – damn her! Damn all of them!

I didn't have to ring for the butler. The butler rang for me. He rang for us both, by way of the front doorbell, and Nicholas and the rat went scrambling off the chaise to loiter in the next room. Sweet innocent, he plainly hoped the caller might be Division Sergeant Septimus, or even the Director herself. But if she'd come, she might have offered an apology, or allied herself to us, or –

Or done anything, in short, but stagger into the room in clomping country walking-boots, cock a pose on my hearthrug the way you'd cock a pistol, and announce herself in triumphal vicious drawl to be none other than Miss Rosamond Pleasant Myfanwy Earlyfate Nettleblack.

Nicholas, I hoped, would hear the ridiculous proclamation, and have the good sense to stay hidden.

I, fool that I was, supposed her to have manifested at the behest of her elder sister. Perhaps she wished me to escort her to the Division and her renegade sibling? The impossibility of doing *that*, whilst still avoiding the Director, was the only stress that scythed through my mind, as I proffered her the expected pleasantries –

"Oh, enough of that, Mr. Adelstein," – and I quote her, actually quote her! – "Not much of a detective, are you, if you think I'm part of Eddie's grand plan?"

I confess this beginning startled me, not that I intended to let her notice. What, then, I retorted evenly, might be the purpose of her unexpected visit?

She was wearing nonsense by way of attire: some sort of Morris & Co. trash cut vaguely to a short gown, like a child, and a greatcoat too wide for her narrow shoulders. Out of this coat she tugged a crumpled envelope – nothing less than the same one I had sent to Edwina Nettleblack an hour or so earlier. Cracked at the seal, but plainly not by Edwina Nettleblack.

"Diolch for the letter," she spat, which I can only surmise from her tone is some ferocious Welsh curse. "So Henry's hiding out in the Division, is she? And never you fear, my dear *Miss Nettleblack*," – she was paraphrasing my letter, albeit rather loosely – "I have the perfect plan to lure her out and back into your clutches, all before you can say *pheasant-shoot*. Yours fawningly, Matthew Adelstein – yes?"

There was hardly time even to panic. I knew, though she couldn't have envisioned the additional consequence, precisely what such an utterance would do to our eavesdropper, though I would have given the very roof to be wrong. Nicholas and his rat came ricocheting through the door, his hair tugged to agitated corkscrews, his wide hazel eyes staring me out with a look of incredulous accusation that I could hardly bear, even without Rosamond Nettleblack gaping as witness.

The onslaught was as expected. What had I done, what was I thinking, why had I not told him –?

"Interesting," Miss Rosamond muttered. Nicholas ignored her, still clutching at my shoulders; I was doing all I could to compose him with a look. "I'd no idea you had a partner."

I snatched Nicholas at the elbows, steered him firmly behind me. Apologies could follow later. "If you would explain your purpose here, Miss Rosamond? Am I to take you to your sibling?"

She considered me – us – a moment, her sharp face tilted into her mass of writhing ebony curls. I frowned: my own consideration of her was hardly proving successful, an uncomfortable truth which irked me all the more given her evident determination to scrutinise me. I knew hardly anything of Rosamond Nettleblack, beyond the facts of her being Welsh and rebellious and somehow too much of a scandal to be trusted with a brilliant marriage. Miss Edwina had firmly refused to provide any further information on the subject. I hadn't thought to press for it, with the youngest of the three proving so troublesome. But now I had nothing on Miss Rosamond, nothing I could summon from my casebooks, nothing I could use –

"No, you're not to take me to my sibling. You're not to take anyone to my sibling, least of all my eldest sister."

And, without so much as following it with her unnerving green eyes, she threw my envelope into the fireplace.

There was no point in starting after it, or towards her, though had I been of a more volatile disposition I would gladly have done both. The flames had flayed the envelope from the letter already, and the pages were ash on the coals before any of us spoke again. I thought it best to remain silent until I was sure of my voice remaining steady under my words, Nicholas was apparently dumbfounded by the turn the exchange had taken, and Miss Rosamond plainly intended to wait, to make me retort.

I managed, eventually, to enquire what she meant by destroying the correspondence thus. My tone, I must add (for I fear I will require some defending where my composure is concerned), was perfectly cold.

"I mean," she explained, somewhere between a snarl and a sneer, "that this is the end of it. I don't care what Eddie's promising you and that Division of yours. Case closed. God knows I've not done much of late to make Henry happy – and it won't be easy for me to manage it in the future, not after tonight – so here's my last bit of chivalry for chwaerlet fach: you're going to leave her be. You never found her. She wasn't here. Tell Edwina whatever mad invention you want to make up."

Nicholas was clinging to my sleeve. I shook him off. I was almost – I say almost – *almost* incensed, for reasons which should be patently obvious.

"I intend," I informed the conniving trollop in no uncertain terms, "to tell Edwina the truth."

She grinned at me. Perhaps it would be more accurate to say that she bared her teeth; the sentiment was purely vicious. One of her teeth was made of porcelain, which was disconcerting in the extreme considering the colour of the rest of them.

"Are we all going to be telling Eddie the truth, then?"

Nicholas, brilliant (fatally so), saw what she was about before I did, and caught my arm again. "Matty, don't – "

"The truth about you and your lover?" she added, her eyes skidding between Nicholas and I. "Matty?"

It was my fault. Nicholas had always been able to pass off the nickname as careless unromantic affection, and he could easily have done as much again. *I*, who had prepared in theory for every variation on this moment, ought to have snapped straight into the pre-conceived story: that she was mistaken, that Nicholas was my relation, my ward, my apprentice. I hardly know whether it's to my shame or my credit that, in the event, I simply couldn't. Instead, I flushed with insufferable violence – part of it accreditable to the mere fact of hearing his name for me in someone else's voice – and launched into snivelling, unscripted nonsense.

"This was my idea – he isn't to blame – "

Nicholas, with his indefatigable generosity, was intent on the same course. "No, listen, it was me, I encouraged him – "

Rosamond Nettleblack flapped her hand at us, exasperated. "Oh, shut up! There's no one to *blame!* No blame to be found, and nothing wrong or revolting or despicable about the pair of you!"

I was far too stunned to speak. Nicholas managed the question for us, lashing his ratless hand through mine as he did so (for which I could have sobbed, had I been anywhere but under scrutiny). "Then – what – ?"

She shrugged. "People who aren't me won't think the same.

What you're doing is still illegal. And I despise that law a thousand times over – but if it's the only threat that's going to stop you destroying Henry's life – well – you're not leaving me many other options, are you?"

I would have been less horrified had she – well, had she relished her victory, rather more than she actually did. She looked, once the sneers had dropped off, nothing so much as truly pained by her coup de grace, and by the final words even her voice was faltering. Not that it gave me any confidence to take the chance – the risk – that her evident sympathy might get the better of her. If she, who clearly felt the agony of our position as if it were her own – why, I couldn't fathom – if she could still bear to voice the threat, she could not be trusted. It was a ghastly testament to how far she would go for her wretched little sister. Not that there was anything commendable in it.

She blinked, too sharply for an ordinary blink. Her smile, when it returned, was shaking at the edges.

"Drop the case, and I swear you'll get nothing but silence and support from me. Otherwise – look at me! Disappointed one sister, pushed the other away, and about to fling off the remnants of my family forever – gentlemen, I've crossed every line in the book – so don't you think I wouldn't!"

She stumbled around on her heel and crashed out of the room, one of her skinny hands jerking up to cover her face. Nicholas flung himself into my arms, his chin gouging into my shoulder, gripping me so tightly I hoped it would snap us both. The rat curled up at my jaw, absurdly comforting.

Nicholas is burrowed against my collarbone now. He won't leave my side, not even whilst I write. He has his wish, in the most dreadful manner conceivable: I shan't be pursuing Nettleblack anymore. I don't know what I shall tell her eldest sister. I must say something quickly. Though – if what Miss Rosamond said is to be believed – Edwina Nettleblack will have new family troubles to occupy her for the immediate future, at yet another sister's instigation.

Nicholas's voice is plaintive, murmuring in my ear: even if he's glad of it, he still doesn't wish to be the reason I have to throw over the case.

How to tell him that the case could never matter when set against this, that I care far more for him than any case there could ever possibly be?

Write it, out of the usual code, and let him lean over the book and read it for himself. And, while he's watching –

We will get through this, Nicholas. We will. It's going to require a considerable change of plan, but I'm nothing if not an inveterate schemer, and you've always been admirably cavalier in the face of disaster.

And yes – of course I will be sending the butler away tonight.

19.

IN WHICH MORE EXPLANATIONS ARRIVE
THAN WERE STRICTLY ANTICIPATED

Correspondence (from the past)

<u>*22nd Aug, 1893*</u>

Fiancée mine (now THIS endearment looks as good as it sounds!!) –

*I know we said you were coming this Friday – can we push it back a week?
Something's happened – Sept needs to stay here for a bit. Also – I know this
is probably a stupid question, but – any chance you've got a spare bottle of
Nettleblack's?*

*

<u>25th August 1893</u>

Of course. Tincture enclosed. If our extensive advertising is to be
believed, it should work wonders for all painful, nervous and drugbaffling cases. All my (anonymous) good wishes to your sister.

This coming month will be the first September in years that has
not been swallowed up with preparations for Henrietta's return to
Girton. I fear the endeavour was not as successful as I would have
hoped. But it is no matter – I can at last begin finding her opportunities a little closer to home.

<u>*28th Aug, 1893*</u>

Thank absolutely everything – Sept's on the mend and back at work. Obviously I wasn't worried. Well – I was worried – she was in a bad way – and she didn't even want the Div to know. I don't know what she's told them – if she's told them anything at all. But I didn't seriously think they'd dismiss her. And she seems to be getting better now. I hope.

Also – more news. You know I've got that costume thing going with the Dallyangle Theatre – well, they gave me an advert today. Pirates of Penzance – coming to Dallyangle this autumn – and they want more chorus. The fact I'd be able to fix any costume chaos will count in my favour – and – auditions this week.

...would it scupper everything if I...?

*

<u>1st September 1893</u>

Of course you must audition! If your sister can have the career of her dreams, why should you not seek out the same? We will be waiting at least a few months before there is any movement on the Henrietta front anyway.

Best of luck, my dearest. I greatly look forward to hearing of your inevitable success.

*

<u>*22nd Sept, 1893*</u>

!!!!!

I... am a pirate CHORUS! I AM! HURRAH FOR THE PIRATE CHORUS!!!

*

<u>18th October 1893</u>

I have booked a box. I have it until at least the eighteenth of November, so I can assure you I will be in attendance as much as I can get away with. Starting tonight.

*

<u>*The same, in haste*</u>

I love you. I'm singing it for you, you know that?

Septimus's notebook

Well. The Sweetings had a mind to have it otherwise, but I'm still here. And I've still got a book to write in. Not that there'll be many pages left once I'm done with this.

I'm awake later than I ought to be, and – damn it – far too much hurts. My head, my throat, the cut at my temple. My injuries ain't as bad as last time – they didn't get their fists involved, and the lamp didn't hit me, even if a chip of the glass did – but I didn't have anyone last night to fling me into a bath, to clean me up with fancy bottles and useless apologies. Gertie shoved some Nettleblack's at me, but it ain't done much. I fell asleep too quick, with all my hair still up. My mattress ain't soft, and there's a mort of jumbled pins jabbing into my scalp. That glass-cut at my temple's scabbed over, but it still stings something awful. My jacket sleeve wafts down where I've draped it on the chair, stinking of tallow, nowhere near dry. So much for all that waterproofing.

I groan myself up. Not upright, just – off, sideways, 'til I'm curled on the freezing floor in the murky dark, and my desk-leg's digging at my knee. Outside's a bustle of noise. I don't know every bit of our new plan, but clearly I ain't an urgent part of it, if no one's come to wake me. The Director stayed in late last night, her door smudging gaslight down the corridor. With the head and the Sweetings, it's no wonder she's stretched taut. Maggie and Norman picked their bloody moment to get hold of a gun.

I fling myself on my feet, shoulder into the corridor. Hair – never mind, I can fix it later. Just a glance round into reception, see what's happening. The Director's at the desk, nabbing Gertie and her gang one by one as they trudge past, instructions murmured to each in turn like they're lining up for gruel. Cassandra's at her mother's side, proofing her ledgers, dodging her gaze. All the gaslights are on. Ain't enough light from the windows, not even the smashed one. Wood-burner's just clumps of ash – no one's set it going. My fingers are red as bricks, numb with chill already –

There's Henry! Fidgeting in the dormitory doorway, shivering in her uniform – her clothes can't be dry either – catching my eye with a blink and a smile. It's straight through the bruises and sharp to my heart, how pleased she looks. Her nervous eyebrows furrow in a question – what's the plan?

Well. The plan's there in her outfit. She's unbuttoned the panel on her skirt, folded it back – that tailoring trick Lorrie spent full days working out – and now she's bright in culottes. God, it suits her. As I stare, she fidgets with one of the buttons, nervous and elated all at once.

Cycling clothes! Yes! Getting her on a bike! That's the first bit!

I bite my lip hard, else I'd be grinning. Henry saw me wretched yesterday, listened wide-eyed to all I never thought I'd tell her. She held my hand steady in her slim cold fingers – damn it, she saved my life! And now here she is, still on my side, asking what's next. It don't make a bit of sense, but my feeble show with the Sweetings ain't made her despise me.

I lift a hand, raw splayed fingers – *give me five minutes*. Dart back for my jacket. Taper struck, fingers up and into my hair – I've the oddest feeling she'd not hate me even if I left it scruffy, but even so – 'til the pins I've still got sit right. No time for the hundred strokes. Quicker we can get out, the better.

It ain't raining today, which is a scrap of mercy. My jacket's clammy on my arms, the damp seeping through my shirt. The market square's back at a bustle, but that's not our route. First it's round the building to the cycle-shed, keys in my fist, gesturing Henry in to choose her transport.

No one's touched my cycle – wise of 'em – and a sleepy spider's taken over the handlebars, legs splaying like bent pins. I flick it off, pivot to check Henry's. It's still mud-caked and scuffed from what-ever she did to it on the towpath, but there's nothing that'll stop her riding it. From her pallid stare, it looks like the only thing stopping her's her own imagination.

"It won't bite," I assure her, as she skitters at my elbow. It's the first thing I've said to her all morning. Seems a bit of an odd start, after last night, but I don't think anything I say now could match that handclasp. "And you won't fall off. I won't let you, alright?"

No idea how I'm going to manage that with me on my own cycle, but I want to say it. She's so shivery, so sickly-looking, like one slap against the cobbles'd be enough to snap her – though I was wrong to ever think her delicate. Well. No. She is delicate, but it don't stop her firing a pistol, or facing down the Sweetings, or turning up at the Div desk every morning.

She glances at me, twitches a smile. Too nervous to be really wry, but closer than she's ever managed – and closer to me, too, given how much I've got to stoop in the cycle-shed. There's a lantern skewered inches above my head, flickering strangely in the morning breeze, skewing weird shadows down her cheeks. She's got the slightest of dimples when she smiles. Without the snag of the shadows, I might not've noticed it.

"I – I fear I've already done as much – rather too much – since I first attempted to – erm – conquer this particular Division requirement – "

The smile's at me too. "Well. I did warn you Div work was hard."

"Figs," she concedes grimly, "You quite weren't wrong."

Cycling'll massively cut our timings when I can get her up to speed. We'll be scorching from the Div to Pole Place in two minutes. For the first bit of today's trek, though, we're slow as walking ever was. In the end, I'm barely on my own cycle. If I swing a leg over and turn my head, Henry's toppled sideways by the time I glance back at her.

Since I've all but vowed not to let her hit the stones, I change tack once we're in Lorrie's street. I vault off, keep my cycle steady with one hand, clasp my other arm round Henry's waist to keep her up. She don't fall again.

Concentrate. Get her proficient. That's the job. Safer for us both if we can stick to cycles. It ain't supposed to matter whether I enjoy teaching her –

But it's her. 'Course I do. 'Course *we* do. The freezing morning around us cracks and melts for the warmth of her, the twitch of her heartbeat, the jab of her elbow in my ribs – well, it ain't all an idyll. Then there's the jolts, as she loses her handlebars, and her face suddenly tips towards mine –

Stop it! She ain't *meant* to skid into you!

But she's given up on tremulous apologies. She's gasping, laughing, catching my eye with a weary smile: *figs, but what did you expect?* And then it's my turn to laugh, to shove her back to where she's meant to balance. To force myself to slacken my hold, blushing fit to mist away my breath. To get her standing on her own. To step away 'til I'm just a ghost of a hand between her shoulder-blades, trembling for their every twinge.

By the time we've done a few loops of Lorrie's road, she's got it. Enough of it, at any rate. She won't be scorching any time soon, but she can keep the cycle up, and make it turn, and fling out her arms to point the way she's headed. I kick back into my saddle then, race up to her inside. Show off a bit, if I'm honest. Keep pace, then sprint into a lap, tip my front wheel off the ground, plait my fingers behind my head and grin at her staring amazement. For some vague space of time between church-bells, we're every nightmare lady cyclist your *Punch* warned you about. *Watch this! – wait, don't copy it – Henry! Steady! Point the wheel where you want it to go!*

It'd be a dream too peach-tinted for the day to have Lorrie stroll out across his doorstep, hands tucked in his elbows, chuckling for my antics. He used to. When the Div first gave me a cycle he'd sit on the front steps, some heap of green mending splayed over his knees, breaking off his smile only to yell a warning before I scorched some idiot pedestrian out of the street. If he came out now – what'd he think, to see it ain't just me on a bicycle this time?

What am I going to tell him about me and Henry?

I bite my lip, swoop to a stop at his steps.

You ain't so much as kissed her yet, and already you're dreaming up how to introduce her to the family. You've not even summoned the word *sweetheart*. You've not even met his sweetheart. One thing at a time.

And the thing for this morning ain't me anyway – it's Lorrie. Then back to the Div to pick up some reinforcements, and up to scope out anything else the Sweetings' attic wants to give us. Because – and I've got to glare, guilt pinching in my face – we've our two biggest cases still unsolved, and I've snatched far too much time to enjoy myself already.

Henry skids to a halt beside me, follows my stare. All the floors in the house've chucked out their Hallowe'en turnips, left 'em to fester on the outside windowsills. Half the rotten turnips are still brimming with yesterday's rainwater. There ain't a light on in the place, just red brick and dull blank windows. The church-bell strikes up in the sudden hush – we're grazing seven thirty. Most of his neighbours work the market. They'll all've gone out. If Lorrie's still in, he don't want to be disturbed.

Well! So much for that!

I prop the cycle on the bricks, march to the door, rap it 'til it shakes. Not a sound beyond it. The wood's swollen in the rain, 'til there ain't even much of a crack at the bottom to peer under.

"Lorrie? It's me! God's sake – open the door!"

Not even a twitch of his window-drape. Henry edges up the steps behind me, her face tense in an anxious frown.

"Maybe – erm – he's already gone to the theatre – and – ?"

"I've got to be sure," I mutter. "He said he never got called this early. It's fine – we'll go round the back. The idiots he lives with always forget to lock that door."

Henry blinks at me. "You – erm – plums – you intend to break in?"

I don't even want to imagine Cassandra's quips. "Problem with that?"

"No!" She's already darting back down the steps, a start of blush under her eyes. "After all that I've done – I – I quite can't lecture you – "

298

It's short bristly work to climb the back fence. The grass in the garden's thick to my ankles, matted by the rain into soft rumpled heaps. None of the tenants know what to do with it – an actor-tailor-flower-seller and a couple of eel-merchants ain't got much use for a lawn. They have got a back gate, though, set into the wood of the fence, a latch I can flick up and a path I can drag our cycles through.

The back door lantern's not lit, but we've just about got a sunrise. Once I've latched the gate, and found wall enough to prop the cycles, I'm grabbing for the door-handle – there! It gives with a quick shove, and we're in.

Damp stone walls, the brittle edge of the metal banister, stark under the skylight. I take the stairs two at a time. Henry clatters up behind me. We jolt to a halt at his door. Nothing but more damned silence.

"Lorrie," I hiss, nose to the frame. "Lorrie, it's Sept. Open up."

I'm half-tempted to start singing. He'd be at the door in a flash if he heard me filching one of his blessed Frederic solos.

If he's there. If he's there, he can have all the solos he wants.

"Ah, must I leave thee here, in endless night to dream? – "

The door gives. So sharp it nearly knocks me over. Lorrie's haggard in the shadows, filthy-haired, huge-eyed, wrapped in a moth-eaten cardigan. There's a dingy candle at his back, nothing more. He's not got shoes on. He looks – dear God – like every devil in hell or Surrey's clustering up at his curtained windows, ready to strike him down the instant they spot a flinting of life within.

My jaw drops. What's done this to him?

"Sept," he gasps, and hurtles into my arms.

I wrestle him into his favourite chair, tell him he ain't to move. Get the drapes open, let some dingy morning light in. Strike up the fire. Drape mine and Henry's jackets next to it. Fling a blanket over his legs. He flinches for everything I do, though I've told him there's no need – I'm here now, and whatever's scaring him can't get past me. The Div needs me – but Lorrie needs me too – and there's clearly not been enough of me these last few days to protect both of 'em.

Henry's a pallid gem. She's frowning over his tin kettle at the fire-side, faffing about with tea-leaves and a spirit-lamp, prising mugs and plates off cluttered shelves. Somehow, she's found a loaf of bread, a chipped pot of jam, a rickety knife. I blink at her as she sets to work – here she is, chasing down food for me.

Lorrie's made no objection. If he's surprised she's here, he don't show it.

"I shouldn't've hid," he mutters, hands deep in his cardigan sleeves. "I just – there weren't a way of getting word to you – and I couldn't go out – and she knows you work at the Div – with all the bile you're getting there, and how much she already hates the place, I didn't want to make it worse for you – but she doesn't know where I live, and if I just wait it out it'll all go away – "

I wrench the last curtain back, grab his spare chair and drag it close to him. "She? What she? What's going on?"

He stares at me. Strained and helpless, like he don't know where to begin.

"Lorrie." I snatch for his icy hand, shove up a raft of straggly wool to get to it. "You ain't to worry, alright? I know you ain't the Head-Hider. And I've told the Director you never had anything to do with – "

"What?" He frowns, stunned. "Who – what – who thinks I'm the Head-Hider?"

But – if this ain't that, then what – ?

"No one," I blurt. "Never mind. What is it, then? Can't be worse than anything I've done."

"It is," he admits wretchedly, eyes on our fingers. "And it should be good, that's the worst of it. I wanted it to be perfect when I told you. I never meant it to come like this! But now she knows – and what she'll do to me – and – worse – what she'll do to her – "

"Who's *she?*" I spit through my teeth.

He swallows. Still won't look up. Whatever this is, he's afraid of my reaction. It twists in me, a kick to the stomach. He knows how much I care for him. Surely he knows not to be scared of me – not even –

Not even what? How can I think a damn thing when I don't *know?*

Henry taps his shoulder, eases a mug of tea into his hands.

"Drink," I order him. I ain't got many words left. "And then tell me."

He downs the lot in horrible violent gulps. Henry drops two plates of jam sandwiches onto our knees, edges behind my chair, curls her fingers round the wooden curve of the back-rest. I wish she'd the nerve of last night – that she'd lift her hands and cup my shoulders with 'em.

"It'll be a lot."

Lorrie. Tea dribbling off his lips. But looking me in the eye.

"And it's about my sweetheart."

I set my face steady. If I frown, even slightly, he'll not carry on.

"Well. It ain't just her. It's – I – I don't even – "

I want to snatch for Henry's hand and wring it taut. I don't dare. "Tell me?"

He sighs. It won't be a quick blow, I can tell.

"I can't give you her name 'til it's safe. Swore to her I wouldn't. Ain't like you won't know who she is soon enough, if Lady Miltonwaters gets her way."

If I didn't need the other half of the explanation, I'd shake him 'til the chair rattled. I've never pried on this. I know he wants to keep this woman secret – and he's been with her long enough for me to trust it. But – when he's in this state – why's it that I still only get half-answers, moth-eaten confessions with the details gnawed out?

I tear up the sandwich, eat it bite by bite. Might keep me calm. "Go on."

"I was going to wait for her." Even now, his eyes've got a glint in 'em. I know that look. I'd done the same this morning, when Henry smiled at me across reception. "'Long as she needed. But now – I – oh, God, Sept – I don't know how to tell you – we – "

"But now you're running away with her?"

Even saying it's torn a rent in my chest.

'Course I've no right to stop him. I wouldn't want to stop him, if it's what'll make him happy. But to have it flung at my head so sudden –

"No!"

He's seen it, the panic, before I can smooth it off. His hand shoots out and grips mine, too firm to doubt.

"Sept, I ain't going anywhere. That's never been the plan!"

"What? What plan?"

He squeezes my hands. "We've been working it out for years. She's got duties beyond what I can imagine, you see. A whole inheritance she's got to protect. She's going to marry me, but she can't just run off and do it yet – not 'til she's sorted out the rest of her family!"

Henry's fingers spasm to fists at the back of my neck, clutching the chair fit to warp it. She's astonished enough, hearing this about someone else's sibling.

But it's happening to me, and I'm thrice as struck as her. The room clusters stiflingly close round me, full of stuff that ain't mine. Even the furnishings I helped pay for ain't got the look of me anymore. The chairs and table'll seat a new family. The sheet-music'll have its proper purpose, and serenade this stranger and her strange relations. The bits that mark where I was – the tiny box of clothes, the old scythe – I can't see 'em – they've all been buried and shoved away. And I'll be the same. The scuffed floor'll open under my feet, spit me into the emptiness beneath, while Lorrie and his faceless fiancée kick the boards back into place.

No. That's just first-instinct panic. He always meant to tell me. He said as much. He always planned to bring me in, to whatever new family he's making.

Stop shrivelling up with terror, then, and *say* something!

"Then why're you hiding?"

My voice's too strained, rasping up my gullet. If Henry'd not seen me so pitiful yesterday, I'd never dare mewl like this in front of her.

"If you're happy with her – and she with you – and you – you're engaged – and you've got this *plan* to make it all work out – why ain't you – ?"

Why ain't you just introduced me to her?

"Why ain't you – done it yet?"

He groans, right down 'til his lips dash off my knuckles. "I ain't hiding from her, Sept. It's Lady Miltonwaters. Lady Miltonwaters called on her – when I was there – and she heard us talking – and now she knows. She came for me that same night after the show. She said – all that I've done for you, all that I've done for her – she wanted charge of me, she was about to get me a Frederic audition – and – I don't know – something about helping with my fiancée's sister – and forgiving some wrong she'd done – and this was how we repaid her – and she'd see us both in the gutter, and she knew just the person to do it for her! And I don't doubt she does. My fiancée's rich, but Lady Miltonwaters has a *title* – and her uncle practically owns Dallyangle – and neither of us've got any idea how to stand up to that. So I ran – and I've been off sick from the market ever since – and from *Pirates* – and I know Lady Miltonwaters ain't done anything yet, but – it's only 'cause we ain't giving her chance – and we don't have a new plan – and I don't know what to do – and neither does she – and I'm sorry, Sept, I'm so very sorry – "

His face crumples.

The shock, the guilty fear, the lingering nightmare visions, all of it shatters in my head. I ain't got breaths to take anything in, beyond the fact that he's Lorrie, and he's crying, and I've not yet tugged his face into my shoulder. The rest – Lady Miltonwaters, and her plan to chase down my brother – I can't think of it as real. Not 'til he's stopped sobbing. Not 'til the Div's – and Henry's – and I can't hold it all in me at once, I can't –

I drag him into my arms. One thing at a time.

Now – what's happening now – right now? The light's getting stronger at the window. The street's quiet, but we ain't stagnant anymore – the stale air's been yanked out up the chimney. He's shivering, all sour sweat and damp wool. His cheek's rough as it skids past mine – he ain't shaved. Over his shoulder, the fire's blazing proper at last. There's a heady damp smell from the drying jackets. Two spare mugs of tea – they'd've been mine, and Henry's – sit forgotten and cooling on the mantelpiece. Somewhere behind me, still gripping the chair-back, Henry's gasping short frantic breaths.

Second question, then. What can I do?

"You're going back to *Pirates* tonight," I declare, firm as I can get it. "You can't hide here forever. I'll be there with you, and I'll not let anything happen. And – if you tell me her name – whoever she is – I can report the threats to the Div, sort out some protection for her too – "

All the while, it's hammering on my skull: but what about the head? What about the Sweetings? What about the Div? It's too much for 'em, in our broken state. It's too much indulgence to ask this of the Director. It'll distract me. If I stretch myself too thin for Lorrie, there's too much chance I'll lose everything –

But how can I do anything else? How can I not at least try?

"I'll ask her if I can tell you," he whispers faintly. "I can't imagine she'll say no, not now. But – look – no more secrets from this point on, Sept – I swear – "

There must be a way to manage it. If Henry and I spend today doing everything we can to find the Sweetings, I can slip out tonight. Watch him in the show, walk him home safe. Get back out and keep looking, once he's locked the door behind him. And it ain't like this and the cases don't overlap, sort of – going to the theatre's as good as returning to where we found the head, ain't it?

And that'll be what you say, I snarl at myself, terse between my temples, *when the Director finds out you're pushing into Cassandra's case, and rightly dismisses you.*

"You're coming, then?" Lorrie pleads at my ear. "Both of you?"

No. Not Henry. She can't. Not even if I want her to. I can't risk her job alongside mine. And if I feel I can hardly stand without her beside me tonight, that's just damned selfishness –

Henry clears her throat. "Well – I – erm – only if I'm not in the way."

So tell her she'd be in the way – tell her whatever – protect her, damn you –

I wrestle for the words, but they won't come. There's just the logs, snapping in the grate.

"I'll get you two comps," Lorrie adds feebly.

And I love him, and I'll do everything to help him, and I've just set my livelihood on the line for him, but in that moment I want nothing more than to lash an arm round his waist and hurl him straight out of his wretched dirty window.

20.

OF CARNAGE IN A THEATRE

Septimus in straits

My cycle's propped in the shed – to sit there in the thickening blue dusk for all of five minutes, if I'm lucky – and the front doors of the Div're looming before me. I ain't been scared to go in for months. I've only hovered outside once before – I didn't know if it was the last time I'd ever open the doors, and I wanted to cling to the moment. But the Director trusted me. She didn't dismiss me. She gave me a chance I ain't sure I deserved, and I'm about to throw it back in her face.

The day's been stuffed with its usual dead ends. Nothing to report from the Sweetings' attic. Like as not, the place weren't even theirs – they just knew it was empty, had some practised shove to get the door open. We've given up on Dallyangle for 'em now. More likely, they're hiding out in the fields. I've sent Gertie, Millicent and Oliver further than we've gone since the Div's earliest days: out to the far-flung farms, lanterns swinging from their belts, to peer into barns and under hedges and see what they can find. I don't want 'em trying to start a fight, but if we can work out where the Sweetings are living – that'd be a start.

And if the three of 'em are out chasing Sweetings, stands to reason Henry and I ought to stay in town and switch over to the Head-Hider for a night. Even if I ain't meant to be on that case. Even if my plan's only to get on that case *after* making sure Lorrie's had his stage-time.

Even if I've got to get permission from Cassandra to do any of it.

If Cassandra weren't such a wreck right now, I reckon she'd love this. Me, twitching and wheedling at her desk, hoping she'll deign to make my life easier for once. At least Henry's gone back to Lorrie's. I don't want to drag her into this grovelling as well. If Cassandra says no and I've got to sneak off for Lorrie anyway, Henry can just about say she didn't know I was going to do it.

But Cassandra might not gloat. She might be all for it. She's barely said a word since that night in the Director's office – certainly not to me. And what'd she said, that same night, when the Director flung the case at her? *Give me the Sweetings, give me anything else, but not the Head-Hider.* Maybe she'll stick by that.

Clutching at straws now, I am.

Right. Both hands flat on the doors, the back of my knuckles yellow in the lamplight. In we go.

"No!"

Wait. Cassandra's voice. Spiking out through the hole in the windowpane.

"I'm the only person on this case! You have to tell me where it is – before Mother gets back!"

What?

I drop my hands, flatten my breath to silent gulps. Dash two steps sideways, close to the window as I can get without being seen through it. It's dark out here – and bright in there – but there's still a few lanterns close enough to pick me out in.

"Come now, Cassie. That's not going to help anything, is it? How would you even begin to explain the leaps of detective-work that led you to such a revelation?"

Who's that? The faint familiar shape of a voice – colder than Cassandra, with a strange lilt that sounds more like Henry – but Henry's waiting for me at Lorrie's. Henry's got a stammer. These words are flying fast and sharp as a sewing-needle.

"I could invent something," Cassandra retorts shakily. "It doesn't have to involve you. That's what I do – invent things – "

"And hasn't *inventing things* got you into enough trouble already?"

Cassandra's trying to be snappish, but there's too much tremble in her voice to carry it off. "Only when you post them to me. Only when you – when you imitate them – and make it look like I'm some kind of handbook for murder – "

A wry little laugh. "I don't care a whit about your novel. Your mother, on the other hand – well. If she simply accepted what you wanted to do, and you weren't so mortally terrified of upsetting her – where is she, incidentally? Run away in shame?"

"She's with the council," Cassandra hisses. I'm straining to catch her voice. "And she'll be back any minute now. So will you *please* stop trying to confuse me, and breaking your word, and generally being awful, and just tell me where the damned thing – "

"Breaking my word?" The other voice files itself down, pinches around Cassandra's ragged breathing. "Only because you were stupid enough to let me. But that's what all these people think of you, you know. Stupid frivolous *Cassandra*, too lackadaisical even to flaunt her family surname. But that won't be the case for much longer. I'll be interested to see what you become when all of this is over, when there's not a colleague in sight to show up your failings."

"Over?" Cassandra gasps, skidding out of her whisper. "What do you mean?"

"Well, it has to end somewhere, doesn't it?" her companion tosses back, airy and cold as a draught under a door. "You surely didn't think you and the Division were going to be stuck in a danse macabre for the rest of your life? It's simply the logical consequence, Cassie – and you must admit, it's a fair conclusion. You're all distracted – missing deadlines at every turn, as Lady Miltonwaters always said you would – and she means to say it again, so I wouldn't trust your mother's little council meeting to sort everything out for you – "

"What – who – *what?*"

" – not when you can't even be trusted to keep hold of your evidence – "

Cassandra's voice twists, writhes, struggling out of her fear into something more familiar. Anger. Sharp and fierce as the snap of a log in the wood-burner – sharper and fiercer than anything she's flung at me.

"*That*'s what you're doing. You planned this. You mean to – with – "

Then the words break off. I start, jolt upright, but it's too late. Cassandra must've seen an edge of me at the window, must've let the sight cross her face.

Right. Well. There's one answer I can get, and I'll have it the moment I shove in the doors –

The warmth and the gaslight slap me to a halt, a smarting change from the dark chill outside, scrape a mort of sweat up my back as I squint off the brightness. Cassandra's sat in her usual spot, staring at me like she wants to set the room on fire and thwack me into the flames, and there's a pale-faced girl leant on the desk, glancing round. Hair the colour of eel bone, ashen and silvery above a neat grey dress. Pointless frill of lace at her collar. Wide green eyes, that widen and blink 'til I gasp – they're Henry's eyes. Poked into this stranger's face like something out of Tam Lin. But she ain't Henry.

I do know her – though we've not spoken, and I ain't seen her this close before. She's the Ballestas governess. The revenant who never eats. The one who keeps staring at the Div.

"Division Sergeant Septimus, is it?" she asks, settling to an icy

306

smile, cold enough to freeze the sweat under my collar. "Cassie's told me wonderful things."

Did she see me at the window? Can I get away with a brusque nod?

Get away with? That ain't – I ought to confront her! Whatever she's doing, whatever Cassandra knows about her, it ain't to the Div's good. And if the Director's off with the council, I'm the only one here to intervene. And she's flimsy, little more than a teenager. If I block the doors, she ain't getting past me.

"Right. You – "

"What's happening, Javert?" Cassandra interrupts hastily. Her voice splinters beneath her as she forces it taut over a smirk. Eyes skewering me: it's a warning, stark and unmistakable. "Have you poached my assistant? Are Gertie and the rest coming back tonight, or have you eaten them all?"

I frown. Does she think I've not heard 'em? "I – "

"Excuse us, Adelaide," she adds, still frozen in her smirk-mask. Flicks her eyes to the governess, softens 'em mid-flight, all taut innocence. "Javert's probably done something ghastly again. It's only charitable to spare her the humiliation of telling you about it."

Cassandra! You can't hear what she said and just let her walk!

"But – "

"As you wish," Adelaide returns smoothly. "And you're quite right – I ought to return to Johannes. You don't want your brother left on his own."

She weaves past me as she says it, freezing-elbowed as she brushes my arm, steps out between swings in the double doors. The doors don't even jolt for it. It's like watching a ghost slip through a wall. Her dress vanishes into the gloom outside, but you can still make out that pallid hair right across the empty market, weaving silently between the deserted awnings. I have to tense my fists to stop 'em lashing out for her, yanking her back from her easy escape. All the while, Cassandra's pinning me to the spot with her glare, the tiny frantic shake of her head.

I wait 'til the doors stop swinging, 'til I'm sure the governess must be gone, 'til the last glimpses out don't even give me the hair anymore. Then I dash over the floorboards, as close to Cassandra as the desk'll allow me to get. I need to be close enough to whisper, and even hushed voices make it out through that smashed window.

"The hell's going on?"

Not that I expect her to tell me. 'Course she won't tell me. She despises me – it's there every time she speaks to me, in the snarl curling between the sarcasm. She must've known I wanted answers – and she just let her go –

But she tips forward on her stool 'til she's got her elbows on the desk. Notches her voice to a whisper, matching mine. All her sardonicism's sliding off, straggling into the spirals of her hair.

"I had to get rid of her, however impossible you were making it. Are you going to do a Mother and lecture me for my idiocy, or are you going to listen to why I did it?"

I stare at her. It's closer to answers than she's ever given me.

"Alright. Why'd you do it?"

"Because I've worked something out," she breathes. No – it's spikier than a breath, the anger bunching under her words. "I've been trying, but – I didn't put it together for far too long – I – I don't know what I thought. Between this, and what happened yesterday, with your little bout of perfection in turning up the head a second time – "

"I ain't perfect," I snap. There ain't time for this. "What's your point?"

She sighs. There's the scrawniest ghost of her old smirk. "No, you're not, are you? And now I'm the same. I let this happen. I could have stopped it, but I didn't. I thought – well, if you still haven't told my mother why you sat back and let the Sweetings rob every other house in Dallyangle, I can certainly be forgiven for sitting back and – and hoping that someone else can sort this out, until I've got something better to work with, until it's not just my – but – "

Her hands press to the counter, flat and splayed, 'til they stop shaking. "But I've got it now. She doesn't know that you heard – that anyone heard. We have a chance. *I* have a chance."

"To do what?"

She spits a mirthless laugh, scrunches her eyes shut a moment. When she meets my gaze again, her stare's blazing.

"To show initiative."

"What?"

"I'm bringing you back onto the Head-Hider case," she declares, scrabbling for a ledger below the counter. She slams it open so hard the spine cracks. Grabs a pen and gouges it into the page. Her eyes drop, tracing her scribble as she speaks. "You and Hyssop, and – Gertie et al, where are they?"

I swallow. Cassandra, voluntarily handing me an excuse for tonight – it's about the best change of heart I could hope for. Give her the facts, then, see how many she'll give you back.

"Gertie's out of town with Millicent and Oliver. The three of 'em're trawling barns for the Sweetings. And – look, if you want me and Henry – I think we should go back to the Dallyangle Theatre. It's where the head thing started. We can – "

"No point." She cuts me off like she's biting a thread, and I'm startled enough to let her. "You won't find anything there. You need to go to Lady Miltonwaters's house in Catfish Crescent. You need to ask her what connection she has to Adelaide Danadlenddu. And you need to make sure Adelaide doesn't find out you're doing it."

Now I'm lost. "Why?"

"Because Adelaide has no reason to destroy the Division," she murmurs, her fingers bunching into her palm as she scrawls in the ledger, "But Lady Miltonwaters does. And if the two are working together – I didn't know they were even on speaking terms! That's how I missed it. I can't be expected to know everything!"

I want to shake her. "God's sake, Cassandra, no one ever said you did!"

"Nothing else is enough, though, is it?" she mutters. "Not for Mother. Not next to you, and her, and Miss Hyssop the Scribbler Extraordinaire, and Perfect Skiving Matthew Adelstein. I can't beat any of you – but I can beat myself. I can do better. I *will*. Now get out there and get me proof that Miltonwaters and Adelaide know each other – that they know each other well. Too well for either of them to deny. If it really is some joint design with the Marquess's niece, we're going to need all the evidence we can get."

She tears half a page from the ledger, shoves it at me. I glance down – 'course she's written in huge capitals, a nice little show of how much she thinks I can't read. *ADELAIDE DANADLENDDU*. Brackets underneath the surname: the pronunciation, spelt out, a note to say it's Welsh.

"Mother!"

I skid round just as Cassandra scrambles out from behind the desk, so tense I can pick out her shoulder-blades beneath her jacket. The Director's halfway through the double doors, slackening her pace as Cassandra dashes to meet her. "Mother, I need to talk to you. Ideally right now."

Her mother's all puzzled scowl, but there's no annoyance in it. If anything, she looks almost relieved. The doors sling shut behind her, snapping off the draught. "Cassandra. Perfect timing. I have actually been meaning to discuss something with you, and in light of the council meeting, I – Septimus, what are you doing here?"

Cassandra sprints me to it, wins. "I'm sending Ja– Septimus and her assistant to investigate something on the Head-Hider case. She's already arranged for Gertie's lot to follow up on the Sweetings."

The Director blinks at her. "I – I see. Well, Cassandra, if you think it best, although I would suggest – "

"I do," Cassandra blurts. "I do think it best. I've – ah – I've considered all the options, and I think this is the most productive way forward."

If ever phrase could dash straight to her mother's heart, it's this one. The Director's startled frown smooths off, leaves just her careful smile. Not seen that smile for days. In the midst of this chaos, it's weirdly comforting.

"Very well. In which case – " – and her smile darts over to me, wavers – "Septimus, I wish you every success. And when you return – there is something I need to explain to you, too. The same thing, in fact. I – well – "

"What is it?" Cassandra looks ready to strangle me for hovering too long, but I can't race off without checking. "You'd not rather I waited, so you could tell us both?"

The Director sighs, drops her gaze and her smile as one. "No. Individual discussions will work best, I think. Don't worry about it now, Septimus – you have your work, and that must take priority."

'Course that makes me want to plummet through the floor.

No. I can manage this. I can make it all fit together. If I'm delaying Lady Miltonwaters with Cassandra's questions – if I keep her busy – she'll not have time to go after Lorrie. He can have his show without worrying she'll scupper it.

I nod. Half to the Director – and half to Cassandra, watching me with her jaw set. She'd better know what she's doing.

"Right. 'Course. I'll be back later, then."

Thank everything I taught Henry to cycle. I scorch to Lorrie's, scattering pedestrians with every spin of the wheels, explain as much as I can to him and Henry in words with barely any syllables. Then we're off into the dark, scouring down the journey-time. Lorrie crams two tickets into my hands – someone must've dropped 'em off with him, he don't look like he's left the house – just in case. I've not heart nor time to tell him we won't make it now. I just let him know he's safe.

There's no problems racing across town. If anyone's of a mind to heckle us, they think better when they see our speed – or, more like, they ain't had time to grab an insult before we rattle past. No one's around for heckling or otherwise once we hit Catfish Crescent, but there's a faint gasp just past my shoulder. Henry, slipping on the handlebars for a juddering moment, face taut with panic as she steadies herself.

Even when we're off the cycles, she don't relax. We plunge through the dark, sprint under a lantern that turns the leaves in the Nettleblack door-crest to grasping ragged hands, leap up the steps to the fish-hook carved in stone over Lady Miltonwaters's vast threshold – and with every step she only bristles further. I've seen that look on her before, and I don't like it.

"You alright?" I murmur. "Explanation made sense?"

She nods sharply. Her eyes are gleaming wide and white round the green, and her breaths are fast, knifing the air.

"Henry. If you're choking again, I won't force you to – "

"I won't," she blurts. She clenches her teeth, whistles a slower breath through 'em. "I – I quite won't panic – please – the quicker we do this – the quicker we can get away – "

"If you're sure. You change your mind, you tell me, alright?"

Another nod. A rigid revenant of a smile. "I – quite. I will be fine – now – erm – what was the question for Lady Miltonwaters?"

Fair ask. My summary of Cassandra's logic, bouncing off Lorrie's walls while he did his best to shove a cold pie down my throat, weren't exactly the clearest description I've ever offered.

"What's going on with her and the Ballestas governess. How they know each other. Cassandra thinks we need to find out – that the two're scheming some threat to the Div. If it keeps Miltonwaters back from the theatre, I'm all for it."

"The Ballestas governess," she echoes dazedly. "Well – quite!"

The huge brass knocker's got the same crest as the door. Barbed fish-hook. I thwack it harder than it needs, see if I can blunt the hook a bit. It ain't really Lady Miltonwaters's crest, not the way the Nettleblack nettles are. The fish-hook heads up every bit of paper we've got from the council, juts on the stones above the church door. If you could sweep away the stalls and fling yourself into the sky – you more or less can, when you're looking at my map – you'd see it picked out in the cobblestones of the market square, in the shape of half the streets in the town. It's Dallyangle's crest. And our lady of the interrogations tonight, she thinks she can have it because she's got family in the estate. She thinks she can have anything, Lorrie included.

Well. I ain't seen the estate. I ain't met her family. And if she thinks any of that gives her rights to wreck mine, she ain't reckoned on me.

"Be off with you!"

It ain't far off what I've a mind to yell at her – but the voice ain't mine. Or hers. There's some crystal-cut scowl of a maid in the plush purple hallway, already slamming the door on us, pale-capped and perfect-cuffed. Like some drawing of a maid in a fancy novel, fancier than any real maid I've ever seen.

Not stronger, though. I shove my foot between the door and the frame, and the wood just bounces off.

"'Fraid not. Your mistress in?"

The illustrated maid gapes up at me. Just at me, for now. Henry's shrunk behind me. I'm glad of it. The last person out of this bloated house tried to wring the skin from her jaw, and I ain't forgiven any of 'em.

"Even if she were, she would never admit the likes of you!" the maid cries. "No riff-raff from the *Division* is permitted to cross this threshold!"

I dash a glance down to my boot-toe, scuffing the carpet. *Crossed it already, worse luck to you.* "So she ain't in. Where is she?"

"Is everything alright, Gardewes?"

Another voice. Another servant. This one's older, taller, with the face of a china bulldog and a shirtfront like a fresh-made featherbed, yanking the door wider to glower me out. Butler, most like.

Well. He'll hate it as much as the maid will, but –

"In the name of the Dallyangle Division, I've got to talk to Lady Miltonwaters. Maid says she ain't at home?"

The butler sniffs. "She is not. As she will refuse to speak to you, perhaps it is a mercy that you timed your call so ineptly. Now, unless you wish me to send someone for the police, you will leave Milady's house and not return."

I grit my teeth. His threat's stupid as they come – he must know it's twenty minutes in a cart to Gulmere, just to hunt the one constable who edges in and out at the tip of his beat – but I can't give this lot reason to turn any accusations on the Div. Not when Cassandra's so sure.

"Alright. Fine. Tell me where *Milady* is, and I won't come back."

His eyes narrow. "You are hardly in a position to make demands – "

"Look." I fold my arms, skewer him on a glare even his scorn can't dodge. "Either you tell me, or I'll have to race through every shop, hall and public-house in Dallyangle. D'you really think your mistress'll appreciate you starting a whole town's-worth of gossip about where she might be of a Saturday evening?"

He's clearly out to scoff when I start talking, but by the end he's choked it off. Now those narrowed eyes are bulging. The maid's darting anxious glances up his angry porcelain face, watching it spot red in a furious new willow-pattern.

"As you wish," he spits. "In her present location, you will not be able to disturb her. Milady is at the theatre."

"Again," the maid mutters pertly. He's rattled enough to let her have it.

"I would wish you a pleasant evening," he adds. "But Milady would disapprove."

And I've half a second to tug my foot back before he slams the door, hard enough to set the knocker snarling.

The theatre.

She's already there.

'Course she is. She's the bloody patron, ain't she?

And Lorrie – I told him it was safe –

"We – erm – we have the tickets," Henry splutters, already scrambling onto her cycle. "The church – it – seven o'clock hasn't chimed – we can make it – "

I fling her a nod. There ain't space in my throat for anything else.

I pedal like a dervish, and still my boots are full of lead. No time for quiet streets and a safer route. We've got to streak straight down the middle of Angle Drag, the biggest street in the town, seething with carriages and farm-carts and the stupidest pedestrians known to Surrey. I cut our path for us, a minnow on a cycle against the whole damned shoal, yell myself raw to make the gigs swerve round our wheels, barge full-tilt through the idiots who won't amble out of our way. All the air's crammed with sound. Every crash of horseshoes on the cobbles – every snap of the reins and whips – every shout from the shying passersby – every screaming whinny and snort – every crack of the bicycle-chain – everything thwacks like it's a church-bell, chiming Lorrie's fate. Lorrie and his fiancée. And Cassandra, counting on her evidence. And the Director, unravelling her secrets. And Henry, desperately struggling to keep pace with me, hurtling breathless on a wobbling cycle.

I'm failing all of 'em. Some not for the first time.

No. No time to think like that. Get to the theatre – ain't time to place the cycles properly, just leave 'em by the stage door and hope they stay there – and head Miltonwaters off. Will she go backstage? Will they let her? Or will she watch the show and look for him afterwards? What if she's already done – whatever it is she wants to do? And how do I get her alone to ask Cassandra's question?

We prop the cycles in the lane. Henry grabs for the wall, doubles over, then forces herself up with yellow lamplight scouring her pale face. My hand grips at her shoulder, though it can't be that steadying. Even my legs are shaking under me after that sprint. I want to pull her close, want to press my lips to her hair and splutter apologies into her curls – but we can't stop. Lorrie's tickets buckle in my fist, minutes away from slipping out of date.

The theatre lobby's a crush again. Don't think I've ever seen it quiet. How's there even enough of Dallyangle to pack this place night after night? It's all sorts of Dallyangle too, from your market-traders right up to Catfish Crescent. There's elbows and raucous voices and sudden shocks of heat all around us as we dive in from the cold. I get an elbow in my side, elbow straight back at it. The sweat's slick on my neck again. It's too many people – too many, too close – I want to clamp my eyes shut and push the whole damned clamour away –

But I can't. Miltonwaters – here – somewhere – where?

Nowhere I can see. I twist against the crowd, still clinging to Henry, wrench my neck taut peering over heads. There's Nick's rook-suited family – minus Nick, for years – trudging up the plush red steps towards the gallery. Some more of the Skulls – there are so many Skulls – fresh from their farm and ready to fill the stalls, bulky as hay bales in their Sunday best. Just in through the front doors – and don't the throng part like a ploughed field for her – there's that Welsh tincture-heiress in her heavy green gown, her face pallid and perturbed, walking fast, up to one of the varnished wooden doors that lead to private boxes.

Henry tugs my sleeve, spins me away from the last flick of Miss Nettleblack's mossy velvet skirts. She's studying the tickets – she ain't looked up since we got in. The curls of her fringe've started to flatten, limp with sweat. "I – if I – if this is correct – your brother appears to have obtained us seats – erm – in the grand circle – "

Bloody hell. "D'you reckon Miltonwaters'll sit there?"

She frowns. "I – I would imagine that Lady Miltonwaters – erm – has a box of her own – we could try knocking – perhaps – "

She's gesturing up the stairs to the nearest polished door – the one Miss Nettleblack vanished into. Must not've seen her go past.

"See any others? It won't be that one, 'less Miltonwaters don't mind sharing with – "

"Ladies and gentlemen!" someone bellows, a florid youth in an usher's bright jacket, leaping up the steps to tower over the crowd. Somewhere in the lobby, there's a drawling scoff. (That'll be – no. Not you. Not now. Even if you are here – *please*, just stay out of my way, for once.) "If you would take your seats – tonight's performance of *The Pirates of Penzance* is about to begin!"

Henry tips to her toes, hisses in my ear. "If – erm – if Lady Miltonwaters is in a box – we'll be able to see it from the grand circle – and – there's no chance of us getting thrown out – trying to knock on every door – "

"And Lorrie's on in the first scene," I murmur back. "She won't find him backstage. And if she ain't in the auditorium – we can get out and find her first."

Up the stairs it is, then, past flapping attendants and dawdling theatregoers, above the thicket of double-taking Skulls. Through doors so shiny and mirrored you can make out your fetch in 'em, blurred and softened to a spirit-photograph. Then – beyond it – and, alright, I know I ain't to be distracted – and it's hardly as if I'm here to enjoy the show – but –

But there's the *stage!*

Well. There's the curtain, the sort of bottomless scarlet you can only have a mind to press your cheek to. Where we're sat, a few rows back from the circle's edge, you can peer down into the pit. Everything looks thrice the size of the dim-lit disaster I saw a week ago, huge and sumptuous and defiant. And if that's just the width and the depth, what'll it be like when the curtain rises?

Down in the pit, I can pick out specks of candle, set on rustling music-stands split between a mort of string-players. A chap with a fancy clarinet sucks his reed like a cigar before he clips it in place. A timpanist skimreads a programme. A skinny cellist wrestles round her instrument. They're grinning and chatting and sneaking pieces of clementine, all the show still before 'em. Above, there's the foot-lights, and their gleam on the velvet. And below us, cupped in the plaster cherubs round the circle, you've got the stalls – more bustling heads than plush seats now, and filling fast. More programmes, fanning the stuffy air. The faintest twitch behind the curtain. A streak of an arpeggio from one of the violins, petering into a scrap of a phrase from Cat-Like Tread.

Henry's seen my face before I can frown it back. "You – do you – erm – particularly enjoy the theatre?"

"I've never been," I admit. I'm a bit breathless. "Before this. But – I – well – yes. I think I would. Yes."

She's gleam-eyed as me. "We – if you wanted – we could come back – properly – once I've been paid – I mean – the seats wouldn't be as good – and – you'd probably never want to think about *The Pirates of Penzance* again – but – if you did – "

If I did? To have a night when I was off-duty proper, jostled close to Henry in the gallery, staying for the whole show, with nothing more stressful to think about than picking Lorrie's voice out of the chorus? What the hell's there to *if* about that?

"There," she gasps suddenly, before I can say any of it. "Lady Miltonwaters – red dress – this level – though no sign of any governess – "

I see it. There's the wretched aristo, fiddling with her glossy silver lorgnette, drenched in port-stained silk. The opposite box to Miss Nettleblack. Miltonwaters must've come early, been already sat down by the time we got in. But she couldn't've found him back-stage. Lorrie only left just before we did, tricked up in his pirate costume, too scared to change in the dressing-room.

He's dodged her, then. And now we can see her.

What now? Knock on her? Wait 'til the interval? Watch her through Lorrie's bits, check she stays still?

Then the whole house's applauding, though there ain't a whit of music yet. The curtain's still down, and the lights are slowly dimming. There's a new head bobbing in the pit, swinging their arms out to scoop up the audience. Their arms drop – the instruments jolt – and then –

I'm sheer open-mouthed. Can only hope Henry ain't watching me, that she's keeping her eyes pinned to Miltonwaters. But I can't not gawp. That's an *orchestra*, a real one, loud and rollicking and rich as anything. Richer than anything. I can't think, not with this swelling at the air. It's just music, bits of songs I recognise – *just* music! It's music so thick you could snatch it, and it'd still burst out of your fist. I gasp it in, and it's got a taste, a smell – candlewax and resin and sharp gaudy scents I can't name. And Lorrie gets this every evening! Does that dull it for him? Could anything dull this?

It swoops to its close, and I grab the chair-arms to stop myself leaping into a standing ovation. Much as I want to give the musicians credit where it's due, I can't risk Miltonwaters spotting me. I tug my eyes off the stage, squint through the dark to her box – good, she's still there. Eyes pouring through her lorgnette. Dead to anything outside of it.

And the curtain's rising, flinging a bright painted world down the boards towards us. Choppy wooden waves in neat rows, champing back and forth, in front of a swirling coastal backdrop. A ship and its swooning figurehead, flat as a canvas, with a muslin mast billowing above it. Hollering chaps in frock-coats and stripes and glossy black boots – and I nearly yell myself – there's Lorrie, right out at front! Lorrie as a pirate, in a sea-blue sleeveless jerkin with that tattoo painted on his arm! Lorrie in Penzance, safe as he could ever be, hauling a tankard above his head, singing like his life don't depend on anything but pouring the pirate sherry –

And I can hear him! Whatever he can see of the audience, beaming out from the stage, his voice ain't shaken. It grabs the notes and hurls 'em up, stronger and louder than he's ever dared in the flat. 'Course I always knew he was brilliant – but this is something else. It's happier than I've ever seen him look. Terrified as he must be – as he was in his room – the elation's still swept him up.

And to make us more than merry, let the pirate bumper pass!

Miltonwaters won't have this. Won't take this away from him.

Something's moving. Too close. Here, in the darkness, not out with Lorrie and his pirates on their painted ocean. It jolts me back, flings the bile into my throat. Idiot – as if you're here to lose yourself in the show!

Henry. Her head's tilted round, and her knuckles are ashen on the seat. Taut fingers, nails gouging into the plush. Her breaths have turned to rasps again, tearing up her gullet, her jacket buttons glinting oddly as her chest heaves.

I follow her gaze. It ain't Miltonwaters she's staring at. It's Miss Nettleblack.

The pirates are into dialogue now. Voices like orange slices, bursting on their tongues. *Yes, Frederic, from to-day you rank as a full-blown member of our band! Hurrah!*

"What is it?" I whisper. "D'you need to leave?"

Henry's voice comes in shards. "I – I'm fine – I – I have to be fine – "

There's a sudden stab of light at my gaze's edge, enough to drag my eyes to Miltonwaters's box. The door's open, raking corridor-gaslight over the folds of her padded chignon. A shadow flits into the box – ghost-coloured – dipping down beside her. The two heads bend together, whispering.

Ghost-coloured.

That sly furtive smile across reception. The frail lace collar and snow-pale hair. The name scrawled across the paper in my pocket. Cassandra's suspicions.

Nay, Frederic, a wiry woman cries from the stage, *My mind has long been gnawed by the cankering tooth of mystery. Better have it out at once!*

I'm off my seat, tugging Henry after me, writhing towards the closest aisle. There's angry hisses from our neighbours, crackles as I kick through someone's floor-bound interval snacks – but there ain't time to worry about that. We need to go, now, to catch 'em together. Adelaide and Miltonwaters, doing whatever Cassandra's so afraid of. Before they can actually do it.

But the moment we hit the corridor, Henry almost collapses. Gasping for breath, palms flat on the flocked wallpaper, legs buckling even as she tries to stand. I dart back, get my shoulder under her arm, fold her down to the carpet before she falls. Beyond the gilt doors, there's the muffled moan of the orchestra, a lone contralto tracing a mournful tune. No sound from Lorrie anymore.

"What – what is it? What's wrong?"

"I – I'm sorry," Henry splutters, piecing the words across shuddering breaths. "I – I didn't – expect to see – figs – it was – my own idiocy – please – don't worry – go after them – I – just let me – "

Down the corridor, another door bangs open. Henry yelps, scrambles against the wallpaper like she's a mind for it to swallow her. I start to my feet, skid round – if it's Miltonwaters, or Adelaide, I –

It ain't.

Dear God, it's Property.

White tie. Slick-haired. Smirking. Some velvety flower at their lapel. Easy languid strides round the curve of the corridor. A flick of a glance to us. Scrutiny. But – scrutiny with an eyebrow, like they hardly care what they find, as long as there's something to laugh at in it. Bronze-brown eyes, warm across my face.

The same wry look as always. And the same damned effect. All they'd need do is slip a finger behind my ear, and it'd be the first time I met 'em all over again. *How long is that glorious hair of yours*, they'd asked, *when you're not so intent on restraining it?*

I open my mouth. Any beginning'll do. Tell 'em to stay away from us. Warn 'em I ain't got the time for 'em, not tonight.

They shoot me a wink that makes me flush – rage, mostly – and then they're gone, stalking away past us, without a word. When they hit the stairs, of all things, they break into a sprint, as raffish and elegant as they can manage.

Henry wrings out a rattling breath. "Oh – erm – figs – I thought it was – "

A sharp twist of someone's throat at my ear, enough to spin us both round.

Come from the other end of the corridor – now we've got Miss Nettleblack. Up close, she's tall, pin-neat, taut blonde hair greying like streaks of lead pencil. Stern as she usually looks, if you get a glimpse of her striding out of her carriage. Even if she's not quite looking me in the eye, she's glancing a right side closer than I've ever seen her do for anyone in the street.

What the hell, I think dazedly, does she want with me?

"Excuse me," she begins curtly, voice like the snap of a stick. With an accent that clean-broken, you'd never tell she was from anywhere. "Have you seen a lady in a scarlet evening gown pass through this corridor?"

I set my teeth. I ain't intimidated, it's just – with Miltonwaters and Adelaide still not out of their box – and after that weird little glimpse of Property – and with Henry half-dead, and getting worse – it's all enough to set me on edge. To Miss Nettleblack's strict green glare, I may well look scared.

"No. Not yet." Won't make any sense to her, but I've said it now. "If it's Miltonwaters you're after, she can't get out of her box without coming this way. You'll have to wait, though. I'm from the Division, and I've got to talk to her and that governess first."

Her eyes widen, the whole stern statue-face crumbling past her shoulders. Stunned flickering green – I've had my life's share of green eyes today – struggles across my features, 'til her mouth drops open, and the woollen collar buckles inwards at her throat.

"Septimus. You are Septimus."

How – what – ?

Oh.

My voice shrivels on my tongue. "And – you're – "

Something barrels past me, knocks my eyes away from her. The flocked wallpaper's bare, the crimson carpet scuffed. Footsteps softened in plush, all the way down the stairs. I skid about, just in time – and get a second's glimpse of Henry, hurling herself round the corner, straight for the lobby and the street beyond it, clutching at her chest like every rib's about to crack.

"Keep him safe," I blurt to Miss Nettleblack. Then I kick off the wall and sprint after Henry.

The plan ain't scuppered yet. Adelaide and Miltonwaters can't leave, not without following this route. I can fix this. Find Henry, calm her down, get us back in, all without missing 'em.

The polished banister's hot under my hands, 'til Henry shoulders the front doors open and a shock of cold smacks through the lobby. Outside – I thought she'd stop when we got outside! – but she's still scrambling over the cobbles, faster than usual in her culottes. She skeins under a lantern, headed for Angle Drag, shaking so violently it's a wonder she's still upright. I've a blink of her breath in a frozen cloud, smarting out either side of her wild cropped curls.

"Wait!" I hear myself yell – cracked, splintery, desperate. "Whatever it is – I don't care – I'll help – I – "

Something hurtles out of Weeping Alley, strikes Henry off her feet.

She goes sprawling with a shriek, face-first to the cobbles, arms sickling up to break her fall. I grab the air in two fists to fling myself forward. It's a dream, every inch a dream, and I can't run fast enough. There's someone closing on her. Dragging her up at the wrists, lashing something over her head, scraping her into the shadows 'til she's half-swallowed by the dark –

And then I can't see her. Can't see anything. My eyes are knocked in, and all my senses are blazing on my skin.

I'm a thing in pieces. They ain't holding together. After the rush of the theatre – of the day – of whatever just happened to me – of everything – all of a sudden, the world's just stopped. I ain't even standing up anymore. There's the cold throb of the cobblestones, knuckling at my cheek, digging in my chest. And a screech of pain across my face that don't make any sense. And something's gushing, down into my mouth where I can't get it shut, swollen and salty and thick in my throat.

"Doesn't look much like you're helping!"

It's Maggie Sweeting's voice, singsong-smug over my head.

A boot-heel flips me over, my back pressed to the cobbles, my broken face jutting blind up into the freezing air. I can't move. Can't open my eyes for the smart between 'em. *Smart* ain't enough of a word. Something's snapped there, and just the feel of it clogs me with nausea. Blood's all I can taste.

Cold metal jabbing at my temple. Maggie. Closer. A scraping whisper.

"Good of you both to come out this quick. Most grateful to you, dearie, for saving us the trouble of waiting. And lucky for you we need to sneak, eh? Can't have all the racket of shooting you in the street. But don't you fret. We'll come for you soon enough."

Her heels ring sharp over the stones, away from me. The brief jolt of gunmetal vanishes with her.

They're done with me for now. They're leaving. And if they're leaving, I won't be stuck here for long, not right outside the theatre. Someone else can find me. I don't have to get up. I've just got to stop, and sprawl, and cringe, and let the knife-cold cut up all the smashed edges of my face –

But no one'll find Henry.

Henry.

Right. Never mind that. I can damn well start again.

I wrench my hands over the cobbles – snarl, though it's flint to the break and the bruising – and shove, hard as I can bear, 'til I've got my feet back. My eyes are worse, smeary with daze and tears, but four agonising blinks give me the street. There's something else in it, hammering on the cobblestones, getting louder. I shove myself around, hand collaring my own shoulder to make the turn –

It's a carriage, with one mad-eyed horse and Norman jolting haphazard at the reins, and it's got more than a mind to run me down.

Just you try it! I yell in my head. Can't move my face enough to speak.

I fling myself at the closest wall – and he laughs, as he blazes past, because he ain't got any idea what I'm about to do next –

The wall shunts me away, and I grab. Not the air, this time, but the rail on the back of the carriage, where you'd sling your luggage. The rack slams into my knees, rips through the fabric. I curl up, clinging to the rail both-handed, swallow down my breath – but the carriage don't stop. They ain't noticed my jump.

I'd grin, if I could. That's something, then!

One tentative hand to my face, bloody at the fingertips. Splinters of pain through my skull. A grating slackness where there shouldn't be, enough to flip my stomach and make me retch. Whatever Maggie hit me with – three damned guesses – it's broken my nose.

But how'd the Sweetings get a *carriage?*
Unless –
Damn you! It's never just a wink with you, is it?

21.

IN WHICH YOU'D BE HARD-PRESSED
TO ASTONISH ME MORE

Myself in delirium

Figs, an endless night

Well, to begin with, I was an idiot. I was your feeble-blooded, free-ranging, indisputable definition of wanton stupidity. The panic-attack – mine, that is, spurred by a chest-clenching terror that's impossible to control – had been brewing since we reached Lady Miltonwaters's house, and Septimus had given me every available opportunity to stop, to step out, to gasp for my breathing until I had it back. But the crisis was so urgent, and her plan so sure and steady between her temples, that I hardly felt I could start hurling my own inadequacies at it again. And so we left Catfish Crescent, and the world settled back to its usual sharp edges – and if it were only Lady Miltonwaters and a menacing governess we'd been obliged to confront, I could have made it –

But it wasn't. I had two glimpses of Edwina – first in her box, then towering over us in that corridor, with fury and frustration and heaven knows what else crackling down her leg-o'-mutton sleeves – and it was quite as if all my experiences outside the Nettleblack house had shattered like so many dropped inkwells. I entirely forgot what happened the last time I went sprinting off alone into the Dallyanglian darkness. I'd not even the faintest what I hoped to achieve with a reprise, other than air – breathing – and many substantial miles between me and my sister. In those horrible gasping moments, I was just fear, and squirming cowardice, and everything of the old self I'd been fool enough to imagine I could scour away. As if one could just step out of one's mortal terrors, like shrugging off a greatcoat!

I couldn't, at any rate. Quite the contrary. The sight of Edwina lit a flame beneath my crackling panic, sent it shrieking up to my head until I couldn't breathe, couldn't speak, couldn't think in anything resembling sense. Of course Lorrie's every murmur had struck me sideways. Of course it was Edwina, Edwina with her family and her *plans*, that he'd fallen in love with. Of course her determination to marry me off had been blazing tenfold brighter than ever, if she had decided to stake her life on it! And now – even if I could dare to presume that the pheasant-shooting was well and truly avoided – *nothing* would stop her from pursuing me, and dragging me back, and dismembering me into whatever shape she deemed most convenient! Figs – never mind that it isn't what I want! Never mind that there must be a way – some way to help her and Lorrie – that doesn't just spring up from the dust of everything else!

She wouldn't confide in us. She wouldn't listen to us. Not when there was still a chance I might be found. Not as long as she could fit me to her vision, and wait for me to thank her for it. Even so – there had to be something I could do. Some means of pushing back Lady Miltonwaters, at least –

But then there was Edwina in the very flesh, ramrod in her opera-box!

I ran. I couldn't stop, not even for Septimus. Not until she cried out, and the raw snap of her voice cleaved through my panic and threw me back into myself. And I would have turned – would have forced myself towards her, through the strangling fog and the wild urge to vomit, and spluttered out everything – but the blow was too quick. I was glancing off the floor – or, rather, the floor was glancing off me, as if the whole of Dallyangle was malignantly upending itself – and my feet were scrabbling under me, my arms twisted at my back, a strip of something slippery and cold snaking across my eyes.

And it quite wasn't the moment for polite acquiescence – but heavy shoulders were shoving at mine, marching me forward, and Septimus had vanished, and I couldn't see a scrap of a thing, and my wretched throat was choking off my scream –

My head struck against something soft, a snag of mounted velvet caught against its pile. The floor – a new floor, flatter than the cobble-stones – swayed under my feet. A clockwork-trick of rattles and snaps only urged it to sway more, flicking a chill draught across my face.

It was a carriage.

My hands sprang up, grabbing wildly for the blindfold. Heavy fingers clamped around my wrists, wrenched until they were down at my sides again – all in horrendous thick silence, but for the clatter of the wheels. And even if I tried screaming now, who would hear me? Who would stop the unknown fingers from simply throttling it out of me?

For a moment, the carriage slowed around us, rocked and dipped to one side. The sensation was familiar. That was someone else outside, vaulting up into the driver's seat. Were there *more* of them?

"Please," I heard myself gasp, out into darkened oblivion, as the carriage rattled forward again. The draught through its joints grew sharper, colder – we were speeding up. "I – I quite don't know what you want – but I almost certainly haven't got it – "

But how could I know that? What if it was Edwina holding my wrists down, too livid even to strike me? What if it was Mr. Adelstein?

"Oh, you've got it, Morfydd, as long as you've still got ten fingers!"

My twisting hands quite froze.

And I would have leapt, entirely blind, in whatever unknowable direction faintly suggested *escape* – but Maggie pinned me taut to the seat with one arm, all the weight of her tipping across the carriage towards me, until I'd barely strength even to breathe. It was thrice as ghastly with my breaths already half-choked, with the horrible waxy smell of her waterproof jacket pressed thick and close.

"No room for your tricks now, dearie! You get one last scrap of respite, and then you're all ours. And you can try yelling for the sham sergeant all you like – 'fraid she's not in a state to be of much assistance."

"*What?* I – what have you done to her?"

She shunted closer, every word a clout on the ear. "Nothing next to what we're planning for you."

The carriage kicked to a halt, struck my gasp out before I could get it halfway to a real scream. We dipped again, as the drivers jumped down, and two sets of footsteps strode away outside. The sound of them cut off more swiftly than I expected, vanishing beyond the faint creak of a door.

If I could wrest myself from Maggie now, whilst she bundled me down the steps into the freezing night – as if I could! As if I had any hope of outmatching her without a pistol, without anything more than my own paltry frailty! I cried out – better late than never – until an elbow to the chest doubled me over, my boots scraping under me as she hauled me across the cobblestones. There was another sound under my rasping breaths, a sound that had a thick muddy scent to it – the champing of the river, rifling through the weeds at its banks, swollen and booming with its glut of rainwater. Then the cobbles were gone, and the river's rush stifled, and the floor turned to something soft and draughty and deadening, and there were steps catching at my shins –

A sudden shock of warmth at my face. Maggie dropped me, and a door slammed. The force shoved me forward, struggling both-fisted with the knot of the blindfold – until soft hands settled over mine, worked it loose in three deft twists.

Too-soft hands. That wasn't flesh, it was fabric. Gloves.

I yanked the blindfold down to my neck – and, scorched vermilion in a lurid little fire, Pip Property's lean freckled face gazed worriedly down at me.

I quite defy any human alive to have known how to begin. Not a whit of the immediate world made any sense, besides what I could see (and heaven knew why I was seeing it!): all the perfect edges of their evening dress, their starched collar gleaming hearth-reddish against their olive neck, their cravat replaced with a narrow bow-tie, their shirt fastened with glinting studs. Their room – could it really belong to them? – a veritable chasm away from the bright-patterned excitement of their house, wooden-walled and nondescript, with a dour double-bed under a dirty skylight, and the shabbiest of rag-rugs smudged over the floorboards. A tiny greasy hearth, a cracked jug beside it – no elegant wardrobe, no hoard of cravat-designs – nothing, in short, to connect the impeccable dandy before me with the drab lodgings that surrounded us!

"Gracious, Hylas, are you hurt?"

I'd not a scrap of speech left, but this didn't seem to faze them. They tugged off their white gloves, slipped both into their trouser pockets, and snatched me up in an examination – hands darting along my shoulders, down my arms, around my wrists where the bruises were beginning to smart.

"Wretched creatures! How explicitly must one specify that they don't want you harmed? You were inside the carriage! The seats are plush!"

By now, their hand had crawled up to cup my cheek, the tip of their finger tracing absently round the back of my ear. Plums – and what – *what* was I supposed to say?

You don't think me villainous, do you?, they'd asked me, whilst their scissors glanced through my hair. And I quite hadn't – for all of Septimus's morose inclinations to the contrary –

"Sit down," they ordered suddenly, sliding their free hand round my elbow and ushering me to the bed. "I would offer you a chair, but I'm afraid we're rather in the wrong residence for that. I can try to ring for tea and biscuits, but – " – and they actually grinned at me, skittery and nervous, as if we were in any position whatsoever to be sharing a joke – "it'll have to come to you via the Sweetings, and I very much doubt they've made decent tea in their lives. They are many things, but they are certainly not servants, as I'm sure their pretence tonight must have confirmed. I couldn't even trust Norman to drive the carriage properly – not after enduring his hammish attempts to steer me to the theatre. My own efforts in the carriage-handling department may be entirely self-taught, but they do at least keep the horse at an acceptable angle."

In retrospect, I ought to have been grateful for their wild audacious patter; it was startling enough to shunt me back to words. "I – what – what is this?"

Property blinked. "It's an attic, sweet Hylas. In a less Sweeting-laden world, I would never have flung away rent on a room like this, but when one has Maggie and Norman breathing down one's collar it becomes rather more difficult to say no."

"I'm quite aware of the attic!" I wish I hadn't flushed quite so violently, but I was hardly in a state to be conjuring a measured response. My amazement had jolted the worst breathlessness out of me, but the panic was still plucking at my nerves. "But – *this!* What – what am I doing here? What – you – Maggie – Norman – what?"

A long skein of a sigh, twirling upwards between us. Their hand was still at my ear, thumbing distractedly at the lobe.

"Quite right. I do owe you an explanation, don't I?"

I swallowed. I wasn't entirely sure I wanted to hear it, but – persimmons – when the alternative was this dark sardonic suspense –

"It's infinitely more encouraging than it looks," they added hastily. "I said you would be the first to know if I could devise a means of helping the Division, and now – well, here you are! And in tremendously fashionable split skirts!"

"I – what – how – how is this supposed to – ?"

"I'll come to that. The premise of the situation stands thus: I intend, this evening, to quit this little sceptred isle, and I'm not certain when I'll be returning."

It must have been horrendously evident on my face: the sudden ghastly thought that they intended to take me with them, in a swoop of malevolent logic that made absolutely no sense, but fitted tenfold to the dangerous persona Septimus feared they possessed –

Property caught my terror, and flung a laugh at it. "Gracious, what's that trembling lip for? You're not going to miss me that much, are you? And there I was, writing you off as a stalwart admirer of Division Sergeant Septimus."

"I just don't – erm – understand," I spluttered out, somewhere taut between incredulity and fear, " – what this – what I – why I'm – ?"

They pinched my earlobe – gently, but with the slightest edge of nail to it. Apricots, and it shivered my voice right back down my gullet.

"You see – if it were simply a matter of me trotting off to the Continent to embarrass mamma at one of her open-ca's, I wouldn't need to take precautions – but it isn't. The manner in which I intend to leave England – specifically, the identity of my travelling companion – is going to cause nothing short of a minor explosion in certain exalted circles, circles famously inclined to send blood-hounds after any doves that fly the nest. I don't intend to have anyone chasing me down, thank you very much – and I can only trust our old friend Monsieur Ticket Register to provide the flimsiest of alibis – so it seems I'm in need of your assistance."

I gaped at them. "I – I don't – "

"*Must* we resort to vulgarisms, sweet Hylas?"

They rolled their eyes. Then, so abruptly it made me gasp, they snatched my face in both hands, held me steady and shoved their words at me one by one.

"I need the Division on my side, and you're going to make that happen. I want every Divisioner in this town disguising my absence, refusing to chase me and my companion – and scuppering anyone who tries to stop me."

What? was quite my sole articulate thought.

That, and – churning, relentless, inevitable as giddiness – fear. Petrifying, throttling fear. The ghost of the panic-attack, thickening in my throat.

"So I'm giving you something in exchange!" they continued, snatching at a smile. Their voice dropped to a whisper, dipped close enough for me to feel their lips twitch at my ear. "Namely, the perfect circumstances under which to thoroughly curtail Maggie and Norman Sweeting. *They'll* never let me go unless I destroy them in the doing, and it's more than about time somebody facilitated that destruction. Hence why I had to send them after you tonight, with your sweet sergeant watching on. She'll muster the entire Division whilst we keep the Sweetings suitably sedentary here, your valiant chaotic militia can storm us – I can rush outside, the innocent neigh-bour, and draw them into the relevant room – the Sweetings can be decidedly outnumbered – my companion and I can dash off in the fray – and you can tell them all afterwards what a consummate patron saint Pip Property really is!"

"I – sorry – what – "

"And I'd appreciate it," they blurted, as if talking even faster would somehow whisk all my bafflement out of me, "if you could water my ferns whilst I'm gone. The cases aren't locked – once a week – it's easy enough. Much easier than your ferret. And you shall receive quite possibly the best compensation of all for your services, and for putting up with such treatment. In fact, I've already given it to you. Look!"

They slipped a hand down my neck, to where the blindfold was tangled at my collar, tugged until a swathe of it curled over their palm, and tipped it up to the light. "Amber and green, as I said. I couldn't resist a little bronze, too."

It was – and what was I to make of it? – a cravat. *The* cravat. The same cravat they'd drawn in the air for me, the first time we met: rippling silk, elegant paisley, all the colours to bring out my eyes. The fabric was a little crinkled, where the knot of the blindfold had crumpled it, but in every other respect it was consummately, maddeningly perfect.

"It's yours," they murmured, feathery-soft. "Let's see how it looks, shall we?"

I didn't have a shirt-collar. It didn't seem to matter. They looped the silk round my neck, just above where my jacket collar cut off, twisted finger over deft finger to fasten a jaunty knot, smoothed the ends until they gushed bright over my uniform.

Was I breathing? The cravat was trembling, so I must have been – or perhaps it was just that – trembling, and far too much of it. They'd let their hands linger against the paisley fabric, but their eyes darted up, caught mine with a gentle smile. *I made this for you*, it seemed to assure me – it was precisely the sort of look Rosamond used to proffer when she brought me my pistols on the cliffs. *I remembered you, and I thought of you, and I made this for you, and I have a plan to fix things for you, and I fully intend to keep you safe –*

And whether or not they slipped away – figs, what was that to me? They weren't the Head-Hider. They had no designs on the Division. Septimus might have been wary of them, but – but – but surely, if anything, it would be *better* for Septimus this way, with an ocean between her and Property's tinderbox smirks? And – it was their wonderful bathroom and those flashing silver scissors again – I could feel it, lapping at my nerves, the languid ease of giving myself up to someone else's decisions! How easy it was to embrace it, in this hearthy little room, with all the menace of the situation stripped out, and their smile so close, and the perfect cravat slippery as fish-scales at my neck! Nobody would blame me for not resisting. Hadn't I been snatched off the very street, as stunned and stricken and helpless as anyone might reasonably expect, with Septimus herself as witness?

Septimus.

Whatever it is, she had yelled after me, *I don't care. I'll help.*

And I – selfish decadent idiot! – didn't know what the Sweetings had done to her, what state they'd left her in – whether they'd even left her alive –

"What happened to Septimus?"

For quite the first time in our tangled existences, it was Property's turn to gape at me.

"She – figs, I don't know – if she can even get back to the Division – and if the Sweetings have hurt her, I – "

"Are you trying to threaten them?"

"I'm quite not doing this until I know she's alright!"

Their eyebrows soared – but the suavity was gone. This was something else. This – and it tipped a dram of fear back into me, for all my sudden bravado – this, even in the cosy light, was positively menacing.

"Hylas. I don't want to frighten you, but – "

The starkest of horrendous pauses.

"You don't exactly have a choice. There are two armed criminals outside that door, currently under the impression that I intend to hand you over to them for spontaneous dismemberment. Your beloved ferret is asleep amidst my luggage, but as I seem to recall Maggie and Norman have a score to settle with him too. The only thing currently standing between you and a truly alarming amount of imminent doom is me – and therefore, sweet friend, I rather need you to cooperate. For your sake, and for the Division's, and for mine. Please."

They'd reeled off the sentiments with their usual drawling lightness, but there wasn't a whit of sarcasm left to soften it. Everything of them – their sharp handsome face, the neat arch of their thumb against my cravat, the desperate glint in their heady brown eyes – it was a warning.

And they were on the same side of it as me. I saw it now, however carefully they had been trying to disguise it: the panic twitching at their eyelashes, the scald of hope under their skin. *Please.*

"What – why – the Sweetings – why do they trust you – what have you done?"

Property sighed, dragged it out through a brittle eye-roll. "Sweet Hylas, how do I even begin to explain?"

I swallowed. Waited. Let the fire slump a notch, scatter a few tentative sparks towards the rag-rug at our feet. They were going to give me a testimony – a proper one, this time – and Septimus was going to be safely alive to hear me relay it back. Quite.

"Cravats," Property declared, weary and wry, "are only lucrative up to a point. Heretofore, I had my inheritance from Father to supplement that point. But – for all that my overindulgence of a bathroom and my fine paternal furnishings might suggest otherwise – I am not at all wealthy anymore, and the little I have left is fast sprinting away from me. Mamma carissima cut me off years ago. It's a test, damn her. She's quite determined that I shan't have any support from her until the day I grow my hair out and start calling myself *signorina*, also known as a day that decidedly shan't ever come. I was endeavouring to sort it out on my own, to find some perfectly legal means of increasing my income. But then I found myself in the process of getting burgled by our dear friends the Sweetings, and it came to a choice: let those muddle-headed ruffians steal everything I still had, or convince them I had more to offer."

"I – I don't understand – "

They laughed, bitterly. Twitched their hand up, over my cravat, to where my curls clung close-cropped to the nape of my neck.

"I'm afraid I stole your hair, my dear. I'm afraid I've been press-ganged into stealing everyone's hair, starting with my own. The Sweetings are the proverbial scissors out on the streets, and then I sort it out and sell it on for them. They give me a share of the profits – a polite way of pretending my part in it is at all voluntary. But it has to stop. I've been trying to stop it ever since I saw how they did it – which is something of an impossible task when one's stuck between a Division Sergeant and a hard place that's just bought itself a pistol – "

It snatched me by the throat then, far more vigorously than any belated revelations about my own turbulent history with the hair-thieves. "Septimus – she said you would know about Dallyangle criminals and – and she was right – but how – how did she – ?"

I quite didn't even need to finish.

Property grimaced. "How do you think?"

I'd been tricked. Not by those two – they ain't got wit enough to trick.

"I thought I had it in hand. Septimus was such a trusting flower, and so hopelessly infatuated with me. A state I was at perfect liberty to encourage, I must stress – my companion and I are what you might call flexible with our additional dalliances. Well, the Sweetings were demanding I find them a new target – and I was in no position to refuse – so I asked her to dinner, her and her magnificent hair. Of course, she was to brush past the Sweetings and lose said hair en route to Pole Place, after which I meant to compensate her in abundance with all that she came for! But – gracious – how was I to know she was meant to be guarding the town? How was I to know the Sweetings would thrash her like fighting-dogs? It was all I could do to find them, to prise them off her, to persuade them she wasn't worth the trouble. She could hardly stand – of course I wasn't leaving her there! – so back to my house it was, to hurl her into the bath, to give her a blanket and a chaise to sleep it off on. And then the Sweetings, perverse goblins that they are, chose *that* night for their streak of burglaries!"

Roasted, merciful figs. Of course.

"But everything subsequent is her own insanity. She could have told her Director of my involvement a thousand times over – and yet no one at the Division even seems to know where she was that night. Clearly, she prefers to torture me. She won't just give me up, and she won't just leave me be, and she resoundingly *will* try to catch me out on every other possible front, until all her bright Divisionary prospects wither around her! I ask you, Hylas – is that really the thanks I deserve, for saving her feral little life?"

No one's ever forgiven me for it. And I – I've not forgiven me either.

"Sainted conference pears!"

I was at a legitimate snarl. No – more than that – I was up off the bed and square on my feet, my nails clustered into my palms.

"Septimus doesn't think like that! She – she would have believed in you – and you knew it – and you led her straight into the Sweetings' clutches! And you may well tune yourself to me – and promise me cravats – but you have quite no guarantee the Sweetings aren't simply going to explode your plan from the inside – and shatter all of us – if they haven't shattered her already! You've put Septimus in mortal danger – *again* – and I'm quite not letting you get away with it this time!"

Property seized my arm as I hurled myself past them, twisting desperately enough to wrench me to a halt. Their voice, sharp in my ear, was even more frantic than I had been expecting. "Hylas, wait, you can't simply leave – "

"Henry?"

I froze.

The door of the hearth-room had opened, and all the heat had been sucked out, past one narrow set of ankles in the doorway that decidedly didn't belong to the Sweetings. In a terrible daze, I gasped in the walking-boots, the wild patterned fabric, the crested suitcase, the bramblebush of ink-black hair.

A scandalous travelling companion, with fearsome relations well-known for mounting searches. I really should have guessed it, shouldn't I?

"Beth sy'n bod, chwaerlet?" Rosamond offered feebly from the doorway.

22.

IN WHICH KETURAH BALLESTAS
TAKES HER BADGE OFF

Septimus, dishevelled

It's a mort of distance, wherever they're taking her. I couldn't've kept up with the carriage, even if they stop to pick up Property, stalking down the street in white tie like that's any less suspicious. I've got to make some allowances for the state of my face – I bleed from my broken nose 'til my sleeves are sodden. Never swooned in my life, but this probably would've done it, if I'd had to do anything more than cling to the luggage rack and grit my teeth. It's maddening to think, but I can't climb over the carriage and fight 'em. Not when another blow to the face'll knock me out proper.

We pull up at one of the tall new tenements, out on the edge of town. I know the street. I can mark it, scribbled with a pencil, on the map in my notebook. Right next to the river, though just listening tells you that – the water's fast and churning, but I can't pick out its smell over the blood. Property and Norman get out first, jumping down from the driver's seat, unlocking a front door and stalking in. Maggie's next, tugging Henry with her. Her breathing's ragged, scraping through one of her attacks.

Damn 'em. Damn the whole bloody lot, anyone who'd dare hurt her!

The question is, what the hell do they want with Henry? There ain't much more hair on her for stealing – and she's only met Property once, damn it! –

Unless that ain't the case. Unless they've somehow – I don't know! – but what if it's all a plot? Fake a kidnap, so they can run away together?

What? No – that's mad – she wouldn't!

But – if Property – the lengths they went to just to trick me – how much further'd they go, if it were for someone they actually cared for? And they'd not be shy about it, too. None of my awkwardness, no terrified handclasps in the gloom. They'd just give Henry everything. At least, they'd try – even if they've run out of money as much as they said. And I couldn't even resent Henry for falling for 'em. Not when I'd only gone and done exactly the same.

I slam a fist into the carriage. I can't cry – can't even breathe properly. Not a single window-curtain twitches for the noise, all the way up the building. 'Course not. As far as that lot care, I've bled out back at the theatre.

Might as well be true. I can't go in after 'em. I've tried it enough to know: I can't beat the Sweetings in a fight. *Definitely* not in this state.

So what, then? Back to the theatre? Back to the Div?

Doubting Henry? Running away again?

No.

It's a jolt up my ribs, shunting me off the carriage, back to my feet. There's a sharp crunch in my nose – I hear it more than feel it – as my heels hit the cobbles. I've barely taken a step before I'm swerving sideways, stumbling for a balance that ain't set on its usual compass. Well! I can still work with it. I might be a wreck, but – whatever's up there – Henry ain't a part of it. She ain't Property's – or anyone's. 'Course she ain't. She never was.

I breathe out, the only way I can right now, bite the sodden copper from my lips. One thing at a time. You know where they are – you're the only one – and now you've got the map – you could direct people here. So get back to the Div. Get the Director. Get as many of 'em as you can find. Save Henry.

Maybe even manage another chunk of your impossible to-do: find the missing head, fix everything for Lorrie and Miss Nettleblack, question Lady Miltonwaters and Adelaide Danadlenddu, yank the public onto the Div's side, actually get rid of the Sweetings –

Damn it! This night ain't ever going to end, is it?

The cycles're still at the theatre. Not my best luck. It's just me and my legs and my skewed balance, and too many cobblestones, and the freezing wind chafing my bruises. The clouds've split down the middle, and now the sky's liquid black, crow-wing black, so black it's almost bright. Gouged out of the black's a narrow sickle of white – there's our moon, all we've got of it, cutting weird cracks into the slates on the roofs.

It hurts to walk. Not enough to stop me, though. All the strength the matrons used to hate, yanking at my muscles to keep me moving. The bleeding from my nose has finally dried up, but the break smarts for every chatter of my teeth, and my throat's turned to stiff bark from the gasps of cold air. Lorrie'll scold me for it, out the other side of tonight, if we both make it. *Stop, Sept – stop pushing and rest, for once in your life!* And I will, I promise him. I'll save Henry, and then I will. Probably. My feet skid between the cobblestones, catching in the cracks. There's no one to prop me up this time, no skinny arm tugging round my waist, no frantic whispers at my ear: *gracious, sweet Septimus, I will not let you collapse!* I'm the only one keeping my legs steady – and I – I don't know if I can –

The cottage wall tips towards me, then strikes like an elbow to the ribs. I grab for the bricks, dig my fingers in 'til my boots stop sliding, the cold stinging in my palms. I can't slump down in someone's front garden. I can't slump at all.

"Please," I hiss into the bricks. My jaw's taut against the pain, squashing the word to a strangled rasp. "Can't stop – Henry – "

I'm answered. A chime on the air – then another – the full soft church-peal that marks quarter to eight, every piece of the sound hanging in midair like a hovering buzzard. I cling to the wall, counting out the time, steadying myself to it. 'Til it's done, it's just me and the chimes. Everything else is eerie and still. My breaths are misty in the sallow lamplight. If it weren't for the candles behind the windows, in the cluster of cottages that hems me in, I'd seem the only breathing thing in the world.

But the chimes are close. Loud enough for the church to be just a street away. And the cottages – they're not new-built or hollowed into tenements, they're the pretty rustic stuff – burrowing in on themselves against the freezing night air. Winter primroses planted in the windowboxes. Smoke in the chimneys. And if I'm in the midst of this chilly little picture-postcard, I must be nearly at the market square.

In the end, I hit the Div from the side. I snatch for its nearest wall, a last bit of steadying before I've got to struggle round to the doors – but this time, it ain't the scrape of bricks under my hands. It's the edge of a windowsill, the gaslight inside spilling out onto the cobblestones. I don't have to squint through it to know what I've found. This window's always lit, deep into the night. I can bet she ain't slept a wink since the head first went missing.

Mad it may well be, but I just knock.

It scares me as much as her, making the Director jump. She's sat at her desk, wrist-deep in papers, and I'm a wraith tapping bloody-knuckled on her window. She springs up – it's all I can do not to leap back – and she don't settle to calm, not even when she's recovered enough to dash across the room and wrench up the sash for me. She looks ready to collapse. Gold spectacles dangling from one ear, straggles of thick hair veining her black forehead, the top three buttons of her perfect jacket tugged loose –

Her badge. She ain't got it on. It's gleaming on the desk, but it's the pin that's facing up to us.

I'm straight to my knees once I've twisted through the window. Shaking hands – and they're hers – grab my elbows, drag me up, set me in the spare chair. She drops into focus in front of me, wide-eyed. I've no clue at all where to start.

By the look of it, neither does she. We've a moment to share a dazed silence – then she hooks her glasses on, lifts her thumb, smudges a tendril of hair off my face. Catches my cheek when I flinch, holds me steady, makes me stare her out.

"You look like my conscience, Septimus," she mutters eventually. Gasps a breath, furrows her eyes shut, opens 'em again. "You're my responsibility – you're all my responsibility – and I can't even stop these vicious people reducing you to this. I can't protect you – any of you."

I want to tell her that I chose the job, and that my wrecked face's my own stupid fault, and that she can't take that damned badge off when there's still far too much we need to sort out together. I've opened my mouth to do as much, 'til I realise I'll never get it out without sobbing. And I can't. If I cry in front of her now, with her confidence shot through, that'll be the end of it.

"Who did this to you?" she demands, peering between my eyes. "What happened? Did you see their faces?"

Speak to her, damn it!

"It ain't what you think," I blurt. Spitting words stings a web of pain across my face, blurs her shock into tears for a few frantic blinks. My voice sounds like it's crawled from a rock, grating and stifled and not even slightly familiar. From her quiet gasp, I guess she's noticed the change too. "Wasn't – because of the Div. Wasn't to do with the Head-Hider. It – the Sweetings – "

I lose the sentence to a snarl. She shoves herself out of her crouch, scrabbles through the madness of the desk. Paper, she's after, a quill that ain't snapped. "Don't try to talk. Write it – "

No time! I grab my notebook instead, splay it wide to the map, jab a frantic finger down on my own scribbly streets. "Listen – here – Property – "

It's like I've turned her to stone. The paper skids out of her hand, off the edge of the desk. She ain't looking at my map. Even through the smart in my eyes, I can see her jaw clenching.

"Septimus. The Division is already stretched to its limits. I appreciate – look at you! How can I do otherwise? – that you have suffered a terrible shock, but if you truly think that now is the time to be reviving your obsession with Pip Property – "

Months on end of me shoving 'em at her every five minutes, too ashamed to tell her what I knew – or how I knew it. No wonder it's come to this. No wonder – and I could strangle myself – and all the while, Henry's still out there –

"Please! Look – this ain't like that – I know what they're – "

She slumps back to her knees on the creaking floorboards, lashes her hands up and buries her face in 'em, knuckles taut to her eyes. The sight kicks the words out of me. Every edge of her's rigid – with fury, with fear, with disappointment, with all of it.

"I can't fight you now," she whispers. "I can't. I can only fight so much. I have set myself against everything. I have put all of you in danger – my family, my Divisioners – my son, alone with that viper Adelaide – and as for you, who were once the best hope I had – well. Here you are. Here's what I've made of you. Here's what I've made of everything. And I – I thought the endeavour would be so easy – because that's what you do, when you see where everyone's gone wrong, when you know just what to do to make it all right. You think you can manage it, even if you have to fight yourself and your family and your detractors and anything and everything that can't see what you see, for the rest of your life – until you try it."

The sob cracks at my face, sharp as another blow. "But – you're – "

"Tired."

There ain't a gasp of hesitation. She lets the word drop through her hands like a plummet. One of her elbows cricks against the desk, propping her up where her shoulders sag.

"And I shouldn't even say it, shouldn't look it, not for a moment, with the rest of the Division depending on me. Not when we are almost out of time."

"What?"

She's still staring blank through the cracks in the floor. Every sentence slips out like a thing she's lost her hold on, piling on the boards around her crumpled skirts.

"The matter I intended to discuss with you – that I told Cassandra earlier. It – I hoped never to have to mention it. I hoped we would get rid of it before even having to confront it. But we haven't. We haven't stopped the Sweetings, and it is almost the sixth of November – and the council warned me, three weeks ago, that if we failed to master the Sweetings' situation by that date they would withdraw our funding. I didn't wish to frighten you all out of your efficiency by telling you too soon. I thought we would manage it. I can only hope we might still manage it, though with all that I know now, I just can't see – "

She breaks off, slumping into the hand that clutches her forehead. Around us, the whole building's suddenly, horribly quiet.

I blink, grind my lashes together as much as the break'll let me, 'til the tears scrub off and I can see her properly. For a moment, staring at her's all I can manage. I just – I don't understand. If she's known about this ultimatum for weeks – if this was the same news she had to tell Cassandra – it didn't break her then! When she was summoning Cassandra into the office, encouraging me out of the door, assuring me I'd no need to worry – it was Div business as usual, nothing we couldn't sort out, certainly not a thing to sob over. But now –

When she was telling Cassandra. And Cassandra had something to tell her too. And the only thing that could've made it worse since this afternoon is – whatever happened in their conversation.

So – what to say to her now? Shape myself to simpering patter, and tell her everything'll be fine? Wax on how brilliant she is – what a thing she's managed – so commendable she gives up all her sleep to it – inspirational – pedestal-perfect – patron saint of provincial institutions? Oh, because *that'll* drag her out of her isolation, won't it! *That'll* shove the weight off her shoulders!

"Now just you wait!"

I grab her hand, the one that's at her eyes, wrench it down. She made me look at her – right! Well! My turn!

"It ain't your responsibility to sort it all on your own. To protect us, protect Dallyangle, meet a deadline slapped on you by someone with no idea what we're dealing with – everything. Look – I know where the Sweetings are, right now, and I need your help. I don't need you to be perfect. I just – these ain't things anyone should be trying to manage alone!"

I don't have to make her look at me. She's staring in earnest now.

"It *was* the Sweetings did this to me. They did it so Property could take Henry. And it ain't the first time those three've worked together. I never told you, alright – I just let you suspend me – I was too ashamed – and scared – and it felt better to let you think I didn't even see the Sweetings that night – better'n admitting just how much of an idiot I was! Property wanted to meet me – and I was on duty, so I shouldn't've gone – but I did. It was all a trap – they'd arranged it so the Sweetings could ambush me for my hair. And when I couldn't fight 'em off, Property stepped in – took me back to their house – told me to rest. By the time I woke up, the robberies'd already happened."

It ain't exactly the words I'd want for it. But it's the first time I've said the whole thing aloud. I suppose I can't hope for much better.

"And I – I'm sorry. I know that don't fix it. But what needs fixing ain't me – it's Henry. The Sweetings'll hurt her, and now they're armed Property won't be able to stop 'em. I need – whoever's here – you, me, Cassandra, everyone we can find – to save her – and to get the Sweetings – because we *do* still have time, and I ain't leaving her behind!"

Her hand's trembling against mine, fingers clenching tighter and tighter into my palm. The pain in my face, when I stop, is giddying enough to set my ears ringing.

"You were too scared to tell me that you had been tricked and attacked?" she whispers. Sudden, abrupt, so hoarse it's more a hiss than a question. "And what about yesterday, when it happened again? Would you have told me about that, if Millicent and Oliver hadn't announced it first? What – what are you so afraid of?"

Then her face spasms, taut with new panic. My own must be a mirror for her.

"It's me, isn't it? Like Cassandra. You are afraid of me. Afraid that I will hold you to the same standards that I hold myself, and find you wanting."

Every word's a chokehold. "I – I only – you expect a lot – and – that ain't a bad thing! – it just – "

"Keturah Ballestas?"

The voice smarts on the air, shouted from out in reception.

I know it. So does she.

My first instinct's to spring up and fling the door wide – 'til I remember my face. Another blow and I'll be on the floor. I can't fight anything, can't scare anyone away. Terror skitters up my back, freezing me to the chair. The Director jabs her nail into my palm, lifts one finger to her lips.

There's one creak – then another – it's footsteps. Several sets of footsteps. Crossing past Cassandra's desk – where the hell is Cassandra? – and stalking into the corridor.

There ain't even time to dive across the office and dim the lights. Those footsteps, they'll already've seen the glow under the door. They'll hear the breaths, the dry-mouthed gasps I can't get quieter, scraping through the broken silence. They'll know we're here.

"Come out, now. Quick as you can."

I start, too much. The Director grabs my elbows before I jolt off the chair.

"Cassandra was right," she murmurs.

A sharp rap at the door. "Or must we come in?"

That door. Not even locked. There could be someone – or more – pressed up against it, ready to shoulder it in. Could be armed. Could be – oh, God – and I'm as good as useless – but I can't let her face it alone!

"A moment, please," she calls back, shivering through the words. I stare at her, stiff with fear, helpless to stop her. "This is a conversation for a larger room, is it not?"

I snatch for her. She can't – she can't –

Then her arm's at my waist, easing me silently off the chair, holding me close. Close enough for the lightest of shaky whispers at my ear.

"Henry Hyssop. Get her back here. Don't worry about the deadline. What she is – no, more important, what she does – the writing – tell her she can use it. This is a chance I never dreamed we would have, and we will not get it again."

I – but – what?

Another rap on the door, a brief rattle of the handle. I can despise myself all I like, but I nearly scream for it.

She moves. One hand tugs the makeshift bolt of curtain across the open window. The other marches me with her, step for step, 'til we get to the door, where she presses me against the wall. When she opens it – it opens inwards – it'll hide me. Her last look to me, before she reaches for the handle, is as much an entreaty as it is a warning. I've got to trust her, but – and it's clearly terrifying both of us – she's also got to trust me.

"Well?" she declares briskly, swinging the door wide. In the last glimpse I get of her face, I see anger running taut along the edge of her jaw. "I am sorry to disappoint you, but this is not precisely a surprise. I think it about time you start explaining what you want with me – and what you have done to my daughter."

No one answers, but she's already going. There's a breath or two, enough to make me hold mine – someone's looking in – a rustle on the threshold –

The door slams.

I stay there, frozen and silent, 'til the footsteps clear the corridor. There's still voices – but I can't tell whose anymore. I step to match the sounds, inching across the office, dodging the creaks, shoving my notebook into my jacket. Lift the curtain in trembling hands. Blink to blunt the knife of breeze at my eyes.

I tip myself out in a heap, both hands tense around my nose. It hurts, but it works. If I'd gone feet-first, my boots would have clattered at the cobbles, but now all the sound's swallowed up in fabric. I've got the way back to that tenement scribbled in my notebook. I've got fear, swelling in my gullet – and no plan.

I thought I'd be striding in there with the Div at my side. I ain't got a weapon to match the Sweetings, and my strength for a brawl's all but gone.

Henry – please – what in hell's name do I *do?*

23.

IN WHICH EVERYTHING
IS INFURIATING

Myself, somewhat less than helpful

To continue the attic-based catastrophe

Rosamond. Property. Figs, but why not bring the Sweetings back in, and make one vast delirious carnival of it?

And *beth sy'n bod?* She met me here, on this threshold, doubtless aware to her very marrow that I had been dragged from the street by vengeful burglars with whom she was apparently perfectly prepared to associate – and yet she still had the audacity to summon her old comforting refrain by way of an opening gambit?

Summon! Call it *desecrate!*

I can only hope my seismic outrage provides something of an explanation for quite what happened next. I was slack-faced, fury-headed, gaping at Rosamond whilst she gaped at me – and something in her question struck a flame I wasn't entirely conscious of remembering. Then the words were shrilling headlong up my throat, and they weren't words I'd dared use for full six years.

"Mefus! Beth – wyt ti'n – *gwneud?* Wyt ti eisiau mynd adre – neu ble, Rosamond? – a pham ydw i yma – pam fi? *Pam fi?*"

To summarise the gist, it was incredulity to the eartips, and there wasn't so much as an *erm* in sight nor sound. I don't think I planned for an answer, and I very much doubt I was calm enough to understand one. The door was still open at Rosamond's back, and I was far too furious to care what might sprint into my path beyond it

– after all, Rosamond had clearly managed to get past the Sweetings without being seen! I was halfway onto the stairwell before either of my new tormentors had so much as drawn breath for a retort.

"Stop her!" Property spluttered – which must have been one of the most ungraceful things they had ever been forced to say – and leapt after me, just as Rosamond tossed her suitcases down and snatched for my arms. Either of them alone I could probably have had a fair chance against, but Rosamond only had to struggle with me for a gasp before Property caught up with us, and then I was resoundingly outnumbered. "Back inside, quickly, and lock the door!"

The two shoved as one – the raggedy floorboards thwacked into my knees – and the door slammed behind me again. I scrambled to my feet, but this time they were ready. Property splayed across the locked door like the most debonair of arachnids, gasping for breath, whilst Rosamond grabbed my hands and squeezed them together, as if she thought it remotely possible to calm me by clasp alone.

"Gracious, here's fire!" – and Property may well have intended a sardonical grin, but they were rather too short of breath to manage it. "Now, Hylas, are you going to behave sensibly, or must we make this situation even more ridiculous than it already is?"

Rosamond pressed her thumbs into my palms, flung me a shaky smile. "Da iawn, chwaerlet. Didn't know you remembered that much of the mamiaith."

Was it too much, really, to howl *traitor* at her?

"You quite can't do this!" I cried instead. "I – you – you don't understand – you can't leave! Not now that Edwina – look – you – you have to stay – it has to be you – you're – erm – the best positioned to help her – "

"Narcissus, what is going on?" Property demanded, slicing through the remnants of my explanation. "Why the devil are you clutching the little Divisioner like a Millais made flesh? Is this some quaint Welsh custom I ought to know about?"

An arch of the eyebrow from Rosamond, as she whirled to meet their incredulous stare. My sister seemed more mocking than indignant; plums, even the Welsh jibe hadn't fazed her, not when it danced in Property's drawl.

"Pip fach, dau gwestiwn i ti: un, why have you abducted my sister, a dau, why are you calling her Hylas? Casual seductions are all well and good, cariad, but probably best they aren't related to me!"

My jaw quite dropped. If she was asking this – surely that meant –

"You didn't know?" I heard myself stammer.

Property stiffened against the door, their teeth sharp and gritted beneath an impatient velvety whisper. "What didn't you know, Narcissus?"

Rosamond blinked, green eyes flitting dazedly from face to face. "Ah. Well. Pip. It's – it's rather more what *you* don't know – "

"Is it?" Property was unabashedly snappish, the smirk fading, the last of their sardonicism straining at the edges. "Gracious! And I thought that, after all I've done to mastermind your escape from your family – from breaking into your house to lying to Edwina's face to *making sure we can leave* – I'd be more due for abject gratitude than bilingual mockery!"

Peaches.

I knew the look this tirade struck up in Rosamond all too well. I had last seen it a week ago, just before she flung herself over the chaise, Morris fabric and feral hair and all. The glassy gaze, the languid half-smile, the indifferent amusement – and, this time, it wasn't in the least directed at me.

"You told me," she observed wryly, one skinny hand sliding out of mine to tousle her fringe, "that you were going to make sure the Division and the Sweetings didn't chase us, even if Eddie tried to start a search. I had, I suppose, the vaguest of ideas that you were going to reconcile with the Division by giving them the Sweetings. But I'd no idea how you meant to do it – and, really, if the idea was to drag a Divisioner in as bait, I'm amazed you didn't pick Septimus – "

She quite knew how I felt! I'd told her, every word I could stammer out, and she'd squeezed my knee and called me chwaerlet for it!

"Don't you – I quite won't let you hurt Septimus!"

An irritable chuckle from the doorway. "Do forgive, Narcissus, Hylas is exhaustingly sweet on her."

"Oh, I know," Rosamond agreed cheerily. "I did tell her she was in for an amser anodd with that one – "

"You entirely don't get to lecture me now!" I snarled at her, snatching my hand from her half-hearted hold. I seemed to have discovered a capacity to snarl, and I confess in that maddening instant it was addictive. "I trusted you! I – why do I always trust you?"

It was more than a fair question, and for a moment I watched it strike home. Rosamond blinked at me, her pale lips shrugging off words with several panicky twitches – but she lost her nerve. Before I could demand anything else, she'd ducked my glare and swung her gaze back to Property.

"Well – anyway – Pip – you do rather seem to have snatched up my sister. Henry's been living the vigorous working life as a Divisioner for the past week – " – and, amazingly, her voice sharpened into mocking scorn – " – so why she suddenly sees fit to judge me for wanting to get away from Eddie, I couldn't say."

I gaped at her. It hardly seemed the most appropriate moment to hurl my eldest sister's impending ruin down my middle sister's smirking throat, but neither had left me with anything resembling a better option. "I – I'm quite not *judging* you! It's just – Edwina – she – she's – "

"Not again, chwaerlet," Rosamond groaned. "Eddie's a lost cause, and I can't change that. Just leave it, alright?"

"Narcissus," Property interrupted sharply, their voice a veritable knifeblade, "Do you mean to tell me that this roaring mouse is in fact Harriet Nettleblack? And – more to the point – that you didn't warn me I might need to bear that in mind when dealing with the Division?"

Rosamond rolled her eyes. "How was I to know your melodramatic little mind would jump straight from *lure in the Division* to *actual kidnap?* And what's the plan for when they all arrive, eh? I mean, I say *all* – you'll probably get enough of them to outnumber the Sweetings – though they don't have Mr. Detective anymore, and they've got about five hundred other cases – "

"Thank you for your input *now!*" Property snarled. "Perhaps, if you had been willing to help me come up with a plan in the first place, my melodramatic little mind might have bowed in good time to your Cambrian genius! You do realise that Septimus will not simply give up, where I am concerned? Even if she won't be direct about it, she'll still chase me down to the ends of the known world unless I can find some means of stopping her! And now – *maledizione* – don't you see? Now – now that I've essentially carried off two heiresses in the same night – she and Edwina have all the proof and reason they need to have me arrested!"

Property's voice had risen and risen, clean out of sarcasm, up to a spiky pitch of terror that set me flinching. Their hands were clenched to talons around the edges of the doorframe, taut against the damp-softened wood. Rosamond, perpetually Rosamond, still had her eyebrow hooked up, her lazy sneer coiling across her pale lips – that defiant disdain, carved on with all the stiffness of a mask.

"Calm down, bach, you'll figure something out – "

"I *can't* be arrested!"

It was all but a scream. Rosamond's eyes shot wide.

"Think about it, Rosamond," Property hissed. "*Think.* I will be eaten alive, and not for anything that's happened tonight."

Then, I confess, Rosamond astonished me. She slipped past her suitcase, snatched Property at the bow-tie – and quite entirely kissed them out of panic.

I gasped, but the pair of them ignored me. Rosamond had Property's lower lip between her teeth, their foreheads dipping together, eyelids sinking into lashes. It was nothing I could have dared to imagine, or credit with the capacity for genuine corporeal existence. I had thought, before, that I wanted to kiss Septimus. I thought I'd the slightest idea what kissing Septimus might entail – and I had speculated that the sensation might be an enjoyable one – but – but –

I quite forgot where we were, what had happened, what I was meant to say, how much I'd been furiously intent on cleaving Rosamond into several traitorous pieces. I – I can't say what possessed me – and my face was aflame – but I couldn't in the slightest look away. I had never seen a kiss like this one. My youthful existence had shown me perfunctory hand-kisses, and the old half-smile brush of Rosamond's lips against my forehead, and the chaste fervency of modern novels, and the puffy-faced embraces you could find in paintings from the last century. Not the sort of darting, daring manoeuvres my sister and her lover were currently excelling in – the glints of teeth, tugging at a lip, the fingers trailing up from tie to jawline –

And there were words, too, whispered between them. It was the gentlest I'd heard Rosamond's voice in years.

"Calm, cariad. You're alright. We'll be alright. We'll be away before anyone can stop us, and you'll be beyond all the arrests in the country soon enough."

Property sighed. "And this time, you intend to help me?"

"Just you watch me. Now – you've got Sweetings goblining up and down the stairs, but they were easy enough to sneak past. Let's put my luggage next door with yours, and then we'll sort Henry out – and then, what, be ready to escape when all the Divisioners rush in?"

"Surreptitiously," Property added, shuddering. "I can placate the Sweetings until then, but I would rather they don't notice our retreat."

Persimmons, if anything could have dragged me out of my daze –

"The Sweetings – they – erm – what are you doing about them?"

Rosamond and Property blinked at me as one – still cheek to cheek, reddened at the lips, eyebrows a very proscenium of bemusement. I had undoubtedly not lost my slack look, the blaze under my eyes. Strung on their gazes, I felt quite unbearably young, and no amount of new backbone could have ameliorated it.

"Scuppering them, in theory," Property muttered. "Maggie and Norman are under the impression, courtesy of my own good self, that these antics tonight are some grand revenge orchestrated for their benefit, against the Division that seems so resoundingly to have wronged them over the past few days. I mean to keep them stationary and thinking as much until the Division arrive – at which juncture, even they're bound to spot that I've resigned my role as their pleasant-voiced plaything."

They dropped to a hiss, dark with disdain. "After tonight, if I ever see that motley pair again it'll be too soon."

Rosamond smirked. "See, Pip? You'd be an excellent criminal mastermind!"

Property rolled their eyes. "I prefer *cravat designer under coercion.*"

My sister ignored the correction. "Right! Henry – here's something I *can* fix for you, eh? Imagine that! You just sit tight in here while Pip and I sort it out. Better lock the door, in case the stairwell ghouls come prying. We'll just be – oh, however long it takes until your rescue comes!"

I'd no retort to that beyond open-mouthed bewilderment – but neither of them seemed inclined to wait for me. Property laced their fingers through Rosamond's, whilst their free hand slipped across their waistcoat, along the golden gleam of what I'd assumed to be a watch-chain, drew it out until it roughened into a brace of keys. Rosamond – and it struck me quite as much as the kiss – beat them to the lock, fished an identical key from her coat pocket and twisted the door wide. Either one could have locked me in, once they had both vanished into the peaty darkness of the landing. They could have done it together, and kissed as they turned the key, pallid hands pressed against olive skin and starched collar –

"Rosamond – wait! Listen to me! Edwina – Edwina needs you! She's engaged – to a lyric tenor – and our family tailor – same person – I quite can't explain how I know that, but – I – I just do! And Lady Miltonwaters wants to ruin her for it – and – and Edwina's going to need – at least one of us – to help her – and you're the only one she won't try to force into marriage – so it has to be you!"

It froze them both in the doorway, as I had desperately hoped it would. Property's face jerked into an incredulous smirk, bemused and half-disbelieving, their eyes flicking to Rosamond. And – figs – Rosamond – she didn't doubt me. If anything, the revelation seemed to settle her, until she was perfectly, unnervingly still. Hand-in-hand with Property, wide-eyed and motionless in the scrawny wooden doorframe, she didn't look a whit like any version of her I'd ever known. Not daredevil Gower Rosamond, not decadent Surrey Rosamond, not even the Rosamond who'd sat with me outside Checkley's Tavern and dipped an ear to my infatuation. She was just solemn, and steady-voiced, and resigned.

"Well," she declared. "Da iawn. That would explain it."

"Quite! So – erm – you see – "

"I see she doesn't want us involved, not as anything other than convenient little pieces in her perfect plan. If that's all we can do to *help* her, then – no. Let her have her life, and pob lwc to her, but not at the expense of mine."

"But – Rosamond – "

She squeezed Property's hand – and then she was beside me in three swift steps, slender fingers gripping my sleeves. "Me going doesn't have to mean you staying, chwaerlet. Edwina clearly won't accept help from either of us. If you don't feel safe going back, don't go back. I've made sure you'll never have to, and you should know I hate myself for the way I had to do it."

"What? I – I don't – "

"Exactly. You don't. You don't have to do anything for Edwina, not anymore. Edwina took as much from me as she could, as long as I let her – my home, my freedom, my former self, almost my language – and if you rush off to help her, with your sympathy and your kindliness and your sisterly loyalty, she'll only do the same to you. And you've got things you don't want to lose now! Don't give them up at her insistence, and don't let her leech them out of you. Addo i mi."

She read my confusion in an instant, dredged a weary sigh. "I asked you to promise me, Henry. If it weren't for her, you might have understood that."

And she stalked from the room with Property at her side.

24.

OF CONTINGENCY PLANS

To continue my catastrophe

I couldn't say how long they left me waiting. I staggered over the floorboards, examined every scrap of the rickety room for something to do, something that wasn't a swift descent into abject despair, or tumbling too thoroughly through Rosamond's last words. There was a pile of spindly firewood for the filthy hearth, though the blaze was slumping into its embers now. The rag-rug, on closer inspection, was all cravat: scraps of discarded patterns plaited into colourful chaos. The skylight was the only window, the broad pane of glass clouded to its own patch of fog. I shoved it open just to check that I could, stood up on the bed to poke my head out – though the moment I had it gaping to the night I confess I backed away. I didn't dare try climbing through it in the darkness. It was true country dark out there, utterly stripped of streetlamps – just the fields and the coppices and the river before them, hissing as it slapped against its weedy banks.

I have to admit it – I wanted Rosamond back. I wanted her to sit beside me on the frail metal bed and explain herself in full. I wanted her to blotch up all the rents in my knowledge, and trust me to comprehend them, and steady the ground for me to make my next decisions – not just leave me with cryptic half-confessions, and bitterness, and scraps of broken Welsh! What had Edwina done to her – what had she done to Edwina? Where were she and Property going? Would I ever see her again, once they'd both left me behind?

I was curled on the bed, my knees to my chest, my head locked in my elbows. My thoughts veered off at dead-end angles, or folded in on themselves. Rosamond and my family, Septimus and the

Division, me and my alias – had I lost that? Would I lose it now? Or had Mr. Adelstein, if he'd not forgotten me, already given me up, and I simply didn't know it yet?

Either way, how did any of that translate into action, in this immediate wretched moment?

"Septimus," I whispered, fast, to choke off a sob. "You – you'd know – "

"Henry?"

Pomegranates.

That quite wasn't my fevered mind. That was entirely real.

That was ten bloodstained fingers, clinging taut to the lower frame of the skylight, wrenching until the straggling remnants of a chignon rose into view.

I sprang uncoiled, hurled myself at the window.

She had just enough strength to drag herself up and over the skylight's edge – she hardly needed my frantic scrabbling at her shoulders – before she crumpled down onto the bed, both hands clasped to her face. Quite beyond hesitation, I grabbed her elbows and tugged her upright, across the room and onto the rag-rug, as close to the fire as I could get her. She was stiff and shivering from the freezing night, and the shock of warmth on her skin set her gasping anew.

Beyond that instinctive competence, I could only stare. There's quite not enough rage and terror and desperate protectiveness in *horrified* to encompass it –

I'd seen her angry, scared, helpless. It didn't twitch a candle to this. Her hair was toppling out of its neat folds, shards of heavy chestnut crumpling over her trembling shoulders. Her uniform was filthier than mine had ever been: torn and grey with dust at the elbows and knees, bristling with splinters and mortar – she truly had just climbed the back of the building! – crusted at the sleeves with the dried remnants of blood. And – her face – and how she flinched, and coloured, and dodged my gaze when I prised her hands away from it – her impeccable face was livid with bruises, streaked along her cheekbones, under her eyes, across the crooked bridge of her broken nose –

"Figs," I spluttered out – there weren't better words, or any words – and flung my arms round her.

She started, almost enough to knock me away. I would have hesitated – or asked her permission, or anything more decorous – but with both of our situations so resoundingly unhinged, I'd quite lost the ability. Then she jolted towards me, her forehead pressed to mine, her frozen hands clasping welts of cold into my back. Sharp through my jacket buttons, the bolting rattle of her heartbeat jarred against my ribs. My lips were at her cheek, shuddering on her skin. There wasn't time to consider what I did, whether my convulsive twitches were gasps, or sobs, or kisses –

She flinched, and I could cheerfully have wrenched my own head off. Every touch to her face must have been a shriek of pain. I prised myself back, as gingerly as my nerves could stand, until I could meet her eyes, wider and more terrified than I'd ever seen them. Beneath her bloodied nose, her lips were bitten almost to shreds.

"You were right," I heard myself stammer. "About – about Property – and everything – they want to run away – and – "

She spat a wretched groan. "Oh, Henry, that ain't even the half of it."

She grabbed my shoulders, freezing fingers clinging to me with all the strength left in them, and she told me quite everything. The deadline for catching the Sweetings, about to be missed. Cassandra and her unknown revelation. The Director, alone in her room, refusing to so much as glimpse her own badge. How she had hidden behind the door, on the Director's orders, watching in petrified silence as our leader strode out to meet intruders in the Division. Then her voice cracked, though she cleared her throat with a frantic jerk of the chin: she had left the building, as ordered, and now there was no way of knowing what new threat the Director had to face without her support.

It flung the remnants of my worries over Rosamond out of my head. Figs, of course it did! This was – it couldn't be – it was surely too heightened to credit, too desperate to be true – but even the wildest bout of wishful thinking would have been punctured by her stricken face –

"But she's got a plan," she added suddenly, squeezing my shoulders. "The Director. And we're part of it. Or – you – you are. I ain't had more orders than what she's given me, but there's a message from her to you."

I gaped at her. My expression must have been question enough.

"Your writing." She swallowed, cleared her throat again. Her voice sat strange in her skull, straining to match its usual shape. "She wants you to go back to the Div with it. Something – she said – what you are, but more importantly, what you do, and you can use it. And it has to be right now. I assume that means something to you, that it don't to me?"

She was too urgent to sound exasperated, even when facing down this new gap in her knowledge. *Whatever it is, I don't care, I can help* – and she'd quite meant it.

Except that now, apparently, it was me who had been appointed to do the helping. And – what – what did the Director expect me to do? If she was confronting something fearsome within the Division building, how could my *writing* possibly ameliorate the situation? Did she want my journal – the journal which was still hidden in the dormitory? Was it my identity? And for what?

All the while, Septimus was staring at me, teeth biting down in her bloodied lip, straggles of hair snagging on her eyelashes.

"If she – I can only presume she's referring to – my journal – and it's in the Division – as she says – and there's a back door into the dormitory – "

"Then we've got to get you there," she muttered, wincing into a frown. "And – look – never mind Property. If they're running away, must mean they're breaking with the Sweetings – and it ain't a moment too soon for that. I won't just abandon the Director. Any threat to the Div ain't for her to face alone."

But Rosamond – if she leaves the country, Edwina will only double down on the search for me – and she'll never have the chance to undo whatever made her so resoundingly cavalier about abandoning our family –

I thought it all, stark and fierce as a burn, as the smart in my fingers when they dashed against the metal on the Division's wood-burner. I thought it – and then I blinked, ran my fingers along her arms and clenched her hands in mine.

"Quite."

Behind me, the door rattled against its lock.

"Right!" – and Septimus was on her feet, shaking fists curled up, shunting me behind her. "We'll be out now, Henry, and no damned fop in a suit'll stop us – "

"Oi! Boss! Open up so we can see Morfydd, why don't you?"

Septimus froze. My thoughts were whirling, quite parallel to hers. Property she could have got us past, but the Sweetings were entirely another matter. I'd never get close enough to snatch the pistol this time. For all we knew, the gun was right on the other side of the door, already trained on us –

"You go," Septimus spat through gritted teeth.

"What?"

"Go!" she snarled, skidding about to hold my gaze. Her hand fumbled at her pocket, wrenched out her notebook and shoved it deep into mine. "There's a map in this that'll get you back. I'll distract 'em – all of 'em – follow you when I can. You've got to go – get your journal – it's you the Director needs – "

"I'm quite not leaving you!"

She snatched my arm, dragged me to the bed and the open skylight. All the while, the door-handle juddered and shook. "You've got to trust me. Please. Out the window so I can shut it. Don't you fret for me – there ain't time."

I opened my mouth to inform her that this was lunacy, that under no circumstances was I abandoning her to the mercies of the criminals who'd already maimed her once this evening – but I didn't make it through so much as the first syllable. She still had my arm – she tugged me close – closer – until she was warm breath and the sharp tang of blood – and then she dashed her lips against mine for innumerable giddying seconds – sweet figs, she *kissed* me – fierce and deliberate and entirely indisputable –

Then she hooked an arm under my knees, flung me out onto the roof, and slammed the skylight window behind me.

Well. Quite. Had I not been scrambling over a rooftop in numbing darkness, dodging slates as wobbly as loose teeth, praying I'd survive the skitter down onto the lower floor jutting beneath me, I would have swooned myself to consummate oblivion, and no criminal alive could have reasonably stopped me.

I never would have managed this climbing feat in reverse, even in culottes – injured as she was, her athletic daring shall perpetually amaze me – but lowering myself down the storeys was just about possible, and the windows had candles enough to light my way. The tenement got wider as it got closer to the ground, in a kind of oversized staircase. The whole building was composed primarily of boxy rooms with flat roofs crammed onto the back, swallowing up the square of unkempt garden. In a scrap of luck, it wasn't raining, but – nectarines! – it was cold.

I toppled face-first into the damp grass, shoved myself back to my feet. The rush of the river hung close on the air. I'd been too dazed for fear the whole way down, too dazed for anything but squinting concentration and –

I confess it: and elation.

The icy breeze cracked my lips, stiffened them to a grimace, but I could still feel the throb in them – she'd kissed furiously enough to bruise. But – persimmons – had I, in all my astonished inexperience, managed to sufficiently return it? How was I supposed to communicate, with no words and five seconds and a hallway-ful of criminals about to riddle us with pistol-shot, quite what her kiss had done to me, and how ferociously intent I was on reprising it when I next saw her? To imagine kissing her – to blush and wonder and hesitate myself out of it – that was one thing – but it had *happened*, and it could happen again – and I wanted nothing more than for it to happen again! In that instant, as I sprinted through the house's narrow brick passageway and wrestled open the latch of its brittle back gate, you could have struck a match alight on me!

The ring of the cobblestones through my boots knocked me back to composure, or at least as close as I was going to get. She would escape – she had to – as far as I was concerned, there wasn't an alternative. And I – I had my bewildering orders, never mind that I'd still not the faintest what effect they were intended to have. Get into the Division in a suitably surreptitious fashion, find my journal – or, more ideally, find the Director, work out what she wanted me to do with the aforementioned writing, assuming that she was in any position to –

No! A fig for these wretched worst-case scenarios! Not until I knew something for certain!

Fortunately for my unravelling nerves, it was the work of a few gasping moments to discover just where in Dallyangle I was. Now that I had extricated myself from the shadowy passageway and the gloomy back garden, I was back in the realm of streetlamps, able to wrestle Septimus's notebook from my pocket and tip the map to the light until its geography made sense. Beyond its pages, there was the carriage, parked awkwardly in front of the narrow tenement, the horse eye-deep in a bag of oats, a heap of blankets and a slouching hat propped on the seat in rough imitation of a waiting driver. I'd neither skill nor desire to steal it, but the Divisionary bicycles leant against the opposite housefront were another matter entirely. Septimus must have balanced mine alongside hers, heaved them both through the streets, set the two side by side for our hasty getaway. My footsteps struck up a pealing echo as I staggered towards them – it was the church-bell, tolling nine o'clock from the very direction the front wheels jutted towards. *That* way to the town centre and the market square.

I wrenched out the smaller bicycle, its pedals scouring into my ankles in the old visceral greeting. Septimus's I left where it was. She'd still have need of it.

Figs. Cycling. I had done more today than ever in my life, and I quite wasn't about to forget the knack now.

The voice from the lamplit gloom nearly struck the wheels out from under me. I had only just hit the market square, pedalling as fast as I dared between bouts of map-squinting – wary not just of the terrifying speed, but of the rattle of the bicycle on the cobblestones, horrendously loud against the cottage-windows. I had met not a single human soul on my inexpert scorch past the candlelit homes, but sneak was rather of the essence, and I was determined to be careful. My plan had been to cycle past the Division and double back on foot from the farthest side of the building – the one with the back door into the dormitory. The bicycle could be hidden behind Checkley's Tavern, and I'd lose no time trying to tiptoe the full length of the Division.

But a pale shadow sprang out from the log-shed before I could cross the market square, until my choice was either to clutch at the brakes or run it down. Septimus could have swerved and scorched on, of course, but it was quite all I could do to manage regular turns, never mind emergency skidding.

The bicycle shrieked for me, jolting to a halt so violently I almost pitched clean over the handlebars. The pale shape before me gasped, settling into a face – a corpse-candle of a face, hovering above a dowdy grey gown and a lace collar the very hue of polished bone. Only several dazed blinks turned it from ghoul to girl. Even so, she was distinctly ghoulish in her look: lank wavy hair in a bun, too ashy to really call blonde, and stark green eyes with an eerie paleness to the lashes.

It was a measure of my addled state, perhaps, that my first squinting stare into those eyes gave me the vaguest impression of Rosamond. But Rosamond hadn't followed me, and now the stranger was speaking.

"Division?" she asked briskly. Her eyes didn't follow her voice, detached and staring and quite motionless. "Are you one of Cassie's assistants?"

It was a vain endeavour to stop myself gaping at her. I knew her now, though I'd only ever had the one real glimpse. *She* was the governess, that terrifying young child-minder of the family Ballestas, who had stared me into trembling across this very same square only a matter of days ago. The same governess Septimus and I had been chasing through our pursuit of Lady Miltonwaters, before the Sweetings had blundered in and shattered our original plan. And here she was again, freezing Cassandra's name in her icy voice – Cassandra, who not a matter of hours ago had believed her inextricably connected with some dastardly plot against the Division. At least, that was as much of Septimus's frantic explanation as I could recall –

I swallowed. The governess's face was younger than mine, but she was still half a head taller, even with the teetering height the bicycle gave me. It was the easiest thing in the world to widen my eyes, to pinch words from an intimidated stammer and offer them up to her.

"I – erm – quite – I'm sorry – who – ?"

She blinked at me. Slowed her voice, glacial, as if my answer had been far too stupid to merit a riposte at normal speed. One of her pallid hands reached out to steady my shaking handlebars, long and sharp-nailed at the fingers, searingly cold where her skin brushed against my thumb.

"You must be new. I thought I saw you before, but evidently you didn't notice me. I work as a governess for the Ballestas family – not Cassie, obviously, but her younger brother – she must have mentioned me? Adelaide Danadlenddu?"

Persimmons.

And I was crouched under the Nettleblack drawing-room window again, with Edwina's voice spearing out into the night. *I obtained Adelaide Danadlenddu a respectable post with Lady Miltonwaters some years ago – I advised her not to anglicise her name – I did not think it would be appropriate to have a maid in Lady Miltonwaters's house calling herself Adelaide Nettleblack – but with Rhys as her father I doubt she will remain content –*

This – and that – and – and I'd not even had the wit to make the connection! What a comfort it had been, to think of some vaguely villainous governess aiming her bolts somewhere that wasn't me – and to think of Adelaide Danadlenddu, if I thought of her at all, as a family ghost that no longer applied, a spectre flung off with the Nettleblack surname!

But I clearly wasn't sufficiently devoid of the surname to stop Adelaide Danadlenddu from thwacking me round the head with her mere existence. She was my cousin. She had a post in Lady Miltonwaters's house, courtesy of Edwina. And even if she now worked for the Director, she would have been Lady Miltonwaters's first.

There was Cassandra's link!

But what did Cassandra want to do with the link?

Sweet unplucked sloes, Adelaide Danadlenddu was still watching me.

"Oh – erm – of course," I gasped. "Henry – erm – Hyssop – I – yes – I – I work with Cassandra – "

I quite don't know what stopped *Nettleblack* skidding across my tongue. Those frozen eyes, that steady face – the girl could have leeched truth from a stone. It would have been perfectly natural to crumple beneath the familiar green of her eel-eyed stare, and give her my name, our kinship, in a desperate bid to draw her into some cooperation with me. I had just lost Rosamond – and Adelaide surely shared my position as a walking inconvenience to Edwina's arrangements – and being sent to work for Lady Miltonwaters was no guarantee of anything – and a thousand other such half-plausible reasons –

But, as much as it stung, I couldn't be sure of her. Not until I knew what she meant to tell me, when she dashed up to stop my bicycle. Not with Septimus, and the Director, and the Division, and more than I entirely feared I understood, all hanging on every paltry word I gave her.

Adelaide dropped her hand from the bars, curled her fingers around her elbows, slender arms crossed over her dull gown. "Henry Hyssop. Of course. Well – Cassie has a message for you, and it can't wait."

I tugged at my face until it shaped a smile. My heartbeat shivered in my throat, scaldingly fast. "I – erm – what message?"

Her voice quickened, unmistakeably impatient. "A tip-off, about the Head-Hider. She says to go to Gulmere and knock on every house on Stavinge Lane – she doesn't know which one – but the right one should know you're coming. They should have some information. She wants you to go immediately, though. Apparently there isn't much time."

I blinked at her. There was only one test for it.

"Should I – erm – should I report to the Director first – or – or just go straight there?"

"Straight there," she returned, with not a single twitch of hesitation. "Why else do you suppose she sent me out to watch for you? My young charge is with his father, and the case takes priority over all – such is the Ballestas world. But perhaps you've not been in the Division long enough to get used to it."

Was it desperately foolish of me to feel it like a slap?

"I – yes – no – I mean – that – I'll get right on it – if that's Cassandra's plan and she knows I'm – right – yes – quite – very good – very helpful – thank you – erm – Miss Danadlenddu – "

Just for a moment, her eyes shifted, narrowing as they pinched at my face. I'd quite no intention of waiting out the reason. My feet scrabbled for the pedals, kicking them into my shins, nearly driving the bicycle over her toes as I dragged it around –

"Idiot," she hissed, springing away from me. Her voice was so low, and the clattering of the bicycle so cacophonous, I suppose she imagined I couldn't hear her. "At least that's the last of them."

One final frantic kick got the bicycle moving. I kept it going, shaking all the more for the jab of her contemptuous glare in my back, until I rounded the opposite corner of the market square, and the Ballestas apothecary started out between us, its stack of tincture-bottles blocking me from her sight. Then, brimful of the smarting and the shattered hope and the sheer simmering rage that I quite couldn't permit myself to set into words, I shoved my feet down and sped up. Across the bruised cobbles of Angle Drag, towards where the town's largest houses and their lavish windows swelled out of the gloom.

Figs, but I wasn't in the least headed for Gulmere!

What you are, and what you do, the Director had said. Well. If I couldn't get near the latter with my traitorous relation guarding the door, the former – and all I could wrangle out of it – would have to suffice.

I knocked. Sharp and vigorous as Septimus had done, enough to flake a little more of the paint. The lights on the upper floor were blazing away above my head; Mr. Adelstein was quite evidently in residence.

25.

IN WHICH MR. ADELSTEIN'S BEDTIME READING IS INTERRUPTED

Casebook of Matthew Adelstein

Pertaining to – oh, there's no neat delineation

I f written records are what's wanted now, permit me to add mine to the evening's fray. Not that I was anywhere near my casebook when everything began to unfold at a newly hectic rate. Nicholas and I had retired to bed early, night-clad and curled up with two cups of his most soothing chai. He was reading one of his chirpy novels aloud – specifically one that was very much not *Life and Limbs* – to distract us from the imminent horrible need to thwart the trust of the town's most famous resident. I had attempted to compose, and subsequently burned, no less than six drafts of the letter that would resign me from Edwina Nettleblack's commission, and I still wasn't happy with the contents of the seventh.

We both heard the knocker, even three floors up, bludgeoning the silence out of the evening. Nicholas was in favour of ignoring it, and initially I was of the same opinion. How could I be otherwise, after the events of that ghastly afternoon, which his desperate caresses and relentless good cheer were only just beginning to soften? The butler would have dealt with it, perhaps, but the butler had been dispatched on half-holiday, and the cook and her skivvy knew not to answer the door. And here was Nicholas, his curly head warm through my nightshirt, with a thumb's width of his novel still to read.

But the hammering only continued, louder and more relentless than ever. I began, I confess, to tip back into panic. If Rosamond Nettleblack had been expecting me to break with her elder sister immediately – if she had taken my hesitant silence as disobedience, and arranged her counter-attack accordingly –

This line of thinking left me somewhere poised somewhere relief and incredulity, when the voice came shrieking up the housefront.

"Figs! Mr. Adelstein! I quite know you're in there!"

I recollect myself spluttering, whilst Nicholas gazed at me in equal stupefaction: were the family dispatching sisters here purely to torment us now?

But as my options in that immediate moment seemed to be either let her in and take the consequences, or let her scream the streets awake and take the consequences of her siblings, I had little choice but to spring out of bed and clatter down the stairs at triple-pace, candle in hand. I would, unsurprisingly, have greatly preferred to have strode into a confrontation with Henry Nettleblack in something more substantial than a nightshirt and dressing-gown, but by the time I reached the door she was actually kicking it, leaving me rather no alternative.

Of all the peculiar states I had seen the little wretch in, this was by far the most perplexing. I could only observe her in dimly-lit glimpses, as she shoved past me and sprinted up the stairs to the drawing-room, but her every step left crusts of mud trampled into the carpet. She appeared to still be flaunting her Divisionary disguise, but the uniform was damp and filthy, and now seemed to include an incongruously expensive cravat trailing limply from her neck.

My first instinct, naturally, was to assume that the straits of the Division had finally got too much for her. By the time I'd followed her back up the stairs, Nicholas already had the gaslamps sputtering to life, and she was slumped on our chaise, breathlessly oblivious to the havoc her clothes would wreak on the material, her head tipped forward into hands streaked black with ink and bicycle-grease. Nicholas was on his knees beside her, admirably unfazed by this public disclosure of his novelty rat pyjamas, his questions undeservedly gentle: was she alright, what had happened, could he get her anything (could he get her anything!) –

"What are you doing here?" I demanded, in a more appropriate tone. Nettleblack the youngest jumped like a starling.

"You – erm – " – and she swallowed hard, presumably to amend that clockwork-trick of a stammer – "You don't seem – especially pleased – to have me turn up on your doorstep – "

At which, it became patently obvious that the chit had no idea what Rosamond had done, that she still believed herself to be the ill-fated object of my unshakeable pursuit. If it kept her on edge, and sufficiently wary of me not to wreck any more of my furniture, I wasn't especially inclined to correct her.

Nicholas would have done it regardless, in his mollifying way, had I not glowered him to silence. It was more than enough for now to reiterate to Nettleblack that she hadn't answered my question.

She regarded me a moment, her wide eyes the uncanny spit of her sister's, evidently assessing the situation for herself. Her paltry intellect apparently didn't disappoint. Having worked out that any overt request for my time, help, and patience would have resulted in her instantaneous ejection, through door or window, she flung a new gambit at me, even more insane than the last.

"The Director needs you – there's a plot – erm – against the Division – "

What, I was on the verge of snarling, did I care about the Division – ?

But Nicholas caught my eye, and shook his head. "Listen to the fieldmouse, Matty. Can't tell you why she's here if you don't let her finish the sentence, eh?"

The reprimand was so gentle, so solemn, yet so much firmer than his usual wafting cautions, that it silenced me on the instant. Nettleblack proceeded –

"Forget you've resigned – erm – and help me – something's happening in the building – and the Director has some kind of plan – and – I can't get to her – or Cassandra – and Septimus hasn't got back yet – and Gertie and the others are gone – and you're the only one left in Dallyangle who can assist – so you have to – "

"I don't take orders from you," I snapped. Nicholas waved me frantically to silence again, an absentminded rodent on his wrist flicking its tail across his knuckles. I stared at him: twice in one evening?

"Pretend he's not still sulking, Henry," he blurted, without so much as a wince for my incredulous splutter. "And give him all the facts you've got. Matty enjoys facts, eh, Matty?"

Only sheer love for the man kept me from strangling him.

"Cassandra's deduced something," Nettleblack declared wildly, as if she thought Mrs. Ballestas's scatterbrained author-child in any way capable of doing my job. My former job. Regardless. "As far as I – erm – understand it – there was only so much time to explain – Cassandra seems to think that Lady Miltonwaters and Adelaide Danadlenddu have some connection – erm – to a plot against the Division – and now Adelaide is keeping people out of the Division on false pretences – with the Director inside – and very probably Lady

Miltonwaters too – and – the Director – she – she wants me to – figs, I don't know! – to get into the Division – and do something for her – but I can't work out what – and – and – quite!"

Nicholas patted her shoulder, glanced over to me with the same infectious panic glinting in his eyes. "Matty, we have to help – "

But we had, if anything, to remain within the perimeters of reason, even dishevelled and half-dressed as we were.

"Do you have any proof of this so-called plot?" I demanded. "Or, indeed, proof that anything remotely untoward is happening inside the Division building? Or – most pertinently of all – a sensible and thorough explanation from Cassandra, that sounds less like a semi-devised melodrama and rather more resembles an actual strand of deductive logic?"

Her pale face twitched, evidently with an impatient desire to injure me in some not insignificant way. "I can't *get* to Cassandra without giving the game away to Adelaide – and I don't want to do that until I know what the Director needs! Can you not simply believe me? You have my word!"

I was about to inform her with justified viciousness that, even if what she said was true, yelling at me was not going to make the mystery clearer – but the moment she finished her sentence, her whole expression changed. Where she had been pinched in a glare, she was now startlingly slack, gaping at some unfixed point inside my eyes. Nicholas darted closer; he assumed, reasonably, that she was on the verge of toppling down senseless again.

"My word," she gasped. "That's – that's it! That's her plan! Not the journal! My written word – written tonight – now that they're all at the Division – and she can trick them into explaining themselves – and I know the back way in! She's seen how quickly I can transcribe – how much I can remember – and she wants to catch them with it! Figs! Of course!"

"Whose plan?" – but I asked purely, at this stage, for confirmation of what I already suspected. If anyone could quietly deduce Nettleblack's identity, store it up in her mind until it proved useful, then summon a way to weaponise it against whatever threat happened to arise – of course it would be Keturah Ballestas.

Unsurprisingly, Nettleblack blurted the very same name. "And Septimus said that Adelaide and Lady Miltonwaters just walked in – demanding to speak to the Director – whatever they're saying, I – I need to write it down – merciful peaches, and she must be running out of time!"

Nicholas snatched this moment to ask the question I really ought to have thought of: namely, why had Nettleblack not enlisted her admirer to assist her? At this stage of the evening, it hardly came as a surprise to discover that Septimus was in some sort of danger too, from which she may or may not have extricated herself, but which nonetheless posed a threat to her immediate ability to join the campaign –

"Of course it does," I muttered, until I caught Nicholas glaring at me.

And how, pray tell, did Nettleblack want our help? Her answer to the aforementioned came with an accessory, in the form of a battered little notebook produced from her pocket and proffered in a shuddering hand – which, for the moment, I pointedly ignored. If we – she was evidently planning this on the spot – could stir ourselves to locate Septimus and the other missing Divisioners through strategic use of the marked-up map in the notebook, we could make sure they were protected, acquaint them with the swirling situation, and prepare our next move, all whilst she snuck back into the Division and transcribed whatever sordid conversation was taking place between the Director, her daughter, and whoever (for these wild claims of a conspiracy between an aristocrat and a governess still seemed alarmingly speculative to me) happened to be with them.

"This plan is patently insane," I informed her curtly, when her spluttering had reached its illogical conclusion. She actually gritted her teeth.

"I quite don't see that there's anything insane about making sure Septimus and the others are safe – do you?"

I coloured then, for to be swatted with the righteous wrath of this little matchstick was rather more than I wished to endure. My retort was set in the sharpest possible terms: she still had no guarantee that I was even willing to assist her, given that I had made my resignation from the Division as clear as I –

"That's unfortunate, Matty," Nicholas remarked suddenly, his gaze solemn, his resolution unsettlingly absolute. Before I could stop him, he reached out and clasped hold of the notebook she held out to us, squeezing her hand as he took it from her. "Given that I'll be giving them all the help I've got."

I'm fairly sure that I gasped his name, that I snatched him by his elbows and readied myself for a fruitless attempt at chastising him. The impulse was involuntary, the last flash of anger from Nettleblack's admonishing tone – I knew, as he must have, that there was no more substance left to flesh my retorts. He lifted his hands, tobacco-stained at the fingernails, and laid them against my cheekbones, until all I could breathe was the smell of him. He was smiling gently, his voice soft as his fingers on my skin.

"Matty. This is the Div. They gave you the job you dreamt of, and they're some of the only folk who'll still look me in the eye now I'm waifed and disowned. I can't make you, but – if I can do anything to help – to stop Ballestas and the rest going the way of everything in Dallyangle that's ever been different – I'm going to be doing it."

With that stare, that quiet fervent murmur, the warmth of his hands and the tang of his tobacco, he could have talked me into anything. And – I readily confess it – he was right. Is right. Insufferable as it can be (and has been), I cannot simply sit back and let the Division crumble, not with all it has done and might yet do. I could not forgive myself for that.

Perhaps my cooperation would have been entirely unreserved, had that wretched tincture-heiress not seen fit to add a gloss.

"So – erm – I – we don't have much time – "

I flicked her a glower so severe she started out of the sentence. "You. What do you intend to do with yourself? If you have any sense left in you, you've doubtless realised it's your status as Miss Nettleblack that the Director wishes to call upon for your transcription, not your feeble efforts as Henry Hyssop."

She blinked. She was tremendously pale, even for her. Evidently the logic had occurred to her in the abstract, if not yet the actual. "I – I suppose you – you want to be the one to hand me in – when I – erm – when I have to – "

Change back? I thought, rather nastily – but didn't voice, for which Nicholas must have been tremendously grateful. She really was an absurdly twisted fairytale: the clock would strike midnight, and transform her from a filthy skivvy to the youngest heir of Dallyangle's wealthiest family. The clock, at any rate, hadn't had Rosamond Nettleblack snarling at it all afternoon, and doubtless had far less to lose than Nicholas and I.

"How you unearth yourself," I told her evenly, with a swift glance to Nicholas to ensure that he followed my drift, "is entirely in your hands."

Nicholas, delighted to the point of pure recklessness, tugged me towards him and dashed his lips against mine. Perhaps he was relieved to find me so graciously abandoning the case and vendetta he'd disliked from the start. Or perhaps – to consider every possibility – perhaps it was affection, earnest and simple, and there was no point in trying to decipher every potential nuance in the twitch of his mouth and the taste of smoke on my tongue.

Nettleblack, of all things, looked desperately relieved. Her elaboration wasn't unwelcome in this instance, stammered rather sheepishly to my bewildered stare: "I – just – pleased that you – and Nick

– that neither of you – erm – that there's never been – anything of the sort – between you – or you – and Septimus – "

"Oh, for goodness's sake," I groaned, whilst Nicholas sniggered triumphantly at my shoulder. *I knew it*, he was muttering to me, his eyes glittering in the gaslight, *I could just tell with this one, I detected it way before you, I knew it, I knew it!*

But enough of this. One way or another, during the remainder of this interminable night, Septimus has to be found, and the Division has to be prioritised, and we all have to take up our parts in the Director's half-legible plan. If we emerge, I hardly dare imagine the contrition with which I shall be forced to pen Keturah Ballestas a tentative request for my reinstatement.

And Nettleblack? What can possibly be left to happen to her?

That's a matter for tomorrow. Nicholas is calling me.

26.

OF ROOFTOPS AND
BOTCHED SCHEMES

Septimus (quite possibly battling the world by this point)

Even when I'm halfway to buckling at the legs – even when I've just had to hurl the diarist I'm sweet on out of a window, not five seconds after kissing her – even now, it's still a devil of a thing not to snigger for the Sweetings' faces. They've been out in that corridor far longer than they'd like, bawling for Property to unlock the door for 'em. When it finally swings open, they've clearly planned their entrance, pistol at the ready, both trying to hold it at once. Obviously meant it to scare Henry out of whatever wits this night'll leave her with. *Definitely* didn't expect the same Divisioner they've spent the past two days trying to kill, more upright than anyone'd like her to be, tottering on filthy boots in the centre of the room.

"Aren't you dead yet?" Norman blurts, part fury part fear.

I'm still afraid of 'em – mad not to be – but there's a dash of triumph sparking in me too. Henry's away, and safe, and if I trust her with my life I more than trust her to get to the Director. I've one job right now, and it's to make sure she's got time and space enough to do whatever needs doing.

So I – *me*, who can hardly read sarcasm with the best of 'em! – I tip the Sweetings an ironic salute.

They gape like anything, but Maggie recovers quickest. Four creaking strides and she's up to me, the jut of her chin an inch from my nose.

"Nice of you to come back, dearie! Tonight just keeps getting better and better, doesn't it?"

I won't flinch. Not this time. Not even when she splits to a yellow smile. I keep my face blankly scornful, though I'm all confusion under the skin, and my damned eyes won't stop watering. Property's plan is to run, was what Henry said – so why's that so brilliant for the Sweetings? Why's Maggie so delighted to see me, if the whole scheme's been to keep me away?

"Gracious," Property murmurs from the doorway.

Right.

What'll I give 'em? Blank scorn too. Teeth gritted so taut you couldn't stick a needle between 'em.

The Sweetings, two grimy courtiers, step away to train their pistol at a respectable distance. I snag my eyes on a splintery roof-beam and keep 'em there, as the polished footfalls saunter closer. As if they're getting my gaze, after tonight, after all the maddening inconvenience of their escape attempt –

"Where's Hylas?"

I ain't answering that. Keep your wretched nicknames out of it.

Property grabs my chin – and I gasp. I'd not been expecting it. Now I can't look anywhere but their eyes, twitching a little on the inside edge. There's no smell beyond my blood, but I can *taste* the scent of their pomade.

"I asked you a question, sweet sergeant – and I'd be obliged in the extreme if you answered it."

"What does it matter where Morfydd's gone?" Maggie ventures cheerily, leaning on the doorframe. "This one's worth a thousand of her! We can have the hair – and a bit of revenge while we're at it – we can have the Div at our feet – "

I can't not grin for this, vicious as I can get it. Oh, Maggie, as if you've any idea what's coming for you now! You've only got *days!* As soon as Henry and the Director are done saving it, the whole deadline-driven might of the Dallyangle Division's going to hoist you and your brother straight out of your crime-spree!

Property spots the change on my face, and glares back. Actually glares. Ain't this a tweak at fortune's wheel, to have 'em glaring while I smirk!

"Something amusing, darling?"

Damn. They know right well how to pinch my smile off, and that's it. And don't I hate that they can still play on my nerves easy as Lorrie's piano. I kissed Henry tonight, and all I want's to kiss her again, but even now I can't stop myself flushing for their endearments.

Neck arched above their bow-tie, fingers sharp around my jaw, they lift an eyebrow. 'Course they've noticed.

So retort. Didn't cut out your tongue when they broke your nose, did they?

"I ain't your darling. And you ain't hurting Henry, not tonight and not ever, as long as I'm alive to stop you."

Their glare hardens. "Dio mio! Jealous of Hylas, are we? Would you rather I'd made off with you instead?"

I kissed Henry. She kissed me. You've got no hold on me – not anymore!

"Hate to disappoint you, but – no."

For a moment, Property just stares at me. Fair enough. This snarl's got a real sting to it, not like my old panicky bluster. What's happened, they must be thinking – what's snapped, in my head, to slacken their grip there?

If that's what they're thinking. I never could work it out.

I force a rattling breath. Never mind what they're thinking. You think of Henry, and that'll be enough.

Property drops me, and for a moment I almost think I've won. Almost. But then their hands are up again, past my face and into my crumpling chignon – and I'm stunned, frozen, enough to let 'em – prising and coaxing 'til pins clatter on the floorboards and vanish into the rag-rug. My hair, all of it, topples down over my shoulders. It's tangled, heavy, brushing at my wrists. Hair this long, you can feel it right the way down, feel where it twists and whorls itself out.

I ain't frozen now. I'm shaking, too much to hold their gaze. I watch their slim olive fingers slide through to the ends, catch the knots and pull 'em out, settle at my waist once they've run out of hair.

"Never mind Hylas and Hercules," they mutter, "I should have called you Samson. I underestimated it before, for which I can only apologise. Your thirty-shilling mind can't even imagine the price a latter-day Pre-Raphaelite would gush up for this."

It's one thing to stand here all heroic, and let 'em shear it, and call it a cheap exchange for Henry and the Div. There is a part of me, mercifully, that's thinking that, and smarting for it, and sticking by it. But – I can't lie – it ain't just that, lurking in my mind. I've never had my hair down with anyone else's eyes on it, not since I grew out the orphanage crop. I've never had someone – and for it to be *Property*, with their slick parting and mocking smile! – hold me like this, and study it, and run their fingers through it. If they really wanted it that badly, back when we met, they shouldn't've bothered with the Sweetings. They could've swaggered up to me and prised my hair loose, and (and it stings in my ribs, to admit it) if they'd done it like this I would've let 'em cut off as much as they wanted.

And they'll cut it now. And Henry's not had time to see it loose.

"Sweet Sweetings," Property calls suddenly, eyes still warm and gloating on mine, "Allow me a moment alone with her. Don't fret, I'll be perfectly safe. Just go and check the carriage is still there, would you? There's a pair of scissors under the back seat, if you'd be so kind. Sheep-shears are hardly the most appropriate tools for the job in this instance."

All the while, they're watching me. Even at the heart of that gloat, there's still a glinting wariness in their eyes. Must be in mine too. We ain't had *a moment alone* – not properly alone – not since that night two months ago. But it's rushing up at both of us, and for all that it makes me twitch there's no way to swerve past it. The Sweetings are already almost gone. They've seen my hair unravelled, must think that's me beaten.

Am I beaten? Not if I can outlast this *moment alone.* Not if I can keep Property distracted enough to forget about Henry. Not if –

Then the door's slammed, and Property's dropped my waist to snatch at my shoulders, and their horrified face's about as far away from sarcastic seduction as you'd ever possibly get.

"What are you *doing* here?"

I just blink at 'em. They're actually whispering, of all things.

"Where are the others?" they hiss, shaking me. "What possessed you to come alone? And what have they done to your face? Hylas already had her hair cut – she would have been safer – *you* are not safe! Have you come to wring an apology from my cadaverous hands, in the fraction of a second before you're as much of a cadaver as I'm about to be? Va bene! You have my profuse and reiterated apologies for the attempted appropriation of your hair, all attendant amorous offers, and the poor timing of certain infamous burglaries – there! Was it worth it, sweet sergeant? Was *that* worth your nose and your life?"

I can feel my eyebrows at my hairline. I'm far too stunned even for feigned defiance – and can you blame me?

"The hell're you on about?"

The mad dandy lifts a sharp finger, flicks me at the collarbone, gets a tangle of my hair round their thumb for the trouble. "Don't you see? That was only the preamble – the Sweetings think I want them to kill you! That's ostensibly the plan!"

News to me and Henry both, then. "Thought you were running away?"

"I *am* running away!" Property groans, dragging their pomade off-kilter with – God's sake, a shaking hand, still knotted up in my hair. I yank the strands free, shove shard after shard behind my ears, anywhere to get it out of the way. *This* is why it's never loose, damn it! "But do you really imagine I was fool enough to tell them that? Far more sensible to let them believe tonight to be their grand revenge. I get them blamed for the whole sordid business – and, once you all catch up with them, I don't have them coming after me! So I ask again – why, in the name of your every insane abbreviation, did you not bring the entire Division with you?"

Sensible?

"Oh, right! 'Course! Foolproof plan! 'Cept for the bit where they work out you've double-crossed 'em, and given 'em all the weapons while you're at it!"

They grab my jacket both-fisted, wrench our faces close. There'd better be blood on those spotless white cuffs before they let go of me. "I had no idea they'd invested in a pistol! I discovered this fact this evening, and my world has been nothing but villainous improvisation ever since!"

"How can you not know? They didn't tell you they beat people up to get hair, they didn't tell you they'd got themselves a gun – do they tell you *anything?*"

"If you could gloat at a slightly less suicidal dynamic, I'd be infinitely obliged," they snap, flushing. "I thought your whole wretched family were musicians – can you at least manage a mezzo-piano?"

Oh, as if your damned wit's going to help us now!

"Look. Right. *Right.*" I'm spitting the words, at more or less the same speed as I'm thinking 'em. "You want to leave. Well. Right. How do we get you out, that's question one. I need to not get killed – not before the Div, at any rate – that's number two. Dealing with those maniacs downstairs'll have to wait 'til – "

"What?" Property blurts across me, slack-eyed with surprise. I ain't seen those eyes solemn for months. "What the devil do you mean, *how do we get you out?*"

"I mean, they've got a pistol and you're in your bloody white tie, so – "

"But you don't want to get me out! You've done nothing for the last two months but try to ruin me!"

I gape at 'em. Every second's a risk, but I can't just leave 'em thinking that.

"I – I didn't mean – I only – I wanted to stop the Sweetings, and I knew you know more about 'em than anyone else in Dallyangle! And you weren't telling us any of it! If you'd just come clean – we could even've protected you!"

"What?" They're open-mouthed, stunned, fumbling through words. "Septimus, with all due respect, you did at no point make that clear – "

Because I couldn't. Because you nearly smashed me to pieces, and more'n a part of me wanted to make you smart for it. But there ain't time to admit the lot, even if there's more than enough time for my innards to squirm with it.

"I'm sorry," I stammer. "I – look – I don't want you getting hurt. You can't reason with those two, not since you saved me. They know they've lost their hold on you – that your heart ain't in it. And if they find out you're plotting against 'em, we're both dead. So – please – just take my damned help before I change my mind."

For a moment, they ain't got an answer. When they grab one, it comes sudden, jutted out in a bewildered demand.

"What's happened to you? Why would you saunter into Hylas's place, let me melodrama my way up and down your excellent hair without so much as lifting a finger to stop me, confess a whole litany of sorrowful misunderstandings, and then start devising a spontaneous collaboration with me?"

Five hundred bloody words where one'd do, as ever.

I sigh. "The Div needs me. And Henry. And – I – sneer at me all you like – "

"But if she needs you, what else can you do?" they finish, one eyebrow arched. There's no mocking in it, just dazed agreement. "That, at least, I understand all too well. And – gracious, I suppose the poor fruit-spluttering youth hasn't even told you who she is?"

"What?"

A dazed smirk. "Word of advice, sweet Septimus. When you inevitably take your little Hylas and spirit her away to pastures infinitely less ghoulish, don't ever try to show off your scheming genius to her. She won't be impressed, you'll end up in a ghastly muddle, and sooner or later the armed criminals at the door will come knocking for your head. That's the part I've not yet mentioned, you see – "

"What d'you mean?"

"It's rather not just me you ought to be concerned with protecting tonight – "

I wrench their fists off my jacket. "What the hell do you mean, she hasn't told me who she is?"

"Gracious, will you listen! If you're going to help me, you need to – "

"No! *You* need to finish your damned sentence, and not give me twenty other ones in its place! If there's time for a word of advice, there's time for this!"

"Time for what?"

And now there ain't time for anything. Maggie and Norman're back through the door, scissors in hand.

It's enough to jolt me to fear, watching Property lose it. They spin round, clasp their hands at their back; they're shaking, and trying to hide it. My blood's wrecked their cuffs after all, not that I've much left in me to feel smug about it now.

Ironic as anything, it don't matter if *I* look scared. It's probably better that I do. I drop my gaze, back off, much as the narrow room'll allow. If I can get close to the skylight, I can fling it open, shove Property up onto the roof before either of 'em raise the pistol –

Maggie stalks across the creaking floor 'til she's level with Property. Level, and closer to the skylight. Damn.

"You wanted the scissors?" she asks, pointedly.

If Property took 'em – but it wouldn't help – they'd not stab, and neither'd I –

"Something wrong?" Norman calls, splayed over the doorway, fingers drumming on the pistol he's skewered in his belt.

Property rattles off a strained little laugh. "Oh, nothing for you sweet criminals to concern yourselves with. Just a touch of reluctance, on dear Division Sergeant Septimus's part, to relinquish those marvellous tresses – "

One finger missing, and she ain't even fazed. Maggie lashes up a hand and grabs Property at their perfect starched shirtfront, flicks the scissors open with the other and presses the yawning edge to the freckles on their cheek.

"Lie to our faces, would you?"

And for once in their life, at the worst possible moment, Property can't manage even half a retort. One scathing word would've been enough. A cold look to the scissors, an ironical smirk, a quick twist free –

But they've clearly never been threatened like this. I can't blame 'em.

"Norman picked up your scissors," Maggie explains. It's that same vicious coolness she used on Henry, on me. She's enjoying this. "But I thought I'd have a little listen in. We've been wondering about your loyalties – seemed a good plan to get it proved, one way or t'other."

Property gasps. Still no retorts.

"Leave 'em," I hear myself snap. There ain't more I can do. Maggie could drag the scissors across their throat before I'm close enough to grab at her. Still – they held the Sweetings back when I was in their place, and I've got to try. "It's me you want, ain't it? Just let 'em be!"

Norman barks a sharp laugh from the doorway. "Oh, you're next. Third time's the sodding charm."

I jump, then – Property's finally managed a shaky cry. "Don't! I told you before, the sweet sergeant isn't worth the trouble – "

"You lied," Maggie growls, her fist tightening around the scissors. There's a yelp of pain from Property as she breaks the skin with 'em. "You've been lying all along. And now you want to turn us in and run away! Don't you remember what happens to all those fine heirlooms of yours, if you cross us? To you?"

Norman smirks. "If it's all got a bit too rough for your fine sensibilities, I suggest this time you leave your lady love to us."

Terror or no terror, he can't have that one. "I ain't their sweetheart, damn it!"

"She's right."

A new voice, drawling from the door, sharp shoulders pinching past a baffled Norman. A voice – oh, for God's sake! – that I've heard before, all too recently.

"*I'm* very much the lady love in this scenario, diolch yn fawr!"

Perfect. Sheer bloody perfect.

That's *Rosamond Nettleblack*, sauntering across the room to tug at Property's sleeve, as if Maggie ain't close and ready to massacre the lot of us. Why don't it surprise me, that the maddening Welshwoman's taken up with Property? Or that Property's real taste's for the scandalous girl with the fortune? Or that Nettleblack's here, now, elbow-deep in the carnage without understanding a jot of it?

She spots me before she seems to clock the Sweetings, jolts to a grin. "Shwmae, you! Not chessing fy chwaer heno?"

Norman finds his voice before I can wring her incomprehensible neck. "The hell is this?"

"Narcissus," Property splutters frantically, "Do run – right now –"

Nettleblack stares at 'em – at Maggie, still scouring the scissors down their face – at Norman, back to blocking the door – and she blinks. Fear, at last?

Then she – and I swear, I've no idea how she knows to do it, but this is what she does – swings up her hand, and jabs the sharp nail on her thumb straight for Maggie's eye.

Maggie roars, topples back into Norman. Nettleblack sprints after 'em, grabs the door and slams it round towards 'em. I spot what she's about, hurl myself over and stab an elbow into Maggie's stomach. It's a cheap shot, but we've got to get 'em outside! And then, mad as the odds may be, we *do*. The Sweetings lose their balance, the door's shut, and they and the pistol both are on the other side of it. For now. A moment of surprise for 'em, of dealing with a groaning Maggie. See how she likes it.

Time. Right. Now. How do we use it?

I spit out a mouthful of my hair. 'Course it's all over me. Then there's the slap of *more* damned hair across my neck, blackcurrant-shiny curls, as Nettleblack skids round beside me to smirk at Property. They're still frozen, gaping on the cravat rug.

"I think the word you're after," she declares, "is diolch!"

"Diolch," Property echoes faintly, limp to their skewed hairline.

Thwack on the door, enough to sling my hair into my eyes. I swat it back, brace my heel on a jutting floorboard, hook my fingers round the doorframe. 'Course the time's running out already.

"Got a sequel to this plan, Nettleblack?" I snarl.

The door shudders again. Nettleblack's on her knees, larking about with the keyhole. Property's least helpful of all, stock-still in the middle of the room, one hand clutching at the cut on their cheek.

"There!" Nettleblack grins, leaping back from the door. Damn – no – don't leave it on my strength alone! "Locked. And they'll stay outside, unless they want another stab to the eye – "

I gape at her. "You do realise they've got a gun?"

"Ah." She blanches, not that it's easy to tell with her wraith-pale skin. "Well – your turn for a life-saving scheme now, Pip! I won't even ask where Henry's gone – over the hills and far away, I hope."

Another slam on the door. My legs buckle.

"That's the only way out," Property stammers dazedly. "Down the stairs. And our luggage – my money – all of my savings – it's all through there – "

"Open up!" Maggie bellows, close-pressed to the door. "Or we will!"

Nettleblack shrieks. "Oh, gwell a gwell!"

"Forget the damned luggage!" I spit, flinging myself off the door. "The bed – grab it!"

It's only when they both clock me dragging it single-handed that they dart in to help, 'til we've got something splayed and metal blocking the door. Good thing, too – the lock's all but caved in. I'm at the skylight next, wrenching it open, gasping in the jolt of freezing air, flinching for the spasm of pain between my eyes. No sign of a thing on the back of the house, and no huddled heaps in the garden below. A skinny crescent moon loitering overhead like a stray hair.

A moon and nothing else – so Henry must've made it.

"Figs!" I yell, far too elated for a Divisioner cornered, out into the night.

Property grabs my arm, twists me round. Nettleblack's clinging to their hand, the last of her wild bravado curdling to proper fear. "What are you doing?"

I leap out of my head in the moment, watch it at a distance. There's me, drenched in my hair, hands settled on Property's elbows, muttering the best answer I've got.

"Out the window. I know it works – it's how Henry got out. Leave your stuff. Just come with me if you want to make it. And let all this be a bloody lesson, when you're away. Don't – "

(Fair enough, ain't it, to snatch 'em by the lapels and drag 'em close?)

" – *don't* trick anyone else, and don't steal any more damned hair!"

I drop 'em. Tug open a few of my jacket buttons, shove as much hair as fits under my collar. Vault through the window 'til I'm balanced on the guttering. Two wide-eyed faces, a stricken portrait, still gawping at me.

"Sweet Septimus – you're entirely mad!" Property gasps.

I – *I* do it – I actually wink at 'em.

"Sometimes, Pip, you ain't mad enough!"

And I'm up the slippery tiles, skittering past the chimney, away to shoulder the very moon out of the sky, with my string of ducklings scrambling after me.

27.

OF WRITING

Me again, in all manner of conceivable senses

What was the next step? Mr. Adelstein and Nick – it's quite unbelievable to think that I'd ever imagined them infatuated with anyone but each other – off to deal with the bulk of the practicalities. To find Septimus, to round up Gertie and her contingent, to prepare themselves for – I don't know – but Septimus would! Which left me some taut, frantic, not-quite-settled amount of time to follow the Director's orders, and – but I didn't dare think of the aftermath, not yet.

The orders! Think of the orders! And – pears, but now the orders made sense! The Director – she'd as good as told me she had deduced my identity. And then, as she had said to Septimus: she needed what I was, and what I do – namely, the clout of my family's influence, and my inkstained ability to document things at feral speed. Quite what she proposed to do with either was beyond me, but I'd every intention of giving her the raw materials in veritable spadefuls.

Bear with me, then, and follow me. Round the corner of Pole Place, dragging the bicycle, past Mr. Adelstein and Nick on their front doorstep. Along the gloomy, gaslit, cobblestoned street until it curved and broadened into another street, where my footsteps rung out all the louder for the town-edging silence, catching in weird echoes on plaster pillars and bay windows and writhing brass door-knockers. Up to the green paint, gleaming a strange golden-black in the streetlights, and the nettle-thicket of a crest above the door.

There was a dim light glinting behind the drawing-room curtains. Mercifully, they were closed again. That light was a bridge to be dealt with after everything else was made ready – I was entirely not of a mood to fight past Edwina before the work had even begun.

I propped the bicycle against the front steps, and the shadowy recollection of Septimus whistled past my shoulders with an alternative route inside. I followed the memory, up and over the back wall in a scramble of sodden ivy. It hardly mattered that the effort tore open Lorrie's stitches in my jacket, that the weedy grass was marshy with mud and water where Rosamond had given up tending it, that in the end I had to unlace my boots and leave them lodged in the mire. Not when the sash window beside the back door had only been pulled to – not when all the trembling strength in me was just enough to force it up and topple through. For a moment, I imagined I looked exactly as the Sweetings would have had me: bedraggled and felled and profoundly exhausted, crumpled in a heap of mud and stockings.

Figs, but then I got up.

I crept the stairs two at a time, oozing the garden like a revenant. Around the faint light and soft voices of the drawing-room – not now, not yet, not until I had everything I needed! – and across the upstairs hall, every footstep matting the carpet, feeling my way along the mossy flocking on the wallpaper. The gloom gnawed at the house and left everything hollow: the chandeliers doused and bristling as bird's-nests, the portraits sharp frames with empty shadows inside, the door – my door – so murky I couldn't even squint to make out the handle.

Inside, the curtains were shut, and the darkness was a very blindfold. There was nothing to do but stumble into it, grasping for edges to tug me in deeper. I found a snarl of carved wood for my bed, the jutting metal corner of a chest – there was the clink of handle against drawer, as I slumped into my desk – and then I reached the windows, grabbed for the velvet and wrenched the thin moonlight into the room. With that, it was a sprint to the cupboards – hurling the warmest fabrics onto my bed – matching colours as best I could in the silvery half-light. Kicking out of my slimy stockings, my culottes, my rough collarless shirt and my collapsing jacket.

Part one: a chemise.

I dressed for two rather incongruous purposes – stealth and extravagance. The shirt was oysterish grey, the skirt gloomy forest-green. It was perturbing to return to a skirt proper – so much that I was obliged to reassure myself in a whisper that the switch would not be permanent, that I would find my way back to a pair of culottes, that – that it wasn't the end, even if everything in my known world presently suggested otherwise! I'd no inclination to a corset when I couldn't ring for help, but I decked myself to distraction in every other respect: pearl cufflinks, silk stockings, glossy leather boots, a velvet collar to my coat. My hair I combed to some vague approximation of obedience. I stabbed a pin through Property's cravat, fastened it taut to my shirt – whatever they'd done earlier, they were going to help me now!

I snatched up a new pencil, a sheaf of paper. Correspondence paper, with the crest tooled into the page – a hangover from Father's Nettleblack's Tincture days, when our so-called crest was merely the company logo. It would have to do.

For quite the second time in the last few feverish weeks, I scuttled out into the dark stairwell. No ferret (peaches, Property, good luck with him!) slinked up to intercept me. I stopped for Edwina's study one door down, dived into a musk of leather and book-dust, on a hunt for the last bit of relevant sartorial elegance: the Nettleblack signet ring. Any Nettleblack signet ring would have served the purpose, whether it was hers slipped off, or Father's preserved, or even – though this seemed unlikely – a copy obtained for future presentation to Rosamond or I. But nothing of the sort was forthcoming in the busy shelves and desk-drawers, and there wasn't time to summon a light for a more thorough search. Back down the stairs it was, then, unsteady in longer skirts, determined to at least attempt a genteel exit through an actual door –

"But you said she left!"

That was – *Lorrie*. Strident-voiced, tenor-pitched and unmistakeable, his words slipping out under the drawing-room door.

Septimus's brother, in my sister's house. Bergamots, yes – I'm quite aware that there were greater relations between them to be astonished by – but the sheer physical presence of this one still struck.

"If Lady Miltonwaters couldn't be bothered to wait for us – if she left the theatre before I'd even come off the stage – that's got to be something, eh?"

A shuddering sigh. There was no one else it could have been – though the slumping fear was so far from anything I'd heard in Edwina's voice, it hardly seemed her at all.

"It was the manner in which she left," my sister groaned. "The girl calling her away. Elvira did not have five minutes to spare for me, because of some incentive provided by Adelaide Danadlenddu. That maid's father tried to take my fortune from me before I even had any control over it – and I do not doubt his daughter intends to continue the tradition! And if Elvira is confiding in Adelaide – if she tells the girl that you are an ungrateful rogue and I the treacherous upstart who stole you from her – then Adelaide will know everything – and she – she might – "

She broke off, gasped a breath. "Elvira already wants to ruin us both. To strip me of my reputation and you of your employment. And Adelaide will be all too eager to assist her. It was my arrangement that brought the two of them together – whatever she does will be my fault – "

She stopped. Heart swollen in my gullet, I waited. A matter of seconds, and then the silence would snap, as it always did, shattered at the feet of Edwina's composure. I'd heard it only days ago, when she chided Rosamond. She would break apart the quiet and rebuild herself above it, and when I was sure her panic had calmed I could slip away without –

But the silence held.

And Rosamond wasn't coming back – and I couldn't just –

"She won't."

I saw the movement in a daze, my soul swung out of my limbs and hovering level with the drawing-room chandelier. That velvet-lapelled creature beneath me – which could, against every scrap of logic, have only been myself – shoved the door open and hurled the words at Edwina with all the twitching swagger of another being. My sister was stood at the murky mantelpiece, with Lorrie hunched over his knees on Rosamond's chaise, and it was entirely impossible to discern which of them looked the more profoundly bewildered.

"Because," I added hastily, before either could stiffen into an incredulous exclamation, "If everything proceeds according to plan tonight – she – ah – well – both of them – are about to get quite trapped in their own criminal activity. Quite."

"*Henry?*" Lorrie gasped. "But – I thought you were – "

Edwina's head jerked from me to him and back again, one hand brushing at the edges of her eyes. I knew the movement – I had traced it myself, but – figs – *Edwina* didn't cry!

"Where have you been? What happened to you? Are you hurt? What – ?"

Not now. Not with the Director waiting.

"With all due respect – erm – I quite can't stay. I don't have long at all – I – I don't know how much longer the Director can stall them – "

"Who's getting stalled?" Lorrie burst out. "Lady Miltonwaters? And this Adelaide girl? They're at the Div?"

Edwina cleared her throat with vigour enough to set the curtains trembling. "Wait! Henrietta, I insist that you explain yourself. I cannot have you leave and tell me nothing – I do not think I can bear it again – "

"I'm sorry!" – and I haven't the faintest what wild desperation managed to thicken the reed of my voice, but it shocked her silent.

"I – I promise I'll explain – I just – I can't at this exact second! You – erm – you would like Lady Miltonwaters and Adelaide Danadlenddu to be stopped, yes? Their suddenly being caught in the midst of some dastardly plot against the Division – that – erm – that would be convenient for you and Lorrie – quite?"

Edwina's jaw dropped. "I – but – how do you know – ?"

Lorrie, I noted, was valiantly endeavouring to become one with the chaise.

"I – I simply wished to – ensure that you were – well – to reassure you – that your fears may be cut off before they've begun – but that entirely relies upon you trusting me now – because I'm quite going to do my job, with or without your permission!"

It clambered up my throat and burst out in a shriek before I could catch my voice, my nails sunk in my palms, every edge of me shaking fit to crack the floorboards. After that, I could hardly hold her gaze for my sheepish coda –

"So if I could possibly – erm – borrow your signet ring – yes – that would be – erm – very helpful – quite – "

She folded her arms, drew herself up where the shock had slackened her, arched one pale yellow eyebrow. "You wish to represent the family? Why?"

I swallowed. "It – it might do someone else some good – at least, someone far cleverer than me seems to think so – and – if that's her plan, I quite don't intend to scupper it. But – I really do have to go now – so if you don't want to give it to me, please do say – "

It was consummately insane of me to expect that she would offer it. In the wake of the bravado that had tipped me through the door, I was wilting with every new second into a horrified realisation of quite what I'd done: the time that was being wasted with every question, the anger to which I must have been stirring my all-powerful sister, the awkward questions that would cluster about Lorrie. But I was closest to the door, and the bicycle was just outside. If I had to sprint, they wouldn't catch me. The faint echo of Rosamond plucked at my sleeve, furrowing the rich fabric, urging me away. *Edwina clearly won't accept help from either of us – you've got things you don't want to lose – don't let her leech them out of you –*

Then I blinked. Edwina's face was set, a tight inscrutable scowl down at her hands – but she was slipping the signet from her fourth finger, jutting it out to me.

"I will need it back," she added curtly. "But it seems you need it now."

I stared at her. Lorrie did the same, though the little I could catch of his expression wasn't startled in the slightest. He was grinning, nudging her on as she stalked across the rug and shoved the ring into my hand.

"I – erm – thank you – this will – yes – right – very helpful – good night – "

"You must promise me that this discussion is not over, Henrietta."

Edwina called it after I'd backed away, when I was halfway through the door with the signet shunted precariously up my index finger. "Lady Miltonwaters may have proved herself a disaster narrowly avoided, but you might still have a chance elsewhere if we act quickly. There may be others – "

I set my teeth. As Septimus might well say: *right*.

"Thank you – erm – for your concern – Edwina – but I – I – I quite don't want others. I – I can only apologise if I've not – erm – made that clear. But – I – well – what I *do* want is for you to respect my decision – and stop trying to arrange pheasant-based betrothals for me. I've entirely no intention of being a married woman – in fact, neither of those words fit me in the least. And – erm – I really should have said before – but – whilst it's all springing forth – my name is Henry. Just that. Now – if you'll excuse me – I have a part to play."

I didn't dare glance back. The front door was before me, and my task with it.

My second plan for breaching the Division was, at least, wildly better than my first. Devoid of Septimus's map and battling my skirts, I cycled a demented loop, improvised from the scraps and recollections of my every trudge round the town: a weird parallel route along Dallyangle's outskirts, where the fields lay flat and silent in the moonlight and a seam of housefronts masked me from the market square. I sliced a triangle of cobblestones between the Division and Checkley's – the tavern was threadbare to its last waifs and strays, none of whom looked up from their shivering chats as I wheeled the bicycle past. I had to abandon it at the dormitory's back door, still cricked open at its furtive angle.

I swallowed a gasp. Knelt, shadowed between the door and the gloom beyond, to ease my boots off. Uncurled myself into the first trembling step.

The floorboards inside were quite as cold as I had anticipated, a cold so sharp it seeped through my stockings like water. I had my boots pinched in one hand, my paper and pencil in the other, both arms splayed to force my balance steady as I skirted the boards' creaks. The bolts over the windows hadn't been pinned up, and sickly streaks of yellow street-light cut up the floor. Around me – beside me – behind me, as I crept further in – the dormitory beds were as disordered as they were deserted, sheets heaved back in crumpled huddles, blankets slumped over mattresses to trail on the floor. Gertie, Millicent and Oliver hadn't been back, hadn't had time to make them up.

Yet. But finding them was Mr. Adelstein's responsibility.

"You truly imagine any more ledgers would alter my mind?"

I stifled a shriek with my fist, nearly stunned myself on the boots in my hand. Even with a door between us, that voice was horrendously impossible to mistake. Lady Miltonwaters, unfurling a sneer as heavy and stretched as a hallway rug.

"Do you really not understand what I am telling you – have been telling you for – goodness, over an hour? Are your stunted faculties so incapable – "

Adelaide Danadlenddu's voice knifed under the door, and the temperature shrivelled with it. "They understand you perfectly, Milady. This – this busybodying with the ledgers is simply a design to infuriate you."

"Tush, child, they wouldn't have the wit," Miltonwaters scoffed – before her voice rose to a swell, atop a sudden clatter of footsteps. "You! Girl! What are you and your witless daughter trying to show us *now?*"

A tremendous thump set Gertie's jug rattling in its ablutions bowl. I could have slumped for sheer relief to hear the Director – hoarse, a little breathless, her voice draped in the ragged remnants of her old serenity, but alive. "As you requested, Lady Miltonwaters – "

Adelaide hissed. "She didn't request – "

" – here, the Divisionary records for July of this year!"

Cassandra's voice slipped in beside her mother's, all the sarcasm scraped out, her words light and skittering over a nervous tremor. "And why shouldn't Lady Miltonwaters request, Adelaide? Milady's quite right – as a member of the town council and the niece of our nearest whole entire marquess, she's of course entitled to examine our proceedings and receipts in the most scrupulous detail – "

"She doesn't care about your ridiculous receipts, Cassie," Adelaide snapped. "Whatever you're playing at, it isn't going to change her mind."

Lady Miltonwaters cleared her throat. "I think you are forgetting your place, Danadlenddu. Of course I still want the *Division* disbanded – I told them so, didn't I? – but it shan't hurt to gather even more evidence of their flagrant incompetence, and if these ignorant girls wish to offer it up to me – "

Anger knifed through Adelaide's retort, the most I'd heard my terrifying relation express. "With all due respect, Milady, you have been trawling through the Division's receipts for the best part of an hour, a procedure which is entirely unnecessary when you intend to extract a resignation from its leader. What do you imagine you are going to find – new information to shake your resolve?"

"And what do you imagine *you* are about, speaking to me in such a tone?" Miltonwaters tossed back, her voice curdling. "You have done well, my little sham-governess, but you are still my servant, and I will not tolerate any further insolence. I have already been obliged to overlook your despicable ancestry this week – "

"I am the heir to the Nettleblack fortune, Milady!"

"Precisely," Miltonwaters snarled. "And the Nettleblacks are whores and witches unfit to manage any fortune whatsoever."

Enough of this. The Director – how to get a signal to her? – to let her know that I'd deciphered it, that I was here, that it was time for her to pluck a confession out of the culprits for me to transcribe –

But anything I did – stuck in the shadows, behind a door, without even a window to gesture through – all of them, they'd spot it in an instant!

Silence again. This time, Adelaide wasn't retorting.

"Very well," Miltonwaters declared. "I will examine your ledger, but it shall be the last one I look at this evening. I trust, *Mrs. Ballestas*, that I have given you plenty to think on."

Cassandra's voice was a frantic blurt. "You're not leaving just yet? We're only at July, Milady – if you wanted to wait – "

Sweet nectarines, but her panic was infectious, a visceral thing, seizing me by the hair and shoving me forwards. I quite didn't think. I just unclenched my fist and launched my boots to the floor.

The shoes ricocheted into the yellow-streaked gloom, past my elbows, clattering to rest under Millicent's bed. I flung myself flat to the side of the door, hands and paper and pencil all pressed to my mouth. Out in reception, the stalling prattle and snappish remarks had fallen silent, giving way to stomping footsteps. The door was creaking open, spilling gaslight over the beds, a shadowy silhouette splattered in cameo against the floorboards. If I had calculated wrong – if Adelaide's unblinking stare peered round the door's edge – she'd snatch me at my velvet lapel and drag me into the light, and all that effort with the ledgers would shatter like –

Cassandra blinked at me.

She was hollow-eyed and feverish-looking, her scarf pulled tight to her neck. Exhaustion simmered on every edge of her: in the straggly curls that slumped over her eyebrows, the sag in her hunched shoulders, the tremble of her fingers on the doorframe. Her gaze narrowed to a frown, pinched over everything in my hands – figs, the pencil and paper. Quick as a gasp, she rolled her eyes.

Then she turned away, casting about the shadowy room. Stalked for Millicent's bed, scooped up my boots from underneath and ferried them to the doorway. Her voice was sharp, dour, not a scrap of that frightened syrup left in it. Greengages, but it was easy to conjecture who she was looking at.

"These fell off a bed," she announced. "The bed itself's in a state. Looks like Henry Hyssop's."

If there were immediate responses, I couldn't catch them – she slammed the door so violently that my heart rattled in my ribs. I was shaking fit to dislodge veins, but even I had sense enough left in me to recognise her plan. Like it or not – and I'm not sure she did like it – she'd just proffered me my cue.

I sunk down, gently as I could manage, until I was on my knees at the door's edge. My fingers crawled over the plastered wall – mercifully, it wasn't damp – before I pressed my first page of paper flat to it, the pencil crooked across my palm.

"Perhaps Lady Miltonwaters is right, Cassandra," the Director declared suddenly. My pencil sprinted after her, the faintest rustle of an echo. "She is not under obligation to read any more ledgers than she wishes to. But – before you go, Milady – would you remind me precisely what it was you wanted of me?"

At which juncture, it seems only fitting to give way to the moment, as it were, and offer you up what I actually transcribed.

Keturah St. Clare Ballestas – K. B.
Cassandra Ballestas – C. B.
Elvira Miltonwaters – E. M.
Adelaide Danadlenddu – A. D.

K. B.   Perhaps Lady Miltonwaters is right, Cassandra. She is not under obligation to read any more ledgers than she wishes to. But – before you go, Milady – would you remind me precisely what it was you wanted of me?

E. M.   Good heavens, girl, must we pace you through your situation *again?* And my council deemed you such a clever little rarity, in your exotic way! As I told you, before you began to deluge us with your blotchy paperwork, I have come to advise you in the strongest possible terms to announce your resignation, and the disbanding of the Dallyangle Division.

K. B.   On what grounds, Milady?

E. M.   Saints preserve us! On the grounds of your incompetence!

A. D.   You can't deny that you've done a rather shoddy job of chasing up every criminal currently operating in Dallyangle.

K. B.   Adelaide – if you felt this way, you ought to have spoken to me. Why did you see fit to involve Lady Miltonwaters? Were my family not good to you?

E. M.   She was never working for your family, you fool. Danadlenddu is my maid – has been since that gauche trollop Edwina Nettleblack palmed her off on me. I only hustled her into your household to keep an eye on you – to make sure you couldn't destroy the very fabric of Dallyangle any more than you already have!

A. D.   Milady –

K. B.   I let you care for Johannes. I trusted you with my son.

E. M.   You should consider it a mercy she didn't do worse. She was only there to spy, after all. It was terribly audacious of you to expect that she raise your children for you, whilst you unsex yourself stealing work from the police!

K. B.   Startled as I am, Milady, to learn that you deem me sufficiently important to require surveillance, I don't see why that should have any impact on my Division's ability to solve these cases. We are the only organisation that has even come close to apprehending the Sweetings, and as for the Head-Hider —

E. M.   Oh, I wouldn't go thinking you can stop the Head-Hider.

A. D.   Milady, perhaps not —

K. B.   For all its ghoulish sensationalism, the Head-Hider is nothing more nor less than another case.

E. M.   Are you not listening to me, you overreaching slattern? The Head-Hider is *not* like any of your grubby criminal cases, born from the undeveloped wits of disaffected yokels. You may try all you like, but you will *never* be able to solve the Head-Hider — and as you continue to fail, the town will grow more and more sensible of your Division's deficiencies.

A. D.   This is a kindness, Mrs. Ballestas. You can still resign honourably before it has to go any further.

E. M.   Before you dredge any more effort out of us, you ought to say! I never imagined it would require this much work to get rid of you all — and I certainly don't intend to let it exhaust my energies any longer!

K. B.   Your energies, Milady?

A. D.   Milady simply means that —

E. M.   Milady shall speak for herself, thank you very much!

K. B.   I confess, I am struggling to understand why you should be so certain that the Head-Hider is a lost cause —

C. B.   Because she's the Head-Hider. Both of them are.

E. M. Ha! Topsy speaks!

K. B. That is a very strong accusation, Cassandra –

C. B. Sweet Lord! Can we all just stop tiptoeing around it? It's the pair of them. Adelaide moves the head on Lady Miltonwaters's orders.

A. D. And where did you pluck that theory from, Cassie?

C. B. From – from – I – when I –

E. M. Danadlenddu, you've broken her.

A. D. It sounds to me like you've been reading too many novels. Or should I make that writing them? Which reminds me, Mrs. Ballestas – have you had a proper leaf through your daughter's papers recently? You've made your feelings about – what did you call it? – that *frivolous brain-rot* of a popular fiction so very –

C. B. You're not slipping off the subject this time! I know you're moving the head – because I saw you take it from the morgue that first night it went missing! And if it sounds mad enough to be a novel, then that's you borrowing from me, and not the other way around!

E. M. Danadlenddu – you were *seen*?

C. B. She was seen. I saw her. And she knows it's true.

E. M. Wretched girl, I told you to be careful!

A. D. You didn't see anything, Cassie. I know you would make up any lie just to impress your mother, but this one is simply embarrassing. Don't you think?

C. B. I know what I saw.

A. D. I don't think you do.

C. B. I'm not listening to you this time –

A. D. Cassie, unless you wish things to become very unpleasant, very quickly, I would apologise to everyone here and sit back down with your fictions.

C. B.   No! Not again! You stole the head, and I watched you do it!

A. D.   Very well. Don't you mean that you *let* me do it?

E. M.   Did she really!

C. B.   I –

A. D.   Don't you mean that we stood in that pitiful excuse for a morgue and had a full conversation about letting me do it?

K. B.   Cassandra –

C. B.   Mother, don't listen to her –

A. D.   I was to sneak out with the head, and you were to heroically rediscover it the following day, after – what do you call her? Javert? – had been suitably shamed for her guarding negligence. Only, you see, I didn't want to play along. If someone – and yes, Cassie, I mean you – is so thoroughly pathetic that they have to stage their own triumphs just to look good, they're hardly someone to respect as an ally and friend, are they?

E. M.   Oh, better and better! Danadlenddu, you little fool, you never told me they were *this* useless!

C. B.   It – that wasn't what I – you suggested it –

A. D.   And you ate it up, every last bite of it. You were perfectly willing to let me carry a poor man's mortal remains all around the town for you, so that you might knock your colleague off her shaky pedestal. I ask you, Mrs. Ballestas – with a daughter like that, who I'm sure you feel in some way morally bound to protect, how are any of us in Dallyangle supposed to trust you to keep us safe?

C. B.   It – it wasn't – I didn't – that's not what I –

K. B.   Cassandra, is this true?

E. M.   Now we'll have some sport!

K. B.   You didn't just witness – you were actively *conspiring* –

C. B.   I never meant for it to happen like this! I mean – alright, yes, it was a mistake – but I wasn't just out to scupper Septimus, I swear!

A. D.   Really? Then do explain why you failed to inform your colleagues that you knew exactly who had taken the head –

C. B.   Because I wouldn't get believed! Not without more proof! Which I was trying to get! Otherwise it was just my word against the white girl –

A. D.   Oh, please. You were covering your mistake.

C. B.   I was *fixing* it!

K. B.   Cassandra! Did you truly imagine no one would listen to you? That *I* wouldn't listen to you?

C. B.   I – I couldn't –

K. B.   You put everything at risk. Everything. And for what? I never lost faith in you – I would have believed you – I always –

C. B.   'I never lost faith in you'? You'd look me in the eye and claim that was even slightly true.

K. B.   It –

C. B.   I proofread your Record! I know exactly what you write about me, when you get into your analytical stride, and forget I'm the one who's going to see it! Or do you not forget? Do you scrawl out those dissertations on my *lackadaisical carelessness* and *paltry efforts* and keep your fingers crossed that they might *shock Cassandra into some kind of productive work-ethic?*

K. B.   I –

C. B.   Your words! My words spoil your sensibilities, well – this is what your words do to me. And every time you look at me it's obvious you're still thinking them. Every time you call me *Cassandra*, and set everyone else to believing they should do it too – not *Division Sergeant*, like Javert gets to be, like I ought to be – everything in the way you treat me twists it in. I don't get the surname. I'm not good enough. I can't do it on my own. Well – here we are! Here's where that's led us!

[Silence.]

E. M.   You must tell me, Danadlenddu, why you ever made me believe I needed to bother with angry letters and hidden heads. Perhaps this is what we ought to do with the Nettleblacks next – just leave the wretches to themselves, and watch them bait each other bloody!

K. B.   I – this – this does not distract from – from what you have done –

A. D.   It's your word against ours, Mrs. Ballestas. A disgraced official with a disastrous recent record, trying to cover up her daughter's mismanagement, against the landlord's niece and a lady's maid of spotless character.

E. M.   You will never find that head – not as long as we have any say in it! –

A. D.   And given that any accusation you make relies on Cassie's little misdemeanour to back it up –

E. M.   Just end it while you still can!

A. D.   As Cassie knows all too well, Mrs. Ballestas, I can keep a secret. If you announce your resignation tomorrow, no one ever need know any of this. You can use whatever excuses you deem most appropriate. Perhaps you've decided to divert your energies into supporting the New Police?

E. M.   This contrary town has dodged a proper police force for far too long. There'll be a real constabulary here before the year is out, you mark my words – and *they* won't sit back and let the criminals run wild.

A. D.   You used to work on a police periodical, I believe, Mrs. Ballestas?

K. B.   That was a mistake.

A. D.   Another mistake! Like mother, like daughter, eh, Cassie?

E. M.   And there's no point trying to send her back there. I know the *Constabulary Bulletin* ladies – good girls, very good girls, even if they did choose Bedford College – and they don't want anything more to do with her. Quite right too, I say! If, just to render her unfortunate position more distasteful still, she despises women to the extent that she'd force them to usurp the police and abjure their very womanhood, it's only fitting that true ladies ought to despise her in return! Why is it that you scorn your own sex so much, girl? Is it your innate capacity for malice? Is it your willingness to consort with poisonous deviants? Why is it – do tell! – that you seem so hell-bent on upending the natural order of things?

K. B.   I – I –

E. M.   You, you?

K. B.   I think that – considering – for all I know – you decapitated a man, embalmed his head, and staged an elaborate charade with his remains for weeks – when it comes to upending any 'natural' order –

E. M.   You hear this! Do you! Accusing me of murder!

K. B.   If it wasn't murder, where did you obtain the head?

A. D.   I think that's enough for one evening –

E. M.   If a stupid little under-gardener will go about his work at the wrong time, in the wrong place, in the midst of my uncle's pheasant-shoot –

K. B.   You *shot* him?

E. M.   Murder, again! Owing to Danadlenddu's idiotic relation and her propensity for disappearing-acts, I wasn't even there when the shot was fired!

K. B.   Then – what? You paid off your family's mortician?

C. B.   Probably sent Adelaide to rob his grave.

E. M.   She is lurid, this child! The man was practically a pauper before we raised him up. His body hadn't even been claimed – if I hadn't put him to use, he would have gone straight to the dissection-table –

A. D.   There's something to appeal to you, Cassie.

E. M.   So you see – I didn't shoot him! You have nothing!

A. D.   And I rather think – with all due respect, Milady – that we have nothing more to say. Though I'm sure Cassie and her mother have an awful lot to talk about.

E. M.   Much as I would love to stay and watch you dance, I think my intrepid little maid has hit it spot-on. Resign tomorrow, girl, and spare yourself the humiliation as best you can. Otherwise – and I give you fair warning, though you do not even slightly deserve it – by the time I am finished with you, there will not be a scrap of Dallyanglian air left for you to breathe, nor a single house that will open its doors to you. There is an order to this good English town – to England itself – and it does not set persons like yourself on a par with women like me. I would be disgracing the very concept to let you reduce me thus. So you will banish your vile brood from Dallyangle, or I will do it for you. Let us see if you have been sufficiently civilized to make at least one worthy choice.

Transcribed by Henry Nettleblack, 9.45ish – 10pm

28.

OF EXPLANATIONS, BOTH
DENIED AND PROVIDED

Septimus once more

The grass crashes into my palms, seeps up through my fingers. More force behind it than grass ought to have. It's heavy with damp, every blade a little cord round my knuckles. Not just my hands – I'm crumpled on all fours, and my knees're drenched.

Wait. How'd I end up on the floor?

The building. Climbing down. I jumped. Thought my legs'd catch me a right side better than they seem to've done.

My breaths are more like gasps – too much like. Cold air pours over my lips. Just one more gasp, and my limbs'll stop shaking enough to let me stand. Maybe two more. Fine – three – if I grab for something to help me up. The garden's a bricked-in square. There's got to be a wall in arm's reach.

Moss smudges off the scratch of the bricks on my skin, and I'm up – almost – there. It's the back wall, steadying me to elbow-height. Beyond it, there's the blanket dark of the fields, a shuddering slosh sounding out the river as it champs at the towpath. We're right at the top of the town, backing onto the Angle and beyond. And if Property's had to keep a flat here – well, that works. The Sweetings can hide out deeper in the countryside, cross the river at the nearest bridge, climb this wall and sneak into town via the garden gate.

Could, I should say. Whatever the old arrangement was, it's over now. The Sweetings can't keep forcing Property to make life easier for 'em. That's assuming the two've even a mind to let Property survive the night.

Right. Well. No time for slumping, not with lives still to save.

And here come my charges. Rosamond Nettleblack, damn her, lands neat on her toes like an acrobat, greatcoat whirling behind her as she jumps from the crook where the garden wall meets the ground floor. Her grin's brittle, but there's smug excitement in it even so. "How's that for the Pobbles cliffs?"

I grit my teeth. It's that or groan, or retch. She's still watching me, waiting for applause she ain't going to get, pursing her lips in mock-pity for my staggering state. Well, let her think me as limp as she likes. She ain't had to climb this house upwards, or climb it more than once, or climb it with half her face splintering off. And this ain't a competition. I've just got to get 'em both out.

A wet crash brings Property down after her. No perfect landing this time. They're slumped in the grass like a swatted cranefly, limbs everywhere, the tails of their evening dress flailed into twists. They're spluttering something, too breathless to give the words much shape. "The ferret – maledizione – the ferret will have to save himself – "

I ought to help 'em up – they did it for me – but I – well. I don't think I can let go of this wall yet. Just a second longer, just 'til my legs stop shaking, then I'll be all the help they need.

Nettleblack's distracted, skidding about to peer back up the building. I drag my eyes after hers, blink hard to get the focus –

Oh.

It's the lights. One by one, there's yellow splotches warming up the curtains, every window from attic to ground. The sputtery strike of an extra candle, or a gaslit haze turning brighter and brighter. Spots of light spilling down into the garden, burnishing my bloodied hands where they grip the wall. If you were out in the fields, or jostling with the coppices, you'd see these windows for miles. Is that how the Sweetings've always seen this place, sat under some hedge-cracking tree by the farms – the same view I used to have? All the countryside a swathe of black, and Dallyangle a perfect sitting duck, a neat heap of town speckled with lanterns?

I snarl as I watch the lamps strike up, though I can't say I'd not expected it. Can't keep climbing over someone's lodgings without 'em noticing sooner or later. And I weren't as sleek about it on the way back down. It was – effort, more than I thought it'd be. Too much to leave me room to think about being stealthy.

Never mind that now. Deal with this. If the Sweetings get through the door, and they think to check the skylight, here's our escape-route lit up for the chase.

I dig my heel in the grass, push myself forward a step – another – 'til I ain't got the wall to hold me up anymore. My stomach clenches, squashes the words out on a painful hiss – "We have to go."

Property struggles to their knees, a fistful of grass in each hand. There'll be no saving that shirt. Their eyes widen when they find me, hollowed to skull-sockets from the window-lights, the streak of new-cut scar on their cheek damp with blood and grass-blades. "Septimus, are you – ?"

"I'm fine," I snap. "Out the front. Follow me."

I don't dare throw 'em both over that back wall. Not when the towpath's got no lights – not with the river so close. And what would I do with 'em in the pitch-black fields – how will that make us safer, when the Sweetings'll be headed out that way themselves soon enough? No. We need streets. People. Lanterns. Everything you can stare out for miles – a sitting duck, maybe, but safe enough if you can crawl right inside it. So I set our pace, teeth clenched against the throbbing in my muscles, stagger us through the narrow brick path that cuts between the houses. It ain't open to the sky – just cut through the edge of two terraces. There's a flimsy wooden gate in the middle of the passageway, half-open, slipped free of its latch.

Henry's been here. She's left it ajar.

And – I spot it across the street, dragging myself out of the passage both-handed, palms too numb and scraped to feel any more scraping from the bricks – her bicycle's gone too. She made it out.

She made it out.

Relief wrings straight through me. It's double-edged: I'm glad of it, and I'd never have it any other way – but it acts on my traitorous body like a warm bath, slackening every sinew I've been trying to keep taut. Which – later, perhaps, would be fine – but not yet! I ain't in a bath, ain't even half-safe. I've still got these two idiots to sort out. I can't relax.

Even so – there's no yelling that at my weak-kneed gratitude. One moment I'm stumbling forward across the street, then –

"Septimus!"

Cobblestones. Too close. I must be back on hands and knees.

I peer through gushes of hair, seeping out from where I pinioned it under my jacket. There's tiny specks of plant pushing up around the cobbles, and a sharp-cornered shadow cutting across 'em, blocking the glare from the street-lantern. It's Property's carriage, tugged to a weird diagonal in front of the tenement, the horse untended and stamping. Lucky for 'em it didn't just walk off with their getaway. Nettleblack's inside the carriage already, leant out through the open window like a lady in a sedan-chair, her elbow crooked and pale on

394

the black paint. Property had hold of the reins – but they're dropping 'em now, shaky footsteps stabbing closer to my hands. I squeeze a cobblestone for each palm, spit heavy breaths through my teeth. One stone's heavier than the other. Or is that me, my veering balance, toppling over sideways?

"Narcissus, we can't leave her like this."

Property's voice is trembling, their mud-crusted hands tugging at my shoulders. Heaving me back to my feet. Again. "I don't mean to offend your stoical sensibilities, sweet Septimus, but you truly are keeling over. And – believe me, I am the last individual to suggest venturing back into the jaws of the Sweetings, but my money – "

Nettleblack drums her fingers on the carriage window. Hoisted up, leant on Property's sharp shoulder, I can see her better, though she's all sliced up in strands of my hair. That clambering excitement's drained out – her wide green eyes are bright with fear. "I think it's rather your money or your life at this stage, cariad. What do you want – to take her with us?"

No.

"I said I'm fine," I growl, shoving away from Property's grip. My cycle's just across the street, propped against the opposite house-front. Damn this slumping relief. I can still make it. "You go – I need to be somewhere else – got a cycle – "

"Wait!" Property cries. I ignore 'em, fling out step after step. My cycle tips forward to meet me, pressing under my palms to keep me steady. "You're exhausted! Please – this is insanity – where do you need to be? I can drive you – "

Then we hear it. Even I can hear it. The crash of footsteps, echoes rattling down from every housefront. Sprinting. Too quick. We've no time to hide.

All I can do's stand still. Frozen where I am, my hands scalding-knuckled round my cycle's handlebars. Nettleblack's tucked up in that carriage, and Property's right by the horse. There's a street's-width between me and those two – I can't help 'em this time. I can only wrench my head round, spit out hair, watch in a daze as Property ducks behind the bulk of the carriage.

But – that ain't just footsteps. That's – I know the sound – what the hell is it? *Concentrate.* Push off the fug in your head, the ache in every limb, that damned warm-bath weakness. The sound – it's – like a ticking, but too fast and frantic for a clock – and there's lots of it, all at once –

It's a cycle. More than one cycle. The free-wheel, when someone gets off and walks it along.

"There! Sarge – Septimus!"

I know that voice too. The relief laps up to my shoulders, ready to drown me.

I shunt my gaze up the road, and there they are at last. Gertie, Millicent and Oliver, off their cycles and sprinting along with 'em, spread out across the street and lanterned to the hilt, a barrage of Div from housefront to housefront. Their shadows fling forward, soak over my handlebars before they reach me. And it ain't only the apprentices – there's four figures racing up. The one who breaks from the pack to rush at me ain't got a cycle or a lantern, only a trail of moth-eaten scarf. Scrabbling fingers snatch at my arms, mittened hands shucked out of overlong sleeves. Weirdest of all, it looks like he's holding my notebook.

"Nick?" I rasp. "Gertie? And – how – ?"

Nick Fitzdegu tosses me a feeble grin. "Alright, Septimus? Your map said it was down this street, but finding you in person's about the best we can hope for."

His grin curdles. "Bloody hell, your face – "

I glower at him. Pitying sympathy ain't going to get me out of the bath, is it? "I said I'm fine! – "

Wait. Did I – to him? Or was that Property?

And then I hear the rest of what he's said. Full five seconds after he's said it, with all the younger Divisioners peering worriedly at me as they mark up a semi-circle about my cycle. I flush, snatch my notebook and shove it in my pocket, try to glower 'em all out. Can't keep the glare properly stiff on my face.

"How'd you get my – I gave it to Henry – what – ?"

"Hyssop said you were in danger," Gertie interrupts, her cycle clicking as she wheels closer. Even in this cold, there's stark bumps of sweat on her forehead. "That's what Nick told us. Lucky we met him when we did – that lying little governess would've us right out to Gulmere on a wild goose chase!"

"She was outside the Div," Millicent adds, glaring up the street. "The governess, not Hyssop. Not letting anyone inside. We didn't know it was that at the time – but still. She told us Cass had some lead on the Head-Hider. Just to get us out of the way, Nick reckons."

Oliver nods frantically. "'Pparently there's some scheme in the Div – and Adelstein's on our side again, just in time – " – and even my addled head can spot Nick wincing for that – " – and now we're – "

"Henry," I choke out. "Where's Henry?"

Nick's hands squeeze my elbows. He's warm from his sprint, a right side warmer than the freezing night. The heat's beaming off all four of 'em. "She's gone to the Div. Second time lucky getting past the governess. She said she knew what Mrs. Ballestas wanted her to do, and she was going to do it."

"And you sent her in alone?"

But even as I spit it at him, I know the venom's seeped away. I've seen more than anyone what Henry can do. If she's tracing out something the Director's planned, there won't be a soul in Dallyangle that can stop it.

"No!" Nick blurts. "Matty's gone after her! He's watching the market square – he'll make sure she comes out!"

I give him a nod – and another nod, when I clock that no one looks even slightly reassured. If I'd the energy, I'd roll my eyes. Matthew Adelstein must be the last person in the world Henry wants as a bloody chaperone, and I hope she lets him know it.

"Right. Well – "

"Septimus!"

Next thing I know, Nick's been shoved to the side, and Gertie's got her free arm hooked round my waist. I must've slumped again. For a moment, I can't see – only feel, and blink against the shimmering diamonds that smudge out my vision. Gertie's strong, strong enough to hold me up without a scrap of help from my legs. Her coarse plaited hair scrapes at my cheek, where my chin's hooked over her shoulder, and the edge of her lantern jabs into my thigh. She's got a solid chest on her, and a rock of a corset, squeezing my ribs 'til I can hardly gulp down the breaths I need.

I shouldn't need any of it. I shouldn't be passing out in anyone's arms, not again. But – there's my own voice in my head, a sharp recollection, sprung straight from yelling at the Director: *these ain't things anyone should be trying to manage alone!* And – knifish to admit it, but – I'm almost spent.

"Alright, you lot, we need to get her out of here," Gertie grunts. "Fitzdegu – I assume Mr. High-and-Mightystein's alright with lending us his sofa?"

They're all moving, a shoal with me stumbling at its heart. Someone must've got hold of my cycle. I can feel my fingers prised gently from its handlebars. Gertie's shifted her hold to sling me between her and someone else – from the sharp tobacco smell of 'em, probably Nick – my arms draped over two sets of shoulders. I clear my throat, though it scrapes right round the inside of my neck, shake my head weakly to get my vision back, push the worst of my hair off my face. Even if I've got nothing else to give, the rest of 'em still need to know.

"Wait – the Sweetings – they're in there – have to stop 'em – tonight – there's a – "

I'm not so much cut off as drowned out. Clatters – shouts – too many sounds, springing up from nowhere. I'm too dazed to piece it into bits – 'til Gertie shunts me over to Nick and scrambles away, and her move knocks chaos into sense. I twist about to watch her, blinking off the water at my eyes, dragging Nick with me.

The scene further down the street's big and bombastic as those *Pirates* tableaus. The carriage was moving – was about to move, at any rate, with Property half-scrambled up into the driver's seat. Now it's stuck. Millicent and Oliver, one foot on a pedal and the other swatting furiously at the cobbles, are skidding past it on their cycles, shrieking to a halt to block its path. Gertie's done the same half-cycling trick, only she's gone for the horse, grabbing its harness before it can strike up a proper pace. This is the girl who used to wrangle the Shire horses on her farm; its ears may be flat to its head, but this sleek little town-horse ain't twisting out of her hold. Property nearly tips straight over the reins, snatching for the seat to stay on it, spluttering a panicky curse.

"What the devil do you think you're – I could have run you down!"

Gertie snorts. She's sturdy as a stable-door at the horse's head, glaring up at its would-be driver. "Not likely. Well – look who we've got here! You and your carriage, just *coincidentally* parked right next to your least favourite Division Sergeant, and her broken-nosed and ready to drop. Doesn't take an Adelstein to spur the suspicions, does it?"

Property stares at her, the reins shaking in their grip. I don't think they'd manage it, but they definitely look of a mind to try driving the horse straight over her.

"Maledizione! Will you and your insufferable Division just *leave me be?*"

Their voice is shrill, skidding to a yell. Gertie blinks it off, unfazed. "Septimus? What d'you think?"

I crash into Property's gaze. There's a twitch under their eye, half-pleading and half-defiant. Their jaw's too tense for another rejoinder – which is enough to shock me, even through the thickening fog of my thoughts. Are they not going to try anything else?

Suppose it makes sense they'd be struck wordless. Here's half the Div ready to suspect 'em, a mort of proof, a cluster of eye-witnesses. Even the Director couldn't dispute this. Even if we can't get the Sweetings – this'd be my reputation sorted, my judgment shored up against any more rolled eyes and weary looks. And I don't have to do anything, don't even have to shrug off my exhaustion. Just patch together a few choice words.

I sigh. Thinking it's enough to boil the nausea in my throat.

"Let 'em go, Gertie."

Don't they all stare, now!

I'm inches from collapsing, and every stunned look in the street's gouging into me, ready to push me the last of the way. I've only strength to meet one of the stares. Property's face is suddenly slack – if I'm too tired to scowl, they're clearly too astonished.

"You sure, Sarge?"

"They'll be safer gone." I swallow, scrabble for the rest of my voice. "They're no threat to us anymore. But the Sweetings are. And they're both cornered in there. 'S not much of a chance, but even so."

Gertie's at the edge of my eyes, hesitating. I set my teeth, give her a nod, sharp as I can manage.

Everyone moves then. Millicent and Oliver wheel their cycles out of the way, and Gertie drops the horse's head with a parting glare. The last look I get from Property is swirling and complicated as one of their cravat patterns. A twitch of an arched eyebrow for ghostly bravado – a wary glint in their dark eyes – a curt nod to match mine – and parted lips, just for a moment, as if they've still more to say. But it'll keep. Their mouth tightens to a grim line, and their hands flick at the reins, a brace of practiced tugs to turn the horse about. They're looking ahead now – I've slipped out of their eyeline. The carriage quickens to a clatter, the horse at a brisk trot, rattling to the end of the street and vanishing round the corner.

Drive fast, I will 'em. *Fast and far.*

They've got a whole night to do it. I can hear the clock-chimes on the air, faint and distant, slipping in to fill the sudden quiet: quarter to ten. Plenty of time.

The next thing I know, I ain't on my feet anymore.

There's an arm about my shoulders. My legs sprawl out in front of me, rubbed raw at the trouser-knees, limp as cut hay. Cold stiffness presses at my back – the bricks of a housefront, propping me up in a seat. Ahead of my hazy eyes, there's boots and wheels and jostling shadows. And hair. Too much hair.

"Don't think we'll be finding any Sweetings in there tonight."

Gertie – but when I squint up at her, she ain't looking at me. Nick's crouched beside me, nodding along with her words. "Checked the garden – there's muddy footprints all up that back wall. They could be anywhere on the towpath, probably further off. There was this in the grass, though."

She's holding something down to us. A trim leather wallet with a paisley lining, flapping open, shedding grass-blades as it lolls out of her fist.

'Course it's empty. 'Course the Sweetings took their chance.

And now – the deadline –

No. Made-up dates can shift. It's people need to be protected now, and we can't save anyone from the Sweetings if they just shoot us off the towpath.

I groan, dragging all eyes back to me. Nick jumps – clearly he didn't clock I'd come to.

"No point – going after 'em – in the dark." The words're limp, don't sound like mine. It's what I'm trying to say, anyway. "Need – to check – the Director's – don't know what – Henry's probably – we should – "

I don't remember how the sentence ended. I ain't fully sure it did.

Soft velvet. Sliding up my neck, the back of my head. I ain't known soft velvet since that night on Property's chaise. It's the sort of stuff I stare at from a distance, too plush and perfect to touch.

I heave my eyelids up, squint through darkness tender as a cushion. Shapes fold down from towering walls, dim and yellowed in the flicker of a single candle. Desks. Adelstein's desks. And that's the faint mottle of Adelstein's fancy paintings, smoothed of their stormy details in the gloom.

Adelstein's house. How the hell'd we get up the stairs?

I shudder, mostly just to find my edges. I'm sprawled on a chaise, arms draped across my chest, legs sliding off the end. There's someone hunched over 'em – Nick, tugging my boots off. He folds my feet into the chaise when I'm down to my socks, bending my knees to make 'em fit. Next thing I can tell, there's a heavy woollen blanket, spread over me and tucked up to my chin, my tangling hair swept neatly under it.

I ain't a bloody child, I want to snap. But I weren't treated with anything like this care when I was a child, and the desks around me are blurring at the edges, so I swallow it and close my eyes.

"Are we going back to the Div?"

It's Gertie's voice, high up and far away. Nick's response is closer, hushed in a gentle whisper. "Not yet. Not 'til Henry gets back. Matty'll come home with her – he'll tell us when."

A warm hand smooths straggles of hair off my face. I crack one eye, and Nick's perched at my shoulder, smiling with what looks like wry irritation. "Now – I'd give you some Nettleblack's next, if Matty'd not smashed all the bottles. I'll be having words with him about that. I'd have words with you too, if you didn't need to sleep so much. Saying you're fine, all while looking like you've been dragged through every prize-fight known to Surrey!"

I dig my teeth into my lip. Short sentences, long breaths between 'em. "Had to climb the building. Had to chase the carriage."

"Before or after you broke your nose?"

"Maggie," I hiss. Sort of an explanation, ain't it? "And Nettleblack was there. Climbing like a goblin."

He whistles. Must think I'm delirious. Maybe I am. Didn't seem a mad thing to say, 'til I actually said it.

"And the Div – Henry – is she – ?"

"She'll be fine," he assures me hastily. Hands, or what feel like hands – somewhere between hands and very fleshy spiders – pat my shoulders, swathed under the blanket. "This was her idea, her and the Director."

The question crawls up my throat, quicker than my thoughts. "Why's Adelstein chasing her, Nick?"

"Don't worry." He's kneading with his hands, pressing me into the velvet. The heat thickens, eating through the last scraps of cold. "It's alright. He's not anymore. Now – your job for this eve, m'dear, is rest, rest, and more rest."

"But – "

"*Rest.* You want to help Henry, this is how you'll do it. I'm just going to grab something to clean your face – won't be far – and you're *not* to go staggering off anywhere else, alright?"

By the time I've a breath strong enough to gasp out *Henry* on, he must be gone. My eyes slide under the lids again. The room's starting to rock like a crib, and I'll go mad if I see the ceiling swinging above me. It's the warm bath at last – soft under my chin, on the backs of my hands, about my smarting feet. There's sweat matting my hairline, a scald in my cheeks, crusted blood still blocking my nose. Nick'll deal with that. And he knows about the Div, and Henry knows what she's doing.

What about Lorrie – and Miss Nettleblack?

But that thought's too violent, and it knocks me right out again.

There's a murmur at my head, a chill of breath on my face. The blanket tweaks, lifts. Something soft-edged and solid slips between my arm and my chest. Cold fingertips trace my jawline, patting the blanket back into place.

The words're half-dreamt, jumbled, sliding out of my head as quick as they slide in. I know the voice, soaking over me, a bucket of fresh-heated water for all the coldness of the touches. I want to reply, to find my arms and curl 'em about her. *You're safe. We're safe.*

My limbs stay limp. I ain't wakeful enough to push movement through 'em. It don't worry me, not with all the calm of sleep still wrapped round my head. The cold's drawn back now – she don't mean to wake me properly.

All but one last touch. There's an icy press at my forehead, lips chapped and stiff from the night air.

I sigh, melt out of thoughts and dreams both.

The warmth's almost simmered away when I wake next. Cold grey light spills through my lashes, catches in the whorls of the plastered ceiling. The candle on the nearest desk is burnt to a puddle of wax, the gaslamps dark and empty. Dull mustard yellow clusters under my chin, veined with faded royal blue – the blanket, given colours at last. Past the curl of my legs and the end of the chaise, the desks are steady now. The bay window's uncurtained, framing smudgy clouds and damp slimy rooftops, chimneys sticking out of 'em like broken teeth.

Rare thing for a Dallyangle day, but it ain't raining. The window-panes are bare of drizzle – even the morning frost has faded. In place of the rain, there's a faint mist rubbing out the sharp edges of the opposite roof. Low-hanging fog, everything monochrome as a photograph. Two magpies skitter along the roof-slates, tails tweaking with every leap.

Two for joy.

I groan myself off the cushions. I can sit up. I will.

The room shivers – but not enough to crumple – as I swing my feet over the edge of the chaise. My socks sink deep in the rug, and I dig my toes in to anchor me. I've never been without shoes on a floor this soft. Everything's soft – the light, already darkening again, the blanket heaped across my knees –

The little side-table. That weren't there last night. It's been set down close to the chaise – so carefully, the rug ain't even marked its tracks – and piled with an invalid's bounty: a plate of biscuits, a glass of water, a cooling mug of Nick's chai, a fresh bottle of Nettleblack's. The green of the label's bright and glaring, the glass bottle sharply carved with its spiky leaf-veins. Propped to the side of it's a folded scrap of paper, my name scribbled in a hand I don't recognise.

I reach for the water first, spot in the doing that my jacket's gone. The ends of my shirt-cuffs have a rusty tinge to 'em, but the shirt was never fully white anyway. The jacket's only migrated as far as one of the desks, where it's splayed out in state, all the bloodstains scrubbed off. Beads of water sprint down my shirtfront as I gulp from the glass. There's crumbs to follow 'em when I get hold of the biscuits, hunger smarting back into me with every frantic bite. The lukewarm chai goes the same way, then I've half a mind to eat the note too – still fugged with sleep, I nearly do, my hand snatching and lifting of its own accord. But the feel of the paper stops me: it's like tracing your fingers over a bowl of cream.

Sleep as late as you want, the note scrawls. *I've just gone out to get your brother. And Tom Ballestas, if the apothecary can spare him, to make sure your nose doesn't need setting or anything. Back soon. Everything being taken care of at the Div. Worry not! – Nick.*

I'm in two minds. I want Lorrie – I want him safe with me, safe from Lady Miltonwaters – but seeing me like this'll fling him right into a state. Especially if –

But when I lift my hands to my face, they come away clean, but for a few skeins of my unpinned hair. That's something. Even if the bruises and swelling won't've gone, and I still can't breathe through my nose – 'least the blood's been got rid of. Don't want to worry him too much.

It's only then, as I set the note back down on the table, that I spot it. There's something tangled up with the blanket on my knees, a corner of dark leather poking out from the garish tartan. It sits startlingly familiar in my hand when I ease it free of the blanket's folds – and I know it straightaway.

It's Henry's journal.

I tip it against my palm, and it slumps open to a bookmark, right at the front. There's another sheet of that creamy paper – but this time the writing matches Henry's, wild and spidery.

I can lift it right to my face, squint without fretting about interruption. Trace my finger along the words, for all the world like I'm learning my letters again, guess the shapes and scribbles 'til I can set 'em to a pattern. *I am not coherent,* she's written above a shaky signature, *but this is.* And in the journal itself, at the top of the page she's marked with the paper – that's a date, back in October – and a first line. *To be blunt: I must escape.*

It's her explanation. Not to be rushed or stammered. She's left me alone with it, with all the space and silence I need to take it in.

Whatever it is – whatever it means for us – she wants me to know.

So I curl up my legs again, settle back against the chaise, and start reading.

29.

IN WHICH SOME NEW
DECISIONS ARE MADE

Myself

A date, most likely Sunday, November 5th, 1893

Figs. I now have a whole phase of my flummeried existence to sum up, and I'm quite not even sure how to start.

"'I wish to make an announcement,'" the Director declared. Her voice cracked on the last word, and she cleared her throat, lifting the ledger an inch closer to her spectacles. "'The past few weeks have been, to you, a test of the Division's abilities – to provide you with the security and protection which is your right – and you have been' – Cassandra, what does this word say?"

Cassandra plucked her elbows off the reception desk, wove around it to peer over her shoulder, one hand crooked on the back of the Director's office-chair. "'Sceptical'."

Her mother nodded. The glance between them was tentative – a hesitant smile from the Director, a shaky dip of the head from her daughter. I had said nothing to either of everything I heard last night, when Lady Miltonwaters and Adelaide finally stormed out through the double doors, and I could emerge from the dormitory with transcript in hand, seal off the end of it with some taper-wax and the signet. It had seemed prudent to offer them only my briefest reassurance, a cursory glance over their adversaries' most incriminating speeches – and then hastily take my leave. They did much the same, hastening towards the apothecary with *Johannes* on the Director's lips, and Cassandra staggering in her wake.

Now, we sat in the midst of a peace soft and fragile as an unfinished scarf, still stuck on the end of a knitting-needle. Cassandra had spent the morning in her mother's office. I had heard their voices rising, crashing, tumbling down again, fast frantic talk of a *leave of absence* and *time to consider*. It was only as three o'clock chimed that the pair of them emerged – with the Director's badge pinned in place, and a new-written project in Cassandra's ledger. Even then – even to Gertie and Millicent and Oliver, who had spent the morning resoundingly occupied by other matters – even to Mr. Adelstein, hovering nervously beside the double doors – it was obvious that their conversation had not been smooth, and the joint work in the ledger not entirely placating. But the pair seemed consummately determined to make an effort, to squash things down until their collaboration had run its course. Cassandra had stuck her head round the dormitory door, summoning Gertie and her contingent from their doze on the beds, and I had defied my skirts to cycle across town in search of Mr. Adelstein. Now, the whole Division had gathered in reception – and our opinions were demanded, on the speech just drafted by the Ballestases.

All but Septimus.

Of course I was nervous. Mr. Adelstein, of all people, had proffered me stiff assurances quoted verbatim from Nick: she had rested well, and she would be along when she could, but Mr. Ballestas and Lorrie had to see to her nose first. I was quite amazed that I had energy left to panic. I had barely slept, had simply commandeered an Adelstein desk and scribbled entry after entry until my hands stopped shaking, until there was nothing more to do than leave the journal with Septimus and concede to Nick's attic-bed. She could be reading it now, even as I twitched on the reception bench, the very same bench I had sprawled across the night we first met.

But she had to know. And I wanted her to know properly, in words that wouldn't mangle my feelings to nothing as they struggled out of my throat. And I quite refused to think of it any more than that – for the moment, anyway. The journal – my past, and any potential future she might wish for with me in it – everything was in her hands, and I could do nothing more.

And I was, apparently, the only member of the Division even slightly faltering in careful attendance to the speech. Gertie, Millicent and Oliver filled the bench beside me – the latter with his skinny knees drawn up to his chin, the former gulping down a mug of steaming tea. Cassandra, until her movement, had been sat at the desk, having stuffed the wood-burner almost to bursting. Mr.

Adelstein perched at the doors, trying his best to resemble anything other than a prodigal in disgrace, nodding along to every word with pointed attentiveness. The burner's heat seeped out from behind the desk, clasping tight about the heavy velvets and rich layers I hadn't yet taken off. The stares, from Gertie and her contingent, when I first trembled down beside them in full Heiress Nettleblack attire, had been far too much for me to acknowledge.

Now, Gertie lifted a hand. "D'you reckon it's fair to tell the council they've been sceptical about us? I mean – given they're the ones paying for us to exist? Sorry, I – I mean, it's a great opening, obviously – I just thought –"

"No, you're quite right," the Director returned quickly, levelling an encouraging smile in the bench's direction. Gertie pinked, quite as startled as she was delighted. "This draft is open to suggestions from every Division member. As a Division, we are best when we shoulder the work together – we must try to remember that going forward, myself included. So – Cassandra?"

Cassandra plucked a pencil from behind her ear, twisted it in her fingers. Her voice was studiously measured, carefully devoid of any emotion, pinned in its entirety to the question at hand. "You could say 'you might feel you had reason to doubt us', or something like that. Leave it up to them if they want to agree."

"Very good." The Director proffered the ledger to her, waited with a few careful glances as Cassandra scrawled the edit into the margin. "We do not wish to alienate the council mere seconds into the address, after all. Shall I go on?"

The gaslight shook with nods. Outside, the dusk was thickening, the daylight hours almost pinched away. Not that – persimmons, not that it ought to have plucked at my fears like it did. Septimus's treatment would take as long as it took. There was quite no point pinning any expectations to the time of day.

"'The Metropolitan Police may have years to pursue cases,'" the Director continued, settling back into her chair. She had carried it out of her office – and, cherries, it was peculiar in the extreme to see her folded down into it, no longer the tallest person in any given room. "'To lose their criminals, to never find them in the first place, all whilst armed with resources of which we can only dream. We have had less than a fraction of that time to contend with two difficult and sensitive cases – the business of the Head-Hider, alongside the ongoing problem of the Sweetings' delinquency. Yet a few individuals claim that our rate of play is not good enough when set beside the possibility of bringing in the police – and so the Division is pushed almost to the brink of closure.'"

I felt the bristle of panic skidding down the bench. Gertie and the others were gaping at the Director – even Mr. Adelstein, affecting his usual implacability, had a touch of startled confusion about the slackness of his jaw. I confess, I was surprised to see them all so stunned. When Septimus had told me of the council's deadline, choking the words out in Property's garret, I had assumed the matter to have been – well, rather more widely known than it apparently was.

The Director sighed, catching every glance. "This next part might come as a shock – but it is the very reason why I shall be obliged to make a speech to the council in the first place."

Mr. Adelstein's eyes narrowed – and he spoke, for the first time since skulking back through the doors. "The council have imposed an ultimatum."

"Astute as ever, Matthew." The Director's voice was cool, but not in the least unforgiving. "Continuing: 'As you will recall, one month ago you saw fit to set a deadline for our work, on which our continued funding would depend. We were to rid the town of the Sweetings by November sixth, or else – '"

Millicent all but dropped her tea. "But – that's tomorrow!"

"Precisely," the Director returned calmly. "Which is why I have sent a letter requesting a new meeting at the council's earliest convenience – "

"And why we've got to sort out the speech," Cassandra added, flashing Millicent a quick smile – a glint of reassurance. "Fast."

The Director lifted the ledger again. "'I wish to be clear about where we stand. I cannot deny that the matter of the Sweetings remains unsettled. New developments have forced a major alteration of our tactics.'"

"'Cause they've got a gun!" Gertie burst out. "I say we tell them as much!"

Cassandra grimaced her agreement, tipped down over her mother's shoulder to take up the speech. "Let's put 'New developments – namely, their procurement of dangerous weaponry – have forced a major alteration of our tactics. We will be most effective if we are given chance to regroup, and come back stronger against the heightened threat. With lives at stake, we cannot afford to cut our work short. We cannot be measured by impossible standards – we have to make our own standards, and develop our own strategies. Calling in the police and yet more pistols might solve your problem now, but it won't help anything in the long run.'"

The Director glanced at her, the faintest of tremors threading her voice. "Cassandra, you must write that down!"

The room softened to silence as Cassandra lifted the book – but for the thin scratch of her pencil, a faint scuttling under the floor-boards, the occasional snap and crumple of the logs in the burner. The market had almost closed, leaving bare cobbles and country hush in its wake. Gertie caught my eye, flung me a wry grin. *Just another afternoon at the Div, eh, Hyssop?*

I smiled my agreement, glanced back to the nearest window. The street-lamps were lit against the gloom outside, tipping yellow splashes of light through the panes and the unpatched glass. Surely the meeting with the council wouldn't take place today, before Septimus had a chance to hear the speech? Even if she didn't make it back in time – even if she stayed another night on Mr. Adelstein's chaise, with my journal –

The doors slipped open. Mr. Adelstein started, hastily pressing a scowl away. Even Cassandra glanced up from her writing, the pencil trembling above the page, a spasm of astonished unease skittering across her face.

Septimus blinked at us, nudged the doors shut behind her. She was every inch herself, and every inch something raw-edged and new, in the same faltering moment. Her hair still hung loose, sturdy and heady-textured, arching over her shoulders like nothing so much as polished wood. She had resumed her uniform, with the worst of its dirt scrubbed off, but the elbows and trousers were still torn in holes. Her face was a burst of purpling bruises, stark under her navy eyes, and a plaster had been spread across the sharp new off-set of her nose.

The room stared on, and the colour smarted in her cheeks.

Please. Look at me.

Her gaze darted about, from Cassandra and the Director to the bench – and, plums, where I perched at the end of it.

Nothing left to mask me now. No bedraggled disguise. No tangles of wordy thoughts to thicket myself in. There was only her look, and the careful inscrutability – and, for all I knew, the pain! – keeping her face still, and the realisation jolting in my chest: she couldn't tell me anything yet. Not until we were alone. Not with everyone in the Division still gawping at her.

She blinked – broke our stare – then picked her way past Mr. Adelstein, leaned against the dormitory door, and folded her arms.

The silence stretched on. It was Cassandra's to fill, with one last wary glance at Septimus, her voice rising out of the ledger. The Director slumped against her chair as her daughter took over, closed her eyes with a sigh.

"'But the matter of the Head-Hider has been solved,'" Cassandra announced to the room, straightening up as she did so. "'The Division has been put to the test, but not in the manner determined by yourselves – not in a manner that anyone could have expected.'"

Her face tweaked, a breath's glimpse of her usual smirk. "Think we can say that again."

"Hear, hear," Gertie agreed, grinning at her.

"'There was never a murderer out to plague the town. There was not even a connection with the Sweetings. There was nothing but two individuals, and the severed head they obtained for the express purpose of undermining our abilities, and compromising our chances of meeting your deadline. The names may startle you, but I must give them: Lady Elvira Miltonwaters, General Member of this very council, and her maid Adelaide Danadlenddu – a girl placed under my roof by her employer to disrupt the Division's affairs.'"

Cassandra squared her shoulders, jerked up her chin. "'Both Lady Miltonwaters and Adelaide Danadlenddu have been escorted to Hartgate Gaol by members of the Division, along with the severed head, discovered in a chest in Lady Miltonwaters's bedroom.'"

Gertie snorted. "You should've seen the butler's face – "

"Hang on – you what?"

The room jolted, led in large part by my gasp. It was the first Septimus had spoken since slipping in. Her voice was quite as bruised as her face – though even that hardly softened the smarting incredulity in it.

"You put 'em in a *gaol?*"

Gertie glanced round, plait bristling, defensive. Her contingent did the same, darting anxious looks along the bench. "Didn't exactly have another option! It wasn't like you lot with the pig-stealers – we couldn't just take them to my father."

Her voice sharpened. "We've heard bits of what they said last night. You think we could leave them be, when they all but threatened to kill the Director?"

Oliver gulped. "And Milady didn't want to go quietly."

"Exactly!" Millicent added hotly. "She was there, yelling to the whole street, saying she'd get her marquess uncle to skin us all – "

"But that can't be it!"

Septimus caught the volley of glares, sighed, twitched her words until they softened. "Look. I ain't saying you're wrong about 'em. But – if they're in a gaol – ain't that just fair game for the police to take over?"

Everything skidded into silence. Gertie bit her lip, eyes widening even as they veered away to pucker the floorboards.

"Then what would you suggest, Septimus?"

The Director was watching her, grave and thoughtful. Pomegranates, and she'd only just woken up!

"I – well." Septimus swallowed. "I'd want to come up with something else. I – I don't right know what yet, but – point is, we should. I grew up in gaol, in all but name, and I can tell you – there's nothing good in there."

The Director nodded. "We will reconsider the appropriate response to their situation, and when we have it, we will make sure to see it through."

"And you think – what?" Cassandra muttered, eyes flicking up from the ledger. "That Hartgate Gaol will just give them back to us?"

"I think," her mother returned evenly, "that this is not a matter over which you will be obliged to fret, Cassandra."

Cassandra tugged her shoulders taut. Her gaze darted to Septimus, like a flinch, as if expecting a torrent of quips – not that Septimus seemed to notice. "Of course. I – might as well tell you all – I'm taking some leave from the Div. For my – I mean – that last case – I – I need time to recover. And I'm not – I – right now, you'll do better if I'm not here."

She stared at me then, with the same narrow-eyed wariness she had turned on me ever since I emerged from the dormitory. I had, of course, been careful to boil down the contents of my transcript, at least as far as wider distribution was concerned. No one here had skimread her anguish, or her guilt, unless Mr. Adelstein had snuck a glimpse over my shoulder as I copied at his desks. But I quite couldn't pretend I hadn't heard it all – and she knew that just as sharply as I.

The Director cleared her throat. "The speech, Cassandra?"

"'But we have gathered another piece of evidence against these Head-Hiders.'" Cassandra sighed. "Should warn you, Hyssop, Mother's put quite the spin on you."

This was more than enough to startle words from me. "I – erm – in what – ?"

The Director smiled me to silence. "I simply provide the facts as I see them, Miss Hyssop. Even if you were not precisely hired as a distinguished defender of the Division, you certainly grew into it last night – would you not agree?"

"You'll see," Cassandra added, the slightest prickle about her voice, as she lowered the ledger into her mother's hands.

"'Lady Miltonwaters and Miss Danadlenddu,'" the Director continued, "'did not consider that they might not have been the only impartial observers assessing the Division's capabilities. And, unfortunately for them, not everyone in Dallyangle concurs with their views. Someone else has spent this week observing our workings in secret, unbeknownst to the majority of our members, and documenting her findings in a written record.'"

My mouth fell open. How could I do otherwise? There was the Director, calm and sedate on her office-chair, embellishing my stumble into the Division until it was a glittering tale of espionage, and critical assessment, and motives that I – oh, the enterprising young heiress! – had supposedly held all along –

"'This written record culminates in a transcript of a conversation, in which Lady Miltonwaters and Miss Danadlenddu confess to misusing the remains of a murdered gardener, to fabricate a grisly case which the Division could not have solved as long as they controlled the head's movements. I should stress that the guilty parties did not make their confession unprompted – and give due credit to the work of Division Sergeant Cassandra Ballestas, who endured great personal insult to draw the conversation in the most fruitful direction.'"

Cassandra gasped, her grip on the chair-back tightening in one convulsive clutch. The Director – whose eyes had not been following the content of the ledger for some time – permitted herself a tiny smile.

"'Our observer had no reason to support the Division's endeavours any more than the Head-Hiders did. But she has traced this affair, just as they have, and it has led her to a different conclusion. She is Henry Nettleblack, and she is more than willing to stand by her account of our good work – in fact, she intends to remain a valued member of the Division.'"

It was quite my turn to gasp. The room vanished, sharded to pieces, until I blinked the tears away.

"'To conclude: in recognition of these extraordinary circumstances, and with the matter of the Sweetings now able to receive our undivided attention, I wish to propose that you continue to fund – and stand by – the Dallyangle Division.'"

I ought to recount the swirling particulars of my emotions – of which there were many, and none of them composed – upon hearing the end of the speech, and Keturah Ballestas's retelling of my life. I say *life*, because it's quite the only part of my one-and-twenty years that has resembled life in earnest – not like the sheltered hibernation of Wales, nor the gasping misery of Girton, nor the silent terror of Catfish Crescent, but – something else. Something in which I can – apricots! – hold conversations, and confront my sisters, and just about keep a bicycle upright, and start a fire in a wood-burner, and scramble over a roof, and kiss a wonderful woman with a fantastic chignon – and generally do all manner of incongruous and petrifying and mundane and brilliant things, as if I truly do exist in the midst of them.

Once the session with the speech was concluded, I ended up in Septimus's office. She was still settling matters out in reception – I had left her deep in conversation with the Director and Cassandra – but she was on her way, as soon as she could be.

For my part, to be alone in her office with the gaslamps lit was a startling delight in itself. It was inescapably Septimus. Her desk was far less orderly than the Director's: there were broken-backed books splayed over piles of scrap paper, cheap ink frozen in its inkwell, a bedraggled wooden hairbrush in the pencil pot with half its bristles missing. Under the desk, my boots nudged the edge of a thin mattress, spread with a rough woollen blanket that matched the colours of Lorrie's moth-eaten cardigan. She had signed the inside covers of her books – I was prying rather horrendously – and laid down the letters like strokes in a woodcut, sharp and strident and unnervingly legible. Quite the opposite, in that respect, of myself.

Would it be too much to ask her if I could tear a page free, paste it into my journal, keep the brusque brilliance of her signature?

There was a mirror over the desk, a flimsy quarto-sized thing, mottled like a horsefly's wing. I glanced up to it (for I would have to glare myself out, if I was to regain some control and stop studying her handwriting) – and she was behind me.

Figs.

I whirled about, nearly upended the desk in the process, grabbed the top of the chair to steady my feet. At my back, the pencil pot toppled over. The hairbrush hit the desk with a horribly martial *crack*, enough to make us both jump.

She swallowed. She had my journal in both hands, her fingers twitching on the spine. The door shifted behind her, nudged shut by her boot-heel.

"Miss Nettleblack." She dropped a brusque bow – flushed, clearly thinking better of it – then sprang upright again, nervous and proud all at once. "I – I mean – Henry. I can still – you don't mind if I – "

"Please!" My voice skittered up, shriller than I'd been expecting. "Yes – erm – I'm Henry – and Hyssop is – it's one of my middle names – and I – I don't want it to be *Miss* anymore – so that's Henry Morfydd Hyssop Nettleblack – quite!"

This deluge of appellations sounded infinitely more reassuring in my head. She was staring at me, eyebrows arched in wary bewilderment, clutching my journal so violently that her knuckles smarted. Persimmons, her hands were shaking.

"I – I'm sorry," I stammered. "I'm sorry I – just – for everything. I'm sorry I didn't tell you before – I didn't tell anyone – but – erm – I knew that Mr. Adelstein and the Director had worked it out – and – you – you know far more of me than – erm – any of them – certainly now – "

She was still watching me. Somewhere trembling and strained in my throat, I heard my voice crack.

"I – it entirely isn't an excuse, but – I just – I preferred – I preferred who I was with you. Certainly – erm – I didn't want to be the version of me – the one that everybody was hunting down. And I – I – as I'm sure you'll hardly be surprised to hear – I was scared – scared to tell you sooner – because you met Henry Hyssop, that's quite the person you befriended – "

"More than befriended," she muttered, so swiftly I would have missed it had the stammer not tugged my words back. She was blushing, dull red under her bruises, and only blushed more when the remark struck me to silence. "I – sorry. Interrupted you."

I gulped for the rest of the sentence. "I – well – it – just that you – well. I didn't know how you'd feel about Harriet Nettleblack – I mean – *I* don't really – I don't even think of myself as her. The version of me that existed before the Division – I – I utterly despised her – and so did everyone else – and it seemed only natural you would too. But that's – it isn't – I should have let you decide that for yourself – I should have – I – I'm so sorry – "

If there was more, I quite wasn't up to managing it. I spluttered the last out, dropped my gaze.

"Henry."

Her voice was soft, but it still made me start. I didn't dare meet her eyes. All I could see – all that she must have been forced to look at – were my velvet lapels, and the glinting paisley whorls in my cravat, and the rich green of my coat, and Edwina's signet ring gleaming on my index finger.

"Henry – listen to me. You've got nothing to apologise for."

A snatch of breath above my head. I closed my eyes.

"I don't know," she continued – picking through the words, so carefully – "why it is that you've got me on some sort of pedestal. Like I can judge you, for not wanting to tell me something you didn't want to face. It weren't my right to know, not 'til you were ready to tell me. Like I don't – like – I – "

She broke off – resumed – faster, closer –

"Look. For my part – for what it's worth – God's sake, 'course I don't despise you! I've never despised you! I care for you more than I – more than – there ain't words! It's easier by far to climb a building for you – or defend you – or have some great tumble of a disaster to fend off with you at my side – than put anything into words! I ain't in that opera, I've got no idea how to give you a *Poor Wand'ring One* – take any heart, take mine, and all that – "

I opened my eyes, and she was there. She was inches from my face, and blustering herself into a frenzy, and her gaze was so fervent it was quite past fear –

"Might I kiss you?" I blurted.

She was utterly seamless. "Please – I've no lyrics left – "

I kicked off the chair, dashed my lips against hers. She gasped – I'd forgotten her nose – but then her hand sprang to my face, tilted me back, held me to her mouth and kissed my apologies away. This wasn't the scalding glance of a thing we'd had at the attic window, scrabbling and breathless and over in a heartbeat. Everything of me shot to my lips and settled there, where she eased them apart, or glanced her teeth against them – so tentatively that I shivered in her hands –

And – sweet merciful figs, but if I collapse into this description any further, I quite shan't make it to the end of the journal!

I had no desire in the least for it to end. For far longer than I'd dared imagine possible, it didn't end. It became, slowly and dazedly, a kiss for every other breath, our faces still pressed together, twitching kisses by some strange mutual accord. My hands slid from her shoulders to her waist, the warmth of her hair brushing at my fingers.

I blushed. All my agonising, and she didn't even wear a corset.

Another twitch of a kiss. Her thumb stroked gently along my cheekbone.

"I quite don't deserve this," I murmured.

"Oh, shut up. That's a mad way to think."

"And – and my sisters – "

She dragged her thumb across my lips, her voice wonderfully wry. "Henry. I've just kissed you. I've wanted to kiss you since before I even knew I wanted to kiss you. Can we – shelve your sisters, for a minute?"

It seemed only appropriate to kiss her thumb by way of apology. "I – right – yes – figs – very fair point – "

She shifted our heads, meticulously careful of her nose, until her forehead rested on mine, until all I could see was her solemn navy stare. "Right. Well."

"Well?"

"Was that – alright?"

I gaped at her. "Yes! Alright quite isn't the word! Sweet passion-fruit, I'm entirely infatuated with you!"

She grinned. I had missed her fierce grin. "Right. Yes. Good! And I – you – same to you – so – well. Does this mean – I'm sorry, if this is too quick, I've no real idea how it works – does this mean you'd not object to – maybe having a go at – y'know – being my sweetheart? In – whatever form you'd like that to take? As secret – or as open – as you want?"

She looked so ecstatic, and so tentative, and so desperately gallant, that I simply tugged her closer to me. "I've quite as little idea as you – erm – and I can't say at this instant how – the – as you say – the practicalities – but I want quite nothing more in the known world than to be your sweetheart! Quite!"

I haven't ink or space enough to record it all – and I want, so fervently, to record it all. I can only write it in glimpses. How I kissed her again, rather more carefully this time. How she scooped everything off her desk and tossed it down onto the mattress, so we could sit side by side with our feet on the chair. How there wasn't a whit of hesitation when I slipped my hand through hers – and how she responded, with faltering boldness, by shifting her leg to press against mine. How she suddenly glanced at me, broke into an indignant smile – "Damn it, you ain't eaten! I've had nothing but biscuits!" – and I sprang off the desk and demanded she let me take her to the market. How we dug through her desk-drawer for small change (I must record this, for I certainly owe her that small change back). How she frowned before the mirror, pinning her hair into place. How I caught a strand of it, and blushed in tandem with her, and drifted towards her until we slid back into kissing.

And this – *this* – is happening to me!

And the Division is strong, strong enough to survive. And they know who I am, and the sky's not fallen in, and – perhaps most astonishingly of all – I'm quite not afraid that it will. I feel precisely the opposite of afraid. I felt it as I gazed at Septimus, and I feel it writing this now. Figs, but it's rather an intoxicating experience. One way or another, my position amidst my family and the Division will arrange itself anew – and I will need to speak to Edwina, for her own future trajectory as much as mine – but I don't fear it. And if I can keep myself poised just as I am, decidedly *not* in my usual state of perpetual panic – well, that'll be the next giddy undertaking, won't it?

But where am I now? Precisely where I'd want to run out of pages in this journal, though I couldn't possibly have predicted it. The blue-black darkness – with a new drizzle of rain against the glass, for this is still Dallyangle – is draped across the office window, and all the candles we could scrounge are blazing along the back of the desk, and the shadows are thickening around my ankles. The newspaper that wrapped the pies is crumpled in the corner, picked quite clean. I'm perched at the desk, bundled in velvet collar and Div jacket both, cross-legged in my salvaged culottes. I can glance down, and smile, and see Septimus curled up on her mattress. She insisted she'd only lie down a moment, but she promptly toppled headlong into sleep. I can gaze at her for rather longer than a glance – as I'm doing, I must confess, between every other sentence – and wonder what she thought of my journal. Whether, when she wakes up, I might ask her.

Of course, she might wish to converse of other things. Or schedule our next cycling lesson. Or take my face in her hands and kiss me.

Me. Her sweetheart. Her consummately infatuated sweetheart.

Figs. Quite. Here we are!

ALMOST CERTAINLY NOT THE END
BUT A FAIRLY REASONABLE PLACE AT WHICH TO PAUSE

ACKNOWLEDGEMENTS

Much like its author, this book has gone through quite the transition in its journey to full-blooded novelistic endeavour. Ever aiding it – and, occasionally, just putting up with it – is my dearest Claudia Chapman. Her generous and incisive criticism hoisted the story from innumerable nets of nonsense.

Cipher Press have excelled and exploded my dreams of the *perfect publisher* for this tome of madness and rodents. Jenn and Ellis stared into the face of Dallyangle's odd little soul, and Wolf made magnificent art from it. Thanks also to Jordan Taylor-Jones for publicity worthy of Nettleblack's Tincture, and Laura Jones for marvellous typesetting escapades. I am so lucky to be able to, in Ellis's words, roll forwards with grace and aplomb in such brilliant company.

I was blessed with early readers, and I want to thank them all for indulging my makeshift attempts at email-based serialisation. Gwen Davis (perennial champion of Edwina's cause), Katie Barrowman (she of the crochet ferret), Vanessa Knight (apologies for killing your darling L.L.), and others – I am profoundly grateful. Even if – especially if – you read a ghastly draft. And you, Courtney O'Donnell, are the ferret reading this.

I'm grateful to the English Department at Royal Holloway, for its wonderful world of critics who are creative and creatives who are critical, and to the Cambridge contingent who nudged me into asking how words worked. To all the scholars, researchers and writers who opened up the nineteenth century for me, especially the ones who showed its strangeness and diversity. To TECHNE, who thought they were funding a PhD and got a novel as well. To Adam Roberts, for 'what is book?' and patient reassurance. Diolch yn fawr to M. Wynn Thomas, for double-checking my Welsh – if there are errors remaining, they're quite my fault. To Mark Samuels Lasner, Margaret D. Stetz and the Delawareans, for enthusiasm and a hoard of glorious novel covers. Heartfelt thanks to Preti Taneja, for letting me take prose to a poetry salon, and uplifting my spirits when they threatened to shrivel.

Profoundly, to my parents. My mother, who will do me the highest compliment if she gets the local library to order this book. My late father – I hope he'd be both delighted and relieved (and only slightly perturbed) by the end result.

I have to write these rather early, so I can only apologise tenfold for being insufficiently thorough. Sprawling and fervent gratitude to anyone not named who's done aught to help *Nettleblack*. If you've answered a delirious question, spread the word, enjoyed the book, said something nice about the cover, and so forth – please accept my thanks.

And to Henry, Sept, Pip, Cass, Matty et al – you knew I was queer before I did.